The Giaour
and other poems

The Giaour
and other poems

by

Lord Byron

CAMBRIDGE
SCHOLARS
PUBLISHING
classic texts

The Giaour and other poems, by Lord Byron

This book in its current typographical format first published 2009 by

Cambridge Scholars Publishing

12 Back Chapman Street, Newcastle upon Tyne, NE6 2XX, UK

British Library Cataloguing in Publication Data
A catalogue record for this book is available from the British Library

ISBN (10): 1-4438-0967-5, ISBN (13): 978-1-4438-0967-2

CONTENTS

POEMS 1809–1813

THE GIRL OF CADIZ

1.

Oh never talk again to me
    Of northern climes and British ladies;
It has not been your lot to see,
    Like me, the lovely Girl of Cadiz.
Although her eye be not of blue,
    Nor fair her locks, like English lasses,
How far its own expressive hue
    The languid azure eye surpasses!

2.

Prometheus-like from heaven she stole
    The fire that through those silken lashes
In darkest glances seems to roll,
    From eyes that cannot hide their flashes:
And as along her bosom steal
    In lengthened flow her raven tresses,
You'd swear each clustering lock could feel,
    And curled to give her neck caresses.

3.

Our English maids are long to woo,
    And frigid even in possession;
And if their charms be fair to view,
    Their lips are slow at Love's confession;

But, born beneath a brighter sun,

For love ordained the Spanish maid is,

And who,—when fondly, fairly won,—

Enchants you like the Girl of Cadiz?

4.

The Spanish maid is no coquette,

Nor joys to see a lover tremble,

And if she love, or if she hate,

Alike she knows not to dissemble.

Her heart can ne'er be bought or sold—

Howe'er it beats, it beats sincerely;

And, though it will not bend to gold,

'Twill love you long and love you dearly.

5.

The Spanish girl that meets your love

Ne'er taunts you with a mock denial,

For every thought is bent to prove

Her passion in the hour of trial.

When thronging foemen menace Spain,

She dares the deed and shares the danger;

And should her lover press the plain,

She hurls the spear, her love's avenger.

6.

And when, beneath the evening star,

She mingles in the gay Bolero,

Or sings to her attuned guitar

Of Christian knight or Moorish hero,

Or counts her beads with fairy hand

    Beneath the twinkling rays of Hesper,

Or joins Devotion's choral band,

    To chaunt the sweet and hallowed vesper;—

7.

In each her charms the heart must move

    Of all who venture to behold her;

Then let not maids less fair reprove

    Because her bosom is not colder:

Through many a clime 'tis mine to roam

    Where many a soft and melting maid is,

But none abroad, and few at home,

    May match the dark-eyed Girl of Cadiz.   1809.

LINES WRITTEN IN AN ALBUM, AT MALTA

1.

As o'er the cold sepulchral stone

    Some *name* arrests the passer-by;

Thus, when thou view'st this page alone,

    May *mine* attract thy pensive eye!

2.

And when by thee that name is read,

    Perchance in some succeeding year,

Reflect on *me* as on the *dead,*

    And think my *Heart* is buried *here.*   Malta, *September* 14, 1809.

TO FLORENCE

1.

Oh Lady! when I left the shore,
    The distant shore which gave me birth,
I hardly thought to grieve once more,
    To quit another spot on earth:

2.

Yet here, amidst this barren isle,
    Where panting Nature, droops the head,
Where only thou art seen to smile,
    I view my parting hour with dread.

3.

Though far from Albin's craggy shore,
    Divided by the dark-blue main;
A few, brief, rolling seasons o'er,
    Perchance I view her cliffs again:

4.

But wheresoe'er I now may roam,
    Through scorching clime, and varied sea,
Though Time restore me to my home,
    I ne'er shall bend mine eyes on thee:

5.

On thee, in whom at once conspire
    All charms which heedless hearts can move,
Whom but to see is to admire,
    And, oh! forgive the word—to love.

6.

Forgive the word, in one who ne'er
    With such a word can more offend;
And since thy heart I cannot share,
    Believe me, what I am, thy friend.

7.

And who so cold as look on thee,
    Thou lovely wand'rer, and be less?
Nor be, what man should ever be,
    The friend of Beauty in distress?

8.

Ah! who would think that form had past
    Through Danger's most destructive path,
Had braved the death-winged tempest's blast,
    And 'scaped a Tyrant's fiercer wrath?

9.

Lady! when I shall view the walls
    Where free Byzantium once arose,
And Stamboul's Oriental halls
    The Turkish tyrants now enclose;

10.

Though mightiest in the lists of fame,
    That glorious city still shall be;
On me 'twill hold a dearer claim,
    As spot of thy nativity:

11.

And though I bid thee now farewell,

When I behold that wondrous scene—

Since where thou art I may not dwell—

'Twill soothe to be where thou hast been.   *September,* 1809.

STANZAS COMPOSED DURING A THUNDERSTORM

Composed Octr. 11, 1809, during the night in a thunderstorm, when the guides had lost the road to Zitza, near the range of mountains formerly called Pindus, un Albania.

1.

Chill and mirk is the nightly blast,

Where Pindus' mountains rise,

And angry clouds are pouring fast

The vengeance of the skies.

2.

Our guides are gone, our hope is lost,

And lightnings, as they play,

But show where rocks our path have crost,

Or gild the torrent's spray.

3.

Is yon a cot I saw, though low?

When lightning broke the gloom—

How welcome were its shade!—ah, no!

'Tis but a Turkish tomb.

4.

Through sounds of foaming waterfalls,
    I hear a voice exclaim—
My way-worn countryman, who calls
    On distant England's name.

5.

A shot is fired—by foe or friend?
    Another—'tis to tell
The mountain-peasants to descend,
    And lead us where they dwell.

6.

Oh! who in such a night will dare
    To tempt the wilderness?
And who 'mid thunder-peals can hear
    Our signal of distress?

7.

And who that heard our shouts would rise
    To try the dubious road?
Nor rather deem from nightly cries
    That outlaws were abroad.

8.

Clouds burst, skies flash, oh, dreadful hour
    More fiercely pours the storm!
Yet here one thought has still the power
    To keep my bosom warm.

9.

While wandering through each broken path,
O'er brake and craggy brow;
While elements exhaust their wrath,
Sweet Florence, where art thou?

10.

Not on the sea, not on the sea—
Thy bark hath long been gone:
Oh, may the storm that pours on me,
Bow down my head alone!

11.

Full swiftly blew the swift Siroc,
When last I pressed thy lip;
And long ere now, with foaming shock,
Impelled thy gallant ship.

12.

Now thou art safe; nay, long ere now
Hast trod the shore of Spain;
'Twere hard if aught so fair as thou
Should linger on the main.

13.

And since I now remember thee
In darkness and in dread,
As in those hours of revelry
Which Mirth and Music sped;

14.

Do thou, amid the fair white walls,
　　If Cadiz yet be free,
At times from out her latticed halls
　　Look o'er the dark blue sea;

15.

Then think upon Calypso's isles,
　　Endeared by days gone by;
To others give a thousand smiles,
　　To me a single sigh.

16.

And when the admiring circle mark
　　The paleness of thy face,
A half-formed tear, a transient spark
　　Of melancholy grace,

17.

Again thou'lt smile, and blushing shun
　　Some coxcomb's raillery;
Nor own for once thou thought'st on one,
　　Who ever thinks on thee.

18.

Though smile and sigh alike are vain,
　　When severed hearts repine,
My spirit flies o'er Mount and Main,
　　And mourns in search of *thine.*

October 11, 1809.

STANZAS WRITTEN IN PASSING THE AMBRACIAN GULF

1.

Through cloudless skies, in silvery sheen,
    Full beams the moon on Actium's coast:
And on these waves, for Egypt's queen,
    The ancient world was won and lost.

2.

And now upon the scene I look,
    The azure grave of many a Roman;
Where stern Ambition once forsook
    His wavering crown to follow *Woman.*

3.

Florence! whom I will love as well
    (As ever yet was said or sung,
Since Orpheus sang his spouse from Hell)
    Whilst *thou* art *fair* and *I* am *young*;

4.

Sweet Florence! those were pleasant times,
    When worlds were staked for Ladies' eyes:
Had bards as many realms as rhymes,
    Thy charms might raise new Antonies.

5.

Though Fate forbids such things to be,
    Yet, by thine eyes and ringlets curled!
I cannot *lose* a *world* for thee,
But would not lose *thee* for a *World.*   *November* 14, 1809.

THE SPELL IS BROKE, THE CHARM IS FLOWN!

WRITTEN AT ATHENS, JANUARY 16, 1810

The spell is broke, the charm is flown!

Thus is it with Life's fitful fever:

We madly smile when we should groan;

Delirium is our best deceiver.

Each lucid interval of thought

Recalls the woes of Nature's charter;

And *He* that acts as *wise men ought,*

But *lives*—as Saints have died—a martyr.

WRITTEN AFTER SWIMMING FROM SESTOS TO ABYDOS

On the 3rd of May, 1810, while the *Salsette* (Captain Bathurst) was lying in the Dardanelles, Lieutenant Ekenhead, of that frigate, and the writer of these rhymes, swam from the European shore to the Asiatic—by the by, from Abydos to Sestos would have been more correct. The whole distance, from the place whence we started to our landing on the other side, including the length we were carried by the current, was computed by those on board the frigate at upwards of four English miles, though the actual breadth is barely one. The rapidity of the current is such that no boat can row directly across, and it may, in some measure, be estimated from the circumstance of the whole distance being accomplished by one of the parties in an hour and five, and by the other in an hour and ten minutes. The water was extremely cold, from the melting of the mountain snows. About three weeks before, in April, we had made an attempt; but having ridden all the way from the Troad the same morning, and the water being of an icy dullness, we found it necessary to postpone the completion till the frigate anchored below the castles, when we swam the straits as just stated, entering a considerable way above the European, and landing below the Asiatic, fort. Chevalier says that a young Jew swam the same distance for his mistress; and Olivier mentions its having been done by a Neapolitan; but our consul, Tarragona, remembered neither of these circumstances, and tried to dissuade us from the attempt. A number of the *Salsette's* crew were known to have accomplished a greater distance; and the only thing that surprised me was that, as doubts had been entertained of the truth of Leander's story, no traveller had ever endeavoured to ascertain its practicability.

1.

If, in the month of dark December,

  Leander, who was nightly wont

(What maid will not the tale remember?)

  To cross thy stream, broad Hellespont!

2.

If, when the wintry tempest roared,

  He sped to Hero, nothing loth,

And thus of old thy current poured,

  Fair Venus! how I pity both!

3.

For *me,* degenerate modern wretch,

  Though in the genial month of May,

My dripping limbs I faintly stretch,

  And think I've done a feat to-day.

4.

But since he crossed the rapid tide,

  According to the doubtful story,

To woo,—and—Lord knows what beside,

  And swam for Love, as I for Glory;

5.

'Twere hard to say who fared the best:

  Sad mortals! thus the Gods still plague you!

He lost his labour, I my jest:

  For he was drowned, and I've the ague.   *May* 9, 1810.

LINES IN THE TRAVELLERS' BOOK AT ORCHOMENUS

IN THIS BOOK A TRAVELLER HAD WRITTEN:——

"Fair Albion, smiling, sees her son depart

To trace the birth and nursery of art:

Noble his object, glorious is his aim;

He comes to Athens, and he—writes his name."

BENEATH WHICH LORD BYRON INSERTED THE FOLLOWING:——

The modest bard, like many a bard unknown,

Rhymes on our names, but wisely hides his own;

But yet, whoe'er he be, to say no worse,

His name would bring more credit than his verse.   1810.

MAID OF ATHENS, ERE WE PART

Ζωή μου, σᾶς ἀγαπῶ

1.

Maid of Athens, ere we part,

Give, oh give me back my heart!

Or, since that has left my breast,

Keep it now, and take the rest!

Hear my vow before I go,

Ζωή μου, σᾶς ἀγαπῶ.[i]

i. Romaic expression of tenderness. If I translate it, I shall affront the gentlemen, as it may seem that I supposed they could not; and if I do not, I may affront the ladies. For fear of misconstruction on the part of the latter, I shall do so, begging pardon of the learned. It means, "My life, I love you!" which sounds very prettily in all languages, and is as much in fashion in Greece at this day as, Juvenal tells us, the two first words were amongst the Roman ladies, whose erotic expressions were all Hellenised.

2.

By those tresses unconfined,

Wooed by each Ægean wind;

By those lids whose jetty fringe

Kiss thy soft cheeks' blooming tinge;

By those wild eyes like the roe,

Ζωή μου, σᾶς ἀγαπῶ.

3.

By that lip I long to taste;

By that zone-encircled waist;

By all the token-flowers[i] that tell

What words can never speak so well;

By love's alternate joy and woe,

Ζωή μου, σᾶς ἀγαπῶ.

i. In the East (where ladies are not taught to write, lest they should scribble assignations), flowers, cinders, pebbles, etc., convey the sentiments of the parties, by that universal deputy of Mercury—an old woman. A cinder says, "I burn for thee;" a bunch of flowers tied with hair, "Take me and fly;" but a pebble declares—what nothing else can.

4.

Maid of Athens! I am gone:

Think of me, sweet! when alone.

Though I fly to Istambol,

Athens holds my heart and soul:

Can I cease to love thee? No!

Ζωή μου, σᾶς ἀγαπῶ.   *Athens,* 1810.

FRAGMENT FROM THE "MONK OF ATHOS"

1.

Beside the confines of the Ægean main,
    Where northward Macedonia bounds the flood,
    And views opposed the Asiatic plain,
    Where once the pride of lofty Ilion stood,
    Like the great Father of the giant brood,
    With lowering port majestic Athos stands,
    Crowned with the verdure of eternal wood,
    As yet unspoiled by sacrilegious hands,
And throws his mighty shade o'er seas and distant lands.

2.

And deep embosomed in his shady groves
    Full many a convent rears its glittering spire,
    Mid scenes where Heavenly Contemplation loves
    To kindle in her soul her hallowed fire,
    Where air and sea with rocks and woods conspire
    To breathe a sweet religious calm around,
    Weaning the thoughts from every low desire,
    And the wild waves that break with murmuring sound
Along the rocky shore proclaim it holy ground.

3.

Sequestered shades where Piety has given
    A quiet refuge from each earthly care,
    Whence the rapt spirit may ascend to Heaven!

Oh, ye condemned the ills of life to bear!

As with advancing age your woes increase,

What bliss amidst these solitudes to share

The happy foretaste of eternal Peace,

Till Heaven in mercy bids your pain and sorrows cease.

LINES WRITTEN BENEATH A PICTURE

1.

Dear object of defeated care!

Though now of Love and thee bereft,

To reconcile me with despair

Thine image and my tears are left.

2.

'Tis said with Sorrow Time can cope;

But this I feel can ne'er be true:

For by the death-blow of my Hope

My Memory immortal grew.   *Athens, January,* 1811.

TRANSLATION OF THE FAMOUS GREEK WAR SONG

"Δεῦτε παῖδες τῶν Ἑλλήνων."

The song Δεῦτε παῖδες, etc., was written by Riga, who perished in the attempt to revolutionize Greece. This translation is as literal as the author could make it in verse. It is of the same measure as that of the original.

Sons of the Greeks, arise!

The glorious hour's gone forth,

And, worthy of such ties,

Display who gave us birth.

CHORUS.

Sons of Greeks! let us go
In arms against the foe,
Till their hated blood shall flow
In a river past our feet.

Then manfully despising
    The Turkish tyrant's yoke,
Let your country see you rising,
    And all her chains are broke.
Brave shades of chiefs and sages,
    Behold the coming strife!
Hellénes of past ages,
    Oh, start again to life!
At the sound of my trumpet, breaking
    Your sleep, oh, join with me!
And the seven-hilled city[i] seeking,
    Fight, conquer, till we're free.
            Sons of Greeks, etc.

i. Constantinople. "Επτάλοφος."

Sparta, Sparta, why in slumbers
    Lethargic dost thou lie?
Awake, and join thy numbers
    With Athens, old ally!
Leonidas recalling,
    That chief of ancient song,
Who saved ye once from falling,
    The terrible! the strong!

Who made that bold diversion

In old Thermopylæ,

And warring with the Persian

To keep his country free;

With his three hundred waging

The battle, long he stood,

And like a lion raging,

Expired in seas of blood.

Sons of Greeks, etc.

TRANSLATION OF THE ROMAIC SONG

"Μπένω μεσ' τὸ περιβόλι,
Ὡραιοτάτη Χαηδή," κ.τ.λ.

The song from which this is taken is a great favourite with the young girls of Athens of all classes. Their manner of singing it is by verses in rotation, the whole number present joining in the chorus. I have heard it frequently at our "χόροι" in the winter of 1810–11. The air is plaintive and pretty.

I enter thy garden of roses,

Belovèd and fair Haidee,

Each morning where Flora reposes,

For surely I see her in thee.

Oh, Lovely! thus low I implore thee,

Receive this fond truth from my tongue,

Which utters its song to adore thee,

Yet trembles for what it has sung;

As the branch, at the bidding of Nature,

Adds fragrance and fruit to the tree,

Through her eyes, through her every feature,

Shines the soul of the young Haidée.

But the loveliest garden grows hateful

   When Love has abandoned the bowers;

Bring me hemlock—since mine is ungrateful,

   That herb is more fragrant than flowers.

The poison, when poured from the chalice,

   Will deeply embitter the bowl;

But when drunk to escape from thy malice,

   The draught shall be sweet to my soul.

Too cruel! in vain I implore thee

   My heart from these horrors to save:

Will nought to my bosom restore thee?

   Then open the gates of the grave.

As the chief who to combat advances

   Secure of his conquest before,

Thus thou, with those eyes for thy lances,

   Hast pierced through my heart to its core.

Ah, tell me, my soul! must I perish

   By pangs which a smile would dispel?

Would the hope, which thou once bad'st me cherish,

   For torture repay me too well?

Now sad is the garden of roses,

   Beloved but false Haidée!

There Flora all withered reposes,

   And mourns o'er thine absence with me.   1811.

ON PARTING

1.

The kiss, dear maid! thy lip has left
    Shall never part from mine,
Till happier hours restore the gift
    Untainted back to thine.

2.

Thy parting glance, which fondly beams,
    An equal love may see:
The tear that from thine eyelid streams
    Can weep no change in me.

3.

I ask no pledge to make me blest
    In gazing when alone;
Nor one memorial for a breast,
    Whose thoughts are all tine own.

4.

Nor need I write—to tell the tale
    My pen were doubly weak:
Oh! what can idle words avail,
    Unless the heart could speak?

5.

By day or night, in weal or woe,
    That heart, no longer free,
Must bear the love it cannot show,
    And silent ache for thee.

March, 1811.

FAREWELL TO MALTA

Adieu, ye joys of La Valette!

Adieu, Sirocco, sun, and sweat!

Adieu, thou palace rarely entered!

Adieu, ye mansions where—I've ventured!

Adieu, ye cursèd streets if stairs!

(How surely he who mounts them swears!)

Adieu, ye merchants often failing!

Adieu, thou mob for ever railing!

Adieu, ye packets—without letters!

Adieu, ye fools—who ape your betters!

Adieu, thou damned'st quarantine,

That gave me fever, and the spleen!

Adieu that stage which makes us yawn, Sirs,

Adieu his Excellency's dancers!

Adieu to Peter—whom no fault's in,

But could not teach a colonel waltzing;

Adieu, ye females fraught with graces!

Adieu red coats, and redder faces!

Adieu the supercilious air

Of all that strut *en militaire*!

I go—but God knows when, or why,

To smoky towns and cloudy sky,

To things (the honest truth to say)

As bad—but in a different way.

Farewell to these, but not adieu,
Triumphant sons of truest blue!
While either Adriatic shore,
And fallen chiefs, and fleets no more,
And nightly smiles, and daily dinners,
Proclaim you war and women's winners.
Pardon my Muse, who apt to prate is,
And take my rhyme—because 'tis "gratis."

And now I've got to Mrs. Fraser,
Perhaps you think I mean to praise her—
And were I vain enough to think
My praise was worth this drop of ink,
A line—or two—were no hard matter,
As here, indeed, I need not flatter:
But she must be content to shine
In better praises than in mine,
With lively air, and open heart,
And fashion's ease, without its art;
Her hours can gaily glide along.
Nor ask the aid of idle song.

And now, O Malta! since thou'st got us,
Thou little military hot-house!
I'll not offend with words uncivil,
And wish thee rudely at the Devil,
But only stare from out my casement,
And ask, "for what is such a place meant?"
Then, in my solitary nook,

Return to scribbling, or a book,

Or take my physic while I'm able

(Two spoonfuls hourly, by this label),

Prefer my nightcap to my beaver,

And bless my stars I've got a fever.   May 26, 1811.

NEWSTEAD ABBEY

1.

In the dome of my Sires as the clear moonbeam falls

Through Silence and Shade o'er its desolate walls,

It shines from afar like the glories of old;

It gilds, but it warms not—'tis dazzling, but cold.

2.

Let the Sunbeam be bright for the younger of days:

'Tis the light that should shine on a race that decays,

When the Stars are on high and the dews on the ground,

And the long shadow lingers the ruin around.

3.

And the step that o'erechoes the gray floor of stone

Falls sullenly now, for 'tis only my own;

And sunk are the voices that sounded in mirth,

And empty the goblet, and dreary the hearth.

4.

And vain was each effort to raise and recall

The brightness of old to illumine our Hall;

And vain was the hope to avert our decline,

And the fate of my fathers had faded to mine.

5.

And theirs was the wealth and the fulness of Fame,

And mine to inherit too haughty a name;

And theirs were the times and the triumphs of yore,

And mine to regret, but renew them no more.

6.

And Ruin is fixed on my tower and my wall,

Too hoary to fade, and too massy to fall;

It tells not of Time's or the tempest's decay,

But the wreck of the line that have held it in sway.   August 26, 1811.

EPISTLE TO A FRIEND,

IN ANSWER TO SOME LINES EXHORTING THE AUTHOR TO BE CHEERFUL, AND TO "BANISH CARE."

"Oh! banish care"—such ever be

The motto of *thy* revelry!

Perchance of *mine*, when wassail nights

Renew those riotous delights,

Wherewith the children of Despair

Lull the lone heart, and "banish care."

But not in Morn's reflecting hour,

When present, past, and future lower,

When all I loved is changed or gone,

Mock with such taunts the woes of one,

Whose every thought—but let them pass—

Thou know'st I am not what I was.

But, above all, if thou wouldst hold

Place in a heart that ne'er was cold,

By all the powers that men revere,

By all unto thy bosom dear,
Thy joys below, thy hopes above,
Speak—speak of anything but Love.

'Twere long to tell, and vain to hear,
The tale of one who scorns a tear;
And there is little in that tale
Which better bosoms would bewail.
But mine has suffered more than well
'Twould suit philosophy to tell.
I've seen my bride another's bride,—
Have seen her seated by his side,—
Have seen the infant, which she bore,
Wear the sweet smile the mother wore,
When she and I in youth have smiled,
As fond and faultless as her child;—
Have seen her eyes, in cold disdain,
Ask if I felt no secret pain;
And *I* have acted well my part,
And made my cheek belie my heart,
Returned the freezing glance she gave,
Yet felt the while *that* woman's slave;—
Have kissed, as if without design,
The babe which ought to have been mine,
And showed, alas! in each caress
Time had not made me love the less.

But let this pass—I'll whine no more,
Nor seek again an eastern shore;

The world befits a busy brain,—
I'll hie me to its haunts again.
But if, in some succeeding year,1
When Britain's "May is in the sere,"
Thou hear'st of one, whose deepening crimes
Suit with the sablest of the times,
Of one, whom love nor pity sways,
Nor hope of fame, nor good men's praise;
One, who in stern Ambition's pride,
Perchance not blood shall turn aside;
One ranked in some recording page
With the worst anarchs of the age,
Him wilt thou *know*—and *knowing* pause,
Nor with the *effect* forget the cause.   Newstead Abbey, Oct. 11, 1811.

TO THYRZA

Without a stone to mark the spot,
    And say, what Truth might well have said,
By all, save one, perchance forgot,
    Ah! wherefore art thou lowly laid?
By many a shore and many a sea
    Divided, yet beloved in vain;
The Past, the Future fled to thee,
    To bid us meet—no—ne'er again!
Could this have been—a word, a look,
    That softly said, "We part in peace,"

Had taught my bosom how to brook,

   With fainter sighs, thy soul's release.

And didst thou not, since Death for thee

   Prepared a light and pangless dart,

Once long for him thou ne'er shalt see,

   Who held, and holds thee in his heart?

Oh! who like him had watched thee here?

   Or sadly marked thy glazing eye,

In that dread hour ere Death appear,

   When silent Sorrow fears to sigh,

Till all was past? But when no more

   'Twas thine to reck of human woe,

Affection's heart-drops, gushing o'er,

   Had flowed as fast—as now they flow.

Shall they not flow, when many a day

   In these, to me, deserted towers,

Ere called but for a time away,

   Affection's mingling tears were ours?

Ours too the glance none saw beside;

   The smile none else might understand;

The whispered thought of hearts allied,

   The pressure of the thrilling hand;

The kiss, so guiltless and refined,

   That Love each warmer wish forbore;

Those eyes proclaimed so pure a mind,

   Ev'n Passion blushed to plead for more.

The tone, that taught me to rejoice,

   When prone, unlike thee, to repine;

The song, celestial from thy voice,

But sweet to me from none but thine;

The pledge we wore—*I* wear it still,

But where is thine?—Ah! where art thou?

Oft have I borne the weight of ill, '

But never bent beneath till now!

Well hast thou left in Life's best bloom

The cup of Woe for me to drain.

If rest alone be in the tomb,

I would not wish thee here again:

But if in worlds more blest than this

Thy virtues seek a fitter sphere,

Impart some portion of thy bliss,

To wean me from mine anguish here.

Teach me—too early taught by thee!

To bear, forgiving and forgiven:

On earth thy love was such to me;

It fain would form my hope in Heaven!   October 11, 1811.

AWAY, AWAY, YE NOTES OF WOE!

1.

Away, away, ye notes of Woe!

Be silent, thou once soothing Strain,

Or I must flee from hence—for, oh!

I dare not trust those sounds again.

To me they speak of brighter days—

But lull the chords, for now, alas!

I must not think, I may not gaze,

On what I *am*—on what I *was.*

2.

The voice that made those sounds more sweet

Is hushed, and all their charms are fled;

And now their softest notes repeat

A dirge, an anthem o'er the dead!

Yes, Thyrza! yes, they breathe of thee,

Beloved dust! since dust thou art;

And all that once was Harmony

Is worse than discord to my heart!

3.

'Tis silent all!—but on my ear

The well remembered Echoes thrill;

I hear a voice I would not hear,

A voice that now might well be still:

Yet oft my doubting Soul 'twill shake;

Ev'n Slumber owns its gentle tone,

Till Consciousness will vainly wake

To listen, though the dream be flown.

4.

Sweet Thyrza! waking as in sleep,

Thou art but now a lovely dream;

A Star that trembled o'er the deep,

Then turned from earth its tender beam.

But he who through Life's dreary way

Must pass, when Heaven is veiled in wrath,

Will long lament the vanished ray

That scattered gladness o'er his path.   December 8, 1811.

ONE STRUGGLE MORE, AND I AM FREE

1.

One struggle more, and I am free

From pangs that rend my heart in twain;

One last long sigh to Love and thee,

Then back to busy life again.

It suits me well to mingle now

With things that never pleased before:

Though every joy is fled below,

What future grief can touch me more?

2.

Then bring me wine, the banquet bring;

Man was not formed to live alone:

I'll be that light unmeaning thing

That smiles with all, and weeps with none.

It was not thus in days more dear,

It never would have been, but thou

Hast fled, and left me lonely here;

Thou'rt nothing,—all are nothing now.

3.

In vain my lyre would lightly breathe!
    The smile that Sorrow fain would wear
But mocks the woe that lurks beneath.
    Like roses o'er a sepulchre.
Though gay companions o'er the bowl
    Dispel awhile the sense of ill:
Though Pleasure fires the maddening soul.
    The Heart,—the Heart is lonely still!

4.

On many a lone and lovely night
    It soothed to gaze upon the sky;
For then I deemed the heavenly light
    Shone sweetly on thy pensive eye:
And oft I thought at Cynthia's noon,
    When sailing o'er the Ægean wave,
"Now Thyrza gazes on that moon"—
    Alas, it gleamed upon her grave!

5.

When stretched on Fever's sleepless bed,
    And sickness shrunk my throbbing veins,
"'Tis comfort still," I faintly said,
    "That Thyrza cannot know my pains:"
Like freedom to the time-worn slave—
    A boon 'tis idle then to give—
Relenting Nature vainly gave
    My life, when Thyrza ceased to live!

6.

My Thyrza's pledge in better days,
    When Love and Life alike were new!
How different now thou meet'st my gaze!
    How tinged by time with Sorrow's hue!
The heart that gave itself with thee
    Is silent—ah, were mine as still!
Though cold as e'en the dead can be,
    It feels, it sickens with the chill.

7.

Thou bitter pledge! thou mournful token!
    Though painful, welcome to my breast!
Still, still, preserve that love unbroken,
    Or break the heart to which thou'rt pressed.
Time tempers Love, but not removes,
    More hallowed when its Hope is fled:
Oh! what are thousand living loves
    To that which cannot quit the dead?

EUTHANASIA

1.

When Time, or soon or late, shall bring
    The dreamless sleep that lulls the dead,
Oblivion! may thy languid wing
    Wave gently o'er my dying bed!

2.

No band of friends or heirs be there,
To weep, or wish, the coming blow:
No maiden, with dishevelled hair,
To feel, or feign, decorous woe.

3.

But silent let me sink to Earth,
With no officious mourners near:
I would not mar one hour of mirth,
Nor startle Friendship with a fear.

4.

Yet Love, if Love in such an hour
Could nobly check its useless sighs,
Might then exert its latest power
In her who lives, and him who dies.

5.

'Twere sweet, my Psyche! to the last
Thy features still serene to see:
Forgetful of its struggles past,
E'en Pain itself should smile on thee.

6.

But vain the wish—for Beauty still
Will shrink, as shrinks the ebbing breath;
And Woman's tears, produced at will,
Deceive in life, unman in death.

7.

Then lonely be my latest hour,

Without regret, without a groan;

For thousands Death hath ceased to lower,

And pain been transient or unknown.

8.

"Aye but to die, and go," alas!

Where all have gone, and all must go!

To be the nothing that I was

Ere born to life and living woe!

9.

Count o'er the joys thine hours have seen,

Count o'er thy days from anguish free,

And know, whatever thou hast been,

'Tis something better not to be.

AND THOU ART DEAD, AS YOUNG AND FAIR

"Heu, quanto minus est cum reliquis versari quam tui meminisse!"

1.

And thou art dead, as young and fair

As aught of mortal birth;

And form so soft, and charms so rare,

Too soon returned to Earth!

Though Earth received them in her bed,

And o'er the spot the crowd may tread

In carelessness or mirth,

There is an eye which could not brook

A moment on that grave to look.

2.

I will not ask where thou liest low,
   Nor gaze upon the spot;
There flowers or weeds at will may grow,
   So I behold them not:
It is enough for me to prove
That what I loved, and long must love,
   Like common earth can rot;
To me there needs no stone to tell,
'Tis Nothing that I loved so well.

3.

Yet did I love thee to the last
   As fervently as thou,
Who didst not change through all the past,
   And canst not alter now.
The love where Death has set his seal,
Nor age can chill, nor rival steal
   Nor falsehood disavow:
And, what were worse, thou canst not see
Or wrong, or change, or fault in me.

4.

The better days of life were ours;
   The worst can be but mine:
The sun that cheers, the storm that lowers,
   Shall never more be thine.
The silence of that dreamless sleep
I envy now too much to weep;

Nor need I to repine,
That all those charms have passed away
I might have watched through long decay.

5.

The flower in ripened bloom unmatched
    Must fall the earliest prey;
Though by no hand untimely snatched,
    The leaves must drop away:
And yet it were a greater grief
To watch it withering, leaf by leaf,
    Than see it plucked to-day;
Since earthly eye but ill can bear
To trace the change to foul from fair.

6.

I know not if I could have borne
    To see thy beauties fade;
The night that followed such a morn
    Had worn a deeper shade:
Thy day without a cloud hath passed,
And thou wert lovely to the last;
    Extinguished, not decayed;
As stars that shoot along the sky
Shine brightest as they fall from high.

7.

As once I wept, if I could weep,
    My tears might well be shed,
To think I was not near to keep
    One vigil o'er thy bed;

To gaze, how fondly! on thy face,
To fold thee in a faint embrace,
    Uphold thy drooping head;
And show that love, however vain,
Nor thou nor I can feel again.

                    8.

Yet how much less it were to gain,
    Though thou hast left me free,
The loveliest things that still remain,
    Than thus remember thee!
The all of thine that cannot die
Through dark and dread Eternity
    Returns again to me,
And more thy buried love endears
Than aught, except its living years.   February, 1812.

LINES TO A LADY WEEPING

Weep, daughter of a royal line,
    A Sire's disgrace, a realm's decay;
Ah! happy if each tear of thine
    Could wash a Father's fault away!
Weep—for thy tears are Virtue's tears—
    Auspicious to these suffering Isles;
And be each drop in future years
    Repaid thee by thy People's smiles!   March, 1812.

IF SOMETIMES IN THE HAUNTS OF MEN

1.

If sometimes in the haunts of men
  Thine image from my breast may fade,
The lonely hour presents again
  The semblance of thy gentle shade:
And now that sad and silent hour
  Thus much of thee can still restore,
And sorrow unobserved may pour
  The plaint she dare not speak before.

2.

Oh, pardon that in crowds awhile
  I waste one thought I owe to thee,
And self-condemned, appear to smile,
  Unfaithful to thy memory:
Nor deem that memory less dear,
  That then I seem not to repine;
I would not fools should overhear
  One sigh that should be wholly *thine.*

3.

If not the Goblet pass unquaffed,
  It is not drained to banish care;
The cup must hold a deadlier draught
  That brings a Lethe for despair.
And could Oblivion set my soul
  From all her troubled visions free,
I'd dash to earth the sweetest bowl
  That drowned a single thought of thee.

4.

For wert thou vanished from my mind,
    Where could my vacant bosom turn?
And who would then remain behind
    To honour thine abandoned Urn?
No, no—it is my sorrow's pride
    That last dear duty to fulfil;
Though all the world forget beside,
    'Tis meet that I remember still.

5.

For well I know, that such had been
    Thy gentle care for him, who now
Unmourned shall quit this mortal scene,
    Where none regarded him, but thou:
And, oh! I feel in *that* was given
    A blessing never meant for me;
Thou wert too like a dream of Heaven,
    For earthly Love to merit thee.   March 14, 1812.

ON A CORNELIAN HEART WHICH WAS BROKEN

1.

Ill-fated Heart! and can it be,
    That thou shouldst thus be rent in twain?
Have years of care for thine and thee
    Alike been all employed in vain?

2.

Yet precious seems each shattered part,
And every fragment dearer grown,
Since he who wears thee feels thou art
A fitter emblem of *his own.*

March 16, 1812.

THE CHAIN I GAVE
FROM THE TURKISH

1.

The chain I gave was fair to view,
The lute I added sweet in sound;
The heart that offered both was true,
And ill deserved the fate it found.

2.

These gifts were charmed by secret spell,
Thy truth in absence to divine;
And they have done their duty well,—
Alas! they could not teach thee thine.

3.

That chain was firm in every link,
But not to bear a stranger's touch;
That lute was sweet—till thou couldst think
In other hands its notes were such.

4.

Let him who from thy neck unbound
The chain which shivered in his grasp,
Who saw that lute refuse to sound,
Restring the chords, renew the clasp.

5.

When thou wert changed, they altered too;

The chain is broke, the music mute,

'Tis past—to them and thee adieu—

False heart, frail chain, and silent lute.

LINES WRITTEN ON A BLANK LEAF OF THE PLEASURES OF MEMORY

1.

Absent or present, still to thee,

My friend, what magic spells belong!

As all can tell, who share, like me,

In turn thy converse, and thy song.

2.

But when the dreaded hour shall come

By Friendship ever deemed too nigh,

And "MEMORY" o'er her Druid's tomb

Shall weep that aught of thee can die,

3.

How fondly will she then repay

Thy homage offered at her shrine,

And blend, while ages roll away,

Her name immortally with *thine*!   April 19, 1812.

ADDRESS, SPOKEN AT THE OPENING OF DRURY-LANE THEATRE, SATURDAY, OCTOBER 10, 1812

In one dread night our city saw, and sighed,
Bowed to the dust, the Drama's tower of pride;
In one short hour beheld the blazing fane,
Apollo sink, and Shakespeare cease to reign.

Ye who beheld, (oh! sight admired and mourned,
Whose radiance mocked the ruin it adorned!)
Through clouds of fire the massy fragments riven,
Like Israel's pillar, chase the night from heaven;
Saw the long column of revolving flames
Shake its red shadow o'er the startled Thames,
While thousands, thronged around the burning dome,
Shrank back appalled, and trembled for their home,
As glared the volumed blaze, and ghastly shone
The skies, with lightnings awful as their own,
Till blackening ashes and the lonely wall
Usurped the Muse's realm, and marked her fall;
Say—shall this new, nor less aspiring pile,
Reared where once rose the mightiest in our isle,
Know the same favour which the former knew,
A shrine for Shakespeare—worthy him and *you*?

Yes—it shall be—the magic of that name
Defies the scythe of time, the torch of flame;
On the same spot still consecrates the scene,

And bids the Drama *be* where she hath *been*:
This fabric's birth attests the potent spell—
Indulge our honest pride, and say, *How well*!

As soars this fane to emulate the last,
Oh! might we draw our omens from the past,
Some hour propitious to our prayers may boast
Names such as hallow still the dome we lost.
On Drury first your Siddons' thrilling art
O'erwhelmed the gentlest, stormed the sternest heart.
On Drury, Garrick's latest laurels grew;
Here your last tears retiring Roscius drew,
Sighed his last thanks, and wept his last adieu:
But still for living wit the wreaths may bloom,
That only waste their odours o'er the tomb.
Such Drury claimed and claims—nor you refuse
One tribute to revive his slumbering muse;
With garlands deck your own Menander's head,
Nor hoard your honours idly for the dead!
Dear are the days which made our annals bright,
Ere Garrick fled, or Brinsley ceased to write,
Heirs to their labours, like all high-born heirs,
Vain of *our* ancestry as they of *theirs*;
While thus Remembrance borrows Banquo's glass
To claim the sceptred shadows as they pass,
And we the mirror hold, where imaged shine
Immortal names, emblazoned on our line,
Pause—ere their feebler offspring you condemn,
Reflect how hard the task to rival them!

Friends of the stage! to whom both Players and Plays
Must sue alike for pardon or for praise,
Whose judging voice and eye alone direct
The boundless power to cherish or reject;
If e'er frivolity has led to fame,
And made us blush that you forbore to blame—
If e'er the sinking stage could condescend
To soothe the sickly taste it dare not mend—
All past reproach may present scenes refute,
And censure, wisely loud, be justly mute!
Oh! since your fiat stamps the Drama's laws,
Forbear to mock us with misplaced applause;
So Pride shall doubly nerve the actor's powers,
And Reason's voice be echoed back by ours!

This greeting o'er—the ancient rule obeyed,
The Drama's homage by her herald paid—
Receive *our welcome* too—whose every tone
Springs from our hearts, and fain would win your own.
The curtain rises—may our stage unfold
Scenes not unworthy Drury's days of old!
Britons our judges, Nature for our guide,
Still may *we* please—long, long may *you* preside.

PARENTHETICAL ADDRESS

BY DR. PLAGIARY.

Half stolen, with acknowledgments, to be spoken in an inarticulate voice by Master — at the opening of the next new theatre. (Stolen parts marked with the inverted commas of quotation—thus "—".)

"When energising objects men pursue,"

Then Lord knows what is writ by Lord knows who.

A modest Monologue you here survey,

Hissed from the theatre the "other day,"

As if Sir Fretful wrote "the slumberous" verse,

And gave his son "the rubbish" to rehearse.

"Yet at the thing you'd never be amazed,"

Knew you the rumpus which the Author raised;

"Nor even here your smiles would be represt,"

Knew you these lines—the badness of the best,

"Flame! fire! and flame!" (words borrowed from Lucretius.)

"Dread metaphors" which open wounds like issues!

"And sleeping pangs awake—and— But away"—

(Confound me if I know what next to say).

Lo "Hope reviving re-expands her wings,"

And Master G— recites what Dr. Busby sings!—

"If mighty things with small we may compare,"

(Translated from the Grammar for the fair!)

Dramatic "spirit drives a conquering car,"

And burn'd poor Moscow like a tub of "tar."

"This spirit" "Wellington has shown in Spain,"

To furnish Melodrames for Drury Lane.

"Another Marlborough points to Blenheim's story,"

And George and I will dramatise it for ye.

"In Arts and Sciences our Isle hath shone"

(This deep discovery is mine alone).

Oh "British poesy, whose powers inspire"

My verse—or I'm a fool—and Fame's a liar,

"Thee we invoke, your Sister Arts implore"

With "smiles," and "lyres," and "pencils," and much more.

These, if we win the Graces, too, we gain

Disgraces, too! "inseparable train!"

"Three who have stolen their witching airs from Cupid"

(You all know what I mean, unless you're stupid):

"Harmonious throng" that I have kept *in petto*

Now to produce in a "divine *sestetto*"!!

"While Poesy," with these delightful doxies,

"Sustains her part" in all the "upper" boxes!

"Thus lifted gloriously, you'll sweep along,"

Borne in the vast balloon of Busby's song;

"Shine in your farce, masque, scenery, and play"

(For this last line George had a holiday).

"Old Drury never, never soar'd so high,"

So says the Manager, and so say I.

"But hold," you say, "this self-complacent boast;

"Is this the Poem which the public lost?"

True—true—that lowers at once our mounting pride;

"But lo;—the Papers print what you deride.

"'Tis ours to look on *you—you* hold the prize,"

'Tis *twenty guineas,* as they advertise!

"A *double* blessing your rewards impart"—

I wish I had them, then, with all my heart.

"Our *twofold* feeling *owns* its twofold cause,"

Why son and I both beg for your applause.

"When in your fostering beams you bid us live,"

My next subscription list shall say how much you give!

VERSES FOUND IN A SUMMER-HOUSE AT HALES-OWEN

When Dryden's fool, "unknowing what he sought,"
His hours in whistling spent, "for want of thought,"
This guiltless oaf his vacancy of sense
Supplied, and amply too, by innocence:
Did modern swains, possessed of Cymon's powers,
In Cymon's manner waste their leisure hours,
Th' offended guests would not, with blushing, see
These fair green walks disgraced by infamy.
Severe the fate of modern fools, alas!
When vice and folly mark them as they pass.
Like noxious reptiles o'er the whitened wall,
The filth they leave still points out where they crawl.

REMEMBER THEE! REMEMBER THEE!

1.

Remember thee! remember thee!
   Till Lethe quench life's burning stream
Remorse and Shame shall cling to thee,
   And haunt thee like a feverish dream!

2.

Remember thee! Aye, doubt it not.
   Thy husband too shall think of thee:
By neither shalt thou be forgot,
   Thou *false* to him, thou *fiend* to me!

TO TIME

Time! on whose arbitrary wing
   The varying hours must flag or fly,
Whose tardy winter, fleeting spring,
   But drag or drive us on to die—
Hail thou! who on my birth bestowed
   Those boons to all that know thee known;
Yet better I sustain thy load,
   For now I bear the weight alone.
I would not one fond heart should share
   The bitter moments thou hast given;
And pardon thee—since thou couldst spare
   All that I loved, to peace or Heaven.
To them be joy or rest—on me
   Thy future ills shall press in vain;
I nothing owe but years to thee,
   A debt already paid in pain.
Yet even that pain was some relief;
   It felt, but still forgot thy power:
The active agony of grief
   Retards, but never counts the hour.
In joy I've sighed to think thy flight
   Would soon subside from swift to slow;
Thy cloud could overcast the light,
   But could not add a night to Woe;
For then, however drear and dark,
   My soul was suited to thy sky;
One star alone shot forth a spark

To prove thee—not Eternity.

That beam hath sunk—and now thou art

    A blank—a thing to count and curse

Through each dull tedious trifling part,

    Which all regret, yet all rehearse.

One scene even thou canst not deform—

    The limit of thy sloth or speed

When future wanderers bear the storm

    Which we shall sleep too sound to heed.

And I can smile to think how weak

    Thine efforts shortly shall be shown,

When all the vengeance thou canst wreak

    Must fall upon—a nameless stone.

TRANSLATION OF A ROMAIC LOVE SONG

1.

Ah! Love was never yet without

The pang, the agony, the doubt,

Which rends my heart with ceaseless sigh,

While day and night roll darkling by.

2.

Without one friend to hear my woe,

I faint, I die beneath the blow.

That Love had arrows, well I knew,

Alas! I find them poisoned too.

3.

Birds, yet in freedom, shun the net
Which Love around your haunts hath set;
Or, circled by his fatal fire,
Your hearts shall burn, your hopes expire.

4.

A bird of free and careless wing
Was I, through many a smiling spring;
But caught within the subtle snare,
I burn, and feebly flutter there.

5.

Who ne'er have loved, and loved in vain,
Can neither feel nor pity pain,
The cold repulse, the look askance,
The lightning of Love's angry glance.

6.

In flattering dreams I deemed thee mine;
Now hope, and he who hoped, decline;
Like melting wax, or withering flower,
I feel my passion, and thy power.

7.

My light of Life! ah, tell me why
That pouting lip, and altered eye?
My bird of Love! my beauteous mate!
And art thou changed, and canst thou hate?

8.

Mine eyes like wintry streams o'erflow:

What wretch with me would barter woe?

My bird! relent: one note could give

A charm to bid thy lover live.

9.

My curdling blood, my madd'ning brain,

In silent anguish I sustain;

And still thy heart, without partaking

One pang, exults—while mine is breaking.

10.

Pour me the poison; fear not thou!

Thou canst not murder more than now:

I've lived to curse my natal day,

And Love, that thus can lingering slay.

11.

My wounded soul, my bleeding breast,

Can patience preach thee into rest?

Alas! too late, I dearly know

That Joy is harbinger of Woe.

THOU ART NOT FALSE, BUT THOU ART FICKLE

1.

Thou art not false, but thou art fickle,

  To those thyself so fondly sought;

The tears that thou hast forced to trickle

  Are doubly bitter from that thought:

'Tis this which breaks the heart thou grievest,
Too well thou lov'st—*too soon* thou leavest.

2.

The wholly false the *heart* despises,
   And spurns deceiver and deceit;
But she who not a thought disguises,
   Whose love is as sincere as sweet,—
When *she* can change who loved so truly,
It *feels* what mine has *felt* so newly.

3.

To dream of joy and wake to sorrow
   Is doomed to all who love or live;
And if, when conscious on the morrow,
   We scarce our Fancy can forgive,
That cheated us in slumber only,
To leave the waking soul more lonely,

4.

What must they feel whom no false vision
   But truest, tenderest Passion warmed?
Sincere, but swift in sad transition:
   As if a dream alone had charmed?
Ah! sure such *grief* is *Fancy's* scheming,
And all thy *Change* can be but *dreaming*!

ON BEING ASKED WHAT WAS THE "ORIGIN OF LOVE"

The "Origin of Love!"—Ah, why
That cruel question ask of me,
When thou mayst read in many an eye
He starts to life on seeing thee?
And shouldst thou seek his *end* to know:
My heart forebodes, my fears foresee,
He'll linger long in silent woe;
But live until—I cease to be.

ON THE QUOTATION,

"And my true faith can alter never,
Though thou art gone perhaps for ever."

1.

And "thy true faith can alter never?"—
Indeed it lasted for a—week!
I know the length of Love's forever,
And just expected such a freak.
In peace we met, in peace we parted,
In peace we vowed to meet again,
And though I find thee fickle-hearted
No pang of mine shall make thee vain.

2.

One gone—'twas time to seek a second;
In sooth 'twere hard to blame thy haste.
And whatsoe'er thy love be reckoned,
At least thou hast improved in taste:

Though one was young, the next was younger,

His love was new, mine too well known—

And what might make the charm still stronger,

The youth was present, I was flown.

3.

Seven days and nights of single sorrow!

Too much for human constancy!

A fortnight past, why then to-morrow,

His turn is come to follow me:

And if each week you change a lover,

And so have acted heretofore,

Before a year or two is over

We'll form a very pretty *corps*.

4.

Adieu, fair thing! without upbraiding

I fain would take a decent leave;

Thy beauty still survives unfading,

And undeceived may long deceive.

With him unto thy bosom dearer

Enjoy the moments as they flee;

I only wish his love sincerer

Than thy young heart has been to me.   1812.

REMEMBER HIM, WHOM PASSION'S POWER

1.

Remember him, whom Passion's power

Severely—deeply—vainly proved:

Remember thou that dangerous hour,

When neither fell, though both were loved.

2.

That yielding breast, that melting eye,
    Too much invited to be blessed:
That gentle prayer, that pleading sigh,
    The wilder wish reproved, repressed.

3.

Oh! let me feel that all I lost
    But saved thee all that Consicence fears;
And blush for every pang it cost
    To spare the vain remorse of years.

4.

Yet think of this when many a tongue
    Whose busy accents whisper blame,
Would do the heart that loved thee wrong,
    And brand a nearly blighted name.

5.

Think that, whate'er to others, thou
    Hast seen each selfish thought subdued:
I bless thy purer soul even now,
    Even now, in midnight solitude.

6.

Oh, God! that we had met in time,
    Our hearts as fond, thy hand more free;
When thou hadst loved without a crime,
    And I been less unworthy thee!

7.

Far may thy days, as heretofore,
　　From this our gaudy world be past!
And that too bitter moment o'er,
　　Oh! may such trial be thy last.

8.

This heart, alas! perverted long,
　　Itself destroyed might there destroy;
To meet thee in the glittering throng,
　　Would wake Presumption's hope of joy.

9.

Then to the things whose bliss or woe,
　　Like mine, is wild and worthless all,
That world resign—such scenes forego,
　　Where those who feel must surely fall.

10.

Thy youth, thy charms, thy tenderness—
　　Thy soul from long seclusion pure;
From what even here hath passed, may guess
　　What there thy bosom must endure.

11.

Oh! pardon that imploring tear,
　　Since not by Virtue shed in vain,
My frenzy drew from eyes so dear;
　　For me they shall not weep again.

12.

Though long and mournful must it be,
  The thought that we no more may meet;
Yet I deserve the stern decree,
  And almost deem the sentence sweet.

13.

Still—had I loved thee less—my heart
  Had then less sacrificed to thine;
It felt not half so much to part
  As if its guilt had made thee mine.   1813.

IMPROMPTU, IN REPLY TO A FRIEND

When, from the heart where Sorrow sits,
  Her dusky shadow mounts too high,
And o'er the changing aspect flits,
  And clouds the brow, or fills the eye;
Heed not that gloom, which soon shall sink:
  My Thoughts their dungeon know too well;
Back to my breast the Wanderers shrink,
  And *droop* within their silent cell.   September, 1813.

SONNET

TO GENEVRA

Thine eyes' blue tenderness, thy long fair hair,
  And the warm lustre of thy features—caught
  From contemplation—where serenely wrought,

Seems Sorrow's softness charmed from its despair—
Have thrown such speaking sadness in thine air,
That—but I know thy blessed bosom fraught
With mines of unalloyed and stainless thought—
I should have deemed thee doomed to earthly care.
With such an aspect, by his colours blent,
When from his beauty-breathing pencil born,
(Except that *thou* hast nothing to repent)
The Magdalen of Guido saw the morn—
Such seem'st thou—but how much more excellent!
With nought Remorse can claim—nor Virtue scorn.

December 17, 1813.

SONNET

TO GENEVRA

Thy cheek is pale with thought, but not from woe,
And yet so lovely, that if Mirth could flush
Its rose of whiteness with the brightest blush,
My heart would wish away that ruder glow:
And dazzle not thy deep-blue eyes—but, oh!
While gazing on them sterner eyes will gush,
And into mine my mother's weakness rush,
Soft as the last drops round Heaven's airy bow.
For, through thy long dark lashes low depending,
The soul of melancholy Gentleness
Gleams like a Seraph from the sky descending,
Above all pain, yet pitying all distress;
At once such majesty with sweetness blending,
I worship more, but cannot love thee less.

December 17, 1813.

FROM. THE PORTUGUESE

"TU MI CHAMAS"

1.

In moments to delight devoted,

    "My Life!" with tenderest tone, you cry;

Dear words! on which my heart had doted,

    If Youth could neither fade nor die.

2.

To Death even hours like these must roll,

    Ah! then repeat those accents never;

Or change "my Life!" into " my Soul!"

    Which, like my Love, exists for ever.

ANOTHER VERSION

You call me still your *Life*.—Oh! change the word—

    Life is as transient as the inconstant sigh:

Say rather I'm your Soul; more just that name,

    For, like the soul, my Love can never die.

THE GIAOUR: A FRAGMENT OF A TURKISH TALE

"One fatal remembrance—one sorrow that throws
Its bleak shade alike o'er our joys and our woes—
To which Life nothing darker nor brighter can bring,
For which joy hath no balm—and affliction no sting."
　—MOORE.

TO

SAMUEL ROGERS, ESQ.

AS A SLIGHT BUT MOST SINCERE TOKEN

OF ADMIRATION OF HIS GENIUS,

RESPECT FOR HIS CHARACTER

AND GRATITUDE FOR HIS FRIENDSHIP,

THIS PRODUCTION IS INSCRIBED

BY HIS OBLIGED

AND AFFECTIONATE SERVANT,

BYRON.

London,
May, 1813.

ADVERTISEMENT

The tale which these disjointed fragments present, is founded upon circumstances now less common in the East than formerly; either because the ladies are more circumspect than in the "olden time," or because the Christians have better fortune, or less enterprise. The story, when entire, contained the adventures of a female slave, who was thrown, in the Mussulman manner, into the sea for infidelity, and avenged by a young Venetian, her lover, at the time the Seven Islands were possessed by the Republic of Venice, and soon after the Arnauts were beaten back from the Morea, which they had ravaged for some time subsequent to the Russian invasion. The desertion of the Mainotes, on being refused the plunder of Misitra, led to the abandonment of that enterprise, and to the desolation of the Morea, during which the cruelty exercised on all sides was unparalleled even in the annals of the faithful.

No breath of air to break the wave

That rolls below the Athenian's grave,

That tomb[i] which, gleaming o'er the cliff,

First greets the homeward-veering skiff

High o'er the land he saved in vain;

When shall such Hero live again?

i. A tomb above the rocks on the promontory, by some supposed the sepulchre of Themistocles.

* * * * *

Fair clime! where every season smiles

Benignant o'er those blessed isles,

Which, seen from far Colonna's height,

Make glad the heart that hails the sight,

And lend to loneliness delight.

There mildly dimpling, Ocean's cheek

Reflects the tints of many a peak

Caught by the laughing tides that lave
These Edens of the eastern wave:
And if at times a transient breeze
Break the blue crystal of the seas,
Or sweep one blossom from the trees,
How welcome is each gentle air
That wakes and wafts the odours there!
For there the Rose, o'er crag or vale,
Sultana of the Nightingale,[i]

   The maid for whom his melody,

   His thousand songs are heard on high,
Blooms blushing to her lover's tale:
His queen, the garden queen, his Rose,
Unbent by winds, unchilled by snows,
Far from the winters of the west,
By every breeze and season blest,
Returns the sweets by Nature given
In softest incense back to Heaven;
And grateful yields that smiling sky
Her fairest hue and fragrant sigh.
And many a summer flower is there,
And many a shade that Love might share,
And many a grotto, meant for rest,
That holds the pirate for a guest;
Whose bark in sheltering cove below
Lurks for the passing peaceful prow,
Till the gay mariner's guitar
Is heard, and seen the Evening Star;
Then stealing with the muffled oar,

Far shaded by the rocky shore,

Rush the night-prowlers on the prey,

And turn to groans his roundelay.

Strange—that where Nature loved to trace,

As if for Gods, a dwelling place,

And every charm and grace hath mixed

Within the Paradise she fixed,

There man, enamoured of distress,

Should mar it into wilderness,

And trample, brute-like, o'er each flower

That tasks not one laborious hour;

Nor claims the culture of his hand

To bloom along the fairy land,

But springs as to preclude his care,

And sweetly woos him—but to spare!

Strange—that where all is Peace beside,

There Passion riots in her pride,

And Lust and Rapine wildly reign

To darken o'er the fair domain.

It is as though the Fiends prevailed

Against the Seraphs they assailed,

And, fixed on heavenly thrones, should dwell

The freed inheritors of Hell;

So soft the scene, so formed for joy,

So curst the tyrants that destroy!

i. The attachment of the nightingale to the rose is a well-known Persian fable. If I mistake not, the "Bulbul of a thousand tales" is one of his appellations.

He who hath bent him o'er the dead

Ere the first day of Death is fled,

The first dark day of Nothingness,

The last of Danger and Distress,

(Before Decay's effacing fingers

Have swept the lines where Beauty lingers,)

And marked the mild angelic air,

The rapture of Repose that's there,

The fixed yet tender traits that streak

The languor of the placid cheek,

And—but for that sad shrouded eye,

    That fires not, wins not, weeps not, now,

    And but for that chill, changeless brow,

Where cold Obstruction's apathy[i]

Appals the gazing mourner's heart,

As if to him it could impart

The doom he dreads, yet dwells upon;

Yes, but for these and these alone,

Some moments, aye, one treacherous hour,

He still might doubt the Tyrant's power;

So fair, so calm, so softly sealed,

The first, last look by Death revealed![ii]

Such is the aspect of this shore;

'Tis Greece, but living Greece no more!

So coldly sweet, so deadly fair,

We start, for Soul is wanting there.

Hers is the loveliness in death,

That parts not quite with parting breath;

But beauty with that fearful bloom,

That hue which haunts it to the tomb,

Expression's last receding ray,

A gilded Halo hovering round decay,

The farewell beam of Feeling past away!

Spark of that flame, perchance of heavenly birth,

Which gleams, but warms no more its cherished earth!

i.   "Aye, but to die, and go we know not where;
         To lie in cold obstruction?"
                 Measure for Measure, act iii. sc. 1, lines 115, 116.

ii. I trust that few of my readers have ever had an opportunity of witnessing what is here attempted in description; but those who have will probably retain a painful remembrance of that singular beauty which pervades, with few exceptions, the features of the dead, a few hours, and but for a few hours, after "the spirit is not there." It is to be remarked in cases of violent death by gun-shot wounds, the expression is always that of languor, whatever the natural energy of the sufferer's character; but in death from a stab that countenance preserves its traits of feeling or ferocity, and the mind its bias, to the last.

Clime of the unforgotten brave!

Whose land from plain to mountain-cave

Was Freedom's home or Glory's grave!

Shrine of the mighty! can it be,

That this is all remains of thee?

Approach, thou craven crouching slave:

Say, is not this Thermopylæ?

These waters blue that round you lave,—

Oh servile offspring of the free—

Pronounce what sea, what shore is this?

The gulf, the rock of Salamis!

These scenes, their story not unknown,

Arise, and make again your own;

Snatch from the ashes of your Sires

The embers of their former fires;

And he who in the strife expires

Will add to theirs a name of fear

That Tyranny shall quake to hear,

And leave his sons a hope, a fame,

They too will rather die than shame:
For Freedom's battle once begun,
Bequeathed by bleeding Sire to Son,"
Though baffled oft is ever won.
Bear witness, Greece, thy living page!
Attest it many a deathless age!
While Kings, in dusty darkness hid,
Have left a nameless pyramid,
Thy Heroes, though the general doom
Hath swept the column from their tomb,
A mightier monument command,
The mountains of their native land!
There points thy Muse to stranger's eye
The graves of those that cannot die!
'Twere long to tell, and sad to trace,
Each step from Splendour to Disgrace;
Enough—no foreign foe could quell
Thy soul, till from itself it fell;
Yet! Self-abasement paved the way
To villain-bonds and despot sway.

What can he tell who treads thy shore?
    No legend of thine olden time,
No theme on which the Muse might soar
High as thine own in days of yore,
    When man was worthy of thy clime.
The hearts within thy valleys bred,
The fiery souls that might have led
    Thy sons to deeds sublime,

Now crawl from cradle to the Grave,

Slaves—nay, the bondsmen of a Slave,[i]

   And callous, save to crime;

Stained with each evil that pollutes

Mankind, where least above the brutes;

Without even savage virtue blest,

Without one free or valiant breast,

Still to the neighbouring ports they waft

Proverbial wiles, and ancient craft;

In this the subtle Greek is found,

For this, and this alone, renowned.

In vain might Liberty invoke

The spirit to its bondage broke

Or raise the neck that courts the yoke:

No more her sorrows I bewail,

Yet this will be a mournful tale,

And they who listen may believe,

Who heard it first had cause to grieve.

i. Athens is the property of the Kislar Aga (the slave of the Seraglio and guardian of the women), who appoints the Waywode. A pander and eunuch—these are not polite, yet true appellations—now *governs* the *governor* of Athens!

*   *   *   *   *

Far, dark, along the blue sea glancing,

The shadows of the rocks advancing

Start on the fisher's eye like boat

Of island-pirate or Mainote;

And fearful for his light caïque,

He shuns the near but doubtful creek:

Though worn and weary with his toil,

And cumbered with his scaly spoil,

Slowly, yet strongly, plies the oar,
Till Port Leone's safer shore
Receives him by the lovely light
That best becomes an Eastern night.

        *   *   *   *   *

Who thundering comes on blackest steed,
With slackened bit and hoof of speed?
Beneath the clattering iron's sound
The caverned Echoes wake around
In lash for lash, and bound for bound;
The foam that streaks the courser's side
Seems gathered from the Ocean-tide:
Though weary waves are sunk to rest,
There's none within his rider's breast;
And though to-morrow's tempest lower,
'Tis calmer than thy heart, young Giaour!
I know thee not, I loathe thy race,
But in thy lineaments I trace
What Time shall strengthen, not efface:
Though young and pale, that sallow front
Is scathed by fiery Passion's brunt;
Though bent on earth thine evil eye,
As meteor-like thou glidest by,
Right well I view and deem thee one
Whom Othman's sons should slay or shun.

On—on he hastened, and he drew
My gaze of wonder as he flew:
Though like a Demon of the night

He passed, and vanished from my sight,
His aspect and his air impressed
A troubled memory on my breast,
And long upon my startled ear
Rung his dark courser's hoofs of fear.
He spurs his steed; he nears the steep,
That, jutting, shadows o'er the deep;
He winds around; he hurries by;
The rock relieves him from mine eye;
For, well I ween, unwelcome he
Whose glance is fixed on those that flee;
And not a star but shines too bright
On him who takes such timeless flight.
He wound along; but ere he passed
One glance he snatched, as if his last,
A moment checked his wheeling steed,
A moment breathed him from his speed,
A moment on his stirrup stood—
Why looks he o'er the olive wood?
The Crescent glimmers on the hill,
The Mosque's high lamps are quivering still
Though too remote for sound to wake
In echoes of the far tophaike,[i]
The flashes of each joyous peal
Are seen to prove the Moslem's zeal.
To-night, set Rhamazani's sun;
To-night, the Bairam feast's begun;
To-night—but who and what art thou
Of foreign garb and fearful brow?

And what are these to thine or thee,

That thou shouldst either pause or flee?

i. "Tophaike," musket. The Bairam is announced by the cannon at sunset: the illumination of the mosques, and the firing of all kinds of small arms, loaded with *ball,* proclaim it during the night.

He stood—some dread was on his face,

Soon Hatred settled in its place:

It rose not with the reddening flush

Of transient Anger's hasty blush,

But pale as marble o'er the tomb,

Whose ghastly whiteness aids its gloom.

His brow was bent, his eye was glazed;

He raised his arm, and fiercely raised,

And sternly shook his hand on high,

As doubting to return or fly;

Impatient of his flight delayed,

Here loud his raven charger neighed—

Down glanced that hand, and grasped his blade;

That sound had burst his waking dream,

As Slumber starts at owlet's scream.

The spur hath lanced his courser's sides;

Away—away—for life he rides:

Swift as the hurled on high jerreed[i]

Springs to the touch his startled steed;

The rock is doubled, and the shore

Shakes with the clattering tramp no more;

The crag is won, no more is seen

His Christian crest and haughty mien.

'Twas but an instant he restrained

That fiery barb so sternly reined;

'Twas but a moment that he stood,

Then sped as if by Death pursued;

But in that instant o'er his soul

Winters of Memory seemed to roll,

And gather in that drop of time

A life of pain, an age of crime.

O'er him who loves, or hates, or fears,

Such moment pours the grief of years:

What felt *he* then, at once opprest

By all that most distracts the breast?

That pause, which pondered o'er his fate,

Oh, who its dreary length shall date!

Though in Time's record nearly nought,

It was Eternity to Thought!

For infinite as boundless space

The thought that Conscience must embrace,

Which in itself can comprehend

Woe without name, or hope, or end.

i. Jerreed, or Djerrid, a blunted Turkish javelin, which is darted from horseback with great force and precision. It is a favourite exercise of the Mussulmans; but I know not if it can be called a *manly* one, since the most expert in the art are the Black Eunuchs of Constantinople. I think, next to these, a Mamlouk at Smyrna was the most skilful that came within my observation.

The hour is past, the Giaour is gone:

And did he fly or fall alone?

Woe to that hour he came or went!

The curse for Hassan's sin was sent

To turn a palace to a tomb;

He came, he went, like the Simoom,[i]

That harbinger of Fate and gloom,

Beneath whose widely-wasting breath

The very cypress droops to death—

Dark tree, still sad when others' grief is fled,

The only constant mourner o'er the dead!

i. The blast of the desert, fatal to everything living, and often alluded to in Eastern poetry.

The steed is vanished from the stall;

No serf is seen in Hassan's hall;

The lonely Spider's thin gray pall

Waves slowly widening o'er the wall;

The Bat builds in his Haram bower,

And in the fortress of his power

The Owl usurps the beacon-tower;

The wild-dog howls o'er the fountain's brim,

With baffled thirst, and famine, grim;

For the stream has shrunk from its marble bed,

Where the weeds and the desolate dust are spread.

'Twas sweet of yore to see it play

And chase the sultriness of day,

As springing high the silver dew

In whirls fantastically flew,

And flung luxurious coolness round

The air, and verdure o'er the ground.

'Twas sweet, when cloudless stars were bright,

To view the wave of watery light,

And hear its melody by night.

And oft had Hassan's Childhood played

Around the verge of that cascade;

And oft upon his mother's breast

That sound had harmonized his rest;

And oft had Hassan's Youth along

Its bank been soothed by Beauty's song;
And softer seemed each melting tone
Of Music mingled with its own.
But ne'er shall Hassan's Age repose
Along the brink at Twilight's close:
The stream that filled that font is fled—
The blood that warmed his heart is shed!
And here no more shall human voice
Be heard to rage, regret, rejoice.
The last sad note that swelled the gale
Was woman's wildest funeral wail:
That quenched in silence, all is still,
But the lattice that flaps when the wind is shrill:
Though raves the gust, and floods the rain,
No hand shall close its clasp again.
On desert sands 'twere joy to scan
The rudest steps of fellow man,
So here the very voice of Grief
Might wake an Echo like relief—
At least 'twould say, "All are not gone;
There lingers Life, though but in one"—
For many a gilded chamber's there,
Which Solitude might well forbear;
Within that dome as yet Decay
Hath slowly worked her cankering way—
But gloom is gathered o'er the gate,
Nor there the Fakir's self will wait;
Nor there will wandering Dervise stay,
For Bounty cheers not his delay;

Nor there will weary stranger halt

To bless the sacred "bread and salt."

Alike must Wealth and Poverty

Pass heedless and unheeded by,

For Courtesy and Pity died

With Hassan on the mountain side.

His roof, that refuge unto men,

Is Desolation's hungry den.

The guest flies the hall, and the vassal from labour,

Since his turban was cleft by the infidel's sabre![i]

i. I need hardly observe, that Charity and Hospitality are the first duties enjoined by Mahomet; and to say truth, very generally practised by his disciples. The first praise that can be bestowed on a chief is a panegyric on his bounty; the next, on his valour.

*   *   *   *   *

I hear the sound of coming feet,

But not a voice mine ear to greet;

More near—each turban I can scan,

And silver-sheathèd ataghan;[i]

The foremost of the band is seen

An Emir by his garb of green:[ii]

"Ho! who art thou?"—"This low salam[iii]

Replies of Moslem faith I am.

The burthen ye so gently bear,

Seems one that claims your utmost care,

And, doubtless, holds some precious freight—

My humble bark would gladly wait."

i. The staghan, a long dagger worn with pistols in the belt, in a metal scabbard, generally of silver; and, among that wealthier, gilt, or of gold.

ii. Green is the privileged colour of the prophet's numerous pretended descendants; with them, as here, faith (the family inheritance) is supposed to supersede the necessity of good works: they are the worst of a very indifferent brood.

iii. "Salam aleikounm! aleikoum salam!" peace be with you; be with you peace—the salutation reserved for the faithful:—to a Christian, "Urlarula!" a good journey; or "saban hiresem, saban serula," good morn, good even; and sometimes, "may your end be happy!" are the usual salutes.

"Thou speakest sooth: thy skiff unmoor,

And waft us from the silent shore;

Nay, leave the sail still furled, and ply

The nearest oar that's scattered by,

And midway to those rocks where sleep

The channelled waters dark and deep.

Rest from your task—so—bravely done,

Our course has been right swiftly run;

Yet 'tis the longest voyage, I trow,

That one of—*   *   *

                    *   *   *   *   *

Sullen it plunged, and slowly sank,

The calm wave rippled to the bank;

I watched it as it sank, methought

Some motion from the current caught

Bestirred it more,—'twas but the beam

That checkered o'er the living stream:

I gazed, till vanishing from view,

Like lessening pebble it withdrew;

Still less and less, a speck of white

That gemmed the tide, then mocked the sight;

And all its hidden secrets sleep,

Known but to Genii of the deep,

Which, trembling in their coral caves,

They dare not whisper to the waves.

                    *   *   *   *   *

As rising on its purple wing
The insect-queen[i] of Eastern spring,
O'er emerald meadows of Kashmeer
Invites the young pursuer near,
And leads him on from flower to flower
A weary chase and wasted hour,
Then leaves him, as it soars on high,
With panting heart and tearful eye:
So Beauty lures the full-grown child,
With hue as bright, and wing as wild:
A chase of idle hopes and fears,
Begun in folly, closed in tears.
If won, to equal ills betrayed,
Woe waits the insect and the maid;
A life of pain, the loss of peace;
From infant's play, and man's caprice:
The lovely toy so fiercely sought
Hath lost its charm by being caught,
For every touch that wooed its stay
Hath brushed its brightest hues away,
Till charm, and hue, and beauty gone,
'Tis left to fly or fall alone.
With wounded wing, or bleeding breast,
Ah! where shall either victim rest?
Can this with faded pinion soar
From rose to tulip as before?
Or Beauty, blighted in an hour,
Find joy within her broken bower?
No: gayer insects fluttering by

Ne'er droop the wing o'er those that die,

And lovelier things have mercy shown

To every failing but their own,

And every woe a tear can claim

Except an erring Sister's shame.

i. The Blue-winged butterfly of Kashmeer, the most rare and beautiful of the species.

*　　*　　*　　*　　*

The Mind, that broods o'er guilty woes,

　　Is like the Scorpion girt by fire;

In circle narrowing as it glows,

The flames around their captive close,

Till inly searched by thousand throes,

　　And maddening in her ire,

One sad and sole relief she knows—

The sting she nourished for her foes,

Whose venom never yet was vain,

Gives but one pang, and cures all pain,

And darts into her desperate brain:

So do the dark in soul expire,

Or live like Scorpion girt by fire;[i]

So writhes the mind Remorse hath riven,

Unfit for earth, undoomed for heaven,

Darkness above, despair beneath,

Around it flame, within it death!

i. Alluding to the dubious suicide of the scorpion, so placed for experiment by gentle philosophers. Some maintain that the position of the sting, when turned towards the head, is merely a convulsive movement; but others have actually brought in the verdict "Felo de se." The scorpions are surely interested in a speedy decision of the question; as, if once fairly established as insect Catos, they will probably be allowed to live as long as they think proper, without being martyred for the sake of an hypothesis.

*　　*　　*　　*　　*

Black Hassan from the Haram flies,

Nor bends on woman's form his eyes;

The unwonted chase each hour employs,

Yet shares he not the hunter's joys.

Not thus was Hassan wont to fly

When Leila dwelt in his Serai.

Doth Leila there no longer dwell?

That tale can only Hassan tell:

Strange rumours in our city say

Upon that eve she fled away

When Rhamazan's[i] last sun was set,

And flashing from each Minaret

Millions of lamps proclaimed the feast

Of Bairam through the boundless East.

'Twas then she went as to the bath,

Which Hassan vainly searched in wrath;

For she was flown her master's rage

In likeness of a Georgian page,

And far beyond the Moslem's power

Had wronged him with the faithless Giaour.

Somewhat of this had Hassan deemed;

But still so fond, so fair she seemed,

Too well he trusted to the slave

Whose treachery deserved a grave:

And on that eve had gone to Mosque,

And thence to feast in his Kiosk.

Such is the tale his Nubians tell,

Who did not watch their charge too well;

But others say, that on that night,

By pale Phingari's[ii] trembling light,

The Giaour upon his jet-black steed

Was seen, but seen alone to speed

With bloody spur along the shore,

Nor maid nor page behind him bore.

i. The cannon at sunset close the Rhamazan.

ii. Phingari, the moon.

*   *   *   *   *

Her eye's dark charm 'twere vain to tell,

But gaze on that of the Gazelle,

It will assist thy fancy well;

As large, as languishingly dark,

But Soul beamed forth in every spark

That darted from beneath the lid,

Bright as the jewel of Giamschid.[i]

Yea, *Soul,* and should our prophet say

That form was nought but breathing clay,

By Alla! I would answer nay;

Though on Al-Sirat's[ii] arch I stood,

Which totters o'er the fiery flood,

With Paradise within my view,

And all his Houris beckoning through.

Oh! who young Leila's glance could read

And keep that portion of his creed

Which saith that woman is but dust,

A soulless toy for tyrant's lust?[iii]

On her might Muftis gaze, and own

That through her eye the Immortal shone;

On her fair cheek's unfading hue

The young pomegranate's[iv] blossoms strew

Their bloom in blushes ever new;

Her hair in hyacinthine flow,[v]

When left to roll its folds below,

As midst her handmaids in the hall

She stood superior to them all,

Hath swept the marble where her feet

Gleamed whiter than the mountain sleet

Ere from the cloud that gave it birth

It fell, and caught one stain of earth.

The cygnet nobly walks the water;

So moved on earth Circassia's daughter,

The loveliest bird of Franguestan![vi]

As rears her crest the ruffled Swan,

 And spurns the wave with wings of pride,

When pass the steps of stranger man

 Along the banks that bound her tide;

Thus rose fair Leila's whiter neck:—

Thus armed with beauty would she check

Intrusion's glance, till Folly's gaze

Shrunk from the charms it meant to praise.

Thus high and graceful was her gait;

Her heart as tender to her mate;

Her mate—stern Hassan, who was he?

Alas! that name was not for thee!

i. The celebrated fabulous ruby of Sultan Giamschid, the embellisher of Istakhar; from its splendour, named Schebgerag, "the torch of night;" also "the cup of the sun," etc. In the First Edition, "Giamschid" was written as a word of three syllables; so D'Herbelot has it; but I am told Richardson reduces it to a dissyllable, and writes "Jamshid." I have left in the text the orthography of the one with the pronunciation of the other.

ii. Al-Sirat, the bridge of breadth narrower than the thread of a famished spider, and sharper than the edge of a sword, over which the Mussulmans must *skate* into Paradise, to which it is the only entrance; but this is not the worst, the river beneath being hell itself, into which, as may be expected, the unskilful and tender of foot contrive to tumble with a "facilis descensus Averni," not very pleasing in prospect to the next passenger. There is a shorter cut downwards for the Jews and Christians.

iii. A vulgar error: the Koran allots at least a third of Paradise to well-behaved women; but by far the greater number of Mussulmans interpret the text their own way, and exclude their moieties from heaven. Being enemies to Platonics, they cannot discern "any fitness of things" in the souls of the other sex, conceiving them to be superseded by the Houris.

iv. An Oriental simile, which may, perhaps, though fairly stolen, be deemed "plus Arabe qu'en Arabie."

v. Hyacinthine, in Arabic "Sunbul;" as common a thought in the Eastern poets as it was among the Greeks.

vi. "Franguestan," Cricassia.

*   *   *   *   *

Stern Hassan hath a journey ta'en

With twenty vassals in his train,

Each armed, as best becomes a man,

With arquebuss and ataghan;

The chief before, as decked for war,

Bears in his belt the scimitar

Stained with the best of Arnaut blood,

When in the pass the rebels stood,

And few returned to tell the tale

Of what befell in Parne's vale.

The pistols which his girdle bore

Were those that once a Pasha wore,

Which still, though gemmed and bossed with gold,

Even robbers tremble to behold.

'Tis said he goes to woo a bride

More true than her who left his side;

The faithless slave that broke her bower,

And—worse than faithless—for a Giaour!

*   *   *   *   *

The sun's last rays are on the hill,

And sparkle in the fountain rill,

Whose welcome waters, cool and clear,

Draw blessings from the mountaineer:

Here may the loitering merchant Greek

Find that repose 'twere vain to seek

In cities lodged too near his lord,

And trembling for his secret hoard—

Here may he rest where none can see,

In crowds a slave, in deserts free;

And with forbidden wine may stain

The bowl a Moslem must not drain

*   *   *   *   *

The foremost Tartar's in the gap

Conspicuous by his yellow cap;

The rest in lengthening line the while

Wind slowly through the long defile:

Above, the mountain rears a peak,

Where vultures whet the thirsty beak,

And theirs may be a feast to-night,

Shall tempt them down ere morrow's light;

Beneath, a river's wintry stream

Has shrunk before the summer beam,

And left a channel bleak and bare,

Save shrubs that spring to perish there:

Each side the midway path there lay

Small broken crags of granite gray,
By time, or mountain lightning, riven
From summits clad in mists of heaven;
For where is he that hath beheld
The peak of Liakura unveiled?

        *   *   *   *   *

They reach the grove of pine at last;
"Bismillah!ⁱ now the peril's past;
For yonder view the opening plain,
And there we'll prick our steeds amain:"
The Chiaus, spake, and as he said,
A bullet whistled o'er his head;
The foremost Tartar bites the ground!

    Scarce had they time to check the rein,
Swift from their steeds the riders bound;

    But three shall never mount again:
Unseen the foes that gave the wound,

    The dying ask revenge in vain.
With steel unsheathed, and carbine bent,
Some o'er their courser's harness leant,

    Half sheltered by the steed;
Some fly beneath the nearest rock,
And there await the coming shock,

    Nor tamely stand to bleed
Beneath the shaft of foes unseen,
Who dare not quit their craggy screen.
Stern Hassan only from his horse
Disdains to light, and keeps his course,
Till fiery flashes in the van

Proclaim too sure the robber-clan

Have well secured the only way

Could now avail the promised prey;

Then curled his very beard[ii] with ire,

And glared his eye with fiercer fire;

"Though far and near the bullets hiss,

I've scaped a bloodier hour than this."

And now the foe their covert quit,

And call his vassals to submit;

But Hassan's frown and furious word

Are dreaded more than hostile sword,

Nor of his little band a man

Resigned carbine or ataghan,

Nor raised the craven cry, Amaun![iii]

In fuller sight, more near and near,

The lately ambushed foes appear,

And, issuing from the grove, advance

Some who on battle-charger prance.

Who leads them on with foreign brand

Far flashing in his red right hand?

"'Tis he! 'tis he! I know him now;

I know him by his pallid brow;

I know him by the evil eye[iv]

That aids his envious treachery;

I know him by his jet-black barb;

Though now arrayed in Arnaut garb,

Apostate from his own vile faith,

It shall not save him from the death:

'Tis he! well met in any hour,

Lost Leila's love—accursed Giaour!"

i. "In the name of God;" the commencement of all the chapters of the Koran but one, and of prayer and thanksgiving.

ii. A phenomenon not uncommon with an angry Mussulman. In 1809 the Capitan Pacha's whiskers at a diplomatic audience were no less lively with indignation than a tiger cat's, to the horror of all the dragomans; the portentous mustachios twisted, they stood erect of their own accord, and were expected every moment to change their colour, but at last condescended to subside, which, probably, saved more heads than they contained hairs.

iii. "Amaun," quarter, pardon.

iv. The "evil eye," a common superstition in the Levant, and of which the imaginary effects are yet very singular on those who conceive themselves affected.

As rolls the river into Ocean,

In sable torrent wildly streaming;

As the sea-tide's opposing motion,

In azure column proudly gleaming,

Beats back the current many a rood,

In curling foam and mingling flood,

While eddying whirl, and breaking wave,

Roused by the blast of winter, rave;

Through sparkling spray, in thundering clash,

The lightnings of the waters flash

In awful whiteness o'er the shore,

That shines and shakes beneath the roar;

Thus—as the stream and Ocean greet,

With waves that madden as they meet—

Thus join the bands, whom mutual wrong,

And fate, and fury, drive along.

The bickering sabres' shivering jar;

And pealing wide or ringing near

Its echoes on the throbbing ear,

The deathshot hissing from afar;

The shock, the shout, the groan of war

    Reverberate along that vale,

    More suited to the shepherd's tale:

Though few the numbers—theirs the strife,

That neither spares nor speaks for life!

Ah! fondly youthful hearts can press,

To seize and share the dear caress;

But Love itself could never pant

For all that Beauty sighs to grant

With half the fervour Hate bestows

Upon the last embrace of foes,

When grappling in the fight they fold

Those arms that ne'er shall lose their hold:

Friends meet to part; Love laughs at faith;

True foes, once met, are joined till death!

        *   *   *   *   *

With sabre shivered to the hilt,

Yet dripping with the blood he spilt;

Yet strained within the severed hand

Which quivers round that faithless brand;

His turban far behind him rolled,

And cleft in twain its firmest fold;

His flowing robe by falchion torn,

And crimson as those clouds of morn

That, streaked with dusky red, portend

The day shall have a stormy end;

A stain on every bush that bore

A fragment of his palampore;[i]

His breast with wounds unnumbered riven,

His back to earth, his face to Heaven,

Fall'n Hassan lies—his unclosed eye

Yet lowering on his enemy,

As if the hour that sealed his fate

Surviving left his quenchless hate;

And o'er him bends that foe with brow

As dark as his that bled below.

i. The flowered shawls generally worn by persons of rank.

*   *   *   *   *

"Yes, Leila sleeps beneath the wave,

But his shall be a redder grave;

Her spirit pointed well the steel

Which taught that felon heart to feel.

He called the Prophet, but his power

Was vain against the vengeful Giaour:

He called on Alla—but the word

Arose unheeded or unheard.

Thou Paynim fool! could Leila's prayer

Be passed, and thine accorded there?

I watched my time, I leagued with these,

The traitor in his turn to seize;

My wrath is wreaked, the deed is done,

And now I go—but go alone."

*   *   *   *   *

*   *   *   *   *

The browsing camels' bells are tinkling:

His mother looked from her lattice high—

She saw the dews of eve besprinkling

The pasture green beneath her eye,

    She saw the planets faintly twinkling:

"'Tis twilight—sure his train is nigh."

She could not rest in the garden-bower,

But gazed through the grate of his steepest tower.

"Why comes he not? his steeds are fleet,

Nor shrink they from the summer heat;

Why sends not the Bridegroom his promised gift?

Is his heart more cold, or his barb less swift?

Oh, false reproach! yon Tartar now

Has gained our nearest mountain's brow,

And warily the steep descends,

And now within the valley bends;

And he bears the gift at his saddle bow—

How could I deem his courser slow?

Right well my largess shall repay

His welcome speed, and weary way."

The Tartar lighted at the gate,

But scarce upheld his fainting weight!

His swarthy visage spake distress,

But this might be from weariness;

His garb with sanguine spots was dyed,

But these might be from his courser's side;

He drew the token from his vest—

Angel of Death! 'tis Hassan's cloven crest!

His calpac[i] rent—his caftan red—

"Lady, a fearful bride thy Son hath wed:

Me, not from mercy, did they spare,

But this empurpled pledge to bear.

Peace to the brave! whose blood is spilt:

Woe to the Giaour! for his the guilt."

i. The calpac is the solid cap or centre part of the head-dress; the shawl is wound round it, and forms the turban.

*   *   *   *   *

A Turban[i] carved in coarsest stone,

A Pillar with rank weeds o'ergrown,

Whereon can now be scarcely read

The Koran verse that mourns the dead,

Point out the spot where Hassan fell

A victim in that lonely dell.

There sleeps as true an Osmanlie

As e'er at Mecca bent the knee;

As ever scorned forbidden wine,

Or prayed with face towards the shrine,

In orisons resumed anew

At solemn sound of "Alla Hu!"[ii]

Yet died he by a stranger's hand,

And stranger in his native land;

Yet died he as in arms he stood,

And unavenged, at least in blood.

But him the maids of Paradise

Impatient to their halls invite,

And the dark heaven of Houris' eyes

On him shall glance for ever bright;

They come—their kerchiefs green they wave,[iii]

And welcome with a kiss the brave!

Who falls in battle 'gainst a Giaour

Is worthiest an immortal bower.

i. The turban, pillar, and inscriptive verse, decorate the tombs of the Osmanlies, whether in the cemetery or the wilderness. In the mountains you frequently pass similar mementos; and on inquiry you are informed that they record some victim of rebellion, plunder, or revenge.

ii. "Alla Hu!" the concluding words of the Muezzin's call to prayer from the highest gallery on the exterior of the Minaret. On a still evening, when the Muezzin has a fine voice, which is frequently the case, the effect is solemn and beautiful beyond all the bells in Christendom.

iii. The following is part of a battle-song of the Turks:—"I see—I see a dark-eyed girl of Paradise, and she waves a handkerchief, a kerchief of green; and cries aloud, 'Come, kiss me, for I love thee,'" etc.

*   *   *   *   *

But thou, false Infidel! shall writhe

Beneath avenging Monkir's[i] scythe;

And from its torments 'scape alone

To wander round lost Eblis[ii] throne;

And fire unquenched, unquenchable,

Around, within, thy heart shall dwell;

Nor ear can hear nor tongue can tell

The tortures of that inward hell!

But first, on earth as Vampire[iii] sent,

Thy corse shall from its tomb be rent:

Then ghastly haunt thy native place,

And suck the blood of all thy race;

There from thy daughter, sister, wife,

At midnight drain the stream of life;

Yet loathe the banquet which perforce

Must feed thy livid living corse:

Thy victims ere they yet expire

Shall know the demon for their sire,

As cursing thee, thou cursing them,

Thy flowers are withered on the stem.

But one that for thy crime must fall,

The youngest, most beloved of all,

Shall bless thee with a *fathers* name—

That word shall wrap thy heart in flame!

Yet must thou end thy task, and mark

Her cheek's last tinge, her eye's last spark,

And the last glassy glance must view

Which freezes o'er its lifeless blue;

Then with unhallowed hand shalt tear

The tresses of her yellow hair,

Of which in life a lock when shorn

Affection's fondest pledge was worn,

But now is borne away by thee,

Memorial of thine agony!

Wet with thine own best blood shall drip

Thy gnashing tooth and haggard lip;[iv]

Then stalking to thy sullen grave,

Go—and with Gouls and Afrits rave;

Till these in horror shrink away

From Spectre more accursed than they!

i. Monkir and Nekir are the inquisitors of the dead, before whom the corpse undergoes a slight noviciate and preparatory training for damnation. If the answers are none of the clearest, he is hauled up with a scythe and thumped down with a red-hot mace till properly seasoned, with a variety of subsidiary probations. The office of these angels is no sinecure; there are but two, and the number of orthodox deceased being in a small proportion to the remainder, their hands are always full.—See *Relig. Ceremon.*, v. 290; vii. 59, 68, 118, and *Salt's Preliminary Discourse to the Koran,* p. 101.

ii. Eblis, the Oriental Prince of Darkness.

iii. The Vampire superstition is still general in the Levant. Honest Tournefort tells a long story, which Mr. Southey, in the notes on *Thalaba*, quotes about these "Vroucolochas", as he calls them. The Romaic term is "Vardoulacha." I recollect a whole family being terrified by the scream of a child, which they imagined must proceed from such a visitation. The Greeks never mention the word without horror. I find that "Broucolokas" is an old legitimate Hellenic appellation—at least is so applied to Arsenius, who, according to the Greeks, was after his death animated by the Devil. The moderns, however, use the word I mention.

iv. The freshness of the face and the wetness of the lip with blood, are the never-failing signs of a Vampire. The stories told in Hungary and Greece of these foul feeders are singular, and some of them most *incredibly* attested.

*   *   *   *   *

"How name ye yon lone Caloyer?

   His features I have scanned before

In mine own land: 'tis many a year,

   Since, dashing by the lonely shore,

I saw him urge as fleet a steed

As ever served a horseman's need.

But once I saw that face, yet then

It was so marked with inward pain,

I could not pass it by again;

It breathes the same dark spirit now,

As death were stamped upon his brow.

"'Tis twice three years at summer tide

   Since first among our freres he came;

And here it soothes him to abide

   For some dark deed he will not name.

But never at our Vesper prayer,

Nor e'er before Confession chair

Kneels he, nor recks he when arise

Incense or anthem to the skies,

But broods within his cell alone,

His faith and race alike unknown.

The sea from Paynim land he crost,

And here ascended from the coast;

Yet seems he not of Othman race,
But only Christian in his face:
I'd judge him some stray renegade,
Repentant of the change he made,
Save that he shuns our holy shrine,
Nor tastes the sacred bread and wine.
Great largess to these walls he brought,
And thus our Abbot's favour bought;
But were I Prior, not a day
Should brook such stranger's further stay,
Or pent within our penance cell
Should doom him there for aye to dwell.
Much in his visions mutters he
Of maiden whelmed beneath the sea;
Of sabres clashing, foemen flying,
Wrongs avenged, and Moslem dying.
On cliff he hath been known to stand,
And rave as to some bloody hand
Fresh severed from its parent limb,
Invisible to all but him,
Which beckons onward to his grave,
And lures to leap into the wave."

        *   *   *   *   *

        *   *   *   *   *

Dark and unearthly is the scowl
That glares beneath his dusky cowl:
The flash of that dilating eye
Reveals too much of times gone by;
Though varying, indistinct its hue,

Oft with his glance the gazer rue,

For in it lurks that nameless spell,

Which speaks, itself unspeakable,

A spirit yet unquelled and high,

That claims and keeps ascendancy;

And like the bird whose pinions quake,

But cannot fly the gazing snake,

Will others quail beneath his look,

Nor 'scape the glance they scarce can brook.

From him the half-affrighted Friar

When met alone would fain retire,

As if that eye and bitter smile

Transferred to others fear and guile:

Not oft to smile descendeth he,

And when he doth 'tis sad to see

That he but mocks at Misery.

How that pale lip will curl and quiver!

Then fix once more as if for ever;

As if his sorrow or disdain

Forbade him e'er to smile again.

Well were it so—such ghastly mirth

From joyaunce ne'er derived its birth.

But sadder still it were to trace

What once were feelings in that face:

Time hath not yet the features fixed,

But brighter traits with evil mixed;

And there are hues not always faded,

Which speak a mind not all degraded

Even by the crimes through which it waded:

The common crowd but see the gloom
Of wayward deeds, and fitting doom;
The close observer can espy
A noble soul, and lineage high:
Alas! though both bestowed in vain,
Which Grief could change, and Guilt could stain
It was no vulgar tenement
To which such lofty gifts were lent,
And still with little less than dread
On such the sight is riveted.
The roofless cot, decayed and rent,
      Will scarce delay the passer-by;
The tower by war or tempest bent,
While yet may frown one battlement,
      Demands and daunts the stranger's eye;
Each ivied arch, and pillar lone,
Pleads haughtily for glories gone!

"His floating robe around him folding,
      Slow sweeps he through the columned aisle;
With dread beheld, with gloom beholding
      The rites that sanctify the pile.
But when the anthem shakes the choir,
And kneel the monks, his steps retire;
By yonder lone and wavering torch
His aspect glares within the porch;
There will he pause till all is done—
And hear the prayer, but utter none.
See—by the half-illumined wall

His hood fly back, his dark hair fall,

That pale brow wildly wreathing round,

As if the Gorgon there had bound

The sablest of the serpent-braid

That o'er her fearful forehead strayed:

For he declines the convent oath,

And leaves those locks unhallowed growth,

But wears our garb in all beside;

And, not from piety but pride,

Gives wealth to walls that never heard

Of his one holy vow nor word.

Lo!—mark ye, as the harmony

Peals louder praises to the sky,

That livid cheek, that stony air

Of mixed defiance and despair!

Saint Francis, keep him from the shrine!

Else may we dread the wrath divine

Made manifest by awful sign.

If ever evil angel bore

The form of mortal, such he wore;

By all my hope of sins forgiven,

Such looks are not of earth nor heaven!"

To Love the softest hearts are prone,

But such can ne'er be all his own;

Too timid in his woes to share,

Too meek to meet, or brave despair;

And sterner hearts alone may feel

The wound that Time can never heal.

The rugged metal of the mine

Must burn before its surface shine,

But plunged within the furnace-flame,

It bends and melts—though still the same;

Then tempered to thy want, or will,

'Twill serve thee to defend or kill—

A breast-plate for thine hour of need,

Or blade to bid thy foeman bleed;

But if a dagger's form it bear,

Let those who shape its edge, beware!

Thus Passion's fire, and Woman's art,

Can turn and tame the sterner heart;

From these its form and tone are ta'en,

And what they make it, must remain,

But break—before it bend again.

*   *   *   *   *

*   *   *   *   *

If solitude succeed to grief,

Release from pain is slight relief;

The vacant bosom's wilderness

Might thank the pang that made it less.

We loathe what none are left to share:

Even bliss—'twere woe alone to bear;

The heart once left thus desolate

Must fly at last for ease—to hate.

It is as if the dead could feel

The icy worm around them steal,

And shudder, as the reptiles creep

To revel o'er their rotting sleep,

Without the power to scare away

The cold consumers of their clay!

It is as if the desert bird,[i]

   Whose beak unlocks her bosom's stream

   To still her famished nestlings' scream,

Nor mourns a life to them transferred,

Should rend her rash devoted breast,

And find them flown her empty nest.

The keenest pangs the wretched find

   Are rapture to the dreary void,

The leafless desert of the mind,

   The waste of feelings unemployed.

Who would be doomed to gaze upon

A sky without a cloud or sun?

Less hideous far the tempest's roar,

Than ne'er to brave the billows more—

Thrown, when the war of winds is o'er,

A lonely wreck on Fortune's shore,

'Mid sullen calm, and silent bay,

Unseen to drop by dull decay;—

Better to sink beneath the shock

Than moulder piecemeal on the rock!

i. The pelican is, I believe, the bird so libelled, by the imputation of feeding her chickens with her blood.

    *   *   *   *   *

"Father! thy days have passed in peace,

   'Mid counted beads, and countless prayer;

To bid the sins of others cease,

   Thyself without a crime or care,

Save transient ills that all must bear,

Has been thy lot from youth to age;
And thou wilt bless thee from the rage
Of passions fierce and uncontrolled,
Such as thy penitents unfold,
Whose secret sins and sorrows rest
Within thy pure and pitying breast.
My days, though few, have passed below
In much of Joy, but more of Woe;
Yet still in hours of love or strife,
I've 'scaped the weariness of Life:
Now leagued with friends, now girt by foes,
I loathed the languor of repose.
Now nothing left to love or hate,
No more with hope or pride elate,
I'd rather be the thing that crawls
Most noxious o'er a dungeon's walls,
Than pass my dull, unvarying days,
Condemned to meditate and gaze.
Yet, lurks a wish within my breast
For rest—but not to feel 'tis rest.
Soon shall my Fate that wish fulfil;

   And I shall sleep without the dream
Of what I was, and would be still,

   Dark as to thee my deeds may seem:
My memory now is but the tomb
Of joys long dead; my hope, their doom:
Though better to have died with those
Than bear a life of lingering woes.
My spirit shrunk not to sustain

The searching throes of ceaseless pain;
Nor sought the self-accorded grave
Of ancient fool and modern knave:
Yet death I have not feared to meet;
And in the field it had been sweet,
Had Danger wooed me on to move
The slave of Glory, not of Love.
I've braved it—not for Honour's boast;
I smile at laurels won or lost;
To such let others carve their way,
For high renown, or hireling pay:
But place again before my eyes
Aught that I deem a worthy prize—
The maid I love, the man I hate—
And I will hunt the steps of fate,
To save or slay, as these require,
Through rending steel, and rolling fire:
Nor needst thou doubt this speech from one
Who would but do—what he *hath* done.
Death is but what the haughty brave,
The weak must bear, the wretch must crave;
Then let life go to Him who gave:
I have not quailed to Danger's brow
When high and happy—need I *now*?

       *   *   *   *   *

"I loved her, Friar! nay, adored—
    But these are words that all can use—
I proved it more in deed than word;
There's blood upon that dinted sword,

A stain its steel can never lose:

'Twas shed for her, who died for me,

   It warmed the heart of one abhorred:

Nay, start not—no—nor bend thy knee,

   Nor midst my sin such act record;

Thou wilt absolve me from the deed,

For he was hostile to thy creed!

The very name of Nazarene

Was wormwood to his Paynim spleen.

Ungrateful fool! since but for brands

Well wielded in some hardy hands,

And wounds by Galileans given—

The surest pass to Turkish heaven—

For him his Houris still might wait

Impatient at the Prophet's gate.

I loved her—Love will find its way

Through paths where wolves would fear to prey;

And if it dares enough, 'twere hard

If Passion met not some reward—

No matter how, or where, or why,

I did not vainly seek, nor sigh:

Yet sometimes, with remorse, in vain

I wish she had not loved again.

She died—I dare not tell thee how;

But look—'tis written on my brow!

There read of Cain the curse and crime,

In characters unworn by Time:

Still, ere thou dost condemn me, pause;

Not mine the act, though I the cause.

Yet did he but what I had done

Had she been false to more than one.

Faithless to him—he gave the blow;

But true to me—I laid him low:

Howe'er deserved her doom might be,

Her treachery was truth to me;

To. me she gave her heart, that all

Which Tyranny can ne'er enthrall;

And I, alas! too late to save!

Yet all I then could give, I gave—

'Twas some relief—our foe a grave.

His death sits lightly; but her fate

Has made me—what thou well mayst hate.

    His doom was sealed—he knew it well,

Warned by the voice of stern Taheer,

Deep in whose darkly boding ear[i]

The deathshot pealed of murder near,

    As filed the troop to where they fell!

He died too in the battle broil,

A time that heeds nor pain nor toil;

One cry to Mahomet for aid,

One prayer to Alla all he made:

He knew and crossed me in the fray—

I gazed upon him where he lay,

And watched his spirit ebb away:

Though pierced like pard by hunter's steel,

He felt not half that now I feel.

I searched, but vainly searched, to find

The workings of a wounded mind;

Each feature of that sullen corse

Betrayed his rage, but no remorse.

Oh, what had Vengeance given to trace

Despair upon his dying face!

The late repentance of that hour

When Penitence hath lost her power

To tear one terror from the grave,

And will not soothe, and cannot save.

i. This superstition of a second-hearing (for I never met with downright second-sight in the East) fell once under my own observation. On my third journey to Cape Colonna, early in 1811, as we passed through the defile that leads from the hamlet between Keratia and Colonna, I observed Dervish Tahiri riding rather out of the path and leaning his head upon his hand, as if in pain. I rode up and inquired. "We are in peril," he answered. "What peril? We are not now in Albania, nor in the passes to Ephesus, Messalunghi, or Lepanto; there are plenty of us, well armed, and the Choriates have not courage to be thieves."—"True, Affendi, but nevertheless the shot is ringing in my ears."—"The shot. Not a tophaike has been fired this morning."—"I hear it notwithstanding—Bom—Bom—as plainly as I hear your voice."—"Psha!"—"As you please, Affendi; if it is written, so will it be."—I left this quick-eared predestinarian, and rode up to Basili, his Christian compatriot, whose ears, though not at all prophetic, by no means relished the intelligence. We all arrived at Colonna, remained some hours, and returned leisurely, saying a variety of brilliant things, in more languages than spoiled the building of Babel, upon the mistaken seer. Romaic, Arnaout, Turkish, Italian, and English were all exercised, in various conceits, upon the unfortunate Mussulman. While we were contemplating the beautiful prospect, Dervish was occupied about the columns. I thought he was deranged into an antiquarian, and asked him if he had become a "*Palaocastro*" man? "No," said he; "but these pillars will be useful in making a stand;" and added other remarks, which at least evinced his own belief in his troublesome faculty of *forehearing*. On our return to Athens we heard from Leone (a prisoner set ashore some days after) of the intended attack of the Mainotes, mentioned, with the cause of its not taking place, in the notes to *Childe Harold,* Canto 2nd. I was at some pains to question the man, and he described the dresses, arms, and marks of the horses of our party so accurately, that, with other circumstances, we could not doubt of *his* having been in "villanous company" and ourselves in a bad neighbourhood. Dervish became a soothsayer for life, and I dare say is now hearing more musketry than ever will be fired, to the great refreshment of the Arnaouts of Berat, and his native mountains.—I shall mention one trait more of this singular race. In March, 1811, a remarkably stout and active Arnaout came (I believe the fiftieth on the same errand) to offer himself as an attendant, which was declined. "Well, Affendi," quoth he, "may you live!—you would have found me useful. I shall leave the town for the hills to-morrow; in the winter I return, perhaps you will then receive me."—Dervish, who was present, remarked as a thing of course, and of no consequence, "in the mean time he will join the Klephtes" (robbers), which was true to the letter. If not cut off, they come down in the winter, and pass it unmolested in some town, where they are often as well known as their exploits.

*   *   *   *   *

"The cold in clime are cold in blood,

Their love can scarce deserve the name;

But mine was like the lava flood

   That boils in Ætna's breast of flame.

I cannot prate in puling strain

Of Ladye-love, and Beauty's chain:

If changing cheek, and scorching vein,

Lips taught to writhe, but not complain,

If bursting heart, and maddening brain,

And daring deed, and vengeful steel,

And all that I have felt, and feel,

Betoken love—that love was mine,

And shown by many a bitter sign.

'Tis true, I could not whine nor sigh,

I knew but to obtain or die.

I die—but first I have possessed,

And come what may, I *have been* blessed.

Shall I the doom I sought upbraid?

No—reft of all, yet undismayed

But for the thought of Leila slain,

Give me the pleasure with the pain,

So would I live and love again.

I grieve, but not, my holy Guide!

For him who dies, but her who died:

She sleeps beneath the wandering wave—

Ah! had she but an earthly grave,

This breaking heart and throbbing head

Should seek and share her narrow bed.

She was a form of Life and Light,

That, seen, became a part of sight;

And rose, where'er I turned mine eye,

The Morning-star of Memory!

"Yes, Love indeed is light from heaven;

    A spark of that immortal fire

With angels shared, by Alla given,

    To lift from earth our low desire.

Devotion wafts the mind above,

But Heaven itself descends in Love;

A feeling from the Godhead caught,

To wean from self each sordid thought;

A ray of Him who formed the whole;

A Glory circling round the soul!

I grant *my* love imperfect, all

That mortals by the name miscall;

Then deem it evil, what thou wilt;

But say, oh say, *hers* was not Guilt!

She was my Life's unerring Light:

That quenched—what beam shall break my night?

Oh! would it shone to lead me still,

Although to death or deadliest ill!

Why marvel ye, if they who lose

    This present joy, this future hope,

    No more with Sorrow meekly cope;

In phrensy then their fate accuse;

In madness do those fearful deeds

That seem to add but Guilt to Woe?
Alas! the breast that inly bleeds
Hath nought to dread from outward blow:
Who falls from all he knows of bliss,
Cares little into what abyss.
Fierce as the gloomy vulture's now
To thee, old man, my deeds appear:
I read abhorrence on thy brow,
And this too was I born to bear!
'Tis true, that, like that bird of prey,
With havock have I marked my way:
But this was taught me by the dove,
To die—and know no second love.
This lesson yet hath man to learn,
Taught by the thing he dares to spurn:
The bird that sings within the brake,
The swan that swims upon the lake,
One mate, and one alone, will take.
And let the fool still prone to range,'-
And sneer on all who cannot change,
Partake his jest with boasting boys;
I envy not his varied joys,
But deem such feeble, heartless man,
Less than yon solitary swan;
Far, far beneath the shallow maid
He left believing and betrayed.
Such shame at least was never mine—
Leila! each thought was only thine!
My good, my guilt, my weal, my woe,

My hope on high—my all below.
Each holds no other like to thee,
Or, if it doth, in vain for me:
For worlds I dare not view the dame
Resembling thee, yet not the same.
The very crimes that mar my youth,
This bed of death—attest my truth!
'Tis all too late—thou wert, thou art
The cherished madness of my heart!

"And she was lost—and yet I breathed,
     But not the breath of human life:
A serpent round my heart was wreathed,
     And stung my every thought to strife.
Alike all time, abhorred all place
Shuddering I shrank from Nature's face,
Where every hue that charmed before
The blackness of my bosom wore.
The rest thou dost already know,
And all my sins, and half my woe.
But talk no more of penitence;
Thou seest I soon shall part from hence:
And if thy holy tale were true,
The deed that's done canst *thou* undo?
Think me not thankless—but this grief
Looks not to priesthood for relief.[i]
My soul's estate in secret guess:
But wouldst thou pity more, say less.
When thou canst bid my Leila live,

Then will I sue thee to forgive;

Then plead my cause in that high place

Where purchased masses proffer grace.

Go, when the hunter's hand hath wrung

From forest-cave her shrieking young,

And calm the lonely lioness:

But soothe not—mock not *my* distress!

i. The monk's sermon is omitted. It seems to have had so little effect upon the patient, that it could have no hopes from the reader. It may be sufficient to say that it was of a customary length (as may be perceived from the interruptions and uneasiness of the patient), and was delivered in the usual tone of all orthodox preachers.

"In earlier days, and calmer hours,

When heart with heart delights to blend,

Where bloom my native valley's bowers,"

I had—Ah! have I now?—a friend!

To him this pledge I charge thee send,

Memorial of a youthful vow;

I would remind him of my end:

Though souls absorbed like mine allow

Brief thought to distant Friendship's claim,

Yet dear to him my blighted name.

'Tis strange—he prophesied my doom,

And I have smiled—I then could smile—

When Prudence would his voice assume,

And warn—I recked not what—the while:

But now Remembrance whispers o'er

Those accents scarcely marked before.

Say—that his bodings came to pass,

And he will start to hear their truth,

And wish his words had not been sooth:

Tell him—unheeding as I was,

    Through many a busy bitter scene

    Of all our golden youth had been,

In pain, my faltering tongue had tried

To bless his memory—ere I died;

But Heaven in wrath would turn away,

If Guilt should for the guiltless pray.

I do not ask him not to blame,

Too gentle he to wound my name;

And what have I to do with Fame?

I do not ask him not to mourn,

Such cold request might sound like scorn

And what than Friendship's manly tear

May better grace a brother's bier?

But bear this ring, his own of old,

And tell him—what thou dost behold!

The withered frame, the ruined mind,

The wrack by passion left behind,

A shrivelled scroll, a scattered leaf,

Seared by the autumn blast of Grief!

          *   *   *   *   *

"Tell me no more of Fancy's gleam,

No, father, no, 'twas not a dream;

Alas! the dreamer first must sleep,

I only watched, and wished to weep;

But could not, for my burning brow

Throbbed to the very brain as now:

I wished but for a single tear,

As something welcome, new, and dear:

I wished it then, I wish it still;
Despair is stronger than my will.
Waste not thine orison, despair
Is mightier than thy pious prayer:
I would not, if I might, be blest;
I want no Paradise, but rest.
'Twas then—I tell thee—father! then
I saw her; yes, she lived again;
And shining in her white symar[i]
As through yon pale gray cloud the star
Which now I gaze on, as on her,
Who looked and looks far lovelier;
Dimly I view its trembling spark;
To-morrow's night shall be more dark;
And I, before its rays appear,
That lifeless thing the living fear.
I wander—father! for my soul
Is fleeting towards the final goal.
I saw her—friar! and I rose
Forgetful of our former woes;
And rushing from my couch, I dart,
And clasp her to my desperate heart;
I clasp—what is it that I clasp?
No breathing form within my grasp,
No heart that beats reply to mine—
Yet, Leila! yet the form is thine!
And art thou, dearest, changed so much
As meet my eye, yet mock my touch?
Ah! were thy beauties e'er so cold,

I care not—so my arms enfold

The all they ever wished to hold.

Alas! around a shadow prest

They shrink upon my lonely breast;

Yet still 'tis there! In silence stands,

And beckons with beseeching hands!

With braided hair, and bright-black eye—

I knew 'twas false—she could not die!

But *he* is dead! within the dell

I saw him buried where he fell;

He comes not—for he cannot break

From earth;—why then art *thou* awake?

They told me wild waves rolled above

The face I view—the form I love;

They told me—'twas a hideous tale!—

I'd tell it, but my tongue would fail:

If true, and from thine ocean-cave

Thou com'st to claim a calmer grave,

Oh! pass thy dewy fingers o'er

This brow that then will burn no more;

Or place them on my hopeless heart:

But, Shape or Shade! whate'er thou art,

In mercy ne'er again depart!

Or farther with thee bear my soul

Than winds can waft or waters roll!

i. "Symar," a shroud.

*   *   *   *   *

"Such is my name, and such my tale.

   Confessor! to thy secret ear

I breathe the sorrows I bewail,

And thank thee for the generous tear

This glazing eye could never shed.

Then lay me with the humblest dead,

And, save the cross above my head,

Be neither name nor emblem spread,

By prying stranger to be read,

Or stay the passing pilgrim's tread."[i]

He passed—nor of his name and race

He left a token or a trace,

Save what the Father must not say

Who shrived him on his dying day:

This broken tale was all we knew

Of her he loved, or him he slew.

i. The circumstance to which the above story relates was not very uncommon in Turkey. A few years ago the wife of Muchtar Pacha complained to his father of his son's supposed infidelity; he asked with whom, and she had the barbarity to give in a list of the twelve handsomest women in Yanina. They were seized, fastened up in sacks, and drowned in the lake the same night! One of the guards who was present informed me that not one of the victims uttered a cry, or showed a symptom of terror at so sudden a "wrench from all we know, from all we love." The fate of Phrosine, the fairest of this sacrifice, is the subject of many a Romaic and Arnaout ditty. The story in the text is one told of a young Venetian many years ago, and now nearly forgotten. I heard it by accident recited by one of the coffee-house story-tellers who abound in the Levant, and sing or recite their narratives. The additions and interpolations by the translator will be easily distinguished from the rest, by the want of Eastern imagery; and I regret that my memory has retained so few fragments of the original. For the contents of some of the notes I am indebted partly to D'Herbelot, and partly to that most Eastern, and, as Mr. Weber justly entitles it, "sublime tale," the "Caliph Vathek." I do not know from what source the author of that singular volume may have drawn his materials; some of his incidents are to be found in the *Bibliothèque Orientale*; but for correctness of costume, beauty of description, and power of imagination, it far surpasses all European imitations, and bears such marks of originality that those who have visited the East will find some difficulty in believing it to be more than a translation. As an Eastern tale, even Rasselas must bow before it; his "Happy Valley" will not bear a comparison with the "Hall of Eblis."

THE BRIDE OF ABYDOS. A TURKISH TALE

"Had we never loved sae kindly,
Had we never loved sae blindly,
Never met—or never parted,
We had ne'er been broken-hearted."—
BURNS.

TO

THE RIGHT HONOURABLE

LORD HOLLAND,

THIS TALE IS INSCRIBED, WITH

EVERY SENTIMENT OF REGARD

AND RESPECT,

BY HIS GRATEFULLY OBLIGED

AND SINCERE FRIEND,

BYRON.

CANTO THE FIRST

I.

Know ye the land where the cypress and myrtle

    Are emblems of deeds that are done in their clime?

Where the rage of the vulture, the love of the turtle,

    Now melt into sorrow, now madden to crime?

Know ye the land of the cedar and vine,

Where the flowers ever blossom, the beams ever shine;

Where the light wings of Zephyr, oppressed with perfume,

Wax faint o'er the gardens of Gúl[i] in her bloom;

Where the citron and olive are fairest of fruit,

And the voice of the nightingale never is mute;

Where the tints of the earth, and the hues of the sky,

In colour though varied, in beauty may vie,

And the purple of Ocean is deepest in dye;

Where the virgins are soft as the roses they twine,

And all, save the spirit of man, is divine—

'Tis the clime of the East—'tis the land of the Sun—

Can he smile on such deeds as his children have done?[ii]

Oh! wild as the accents of lovers' farewell

Are the hearts which they bear, and the tales which they tell.

i. "Gúl," the rose.

ii.   "Souls made of fire, and children of the Sun,
        With whom revenge is virtue."
           YOUNG's *Revenge*, act v. sc. 2 (*British Theatre*, 1792, p. 84).

II.

Begirt with many a gallant slave,

Apparelled as becomes the brave,

Awaiting each his Lord's behest

To guide his steps, or guard his rest,

Old Giaffir sate in his Divan:

   Deep thought was in his agèd eye;

And though the face of Mussulman

   Not oft betrays to standers by

The mind within, well skilled to hide

All but unconquerable pride,

His pensive cheek and pondering brow1

 Did more than he was wont avow.

III.

"Let the chamber be cleared."—The train disappeared—

   "Now call me the chief of the Haram guard"—

With Giaffir is none but his only son,

   And the Nubian awaiting the sire's award.

   "Haroun—when all the crowd that wait

   Are passed beyond the outer gate,

   (Woe to the head whose eye beheld

   My child Zuleika's face unveiled!)

   Hence, lead my daughter from her tower—

   Her fate is fixed this very hour;

   Yet not to her repeat my thought—

   By me alone be duty taught!

   "Pacha! to hear is to obey."—

   No more must slave to despot say—

   Then to the tower had ta'en his way:

   But here young Selim silence brake,

      First lowly rendering reverence meet;

And downcast looked, and gently spake,
    Still standing at the Pacha's feet:
For son of Moslem must expire,
Ere dare to sit before his sire!
"Father! for fear that thou shouldst chide
My sister, or her sable guide—
Know—for the fault, if fault there be,
Was mine—then fall thy frowns on me!
So lovelily the morning shone,
    That—let the old and weary sleep—
I could not; and to view alone
    The fairest scenes of land and deep,
With none to listen and reply
To thoughts with which my heart beat high
Were irksome—for whate'er my mood,
In sooth I love not solitude;
I on Zuleika's slumber broke,
    And, as thou knowest that for me
    Soon turns the Haram's grating key,
Before the guardian slaves awoke
We to the cypress groves had flown,
And made earth, main, and heaven our own!
There lingered we, beguiled too long
With Mejnoun's tale, or Sadi's song;[i]
Till I, who heard the deep tambour[ii]
Beat thy Divan's approaching hour,
To thee, and to my duty true,
Warned by the sound, to greet thee flew:
But there Zuleika wanders yet—

Nay, Father, rage not—nor forget

That none can pierce that secret bower

But those who watch the women's tower."

i. Mejnoun and Leila, the Romeo and Juliet of the East. Sadi, the moral poet of Persia.

ii. Tambour. Turkish drum, which sounds at sunrise, noon, and twilight.

IV.

"Son of a slave"—the Pacha said—

"From unbelieving mother bred,

Vain were a father's hope to see

Aught that beseems a man in thee.

Thou, when thine arm should bend the bow,

    And hurl the dart, and curb the steed,

    Thou, Greek in soul if not in creed,

Must pore where babbling waters flow,

And watch unfolding roses blow.

Would that yon Orb, whose matin glow

Thy listless eyes so much admire,

Would lend thee something of his fire!

Thou, who woulds't see this battlement

By Christian cannon piecemeal rent;

Nay, tamely view old Stambol's wall

Before the dogs of Moscow fall,

Nor strike one stroke for life and death

Against the curs of Nazareth!

Go—let thy less than woman's hand

Assume the distaff—not the brand.

But, Haroun!—to my daughter speed:

And hark—of thine own head take heed—

If thus Zuleika oft takes wing—
Thou see'st yon bow—it hath a string!"

V.

No sound from Selim's lip was heard,
    At least that met old Giaffir's ear,
But every frown and every word
Pierced keener than a Christian's sword.
    "Son of a slave!—reproached with fear!
    Those gibes had cost another dear.
Son of a slave!—and *who* my Sire?"
    Thus held his thoughts their dark career;
And glances ev'n of more than ire
    Flash forth, then faintly disappear.
Old Giaffir gazed upon his son
    And started; for within his eye
He read how much his wrath had done;
He saw rebellion there begun:
    "Come hither, boy—what, no reply?
I mark thee—and I know thee too;
But there be deeds thou dar'st not do:
But if thy beard had manlier length,
And if thy hand had skill and strength,
I'd joy to see thee break a lance,
Albeit against my own perchance."
As sneeringly these accents fell,
On Selim's eye he fiercely gazed:
    That eye returned him glance for glance,
And proudly to his Sire's was raised,
    Till Giaffir's quailed and shrunk askance—

And why—he felt, but durst not tell.
"Much I misdoubt this wayward boy
Will one day work me more annoy:
I never loved him from his birth,
And—but his arm is little worth,
And scarcely in the chase could cope
With timid fawn or antelope,
Far less would venture into strife
Where man contends for fame and life—

I would not trust that look or tone:
No—nor the blood so near my own,
That blood—he hath not heard—no more—
I'll watch him closer than before.
He is an Arab[i] to my sight,
Or Christian crouching in the fight—
But hark!—I hear Zuleika's voice;

Like Houris' hymn it meets mine ear:
She is the offspring of my choice

Oh! more than ev'n her mother dear,
With all to hope, and nought to fear—
My Peri! ever welcome here!
Sweet, as the desert fountain's wave
To lips just cooled in time to save—

Such to my longing sight art thou;
Nor can they waft to Mecca's shrine
More thanks for life, than I for thine,

Who blest thy birth and bless thee now."

i. The Turks abhor the Arabs (who return the compliment a hundredfold) even more than they hate the Christians.

VI.

Fair, as the first that fell of womankind,

When on that dread yet lovely serpent smiling,

Whose Image then was stamped upon her mind—

But once beguiled—and ever more beguiling;

Dazzling, as that, oh! too transcendent vision

To Sorrow's phantom-peopled slumber given,

When heart meets heart again in dreams Elysian,

And paints the lost on Earth revived in Heaven;

Soft, as the memory of buried love;

Pure, as the prayer which Childhood wafts above;

Was she—the daughter of that rude old Chief,

Who met the maid with tears—but not of grief.

Who hath not proved how feebly words essay

To fix one spark of Beauty's heavenly ray?

Who doth not feel, until his failing sight

Faints into dimness with its own delight,

His changing cheek, his sinking heart confess

The might—the majesty of Loveliness?

Such was Zuleika—such around her shone

The nameless charms unmarked by her alone—

The light of Love, the purity of Grace,

The mind, the Music[i] breathing from her face,

The heart whose softness harmonized the whole,

And oh! that eye was in itself a Soul!

i. This expression has met with objections. I will not refer to "Him who hath not Music in his soul," but merely request the reader to recollect, for ten seconds, the features of the woman whom he believes to be the most beautiful; and, if he then does not comprehend fully what is feebly expressed in the above line, I shall be sorry for us both. For an eloquent passage in the latest work of the first female writer of this, perhaps of any, age, on the analogy (and the immediate comparison excited by that analogy) between "painting and music," see vol. iii. cap. 10, DE L'ALLEMAGNE.

And is not this connection still stronger with the original than the copy? with the colouring of Nature than of Art? After all, this is rather to be felt than described; still I think there are some who will understand it, at least they would have done had they beheld the countenance whose speaking harmony suggested the idea; for this passage is not drawn from imagination but memory,"'- that mirror which Affliction dashes to the earth, and looking down upon the fragments, only beholds the reflection multiplied!

Her graceful arms in meekness bending

 Across her gently-budding breast;

At one kind word those arms extending

 To clasp the neck of him who blest

 His child caressing and carest,

 Zuleika came—and Giaffir felt

 His purpose, half within him melt:

 Not that against her fancied weal

 His heart though stern could ever feel;

 Affection chained her to that heart;

 Ambition tore the links apart.

VII.

"Zuleika! child of Gentleness!

 How dear this very day must tell,

When I forget my own distress,

 In losing what I love so well,

To bid thee with another dwell:

Another! and a braver man

Was never seen in battle's van.

We Moslem reck not much of blood:

 But yet the line of Carasman[i]

Unchanged, unchangeable hath stood

 First of the bold Timariot bands

That won and well can keep their lands.

Enough that he who comes to woo

Is kinsman of the Bey Oglou:

His years need scarce a thought employ;

I would not have thee wed a boy.

And thou shalt have a noble dower:

And his and my united power

Will laugh to scorn the death-firman,

Which others tremble but to scan,

And teach the messenger[ii] what fate

The bearer of such boon may wait.

And now thou know'st thy father's will;

   All that thy sex hath need to know:

'Twas mine to teach obedience still—

   The way to love, thy Lord may show."

i. Carasman Oglou, or Kara Osman Oglou, is the principal landholder in Turkey; he governs Magnesia: those who, by a kind of feudal tenure, possess land on condition of service, are called Timariots: they serve as Spahis, according to the extent of territory, and bring a certain number into the field, generally cavalry.

ii. When a Pacha is sufficiently strong to resist, the single messenger, who is always the first bearer of the order for his death, is strangled instead, and sometimes five or six, one after the other, on the same errand, by command of the refractory patient; if, on the contrary, he is weak or loyal, he bows, kisses the Sultan's respectable signature, and is bowstrung with great complacency. In 1810, several of these presents were exhibited in the niche of the Seraglio gate; among others, the head of the Pacha of Bagdat, a brave young man, cut off by treachery, after a desperate resistance.

VIII.

In silence bowed the virgin's head;

   And if her eye was filled with tears

That stifled feeling dare not shed,

And changed her cheek from pale to red,

   And red to pale, as through her ears

Those wingèd words like arrows sped,

   What could such be but maiden fears?

So bright the tear in Beauty's eye,

Love half regrets to kiss it dry;

So sweet the blush of Bashfulness,

Even Pity scarce can wish it less!

Whate'er it was the sire forgot:

Or if remembered, marked it not;

Thrice clapped his hands, and called his steed,[i]

   Resigned his gem-adorned chibouque,[ii]

And mounting featly for the mead,

   With Maugrabee[iii] and Mamaluke,

   His way amid his Delis took,[iv]

To witness many an active deed

With sabre keen, or blunt jerreed.

The Kislar only and his Moors

Watch well the Haram's massy doors.

i. Clapping of the hands calls the servants. The Turks hate a superfluous expenditure of voice, and they have no bells.

ii. "Chibouque," the Turkish pipe, of which the amber mouthpiece, and sometimes the ball which contains the leaf, is adorned with precious stones, if in possession of the wealthier orders.

iii. "Maugrabee," Moorish mercenaries.

iv. "Delis," bravos who form the forlorn hope of the cavalry, and always begin the action.

IX.

His head was leant upon his hand,

   His eye looked o'er the dark blue water

That swiftly glides and gently swells

Between the winding Dardanelles;

But yet he saw nor sea nor strand,

Nor even his Pacha's turbaned band

Mix in the game of mimic slaughter,

Careering cleave the folded felt[i]

With sabre stroke right sharply dealt;

Nor marked the javelin-darting crowd,

Nor heard their Ollahs[ii] wild and loud—

He thought but of old Giaffir's daughter!

i. A twisted fold of *felt* is used for scimitar practice by the Turks, and few but Mussulman arms can cut through it at a single stroke: sometimes a tough turban is used for the same purpose. The jerreed [jarid] is a game of blunt javelins, animated and graceful.

ii. "Ollahs," Alla il Allah, the "Leilies," as the Spanish poets call them, the sound is Ollah: a cry of which the Turks, for a silent people, are somewhat profuse, particularly during the jerreed, or in the chase, but mostly in battle. Their animation in the field, and gravity in the chamber, with their pipes and comboloios, form an amusing contrast.

X.

No word from Selim's bosom broke;

One sigh Zuleika's thought bespoke:

Still gazed he through the lattice grate,

Pale, mute, and mournfully sedate.

To him Zuleika's eye was turned,

But little from his aspect learned:

Equal her grief, yet not the same;

Her heart confessed a gentler flame:

But yet that heart, alarmed or weak,

She knew not why, forbade to speak.

Yet speak she must—but when essay?

"How strange he thus should turn away!

Not thus we e'er before have met;

Not thus shall be our parting yet."

Thrice paced she slowly through the room,

And watched his eye—it still was fixed:

She snatched the urn wherein was mixed

The Persian Atar-gul's perfume,[i]

And sprinkled all its odours o'er

The pictured roof[ii] and marble floor:

The drops, that through his glittering vest"

The playful girl's appeal addressed,

Unheeded o'er his bosom flew,

As if that breast were marble too.

"What, sullen yet? it must not be—

Oh! gentle Selim, this from thee!"

She saw in curious order set

The fairest flowers of Eastern land—

"He loved them once; may touch them yet,

If offered by Zuleika's hand."

The childish thought was hardly breathed

Before the rose was plucked and wreathed;

The next fond moment saw her seat

Her fairy form at Selim's feet:

"This rose to calm my brother's cares

A message from the Bulbul[iii] bears;

It says to-night he will prolong

For Selim's ear his sweetest song;

And though his note is somewhat sad,

He'll try for once a strain more glad,

With some faint hope his altered lay

May sing these gloomy thoughts away.

i. "Atar-gul," ottar of roses. The Persian is the finest.

ii. The ceiling and wainscots, or rather walls, of the Mussulman apartments are generally painted, in great houses, with one eternal and highly-coloured view of

Constantinople, wherein the principal feature is a noble contempt of perspective; below, arms, scimitars, etc., are, in general, fancifully and not inelegantly disposed.

iii. It has been much doubted whether the notes of this " Lover of the rose " are sad or merry; and Mr. Fox's remarks on the subject have provoked some learned controversy as to the opinions of the ancients on the subject. I dare not venture a conjecture on the point, though a little inclined to the "errare mallem," etc., *if* Mr. Fox *was* mistaken.

XI.

"What! not receive my foolish flower?

Nay then I am indeed unblest:

On me can thus thy forehead lower?

And know'st thou not who loves thee best?

Oh, Selim dear! oh, more than dearest!

Say, is it me thou hat'st or fearest?

Come, lay thy head upon my breast,

And I will kiss thee into rest,

Since words of mine, and songs must fail,

Ev'n from my fabled nightingale.

I knew our sire at times was stern,

But this from thee had yet to learn:

Too well I know he loves thee not;

But is Zuleika's love forgot?

Ah! deem I right? the Pacha's plan—

This kinsman Bey of Carasman

Perhaps may prove some foe of thine.

If so, I swear by Mecca's shrine,—

If shrines that ne'er approach allow

To woman's step admit her vow,—

Without thy free consent—command—

The Sultan should not have my hand!

Think'st thou that I could bear to part

With thee, and learn to halve my heart?
Ah! were I severed from thy side,
Where were thy friend—and who my guide?
Years have not seen, Time shall not see,
The hour that tears my soul from thee:
Ev'n Azrael,[i] from his deadly quiver
   When flies that shaft, and fly it must,
That parts all else, shall doom for ever
   Our hearts to undivided dust!"

i. "Azrael," the angel of death.

XII.

He lived—he breathed—he moved—he felt;
He raised the maid from where she knelt;
His trance was gone, his keen eye shone
With thoughts that long in darkness dwelt;
With thoughts that burn—in rays that melt.
As the stream late concealed
   By the fringe of its willows,
When it rushes reveal'd
   In the light of its billows;
As the bolt bursts on high
   From the black cloud that bound it,
Flashed the soul of that eye
   Through the long lashes round it.
A war-horse at the trumpet's sound,
A lion roused by heedless hound,
A tyrant waked to sudden strife
By graze of ill-directed knife,
Starts not to more convulsive life

Than he, who heard that vow, displayed,
And all, before repressed, betrayed:
"Now thou art mine, for ever mine,
With life to keep, and scarce with life resign;
Now thou art mine, that sacred oath,
Though sworn by one, hath bound us both.
Yes, fondly, wisely hast thou done;
That vow hath saved more heads than one:
But blench not thou—thy simplest tress
Claims more from me than tenderness;
I would not wrong the slenderest hair
That clusters round thy forehead fair,
For all the treasures buried far
Within the caves of Istakar.[i]
This morning clouds upon me lowered,
Reproaches on my head were showered,
And Giaffir almost called me coward!
Now I have motive to be brave;
The son of his neglected slave,
Nay, start not, 'twas the term he gave,
May show, though little apt to vaunt,
A heart his words nor deeds can daunt.
His son, indeed!—yet, thanks to thee,
Perchance I am, at least shall be;
But let our plighted secret vow
Be only known to us as now.
I know the wretch who dares demand
From Giaffir thy reluctant hand;
More ill-got wealth, a meaner soul

Holds not a Musselim's[ii] control;

Was he not bred in Egripo?[iii]

A viler race let Israel show!

But let that pass—to none be told

Our oath; the rest shall time unfold.

To me and mine leave Osman Bey!

I've partisans for Peril's day:

Think not I am what I appear;

I've arms—and friends—and vengeance near."

i. The treasures of the Pre-Adamite Sultans. See D'Herbelot, article *Istakar*.

ii. "Musselim," a governor, the next in rank after a Pacha; a Waywode is the third; and then come the Agas.

iii. "Egripo," the Negropont. According to the proverb, the Turks of Egripo, the Jews of Salonica, and the Greeks of Athens, are the worst of their respective races.

XIII.

"Think not thou art what thou appearest!

My Selim, thou art sadly changed:

This morn I saw thee gentlest—dearest—

But now thou'rt from thyself estranged.

My love thou surely knew'st before,

It ne'er was less—nor can be more.

To see thee—hear thee—near thee stay—

And hate the night—I know not why,

Save that we meet not but by day;

With thee to live, with thee to die,

I dare not to my hope deny:

Thy cheek—thine eyes—thy lips to kiss—

Like this—and this—no more than this;

For, Allah! sure thy lips are flame:

What fever in thy veins is flushing?

My own have nearly caught the same,

 At least I feel my cheek, too, blushing.

To soothe thy sickness, watch thy health,

Partake, but never waste thy wealth,

Or stand with smiles unmurmuring by,

And lighten half thy poverty;

Do all but close thy dying eye,

For that I could not live to try;

To these alone my thoughts aspire:

More can I do? or thou require?

But, Selim, thou must answer why

We need so much of mystery?

The cause I cannot dream nor tell,

But be it, since thou say'st 'tis well;

Yet what thou mean'st by 'arms' and 'friends,'

Beyond my weaker sense extends.

I meant that Giaffir should have heard

 The very vow I plighted thee;

His wrath would not revoke my word:

 But surely he would leave me free.

 Can this fond wish seem strange in me,

To be what I have ever been?

What other hath Zuleika seen

From simple childhood's earliest hour?

 What other can she seek to see

Than thee, companion of her bower,

 The partner of her infancy?

These cherished thoughts with life begun,

 Say, why must I no more avow?

What change is wrought to make me shun

    The truth—my pride, and thine till now?

To meet the gaze of stranger's eyes

Our law—our creed—our God denies;

Nor shall one wandering thought of mine

At such, our Prophet's will, repine:

No! happier made by that decree,

He left me all in leaving thee.

Deep were my anguish, thus compelled

To wed with one I ne'er beheld:

This wherefore should I not reveal?

Why wilt thou urge me to conceal?

I know the Pacha's haughty mood

To thee hath never boded good;

And he so often storms at nought,

Allah! forbid that e'er he ought!

And why I know not, but within

My heart concealment weighs like sin."

If then such secrecy be crime,

    And such it feels while lurking here;

Oh, Selim! tell me yet in time,

    Nor leave me thus to thoughts of fear.

Ah! yonder see the Tchocadar,[i]

My father leaves the mimic war;

I tremble now to meet his eye—

Say, Selim, canst thou tell me why?"

i. "Tchocadar"—one of the attendants who precedes a man of authority.

XIV.

"Zuleika—to thy tower's retreat

Betake thee—Giaffir I can greet:

And now with him I fain must prate

Of firmans, imposts, levies, state.

There's fearful news from Danube's banks,

Our Vizier nobly thins his ranks

For which the Giaour may give him thanks!

Our Sultan hath a shorter way

Such costly triumph to repay.

But, mark me, when the twilight drum

   Hath warned the troops to food and sleep,

Unto thy cell with Selim come;

   Then softly from the Haram creep

   Where we may wander by the deep:

   Our garden battlements are steep;

Nor these will rash intruder climb

To list our words, or stint our time;

And if he doth, I want not steel

Which some have felt, and more may feel.

Then shalt thou learn of Selim more

Than thou hast heard or thought before:

Trust me, Zuleika—fear not me!

Thou know'st I hold a Haram key."

"Fear thee, my Selim! ne'er till now

Did words like this—"

   "Delay not thou;

I keep the key—and Haroun's guard

Have *some,* and hope of *more* reward.
To-night, Zuleika, thou shalt hear
My tale, my purpose, and my fear:
I am not, love! what I appear."

CANTO THE SECOND

I.

The winds are high on Helle's wave,

    As on that night of stormy water

When Love, who sent, forgot to save

The young—the beautiful—the brave—

    The lonely hope of Sestos' daughter.

Oh! when alone along the sky

Her turret-torch was blazing high,

Though rising gale, and breaking foam,

And shrieking sea-birds warned him home;

And clouds aloft and tides below,

With signs and sounds, forbade to go,

He could not see, he would not hear,

Or sound or sign foreboding fear;

His eye but saw that light of Love,

The only star it hailed above;

His ear but rang with Hero's song,

"Ye waves, divide not lovers long!"—

That tale is old, but Love anew

May nerve young hearts to prove as true.

II.

The winds are high and Helle's tide

    Rolls darkly heaving to the main;

And Night's descending shadows hide

    That field with blood bedewed in vain,

The desert of old Priam's pride;

The tombs, sole relics of his reign,

All—save immortal dreams that could beguile

The blind old man of Scio's rocky isle!

III.

Oh! yet—for there my steps have been;

These feet have pressed the sacred shore,

These limbs that buoyant wave hath borne—

Minstrel! with thee to muse, to mourn,

To trace again those fields of yore,

Believing every hillock green

Contains no fabled hero's ashes,

And that around the undoubted scene

Thine own "broad Hellespont"[i] still dashes,

Be long my lot! and cold were he

Who there could gaze denying thee!

i. The wrangling about this epithet, "the broad Hellespont" or the "boundless Hellespont," whether it means one or the other, or what it means at all, has been beyond all possibility of detail. I have even heard it disputed on the spot; and not foreseeing a speedy conclusion to the controversy, amused myself with swimming across it in the mean time; and probably may again, before the point is settled. Indeed, the question as to the truth of "the tale of Troy divine" still continues, much of it resting upon the talismanic word "ἄπειρος:" probably Homer had the same notion of distance that a coquette has of time; and when he talks of boundless, means half a mile; as the latter, by a like figure, when she says *eternal* attachment, simply specifies three weeks.

IV.

The Night hath closed on Helle's stream,

Nor yet hath risen on Ida's hill

That Moon, which shone on his high theme:

No warrior chides her peaceful beam,

But conscious shepherds bless it still.

Their flocks are grazing on the Mound

Of him who felt the Dardan's arrow:

That mighty heap of gathered ground

Which Amnion's son ran proudly round,[i]

By nations raised, by monarchs crowned,

    Is now a lone and nameless barrow!

Within—thy dwelling-place how narrow!

Without—can only strangers breathe

The name of him that *was* beneath:

Dust long outlasts the storied stone;

But Thou—thy very dust is gone!

i. Before his Persian invasion, and crowned the altar with laurel, etc. He was afterwards imitated by Caracalla in his race. It is believed that the last also poisoned a friend, named Festus, for the sake of new Patroclan games. I have seen the sheep feeding on the tombs of Æyietes and Antilochus: the first is in the centre of the plain.

V.

Late, late to-night will Dian cheer

The swain, and chase the boatman's fear;

Till then—no beacon on the cliff

May shape the course of struggling skiff;

The scattered lights that skirt the bay,

All, one by one, have died away;

The only lamp of this lone hour

Is glimmering in Zuleika's tower.

Yes! there is light in that lone chamber,

    And o'er her silken ottoman

Are thrown the fragrant beads of amber,

    O'er which her fairy fingers ran;[i]

Near these, with emerald rays beset,

(How could she thus that gem forget?)

Her mother's sainted amulet,[ii]

Whereon engraved the Koorsee text,

Could smooth this life, and win the next;

And by her Comboloio[iii] lies

A Koran of illumined dyes;

And many a bright emblazoned rhyme

By Persian scribes redeemed from Time;

And o'er those scrolls, not oft so mute,

Reclines her now neglected lute;

And round her lamp of fretted gold

Bloom flowers in urns of China's mould;

The richest work of Iran's loom,

And Sheeraz' tribute of perfume;

All that can eye or sense delight

 Are gathered in that gorgeous room:

 But yet it hath an air of gloom.

She, of this Peri cell the sprite,

What doth she hence, and on so rude a night?

i. When rubbed, the amber is susceptible of a perfume, which is slight, but *not* disagreeable.

ii. The belief in amulets engraved on gems, or enclosed in gold boxes, containing scraps from the Koran, worn round the neck, wrist, or arm, is still universal in the East. The Koorsee (throne) verse in the second cap. of the Koran describes the attributes of the Most High, and is engraved in this manner, and worn by the pious, as the most esteemed and sublime of all sentences.

iii. "Comboloio"—a Turkish rosary. The MSS., particularly those of the Persians, are richly adorned and illuminated. The Greek females are kept in utter ignorance; but many of the Turkish girls are highly accomplished, though not actually qualified for a Christian coterie. Perhaps some of our own " *blues* " might not be the worse for *bleaching.*

VI.

Wrapt in the darkest sable vest,

 Which none save noblest Moslem wear,

To guard from winds of Heaven the breast,

 As Heaven itself to Selim dear,

With cautious steps the thicket threading,
    And starting oft, as through the glade
    The gust its hollow moanings made,
Till on the smoother pathway treading,
More free her timid bosom beat,
    The maid pursued her silent guide;
And though her terror urged retreat,
    How could she quit her Selim's side?
    How teach her tender lips to chide?

VII.

They reached at length a grotto, hewn
    By nature, but enlarged by art,
Where oft her lute she wont to tune,
    And oft her Koran conned apart;
And oft in youthful reverie
She dreamed what Paradise might be:
Where Woman's parted soul shall go
Her Prophet had disdained to show;
But Selim's mansion was secure,
Nor deemed she, could he long endure
His bower in other worlds of bliss
Without *her,* most beloved in this!
Oh! who so dear with him could dwell?
What Houri soothe him half so well?

VIII.

Since last she visited the spot
Some change seemed wrought within the grot:
It might be only that the night
Disguised things seen by better light:

That brazen lamp but dimly threw

A ray of no celestial hue;

But in a nook within the cell

Her eye on stranger objects fell.

There arms were piled, not such as wield

The turbaned Delis in the field;

But brands of foreign blade and hilt,

And one was red—perchance with guilt!

Ah! how without can blood be spilt?

A cup too on the board was set

That did not seem to hold sherbet

What may this mean? she turned to see

Her Selim—"Oh! can this be he?"

IX.

His robe of pride was thrown aside,

    His brow no high-crowned turban bore.

But in its stead a shawl of red,

    Wreathed lightly round, his temples wore:

That dagger, on whose hilt the gem

Were worthy of a diadeoi,

No longer glittered at his waist

Where pistols unadorned were braced: 620

And from his belt a sabre swung,

And from his shoulder loosely hung

The cloak of white, the thin capote

That decks the wandering Candiote:

Beneath—his golden plated vest

Clung like a cuirass to his breast:

The greaves below his knee that wound

With silvery scales were sheathed and bound.

But were it not that high command

Spake in his eye, and tone, and hand,

All that a careless eye could see

In him was some young Galiongée.[i]

i. "Galiongée"—or Galioagi, a sailor, that is. a Turkish sailor; the Greeks navigate, the Turks work the guns. Their dress is picturesque: and I have seen the Capitan Pacha, more than once, wearing it as a kind of *incog*. Their legs, however, are generally naked. The buskins described in the test as sheathed behind with silver are those of an Arnaut robber, who was my host (he had quitted the profession) at his Pyrgo, near Gastouni in the Morea: they were plated in scales one over the other, like the back of an armadillo.

X.

"I said I was not what 1 seemed;

And now thou see'st my words were true:

I have a tale thou hast not dreamed,

If sooth— its truth must others rue.

My story now 'twere vain to hide,

I must not see thee Osman's bride:

But had:not thine own lips declared

How much of that young heart I shared,

I could not, must not, yet have shown

The darker secret of my own.

In this I speak not now of love;

That—let Time—Truth—and Peril prove:

But first—Oh! never wed another—

Zuleika! I am not thy brother!"

XI.

"Oh! not my brother!—yet unsay—

God! am I left alone on earth

To mourn—I dare not curse—the day

That saw my solitary birth?

Oh! thou wilt love me now no more!

My sinking heart foreboded ill;

But know *me* all I was before,

Thy sister—friend—Zuleika still.

Thou led'st me here perchance to kill;

If thou hast cause for vengeance, see!

My breast is offered—take thy fill!

Far better with the dead to be

Than live thus nothing now to thee:

Perhaps far worse, for now I know

Why Giaffir always seemed thy foe;

And I, alas! am Giaffir's child,

For whom thou wert contemned, reviled.

If not thy sister—would'st thou save

My life—Oh! bid me be thy slave!"

XII.

"My slave, Zuleika!—nay, I'm thine:

But, gentle love, this transport calm,

Thy lot shall yet be linked with mine;

I swear it by our Prophet's shrine,

And be that thought thy sorrow's balm.

So may the Koran[i] verse displayed

Upon its steel direct my blade,

In danger's hour to guard us both,

As I preserve that awful oath!

The name in which thy heart hath prided

Must change; but, my Zuleika, know,

That tie is widened, not divided,

Although thy Sire's my deadliest foe.

My father was to Giaffir all

That Selim late was deemed to thee;

That brother wrought a brother's fall,

But spared, at least, my infancy!

And lulled me with a vain deceit

That yet a like return may meet.

He reared me, not with tender help,

But like the nephew of a Cain;[ii]

He watched me like a lion's whelp,

That gnaws and yet may break his chain.

My father's blood in every vein

Is boiling! but for thy dear sake

No present vengeance will I take;

Though here I must no more remain.

But first, beloved Zuleika! hear

How Giaffir wrought this deed of fear.

i. The characters on all Turkish scimitars contain sometimes the name of the place of their manufacture, but more generally a text from the Koran, in letters of gold. Amongst those in my possession is one with a blade of singular construction: it is very broad, and the edge notched into serpentine curves like the ripple of water, or the wavering of flame. I asked the Armenian who sold it, what possible use such a figure could add: he said, in Italian, that he did not know; but the Mussulmans had an idea that those of this form gave a severer wound; and liked it because it was "piu feroce." I did not much admire the reason, but bought it for its peculiarity.

ii. It is to be observed, that every allusion to any thing or personage in the Old Testament, such as the Ark, or Cain, is equally the privilege of Mussulman and Jew: indeed, the former profess to be much better acquainted with the lives, true and fabulous, of the patriarchs, than is warranted by our own sacred writ; and not content with Adam, they have a biography of Pre-Adamites. Solomon is the monarch of all necromancy, and Moses a prophet inferior only to Christ and Mahomet. Zuleika is the Persian name of Potiphar's wife; and her amour with Joseph constitutes one of the finest poems in their language. It is, therefore, no violation of costume to put the names of Cain, or Noah, into the mouth of a Moslem.

XIII.

"How first their strife to rancour grew,

    If Love or Envy made them foes,

It matters little if I knew;

In fiery spirits, slights, though few

    And thoughtless, will disturb repose.

In war Abdallah's arm was strong,

Remembered yet in Bosniac song,

And Paswan's[i] rebel hordes attest

How little love they bore such guest:

His death is all I need relate,

The stern effect of Giaffir's hate;

And how my birth disclosed to me,

Whate'er beside it makes, hath made me free.

i. Paswan Oglou, the rebel of Widdin; who, for the last years of his life, set the whole power of the Porte at defiance.

XIV.

"When Paswan, after years of strife,

At last for power, but first for life,

In Widdin's walls too proudly sate,

Our Pachas rallied round the state;

Not last nor least in high command,

Each brother led a separate band;

They gave their Horse-tails[i] to the wind,

    And mustering in Sophia's plain

Their tents were pitched, their post assigned;

    To one, alas! assigned in vain!

What need of words? the deadly bowl,

    By Giaffir's order drugged and given,

With venom subtle as his soul,

Dismissed Abdallah's hence to heaven.

Reclined and feverish in the bath,

He, when the hunter's sport was up,

But little deemed a brother's wrath

To quench his thirst had such a cup:

The bowl a bribed attendant bore;

He drank one draught,[ii] nor needed more!

If thou my tale, Zuleika, doubt,

Call Haroun—he can tell it out.

i. "Horse-tail,"—the standard of a Pacha.

ii. Giaffir, Pacha of Argyro Castro, or Scutari, I am not sure which, was actually taken off by the Albanian Ali, in the manner described in the text. Ali Pacha, while I was in the country, married the daughter of his victim, some years after the event had taken place at a bath in Sophia or Adrianople. The poison was mixed in the cup of coffee, which is presented before the sherbet by the bath keeper, after dressing.

XV.

"The deed once done, and Paswan's feud

In part suppressed, though ne'er subdued,

Abdallah's Pachalick was gained:—

Thou know'st not what in our Divan

Can wealth procure for worse than man—

Abdallah's honours were obtained

By him a brother's murder stained;

'Tis true, the purchase nearly drained

His ill-got treasure, soon replaced.

Would'st question whence? Survey the waste,

And ask the squalid peasant how

His gains repay his broiling brow!—

Why me the stern Usurper spared,

Why thus with me his palace shared,

I know not. Shame—regret—remorse—

And little fear from infant's force—
Besides, adoption as a son
By him whom Heaven accorded none,
Or some unknown cabal, caprice,
Preserved me thus:—but not in peace:
He cannot curb his haughty mood,
Nor I forgive a father's blood.

XVI.

"Within thy Father's house are foes;
    Not all who break his bread are true:
To these should I my birth disclose,
    His days—his very hours were few:
They only want a heart to lead,
A hand to point them to the deed.
But Haroun only knows, or knew
    This tale, whose close is almost nigh:
He in Abdallah's palace grew,
    And held that post in his Serai
    Which holds he here—he saw him die;
But what could single slavery do?
Avenge his lord? alas! too late;
Or save his son from such a fate?
He chose the last, and when elate
    With foes subdued, or friends betrayed,
Proud Giaffir in high triumph sate,
He led me helpless to his gate,
    And not in vain it seems essayed
    To save the life for which he prayed.
The knowledge of my birth secured

From all and each, but most from me;
Thus Giaffir's safety was ensured.

Removed he too from Roumelie
To this our Asiatic side,
Far from our seats by Danube's tide,
    With none but Haroun, who retains
Such knowledge—and that Nubian feels
    A Tyrant's secrets are but chains,
From which the captive gladly steals,
And this and more to me reveals:
Such still to guilt just Allah sends—
Slaves, tools, accomplices—no friends!

XVII.

"All this, Zuleika, harshly sounds;
    But harsher still my tale must be:
Howe'er my tongue thy softness wounds,
    Yet I must prove all truth to thee.
    I saw thee start this garb to see,
Yet is it one I oft have worn,
    And long must wear: this Galiongée,
To whom thy plighted vow is sworn,
    Is leader of those pirate hordes,
    Whose laws and lives are on their swords;
To hear whose desolating tale
Would make thy waning cheek more pale:
Those arms thou see'st my band have brought,
The hands that wield are not remote;
This cup too for the rugged knaves
    Is filled—once quaffed, they ne'er repine:

Our Prophet might forgive the slaves;

    They're only infidels in wine.

                XVIII.

"What could I be? Proscribed at home,

And taunted to a wish to roam;

And listless left—for Giaffir's fear

Denied the courser and the spear—

Though oft—Oh, Mahomet! how oft!—

In full Divan the despot scoffed,

As if *my* weak unwilling hand

Refused the bridle or the brand:

He ever went to war alone,

And pent me here untried—unknown;

To Haroun's care with women left,

By hope unblest, of fame bereft,

While thou—whose softness long endeared,

Though it unmanned me, still had cheered—

To Brusa's walls for safety sent,

Awaited'st there the field's event.

Haroun who saw my spirit pining

    Beneath inaction's sluggish yoke,

His captive, though with dread resigning,

    My thraldom for a season broke,

On promise to return before

The day when Giaffir's charge was o'er.

'Tis vain—my tongue can not impart

My almost drunkenness of heart,[i]

When first this liberated eye

Surveyed Earth—Ocean—Sun—and Sky—

As if my Spirit pierced them through,

And all their inmost wonders knew!

One word alone can paint to thee

That more than feeling—I was Free!

E'en for thy presence ceased to pine;

The World—nay, Heaven itself was mine!

i. I must here shelter myself with the Psalmist—is it not David that makes the "Earth reel to and fro like a Drunkard"? If the Globe can be thus lively on seeing its Creator, a liberated captive can hardly feel less on a first view of his work.

XIX.

"The shallop of a trusty Moor

Conveyed me from this idle shore;

I longed to see the isles that gem

Old Ocean's purple diadem:

I sought by turns, and saw them all;[i]

But when and where I joined the crew,

With whom I'm pledged to rise or fall,

When all that we design to do

Is done, 'twill then be time more meet

To tell thee, when the tale's complete.

i. The Turkish notions of almost all islands are confined to the Archipelago, the sea alluded to.

XX.

"'Tis true, they are a lawless brood,

But rough in form, nor mild in mood;

And every creed, and every race,

With them hath found—may find a place:

But open speech, and ready hand,

Obedience to their Chief's command;

A soul for every enterprise,

That never sees with Terror's eyes;
Friendship for each, and faith to all,
And vengeance vowed for those who fall,
Have made them fitting instruments
For more than e'en my own intents.
And some—and I have studied all
    Distinguished from the vulgar rank,
But chiefly to my council call
    The wisdom of the cautious Frank:—
And some to higher thoughts aspire.
    The last of Lambro's[i] patriots there
    Anticipated freedom share;
And oft around the cavern fire
On visionary schemes debate,
To snatch the Rayahs[ii] from their fate.
So let them ease their hearts with prate
Of equal rights, which man ne'er knew;
I have a love for freedom too.
Aye! let me like the ocean-Patriarch[iii] roam,
Or only know on land the Tartar's home![iv]
My tent on shore, my galley on the sea,
Are more than cities and Serais to me:
Borne by my steed, or wafted by my sail,
Across the desert, or before the gale,
Bound where thou wilt, my barb! or glide, my prow!
But be the Star that guides the wanderer, Thou!
Thou, my Zuleika, share and bless my bark;
The Dove of peace and promise to mine ark!
Or, since that hope denied in worlds of strife,

Be thou the rainbow to the storms of life!

The evening beam that smiles the clouds away,

And tints to-morrow with prophetic ray!

Blest—as the Muezzin's strain from Mecca's wall

To pilgrims pure and prostrate at his call;

Soft—as the melody of youthful days,

That steals the trembling tear of speechless praise;

Dear—as his native song to Exile's ears,

Shall sound each tone thy long-loved voice endears.

For thee in those bright isles is built a bower

Blooming as Aden^v in its earliest hour.

A thousand swords, with Selim's heart and hand,

Wait—wave—defend—destroy—at thy command!

Girt by my band, Zuleika at my side,

The spoil of nations shall bedeck my bride.

The Haram's languid years of listless ease

Are well resigned for cares—for joys like these:

Not blind to Fate, I see, where'er I rove,

Unnumbered perils,—but one only love!

Yet well my toils shall that fond breast repay,

Though Fortune frown, or falser friends betray.

How dear the dream in darkest hours of ill,

Should all be changed, to find thee faithful still!

Be but thy soul, like Selim's firmly shown;

To thee be Selim's tender as thine own;

To soothe each sorrow, share in each delight,

Blend every thought, do all—but disunite!

Once free, 'tis mine our horde again to guide;

Friends to each other, foes to aught beside:

Yet there we follow but the bent assigned

By fatal Nature to man's warring kind:

Mark! where his carnage and his conquests cease!

He makes a solitude, and calls it—peace!

I like the rest must use my skill or strength,

But ask no land beyond my sabre's length:

Power sways but by division—her resource

The blest alternative of fraud or force!

Ours be the last; in time Deceit may come

When cities cage us in a social home:

There ev'n thy soul might err—how oft the heart

Corruption shakes which Peril could not part!

And Woman, more than Man, when Death or Woe,

Or even Disgrace, would lay her lover low,

Sunk in the lap of Luxury will shame—

Away suspicion!—*not* Zuleika's name!

But life is hazard at the best; and here

No more remains to win, and much to fear:

Yes, fear!—the doubt, the dread of losing thee,

By Osman's power, and Giaffir's stern decree.

That dread shall vanish with the favouring gale,

Which Love to-night hath promised to my sail:

No danger daunts the pair his smile hath blest,

Their steps still roving, but their hearts at rest.

With thee all toils are sweet, each clime hath charms;

Earth—sea alike—our world within our arms!

Aye—let the loud winds whistle o'er the deck,

So that those arms cling closer round my neck:

The deepest murmur of this lip shall be,

No sigh for safety, but a prayer for thee!

The war of elements no fears impart

To Love, whose deadliest bane is human Art:

There lie the only rocks our course can check;

Here moments menace—*there* are years of wreck!

But hence ye thoughts that rise in Horror's shape!

This hour bestows, or ever bars escape.

Few words remain of mine my tale to close;

Of thine but *one* to waft us from our foes;

Yea—foes—to me will Giaffir's hate decline?

And is not Osman, who would part us, thine?

i. Lambro Canzani, a Greek, famous for his efforts, in 1789–90, for the independence of his country. Abandoned by the Russians, he became a pirate, and the Archipelago was the scene of his enterprises. He is said to be still alive at Petersburgh. He and Riga are the two most celebrated of the Greek revolutionists.

ii. "Rayahs,"—all who pay the capitation tax, called the " Haratch."

iii. This first of voyages is one of the few with which the Mussulmans profess much acquaintance.

iv. The wandering life of the Arabs, Tartars, and Turkomans, will be found well detailed in any book of Eastern travels. That it possesses a charm peculiar to itself, cannot be denied. A young French renegado confessed to Chateaubriand, that he never found himself alone, galloping in the desert, without a sensation approaching to rapture which was indescribable.

v. "Jannat-al-Aden," the perpetual abode, the Mussulman paradise.

XXI.

"His head and faith from doubt and death

Returned in time my guard to save;

Few heard, none told, that o'er the wave

From isle to isle I roved the while:

And since, though parted from my band

Too seldom now I leave the land,

No deed they've done, nor deed shall do,

Ere I have heard and doomed it too:

I form the plan—decree the spoil—
'Tis fit I oftener share the toil.
But now too long I've held thine ear;
Time presses—floats my bark—and here
We leave behind but hate and fear.
To-morrow Osman with his train
Arrives—to-night must break thy chain:
And would'st thou save that haughty Bey,
    Perchance *his* life who gave thee thine,
With me this hour away—away!

    But yet, though thou art plighted mine,
Would'st thou recall thy willing vow,
Appalled by truths imparted now,
Here rest I—not to see thee wed:
But be that peril on *my* head!"

XXII.

Zuleika, mute and motionless,
Stood like that Statue of Distress,
When, her last hope for ever gone,
The Mother hardened into stone;
All in the maid that eye could see
Was but a younger Niobé.
But ere her lip, or even her eye,
Essayed to speak, or look reply,
Beneath the garden's wicket porch
Far flashed on high a blazing torch!
Another—and another—and another—
"Oh! fly—no more—yet now my more than brother!"
Far, wide, through every thicket spread

The fearful lights are gleaming red

Nor these alone—for each right hand

Is ready with a sheathless brand.

They part—pursue—return, and wheel

With searching flambeau, shining steel;

And last of all, his sabre waving,

Stern Giaffir in his fury raving:

And now almost they touch the cave

Oh! must that grot be Selim's grave?

XXIII.

Dauntless he stood—"'Tis come—soon past—

One kiss, Zuleika—'tis my last:

But yet my band not far from shore

May hear this signal, see the flash;

Yet now too few—the attempt were rash:

No matter—yet one effort more."

Forth to the cavern mouth he stept;

His pistol's echo rang on high,

Zuleika started not, nor wept,

Despair benumbed her breast and eye!—

"They hear me not, or if they ply

Their oars, 'tis but to see me die;

That sound hath drawn my foes more nigh.

Then forth my father's scimitar,

Thou ne'er hast seen less equal war!

Farewell, Zuleika!—Sweet! retire:

Yet stay within—here linger safe,

At thee his rage will only chafe.

Stir not—lest even to thee perchance

Some erring blade or ball should glance.
Fear'st thou for him?—may I expire
If in this strife I seek thy sire!
No—though by him that poison poured;
No—though again he call me coward!
But tamely shall I meet their steel?
No—as each crest save *his* may feel!"

XXIV.

One bound he made, and gained the sand:
   Already at his feet hath sunk
The foremost of the prying band,
   A gasping head, a quivering trunk:
Another falls—but round him close
A swarming circle of his foes;
From right to left his path he cleft,
   And almost met the meeting wave:
His boat appears—not five oars' length—
His comrades strain with desperate strength—
   Oh! are they yet in time to save?
   His feet the foremost breakers lave;
His band are plunging in the bay,
Their sabres glitter through the spray;
Wet—wild—unwearied to the strand
They struggle—now they touch the land!
They come—'tis but to add to slaughter—
His heart's best blood is on the water.

XXV.

Escaped from shot, unharmed by steel,
Or scarcely grazed its force to feel,

Had Selim won, betrayed, beset,
To where the strand and billows met;
There as his last step left the land,
And the last death-blow dealt his hand—
Ah! wherefore did he turn to look

   For her his eye but sought in vain?
That pause, that fatal gaze he took,

   Hath doomed his death, or fixed his chain.
Sad proof, in peril and in pain,
How late will Lover's hope remain!
His back was to the dashing spray;
Behind, but close, his comrades lay,
When, at the instant, hissed the ball—
"So may the foes of Giaffir fall!"
Whose voice is heard? whose carbine rang?
Whose bullet through the night-air sang,
Too nearly, deadly aimed to err?
'Tis thine—Abdallah's Murderer!
The father slowly rued thy hate,
The son hath found a quicker fate:
Fast from his breast the blood is bubbling,
The whiteness of the sea-foam troubling—
If aught his lips essayed to groan,
The rushing billows choked the tone!

XXVI.

Morn slowly rolls the clouds away;

   Few trophies of the fight are there:
The shouts that shook the midnight-bay
Are silent; but some signs of fray

That strand of strife may bear,
And fragments of each shivered brand;
Steps stamped; and dashed into the sand
The print of many a struggling hand
   May there be marked; nor far remote
   A broken torch, an oarless boat;
And tangled on the weeds that heap
The beach where shelving to the deep
   There lies a white capote!
'Tis rent in twain—one dark-red stain
The wave yet ripples o'er in vain:
   But where is he who wore?
Ye! who would o'er his relics weep,
Go, seek them where the surges sweep
Their burthen round Sigæum's steep
   And cast on Lemnos' shore:
The sea-birds shriek above the prey,
O'er which their hungry beaks delay,
As shaken on his restless pillow,
His head heaves with the heaving billow;
That hand, whose motion is not life,
Yet feebly seems to menace strife,
Flung by the tossing tide on high,
   Then levelled with the wave—
What recks it, though that corse shall lie
   Within a living grave?
The bird that tears that prostrate form
Hath only robbed the meaner worm;
The only heart, the only eye

Had bled or wept to see him die,

Had seen those scattered limbs composed,

And mourned above his turban-stone,[i]

That heart hath burst—that eye was closed—

Yea—closed before his own!

i. A turban is carved in stone above the graves of *men* only.

XXVII.

By Helle's stream there is a voice of wail!

And Woman's eye is wet—Man's cheek is pale:

Zuleika! last of Giafhr's race,

Thy destined lord is come too late:

He sees not—ne'er shall see thy face!

Can he not hear

The loud Wul-wulleh[i] warn his distant ear?

Thy handmaids weeping at the gate,

The Koran-chanters of the Hymn of Fate,

The silent slaves with folded arms that wait,

Sighs in the hall, and shrieks upon the gale,

Tell him thy tale!

Thou didst not view thy Selim fall!

That fearful moment when he left the cave

Thy heart grew chill:

He was thy hope—thy joy—thy love—thine all,

And that last thought on him thou could'st not save

Sufficed to kill;

Burst forth in one wild cry—and all was still.

Peace to thy broken heart—and virgin grave!

Ah! happy! but of life to lose the worst!

That grief—though deep—though fatal—was thy first!

Thrice happy! ne'er to feel nor fear the force

Of absence—shame—pride—hate—revenge—remorse!

And, oh! that pang where more than Madness lies

The Worm that will not sleep—and never dies;

Thought of the gloomy day and ghastly night,

That dreads the darkness, and yet loathes the light,

That winds around, and tears the quivering heart!

Ah! wherefore not consume it—and depart!

Woe to thee, rash and unrelenting Chief!

    Vainly thou heap'st the dust upon thy head,

    Vainly the sackcloth o'er thy limbs dost spread:

    By that same hand Abdallah—Selim bled.

Now let it tear thy beard in idle grief:

Thy pride of heart, thy bride for Osman's bed,

She, whom thy Sultan had but seen to wed,

       Thy Daughter's dead!

    Hope of thine age, thy twilight's lonely beam,

    The Star hath set that shone on Helle's stream.

What quenched its ray?—the blood that thou hast shed!

Hark! to the hurried question of Despair:

"Where is my child?"—an Echo answers—"Where?"[ii]

i. The death-song of the Turkish women. The "silent slaves" are the men, whose notions of decorum forbid complaint in *public*.

ii. "I came to the place of my birth, and cried, 'The friends of my Youth, where are they?' and an Echo answered, 'Where are they?'"—*From an Arabic MS*. The above quotation (from which the idea in the text is taken) must be already familiar to every reader: it is given in the second annotation, p. 67, of *The Pleasures of Memory*; a poem so well known as to render a reference almost superfluous: but to whose pages all will be delighted to recur.

XXVIII.

Within the place of thousand tombs
   That shine beneath, while dark above
The sad but living cypress glooms
   And withers not, though branch and leaf
Are stamped with an eternal grief,
   Like early unrequited Love,
One spot exists, which ever blooms,
   Ev'n in that deadly grove—
A single rose is shedding there
   Its lonely lustre, meek and pale:
It looks as planted by Despair—
   So white—so faint—the slightest gale
Might whirl the leaves on high;
   And yet, though storms and blight assail,
And hands more rude than wintry sky
   May wring it from the stem—in vain—
To-morrow sees it bloom again!
The stalk some Spirit gently rears,
And waters with celestial tears;
   For well may maids of Helle deem
That this can be no earthly flower,
Which mocks the tempest's withering hour,
And buds unsheltered by a bower;
Nor droops, though Spring refuse her shower,
   Nor woos the Summer beam:
To it the livelong night there sings
   A Bird unseen—but not remote:
Invisible his airy wings,

But soft as harp that Houri strings
 His long entrancing note!
It were the Bulbul; but his throat,
 Though mournful, pours not such a strain
For they who listen cannot leave
The spot, but linger there and grieve,
 As if they loved in vain!
And yet so sweet the tears they shed,
'Tis sorrow so unmixed with dread,
They scarce can bear the morn to break
 That melancholy spell,
And longer yet would weep and wake,
 He sings so wild and well!
But when the day-blush bursts from high
 Expires that magic melody.
And some have been who could believe,
(So fondly youthful dreams deceive,
 Yet harsh be they that blame,)
That note so piercing and profound
Will shape and syllable[i] its sound
 Into Zuleika's name.
'Tis from her cypress summit heard,
That melts in air the liquid word:
'Tis from her lowly virgin earth
That white rose takes its tender birth.
There late was laid a marble stone;
Eve saw it placed—the Morrow gone!
It was no mortal arm that bore
That deep fixed pillar to the shore;

For there, as Helle's legends tell,

Next morn 'twas found where Selim fell:

Lashed by the tumbling tide, whose wave

Denied his bones a holier grave:

And there by night, reclined, 'tis said,

Is seen a ghastly turbaned head:

 And hence extended by the billow,

 'Tis named the "Pirate-phantom's pillow!"

 Where first it lay that mourning flower

 Hath flourished; flourisheth this hour,

Alone and dewy—coldly pure and pale;

As weeping Beauty's cheek at Sorrow's tale!

i. "And airy tongues that *syllable* men's names."
  MILTON, *Comus,* line 208.

For a belief that the souls of the dead inhabit the form of birds, we need not travel to the East. Lord Lyttleton's ghost story, the belief of the Duchess of Kendal, that George I. flew into her window in the shape of a raven (see *Orfords Reminiscences, Lord Orford's Works,* 1798, iv. 283), and many other instances, bring this superstition nearer home. The most singular was the whim of a Worcester lady, who, believing her daughter to exist in the shape of a singing bird, literally furnished her pew in the cathedral with cages full of the kind; and as she was rich, and a benefactress in beautifying the church, no objection was made to her harmless folly. For this anecdote, see *Orford's Letters.*

THE CORSAIR: A TALE

"I suoi pensieri in lui dormir non ponno."
TASSO, *Gerusalemme Liberata,* Canto X.

TO THOMAS MOORE, ESQ.

MY DEAR MOORE,

I dedicate to you the last production with which I shall trespass on public patience, and your indulgence, for some years; and I own that I feel anxious to avail myself of this latest and only opportunity of adorning my pages with a name, consecrated by unshaken public principle, and the most undoubted and various talents. While Ireland ranks you among the firmest of her patriots; while you stand alone the first of her bards in her estimation, and Britain repeats and ratifies the decree, permit one, whose only regret, since our first acquaintance, has been the years he had lost before it commenced, to add the humble but sincere suffrage of friendship, to the voice of more than one nation. It will at least prove to you, that I have neither forgotten the gratification derived from your society, nor abandoned the prospect of its renewal, whenever your leisure or inclination allows you to atone to your friends for too long an absence. It is said among those friends, I trust truly, that you are engaged in the composition of a poem whose scene will be laid in the East; none can do those scenes so much justice. The wrongs of your own country, the magnificent and fiery spirit of her sons, the beauty and feeling of her daughters, may there be found; and Collins, when he denominated his Oriental his Irish Eclogues, was not aware how true, at least, was a part of his parallel. Your imagination will create a warmer sun, and less clouded sky; but wildness, tenderness, and originality, are part of your national claim of oriental descent, to which you have already thus far proved your title more clearly than the most zealous of your country's antiquarians.

May I add a few words on a subject on which all men are supposed to be fluent, and none agreeable?—Self. I have written much, and published more than enough to demand a longer silence than I now meditate; but, for some years to come, it is my intention to tempt no further the award of "Gods, men, nor columns." In the present composition I have attempted not the most difficult, but, perhaps, the best adapted measure to our language, the good old and now neglected heroic couplet. The stanza of Spenser is perhaps too slow and dignified for narrative; though, I confess, it is the measure most after my own heart; Scott alone, of the present generation, has hitherto completely triumphed over the fatal facility of the octosyllabic verse; and this is not the least victory of his fertile and mighty genius: in blank verse, Milton, Thomson, and our dramatists, are the beacons that shine along the deep, but warn us from the rough and barren rock on which they are kindled. The heroic couplet is not the most popular measure certainly; but as I did not deviate into the other from a wish to flatter what is called public opinion, I shall quit it without further apology, and take my chance once more with that versification, in which I have hitherto published nothing but compositions whose former circulation is part of my present, and will be of my future regret.

With regard to my story, and stories in general, I should have been glad to have rendered my personages more perfect and amiable, if possible, inasmuch as I have been sometimes criticised, and considered no less responsible for their deeds and qualities than if all had been personal. Be it so—if I have deviated into the gloomy vanity of "drawing from self," the pictures are probably like, since they are unfavourable: and if not, those who know me are undeceived, and those who do not, I have little interest in undeceiving. I have no particular desire that any but my acquaintance should think the author better than the beings of his imagining; but I cannot help a little surprise, and perhaps amusement, at some odd critical exceptions in the present instance, when I see several bards (far more deserving, I allow) in very reputable plight, and quite exempted from all participation in the faults of those heroes, who, nevertheless, might be found with little more morality than *The Giaour,* and perhaps—but no—I must admit Childe Harold to be a very repulsive personage; and as to his identity, those who like it must give him whatever "alias" they please.

If, however, it were worth while to remove the impression, it might be of some service to me, that the man who is alike the delight of his readers and his friends, the poet of all circles, and the idol of his own, permits me here and elsewhere to subscribe myself,

Most truly,

And affectionately,

His obedient servant,   BYRON.

January 2, 1814.

CANTO THE FIRST

> "—nessun maggior dolore,
> Che ricordarsi del tempo felice
> Nell a miseria,—"
>
> DANTE, *Inferno,* v. 121.

The time in this poem may seem too short for the occurrences, but the whole of the Ægean isles are within a few hours' sail of the continent, and the reader must be kind enough to take the *wind* as I have often found it.

I.

"O'er the glad waters of the dark blue sea,

Our thoughts as boundless, and our souls as free,

Far as the breeze can bear, the billows foam,

Survey our empire, and behold our home!

These are our realms, no limits to their sway—

Our flag the sceptre all who meet obey.

Ours the wild life in tumult still to range

From toil to rest, and joy in every change.

Oh, who can tell? not thou, luxurious slave!

Whose soul would sicken o'er the heaving wave;

Not thou, vain lord of Wantonness and Ease!

Whom Slumber soothes not—Pleasure cannot please—

Oh, who can tell, save he whose heart hath tried,

And danced in triumph o'er the waters wide,

The exulting sense—the pulse's maddening play,

That thrills the wanderer of that trackless way?

That for itself can woo the approaching fight,

And turn what some deem danger to delight;

That seeks what cravens shun with more than zeal,

And where the feebler faint can only feel—

Feel—to the rising bosom's inmost core,

Its hope awaken and its spirit soar?

No dread of Death—if with us die our foes—

Save that it seems even duller than repose;

Come when it will—we snatch the life of Life—

When lost—what recks it by disease or strife?

Let him who crawls, enamoured of decay,

Cling to his couch, and sicken years away;

Heave his thick breath, and shake his palsied head;

Ours the fresh turf, and not the feverish bed,—

While gasp by gasp he falters forth his soul,

Ours with one pang—one bound—escapes control.

His corse may boast its urn and narrow cave,

And they who loathed his life may gild his grave:

Ours are the tears, though few, sincerely shed,

When Ocean shrouds and sepulchres our dead.

For us, even banquets fond regret supply

In the red cup that crowns our memory;

And the brief epitaph in Danger's day,

When those who win at length divide the prey,

And cry, Remembrance saddening o'er each brow,

How had the brave who fell exulted *now*!"

II.

Such were the notes that from the Pirate's isle

Around the kindling watch-fire rang the while:

Such were the sounds that thrilled the rocks along,

And unto ears as rugged seemed a song!

In scattered groups upon the golden sand,

They game—carouse—converse—or whet the brand;

Select the arms—to each his blade assign,

And careless eye the blood that dims its shine
Repair the boat, replace the helm or oar,
While others straggling muse along the shore;
For the wild bird the busy springes set,
Or spread beneath the sun the dripping net:
Gaze where some distant sail a speck supplies,
With all the thirsting eye of Enterprise;
Tell o'er the tales of many a night of toil,
And marvel where they next shall seize a spoil:
No matter where—their chief's allotment this;
Theirs to believe no prey nor plan amiss.
But who that CHIEF? his name on every shore
Is famed and feared—they ask and know no more,
With these he mingles not but to command;
Few are his words, but keen his eye and hand.
Ne'er seasons he with mirth their jovial mess,
But they forgive his silence for success.
Ne'er for his lip the purpling cup they fill,
That goblet passes him untasted still—
And for his fare—the rudest of his crew
Would that, in turn, have passed untasted too ;
Earth's coarsest bread, the garden's homeliest roots,
And scarce the summer luxury of fruits,
His short repast in humbleness supply
With all a hermit's board would scarce deny.
But while he shuns the grosser joys of sense,
His mind seems nourished by that abstinence.
"Steer to that shore!"—they sail. "Do this!"—'tis done:
"Now form and follow me!"—the spoil is won.

Thus prompt his accents and his actions still,

And all obey and few inquire his will; So

To such, brief answer and contemptuous eye

Convey reproof, nor further deign reply.

III.

"A sail!—a sail!"—a promised prize to Hope!

Her nation—flag—how speaks the telescope?

No prize, alas! but yet a welcome sail:

The blood-red signal glitters in the gale.

Yes—she is ours—a home-returning bark—

Blow fair, thou breeze!—she anchors ere the dark.

Already doubled is the cape—our bay

Receives that prow which proudly spurns the spray.

How gloriously her gallant course she goes!

Her white wings flying—never from her foes—

She walks the waters like a thing of Life,

And seems to dare the elements to strife.

Who would not brave the battle-fire, the wreck,

To move the monarch of her peopled deck!

IV.

Hoarse o'er her side the rustling cable rings:

The sails are furled; and anchoring round she swings;

And gathering loiterers on the land discern

Her boat descending from the latticed stem.

'Tis manned—the oars keep concert to the strand,

Till grates her keel upon the shallow sand.

Hail to the welcome shout!—the friendly speech!

When hand grasps hand uniting on the beach;

The smile, the question, and the quick reply,

And the Heart's promise of festivity!

The tidings spread, and gathering grows the crowd:

The hum of voices, and the laughter loud,

And Woman's gentler anxious tone is heard—

Friends'—husbands'—lovers' names in each dear word:

"Oh! are they safe? we ask not of success—

But shall we see them? will their accents bless?

From where the battle roars, the billows chafe,

They doubtless boldly did—but who are safe?

Here let them haste to gladden and surprise,

And kiss the doubt from these delighted eyes!"

VI.

"Where is our Chief? for him we bear report—

And doubt that joy—which hails our coming—short

Yet thus sincere—'tis cheering, though so brief;

But, Juan! instant guide us to our Chief:

Our greeting paid, we'll feast on our return,

And all shall hear what each may wish to learn."

Ascending slowly by the rock-hewn way,

To where his watch-tower beetles o'er the bay,

By bushy brake, the wild flowers blossoming,

And freshness breathing from each silver spring,

Whose scattered streams from granite basins burst,

Leap into life, and sparkling woo your thirst;

From crag to cliff they mount—Near yonder cave,

What lonely straggler looks along the wave?

In pensive posture leaning on the brand,

Not oft a resting-staff to that red hand?

"'Tis he—'tis Conrad—here—as wont—alone;

On—Juan!—on—and make our purpose known.
The bark he views—and tell him we would greet
His ear with tidings he must quickly meet:
We dare not yet approach—thou know'st his mood,
When strange or uninvited steps intrude."

VII.

Him Juan sought, and told of their intent;—
He spake not, but a sign expressed assent,
These Juan calls—they come—to their salute
He bends him slightly, but his lips are mute.
"These letters, Chief, are from the Greek—the spy,
Who still proclaims our spoil or peril nigh:
Whate'er his tidings, we can well report,
Much that"—"Peace, peace!"—he cuts their prating short.
Wondering they turn, abashed, while each to each
Conjecture whispers in his muttering speech:
They watch his glance with many a stealing look,
To gather how that eye the tidings took;
But, this as if he guessed, with head aside,
Perchance from some emotion, doubt, or pride,
He read the scroll—"My tablets, Juan, hark—
Where is Gonsalvo?"

          "In the anchored bark."
"There let him stay—to him this order bear—
Back to your duty—for my course prepare:
Myself this enterprise to-night will share."
"To-night, Lord Conrad?"

          "Aye! at set of sun:
The breeze will freshen when the day is done.

My corslet—cloak—one hour and we are gone.

Sling on thy bugle—see that free from rust

My carbine-lock springs worthy of my trust;

Be the edge sharpened of my boarding-brand,

And give its guard more room to fit my hand.

This let the Armourer with speed dispose;

Last time, .it more fatigued my arm than foes;

Mark that the signal-gun be duly fired,

To tell us when the hour of stay's expired."

VIII.

They make obeisance, and retire in haste,

Too soon to seek again the watery waste:

Yet they repine not—so that Conrad guides;

And who dare question aught that he decides?

That man of loneliness and mystery,

Scarce seen to smile, and seldom heard to sigh;

Whose name appals the fiercest of his crew,

And tints each swarthy cheek with sallower hue;

Still sways their souls with that commanding art

That dazzles, leads, yet chills the vulgar heart.

What is that spell, that thus his lawless train

Confess and envy—yet oppose in vain?

What should it be, that thus their faith can bind?

The power of Thought—the magic of the Mind!

Linked with success, assumed and kept with skill,

That moulds another's weakness to its will;

Wields with their hands, but, still to these unknown

Makes even their mightiest deeds appear his own.

Such hath it been—shall be—beneath the Sun

The many still must labour for the one!

'Tis Nature's doom—but let the wretch who toils,

Accuse not—hate not—*him* who wears the spoils.

Oh! if he knew the weight of splendid chains,

How light the balance of his humbler pains!

IX.

Unlike the heroes of each ancient race,

Demons in act, but Gods at least in face,

In Conrad's form seems little to admire,

Though his dark eyebrow shades a glance of fire:

Robust but not Herculean—to the sight

No giant frame sets forth his common height;

Yet, in the whole, who paused to look again,

Saw more than marks the crowd of vulgar men;

They gaze and marvel how—and still confess

That thus it is, but why they cannot guess.

Sun-burnt his cheek, his forehead high and pale

The sable curls in wild profusion veil;

And oft perforce his rising lip reveals

The haughtier thought it curbs, but scarce conceals.

Though smooth his voice, and calm his general mien,

Still seems there something he would not have seen:

His features' deepening lines and varying hue

At times attracted, yet perplexed the view,

As if within that murkiness of mind

Worked feelings fearful, and yet undefined;

Such might it be—that none could truly tell—

Too close inquiry his stern glance would quell.

There breathe but few whose aspect might defy

The full encounter of his searching eye;

He had the skill, when Cunning's gaze would seek

To probe his heart and watch his changing cheek,

At once the observer's purpose to espy,

And on himself roll back his scrutiny,

Lest he to Conrad rather should betray

Some secret thought, than drag that Chiefs to day.

There was a laughing Devil in his sneer,

That raised emotions both of rage and fear;

And where his frown of hatred darkly fell,

Hope withering fled—and Mercy sighed farewell!

That Conrad is a character not altogether out of nature, I shall attempt to prove by some historical coincidences which I have met with since writing *The Corsair.*

"Eccelin, prisonnier," dit Rolandini, "s'enfermoit dans un silence menaçant; il fixoit sur la terre son visage féroce, et ne donnoit point d'essor à sa profonde indignation. De toutes partes cependant les soldats et les peuples accouroient; ils vouloient voir cet homme, jadis si puissant...et la joie universelle éclatoit de toutes partes.... Eccelino étoit d'une petite taille; mais tout l'aspect de sa personne, tous ses mouvemens, indiquoient un soldat. Son langage étoit amer, son déportement superbe, et par son seul regard, il faisoit trembler les plus hardis."—Simonde de Sismondi, *Histoire des Républiques Italiennes du Moyen Age,* 1809, iii. 219.

Again, "Gizericus...staturâ mediocris, et equi casu claudicans, animo profundus, sermone ratus, luxurias contemptor, iri turbidus, habendi cupidus, ad sollicitandas gentes providentissimus," etc., etc.—Jornandes, *De Geiarum Origine* ("De Rebus Geticis"), cap. 33, *ed.* 1597, p. 92.

I beg leave to quote those gloomy realities to keep in countenance my Giaour and Corsair.

X.

Slight are the outward signs of evil thought,

Within—within—'twas there the spirit wrought!

Love shows all changes—Hate, Ambition, Guile,

Betray no further than the bitter smile;

The lip's least curl, the lightest paleness thrown

Along the governed aspect, speak alone

Of deeper passions; and to judge their mien,

He, who would see, must be himself unseen.

Then—with the hurried tread, the upward eye,

The clenchèd hand, the pause of agony,

That listens, starting, lest the step too near

Approach intrusive on that mood of fear:

Then—with each feature working from the heart,

With feelings, loosed to strengthen—not depart,

That rise—convulse—contend—that freeze or glow,

Flush in the cheek, or damp upon the brow;

Then—Stranger! if thou canst, and tremblest not,

Behold his soul—the rest that soothes his lot!

Mark how that lone and blighted bosom sears

The scathing thought of execrated years!

Behold—but who hath seen, or e'er shall see,

Man as himself—the secret spirit free?

XI.

Yet was not Conrad thus by Nature sent

To lead the guilty—Guilt's worse instrument—

His soul was changed, before his deeds had driven

Him forth to war with Man and forfeit Heaven.

Warped by the world in Disappointment's school,

In words too wise—in conduct *there* a fool;

Too firm to yield, and far too proud to stoop,

Doomed by his very virtues for a dupe,

He cursed those virtues as the cause of ill,

And not the traitors who betrayed him still;

Nor deemed that gifts bestowed on better men

Had left him joy, and means to give again.

Feared—shunned—belied—ere Youth had lost her force,

He hated Man too much to feel remorse,

And thought the voice of Wrath a sacred call,

To pay the injuries of some on all.

He knew himself a villain—but he deemed

The rest no better than the thing he seemed;

And scorned the best as hypocrites who hid

Those deeds the bolder spirit plainly did.

He knew himself detested, but he knew

The hearts that loathed him, crouched and dreaded too.

Lone, wild, and strange, he stood alike exempt

From all affection and from all contempt:

His name could sadden, and his acts surprise;

But they that feared him dared not to despise:

Man spurns the worm, but pauses ere he wake

The slumbering venom of the folded snake:

The first may turn, but not avenge the blow;

The last expires, but leaves no living foe;

Fast to the. doomed offender's form it clings,

And he may crush—not conquer—still it stings!

XII.

None are all evil—quickening round his heart,

One softer feeling would not yet depart;

Oft could he sneer at others as beguiled

By passions worthy of a fool or child;

Yet 'gainst that passion vainly still he strove,

And even in him it asks the name of Love!

Yes, it was love—unchangeable—unchanged,

Felt but for one from whom he never ranged;

Though fairest captives daily met his eye,

He shunned, nor sought, but coldly passed them by;

Though many a beauty drooped in prisoned bower,

None ever soothed his most unguarded hour.

Yes—it was Love—if thoughts of tenderness,

Tried in temptation, strengthened by distress,

Unmoved by absence, firm in every clime,

And yet—Oh more than all!—untired by Time;

Which nor defeated hope, nor baffled wile,

Could render sullen were She near to smile,

Nor rage could fire, nor sickness fret to vent

On her one murmur of his discontent

Which still would meet with joy, with calmness part,

Lest that his look of grief should reach her heart;

Which nought removed, nor menaced to remove—

If there be Love in mortals—this was Love!

He was a villain—aye, reproaches shower

On him—but not the Passion, nor its power,

Which only proved—all other virtues gone—

Not Guilt itself could quench this loveliest one!

XIII.

He paused a moment—till his hastening men

Passed the first winding downward to the glen.

"Strange tidings!—many a peril have I passed,

Nor know I why this next appears the last!

Yet so my heart forebodes, but must not fear,

Nor shall my followers find me falter here.

'Tis rash to meet—but surer death to wait

Till here they hunt us to undoubted fate;

And, if my plan but hold, and Fortune smile,

We'll furnish mourners for our funeral pile.

Aye, let them slumber—peaceful be their dreams!

Morn ne'er awoke them with such brilliant beams

As kindle high to-night (but blow, thou breeze!)

To warm these slow avengers of the seas.

Now to Medora—Oh! my sinking heart,

Long may her own be lighter than thou art!

Yet was I brave—mean boast where all are brave!

Ev'n insects sting for aught they seek to save.

This common courage which with brutes we share,

That owes its deadliest efforts to Despair,

Small merit claims—but 'twas my nobler hope

To teach my few with numbers still to cope;

Long have I led them—not to vainly bleed:

No medium now—we perish or succeed!

So let it be—it irks not me to die;

But thus to urge them whence they cannot fly.

My lot hath long had little of my care,

But chafes my pride thus baffled in the snare:

Is this my skill? my craft? to set at last

Hope, Power and Life upon a single cast?

Oh, Fate!—accuse thy folly—not thy fate;

She may redeem thee still—nor yet too late."

XIV.

Thus with himself communion held he, till

He reached the summit of his tower-crowned hill:

There at the portal paused—for wild and soft

He heard those accents never heard too oft!

Through the high lattice far yet sweet they rung,

And these the notes his Bird of Beauty sung:

1.

"Deep in my soul that tender secret dwells,

Lonely and lost to light for evermore,

Save when to thine my heart responsive swells,

Then trembles into silence as before.

2.

"There, in its centre, a sepulchral lamp

Burns the slow flame, eternal—but unseen;

Which not the darkness of Despair can damp,

Though vain its ray as it had never been.

3.

"Remember me—Oh! pass not thou my grave

Without one thought whose relics there recline:

The only pang my bosom dare not brave

Must be to find forgetfulness in thine.

4.

"My fondest—faintest—latest accents hear—

Grief for the dead not Virtue can reprove;

Then give me all I ever asked—a tear,

The first—last—sole reward of so much love!"

He passed the portal, crossed the corridor,

And reached the chamber as the strain gave o'er:

"My own Medora! sure thy song is sad—"

"In Conrad's absence would'st thou have it glad?

Without thine ear to listen to my lay,

Still must my song my thoughts, my soul betray:

Still must each accent to my bosom suit,

My heart unhushed—although my lips were mute!

Oh! many a night on this lone couch reclined,

My dreaming fear with storms hath winged the wind,

And deemed the breath that faintly fanned thy sail

The murmuring prelude of the ruder gale;

Though soft—it seemed the low prophetic dirge,

That mourned thee floating on the savage surge:

Still would I rise to rouse the beacon fire,

Lest spies less true should let the blaze expire;

And many a restless hour outwatched each star,

And morning came—and still thou wert afar.

Oh! how the chill blast on my bosom blew,

And day broke dreary on my troubled view,

And still I gazed and gazed—and not a prow

Was granted to my tears—my truth—my vow!

At length—'twas noon—I hailed and blest the mast

That met my sight—it neared—Alas! it passed!

Another came—Oh God! 'twas thine at last!

Would that those days were over! wilt thou ne'er,

My Conrad! learn the joys of peace to share?

Sure thou hast more than wealth, and many a home

As bright as this invites us not to roam:

Thou know'st it is not peril that I fear,

I only tremble when thou art not here;

Then not for mine, but that far dearer life,

Which flies from love and languishes for strife—

How strange that heart, to me so tender still,
Should war with Nature and its better will!"

"Yea, strange indeed—that heart hath long been changed;
Worm-like 'twas trampled—adder-like avenged—
Without one hope on earth beyond thy love,
And scarce a glimpse of mercy from above.
Yet the same feeling which thou dost condemn,
My very love to thee is hate to them,
So closely mingling here, that disentwined,
I cease to love thee when I love Mankind:
Yet dread not this—the proof of all the past
Assures the future that my love will last;
But—Oh, Medora! nerve thy gentler heart;
This hour again—but not for long—we part."

"This hour we part!—my heart foreboded this:
Thus ever fade my fairy dreams of bliss.
This hour—it cannot be—this hour away!
Yon bark hath hardly anchored in the bay:
Her consort still is absent, and her crew
Have need of rest before they toil anew;
My Love! thou mock'st my weakness; and wouldst steel
My breast before the time when it must feel;
But trifle now no more with my distress,
Such mirth hath less of play than bitterness.
Be silent, Conrad!—dearest! come and share
The feast these hands delighted to prepare;
Light toil! to cull and dress thy frugal fare!

See, I have plucked the fruit that promised best,

And where not sure, perplexed, but pleased, I guessed

At such as seemed the fairest; thrice the hill

My steps have wound to try the coolest rill;

Yes! thy Sherbet to-night will sweetly flow,

See how it sparkles in its vase of snow!

The grapes' gay juice thy bosom never cheers;

Thou more than Moslem when the cup appears:

Think not I mean to chide—for I rejoice

What others deem a penance is thy choice.

But come, the board is spread; our silver lamp

Is trimmed, and heeds not the Sirocco's damp:

Then shall my handmaids while the time along,

And join with me the dance, or wake the song;

Or my guitar, which still thou lov'st to hear,

Shall soothe or lull—or, should it vex thine ear,

We'll turn the tale, by Ariosto told,

Of fair Olympia loved and left of old.

Why, thou wert worse than he who broke his vow

To that lost damsel, should thou leave me *now*—

Or even that traitor chief—I've seen thee smile,

When the clear sky showed Ariadne's Isle,

Which I have pointed from these cliffs the while:

And thus half sportive—half in fear—I said,

Lest Time should raise that doubt to more than dread,

Thus Conrad, too, will quit me for the main:

And he deceived me—for—he came again!"

"Again, again—and oft again—my Love!
If there be life below, and hope above,
He will return—but now, the moments bring
The time of parting with redoubled wing:
The why, the where—what boots it now to tell?
Since all must end in that wild word—Farewell!
Yet would I fain—did time allow—disclose—
Fear not—these are no formidable foes!
And here shall watch a more than wonted guard,
For sudden siege and long defence prepared:
Nor be thou lonely, though thy Lord's away,
Our matrons and thy handmaids with thee stay;
And this thy comfort—that, when next we meet,
Security shall make repose more sweet.
List!—'tis the bugle!"—Juan shrilly blew—
"One kiss—one more—another—Oh! Adieu!"
She rose—she sprung—she clung to his embrace,
Till his heart heaved beneath her hidden face:
He dared not raise to his that deep-blue eye,
Which downcast drooped in tearless agony.
Her long fair hair lay floating o'er his arms, 470
In all the wildness of dishevelled charms;
Scarce beat that bosom where his image dwelt
So full—*that* feeling seem'd almost unfelt!
Hark—peals the thunder of the signal-gun!
It told 'twas sunset, and he cursed that sun.
Again—again—that form he madly pressed,
Which mutely clasped, imploringly caressed!
And tottering to the couch his bride he bore,

One moment gazed—as if to gaze no more;

Felt that for him Earth held but her alone,

Kissed her cold forehead—turned—is Conrad gone?

XV.

"And is he gone?"—on sudden solitude

How oft that fearful question will intrude!

"'Twas but an instant past, and here he stood!

And now"—without the portal's porch she rushed,

And then at length her tears in freedom gushed;

Big, bright, and fast, unknown to her they fell;

But still her lips refused to send—"Farewell!"

For in that word—that fatal word—howe'er

We promise—hope—believe—there breathes Despair.

O'er every feature of that still, pale face,

Had Sorrow fixed what Time can ne'er erase:

The tender blue of that large loving eye

Grew frozen with its gaze on vacancy,

Till—Oh, how far!—it caught a glimpse of him,

And then it flowed, and phrensied seemed to swim

Through those long, dark, and glistening lashes dewed

With drops of sadness oft to be renewed.

"He's gone!"—against her heart that hand is driven,

Convulsed and quick—then gently raised to Heaven:

She looked and saw the heaving of the main;

The white sail set—she dared not look again;

But turned with sickening soul within the gate—

"It is no dream—and I am desolate!"

XVI.

From crag to crag descending, swiftly sped
Stern Conrad down, nor once he turned his head;
But shrunk whene'er the windings of his way
Forced on his eye what he would not survey,
His lone, but lovely dwelling on the steep,
That hailed him first when homeward from the deep:
And she—the dim and melancholy Star, 1
Whose ray of Beauty reached him from afar,
On her he must not gaze, he must not think—
There he might rest—but on Destruction's brink:
Yet once almost he stopped—and nearly gave
His fate to chance, his projects to the wave:
But no—it must not be—a worthy chief
May melt, but not betray to Woman's grief.
He sees his bark, he notes how fair the wind,
And sternly gathers all his might of mind:
Again he hurries on—and as he hears
The clang of tumult vibrate on his ears,
The busy sounds, the bustle of the shore,
The shout, the signal, and the dashing oar;
As marks his eye the seaboy on the mast,
The anchors rise, the sails unfurling fast,
The waving kerchiefs of the crowd that urge
That mute Adieu to those who stem the surge;
And more than all, his blood-red flag aloft,
Fire in his glance, and wildness in his breast,
He feels of all his former self possest;
He bounds—he flies—until his footsteps reach

The verge where ends the cliff, begins the beach,
There checks his speed; but pauses less to breathe
The breezy freshness of the deep beneath,
Than there his wonted statelier step renew;
Nor rush, disturbed by haste, to vulgar view:
For well had Conrad learned to curb the crowd,
By arts that veil, and oft preserve the proud;
His was the lofty port, the distant mien,
That seems to shun the sight—and awes if seen:
The solemn aspect, and the high-born eye,
That checks low mirth, but lacks not courtesy;
All these he wielded to command assent:
But where he wished to win, so well unbent,
That Kindness cancelled fear in those who heard,
And others' gifts showed mean beside his word,
When echoed to the heart as from his own
His deep yet tender melody of tone:
But such was foreign to his wonted mood,
He cared not what he softened, but subdued;
The evil passions of his youth had made
Him value less who loved—than what obeyed.

XVII.

Around him mustering ranged his ready guard.
Before him Juan stands—"Are all prepared?"
He marvelled how his heart could seem so soft.
"They are—nay more—embarked: the latest boat
Waits but my chief—"

     "My sword, and my capote."
Soon firmly girded on, and lightly slung,

His belt and cloak were o'er his shoulders flung:
"Call Pedro here!" He comes—and Conrad bends,
With all the courtesy he deigned his friends;
"Receive these tablets, and peruse with care,
Words of high trust and truth are graven there;
Double the guard, and when Anselmo's bark
Arrives, let him alike these orders mark:
In three days (serve the breeze) the sun shall shine
On our return—till then all peace be thine!"
This said, his brother Pirate's hand he wrung,
Then to his boat with haughty gesture sprung.
Flashed the dipt oars, and sparkling with the stroke,
Around the waves' phosphoric brightness broke;
They gain the vessel—on the deck he stands,—
Shrieks the shrill whistle, ply the busy hands—
He marks how well the ship her helm obeys,
How gallant all her crew, and deigns to praise.
His eyes of pride to young Gonsalvo turn—
Why doth he start, and inly seem to mourn?
Alas! those eyes beheld his rocky tower,
And live a moment o'er the parting hour;
She—his Medora—did she mark the prow?
Ah! never loved he half so much as now!
But much must yet be done ere dawn of day—
Again he mans himself and turns away;
Down to the cabin with Gonsalvo bends,
And there unfolds his plan—his means, and ends;
Before them burns the lamp, and spreads the chart,
And all that speaks and aids the naval art;

They to the midnight watch protract debate;

To anxious eyes what hour is ever late?

Meantime, the steady breeze serenely blew,

And fast and falcon-like the vessel flew;

Passed the high headlands of each clustering isle,

To gain their port—long—long ere morning smile:

And soon the night-glass through the narrow bay

Discovers where the Pacha's galleys lay.

Count they each sail, and mark how there supine

The lights in vain o'er heedless Moslem shine.

Secure, unnoted, Conrad's prow passed by,

And anchored where his ambush meant to lie;

Screened from espial by the jutting cape,

That rears on high its rude fantastic shape.

Then rose his band to duty—not from sleep—

Equipped for deeds alike on land or deep;

While leaned their Leader o'er the fretting flood,

And calmly talked—and yet he talked of blood!

i. By night, particularly in a warm latitude, every stroke of the oar, every motion of the boat or ship, is followed by a slight flash like sheet lightning from the water.

CANTO THE SECOND

"Conosceste i dubbiosi desiri?"
DANTE, *Inferno*, v. 120.

I.

In Coron's bay floats many a galley light,

Through Coron's lattices the lamps are bright,

For Seyd, the Pacha, makes a feast to-night:

A feast for promised triumph yet to come,

When he shall drag the fettered Rovers home;

This hath he sworn by Allah and his sword,

And faithful to his firman and his word,

His summoned prows collect along the coast, -

And great the gathering crews, and loud the boast;

Already shared the captives and the prize,

Though far the distant foe they thus despise;

'Tis but to sail—no doubt to-morrow's Sun

Will see the Pirates bound—their haven won!

Meantime the watch may slumber, if they will,

Nor only wake to war, but dreaming kill.

Though all, who can, disperse on shore and seek

To flesh their glowing valour on the Greek;

How well such deed becomes the turbaned brave—

To bare the sabre's edge before a slave!

Infest his dwelling—but forbear to slay,

Their arms are strong, yet merciful to-day,

And do not deign to smite because they may!

Unless some gay caprice suggests the blow,

To keep in practice for the coming foe.

Revel and rout the evening hours beguile,

And they who wish to wear a head must smile;

For Moslem mouths produce their choicest cheer,

And hoard their curses, till the coast is clear.

II.

High in his hall reclines the turbaned Seyd;

Around—the bearded chiefs he came to lead.

Removed the banquet, and the last pilaff—

Forbidden draughts, 'tis said, he dared to quaff,

Though to the rest the sober berry's juice[i]

The slaves bear round for rigid Moslems' use;

The long chibouque's[ii] dissolving cloud supply,

While dance the Almas[iii] to wild minstrelsy.

The rising morn will view the chiefs embark;

But waves are somewhat treacherous in the dark:

And revellers may more securely sleep

On silken couch than o'er the rugged deep:

Feast there who can—nor combat till they must,

And less to conquest than to Korans trust;

And yet the numbers crowded in his host

Might warrant more than even the Pacha's boast.

i. Coffee.

ii. "Chibouque," pipe.

iii. Dancing girls.

III.

With cautious reverence from the outer gate

Slow stalks the slave, whose office there to wait,

Bows his bent head—his hand salutes the floor,

Ere yet his tongue the trusted tidings bore:

"A captive Dervise, from the Pirate's nest

Escaped, is here—himself would tell the rest."[i]

He took the sign from Seyd's assenting eye,

And led the holy man in silence nigh.

His arms were folded on his dark-green vest,

His step was feeble, and his look deprest;

Yet worn he seemed of hardship more than years,

And pale his cheek with penance, not from fears.

Vowed to his God—his sable locks he wore,

And these his lofty cap rose proudly o'er:

Around his form his loose long robe was thrown,

And wrapt a breast bestowed on heaven alone;

Submissive, yet with self-possession manned,

He calmly met the curious eyes that scanned;

And question of his coming fain would seek,

Before the Pacha's will allowed to speak.

i. It has been observed, that Conrad's entering disguised as a spy is out of nature. Perhaps so. I find something not unlike it in history.—"Anxious to explore with his own eyes the state of the Vandals, Majorian ventured, after disguising the colour of his hair, to visit Carthage in the character of his own ambassador; and Genseric was afterwards mortified by the discovery, that he had entertained and dismissed the Emperor of the Romans. Such an anecdote may be rejected as an improbable fiction; but it is a fiction which would not have been imagined unless in the life of a hero."— See Gibbon's *Decline and Fall.*

IV.

"Whence com'st thou, Dervise?"

"From the Outlaw's den

A fugitive—"

"Thy capture where and when?"

"From Scalanova's port to Scio's isle,

The Saick was bound; but Allah did not smile

Upon our course—the Moslem merchant's gains

The Rovers won; our limbs have worn their chains.

I had no death to fear, nor wealth to boast,

Beyond the wandering freedom which I lost;

At length a fisher's humble boat by night

Afforded hope, and offered chance of flight;

I seized the hour, and find my safety here—

With thee—most mighty Pacha! who can fear?"

"How speed the outlaws? stand they well prepared,

Their plundered wealth, and robber's rock, to guard?

Dream they of this our preparation, doomed

To view with fire their scorpion nest consumed?"

"Pacha! the fettered captive's mourning eye,

That weeps for flight, but ill can play the spy;

I only heard the reckless waters roar,

Those waves that would not bear me from the shore;

I only marked the glorious Sun and sky,

Too bright—too blue—for my captivity;

And felt that all which Freedom's bosom cheers

Must break my chain before it dried my tears.

This mayst thou judge, at least, from my escape,

They little deem of aught in Peril's shape;

Else vainly had I prayed or sought the Chance

That leads me here—if eyed with vigilance:

The careless guard that did not see me fly,

May watch as idly when thy power is nigh.

Pacha! my limbs are faint—and nature craves

Food for my hunger, rest from tossing waves:

Permit my absence—peace be with thee! Peace
With all around!—now grant repose—release."

"Stay, Dervise! I have more to question—stay,
I do command thee—sit—dost hear?—obey!
More I must ask, and food the slaves shall bring;
Thou shalt not pine where all are banqueting:
The supper done—prepare thee to reply,
Clearly and full—I love not mystery."
'Twere vain to guess what shook the pious man,
Who looked not lovingly on that Divan;
Nor showed high relish for the banquet prest,
And less respect for every fellow guest.
'Twas but a moment's peevish hectic passed
Along his cheek, and tranquillised as fast:
He sate him down in silence, and his look
Resumed the calmness which before forsook:
The feast was ushered in—but sumptuous fare
He shunned as if some poison mingled there.
For one so long condemned to toil and fast,
Methinks he strangely spares the rich repast.
"What ails thee, Dervise? eat—dost thou suppose
This feast a Christian's? or my friends thy foes?
Why dost thou shun the salt? that sacred pledge,
Which, once partaken, blunts the sabre's edge,
Makes even contending tribes in peace unite,
And hated hosts seem brethren to the sight!"

"Salt seasons dainties—and my food is still

The humblest root, my drink the simplest rill;

And my stern vow and Order's[i] laws oppose

To break or mingle bread with friends or foes;

It may seem strange—if there be aught to dread

That peril rests upon my single head;

But for thy sway—nay more—thy Sultan's throne,

I taste nor bread nor banquet—save alone;

Infringed our Order's rule, the Prophet's rage

To Mecca's dome might bar my pilgrimage."

i. The Dervises are in colleges, and of different orders, as the monks.

"Well—as thou wilt—ascetic as thou art—

One question answer; then in peace depart.

How many?—Ha! it cannot sure be day?

What Star—what Sun is bursting on the bay?

It shines a lake of fire!—away—away!

Ho! treachery! my guards! my scimitar!

The galleys feed the flames—and I afar!

Accurse'd Dervise!—these thy tidings—thou

Some villain spy—-seize—cleave him—slay him now!"

Up rose the Dervise with that burst of light,

Nor less his change of form appalled the sight:

Up rose that Dervise—not in saintly garb,

But like a warrior bounding on his barb,

Dashed his high cap, and tore his robe away—

Shone his mailed breast, and flashed his sabre's ray!

His close but glittering casque, and sable plume,

More glittering eye, and black brow's sabler gloom,

Glared on the Moslems' eyes some Afrit Sprite,

Whose demon death-blow left no hope for fight.

The wild confusion, and the swarthy glow

Of flames on high, and torches from below;

The shriek of terror, and the mingling yell—

For swords began to clash, and shouts to swell—

Flung o'er that spot of earth the air of Hell!

Distracted, to and fro, the flying slaves

Behold but bloody shore and fiery waves;

Nought heeded they the Pacha's angry cry,

They seize that Dervise!—seize on Zatanai!ⁱ

He saw their terror—checked the first despair

That urged him but to stand and perish there,

Since far too early and too well obeyed,

The flame was kindled ere the signal made;

He saw their terror—from his baldric drew

His bugle—brief the blast—but shrilly blew;

'Tis answered—"Well ye speed, my gallant crew!

Why did I doubt their quickness of career?

And deem design had left me single here?"

Sweeps his long arm—that sabre's whirling sway

Sheds fast atonement for its first delay;

Completes his fury, what their fear begun,

And makes the many basely quail to one.

The cloven turbans o'er the chamber spread,

And scarce an arm dare rise to guard its head:

Even Seyd, convulsed, o'erwhelmed, with rage, surprise,

Retreats before him, though he still defies.

No craven he—and yet he dreads the blow,

So much Confusion magnifies his foe!

His blazing galleys still distract his sight,

He tore his beard, and foaming fled the fight;[ii]

For now the pirates passed the Haram gate,

And burst within—and it were death to wait;

Where wild Amazement shrieking—kneeling—throws

The sword aside—in vain—the blood o'erflows!

The Corsairs pouring, haste to where within

Invited Conrad's bugle, and the din

Of groaning victims, and wild cries for life,

Proclaimed how well he did the work of strife.

They shout to find him grim and lonely there,

A glutted tiger mangling in his lair!

But short their greeting, shorter his reply—

"'Tis well—but Seyd escapes—and he must die—

Much hath been done—but more remains to do—

Their galleys blaze—why not their city too?"

i. "Zatanai," Satan.

ii. A common and not very novel effect of Mussulman anger. See Prince Eugene's *Mémoires,* 1811, p. 6, "The Seraskier received a wound in the thigh; he plucked up his beard by the roots, because he was obliged to quit the field."

V.

Quick at the word they seized him each a torch,

And fire the dome from minaret to porch.

A stern delight was fixed in Conrad's eye,

But sudden sunk—for on his ear the cry

Of women struck, and like a deadly knell

Knocked at that heart unmoved by Battle's yell.

"Oh! burst the Haram—wrong not on your lives

One female form—remember—*we* have wives.

On them such outrage Vengeance will repay;

Man is our foe, and such 'tis ours to slay:

But still we spared—must spare the weaker prey.

Oh! I forgot—but Heaven will not forgive

If at my word the helpless cease to live;

Follow who will—I go—we yet have time

Our souls to lighten of at least a crime."

He climbs the crackling stair—he bursts the door,

Nor feels his feet glow scorching with the floor;

His breath choked gasping with the volumed smoke,

But still from room to room his way he broke.

They search—they find—they save: with lusty arms

Each bears a prize of unregarded charms;

Calm their loud fears; sustain their sinking frames

With all the care defenceless Beauty claims:

So well could Conrad tame their fiercest mood,

And check the very hands with gore imbrued.

But who is she? whom Conrad's arms convey,

From reeking pile and combat's wreck, away—

Who but the love of him he dooms to bleed?

The Haram queen—but still the slave of Seyd!

VI.

Brief time had Conrad now to greet Gulnare,[i]

Few words to reassure the trembling Fair;

For in that pause Compassion snatched from War,

The foe before retiring, fast and far,

With wonder saw their footsteps unpursued,

First slowlier fled—then rallied—then withstood.

This Seyd perceives, then first perceives how few,

Compared with his, the Corsair's roving crew,

And blushes o'er his error, as he eyes

The ruin wrought by Panic and Surprise.

Alla il Alla! Vengeance swells the cry—

Shame mounts to rage that must atone or die!

And flame for flame and blood for blood must tell,

The tide of triumph ebbs that flowed too well—

When Wrath returns to renovated strife,

And those who fought for conquest strike for life.

Conrad beheld the danger—he beheld

His followers faint by freshening foes repelled:

"One effort—one—to break the circling host!"

They form—unite—charge—waver—all is lost!

Within a narrower ring compressed, beset,

Hopeless, not heartless, strive and struggle yet—

Ah! now they fight in firmest file no more,

Hemmed in—cut off—cleft down and trampled o'er;

But each strikes singly—silently—and home,

And sinks outwearied rather than o'ercome—

His last faint quittance rendering with his breath,

Till the blade glimmers in the grasp of Death!

i. Gulnare, a female name; it means, literally, the flower of the pomegranate.

VII.

But first, ere came the rallying host to blows,

And rank to rank, and hand to hand oppose,

Gulnare and all her Haram handmaids freed,

Safe in the dome of one who held their creed,

By Conrad's mandate safely were bestowed,

And dried those tears for life and fame that flowed:

And when that dark-eyed lady, young Gulnare,

Recalled those thoughts late wandering in despair,

Much did she marvel o'er the courtesy

That smoothed his accents, softened in his eye—

'Twas strange—*that* robber thus with gore bedewed,

Seemed gentler then than Seyd in fondest mood.

The Pacha wooed as if he deemed the slave

Must seem delighted with the heart he gave;

The Corsair vowed protection, soothed affright,

As if his homage were a Woman's right.

"The wish is wrong—nay, worse for female—vain:

Yet much I long to view that Chief again;

If but to thank for, what my fear forgot,

The life—my loving Lord remembered not!"

VIII.

And him she saw, where thickest carnage spread,

But gathered breathing from the happier dead;

Far from his band, and battling with a host

That deem right dearly won the field he lost,

Felled—bleeding—baffled of the death he sought,

And snatched to expiate all the ills he wrought;

Preserved to linger and to live in vain,

While Vengeance pondered o'er new plans of pain,

And stanched the blood she saves to shed again—

But drop by drop, for Seyd's unglutted eye

Would doom him ever dying—ne'er to die!

Can this be he? triumphant late she saw,

When his red hand's wild gesture waved, a law!

'Tis he indeed—disarmed but undeprest,

His sole regret the life he still possest;
His wounds too slight, though taken with that will,
Which would have kissed the hand that then could kill.
Oh were there none, of all the many given,
To send his soul—he scarcely asked to Heaven?
Must he alone of all retain his breath,
Who more than all had striven and struck for death?
He deeply felt—what mortal hearts must feel,
When thus reversed on faithless Fortune's wheel,
For crimes committed, and the victor's threat
Of lingering tortures to repay the debt—
He deeply, darkly felt; but evil Pride
That led to perpetrate—now serves to hide.
Still in his stern and self-collected mien
A conqueror's more than captive's air is seen,
Though faint with wasting toil and stiffening wound,
But few that saw—so calmly gazed around:
Though the far shouting of the distant crowd,
Their tremors o'er, rose insolently loud,
The better warriors who beheld him near,
Insulted not the foe who taught them fear;
And the grim guards that to his durance led,
In silence eyed him with a secret dread.

IX.

The Leech was sent—but not in mercy—there,
To note how much the life yet left could bear;
He found enough to load with heaviest chain,
And promise feeling for the wrench of Pain;
To-morrow—yea—to-morrow's evening Sun

Will, sinking, see Impalement's pangs begun,

And rising with the wonted blush of morn

Behold how well or ill those pangs are borne.

Of torments this the longest and the worst,

Which adds all other agony to thirst,

That day by day Death still forbears to slake,

While famished vultures flit around the stake.

"Oh! water—water!"—smiling Hate denies

The victim's prayer, for if he drinks he dies.

This was his doom;—the Leech, the guard, were gone,

And left proud Conrad fettered and alone.

X.

'Twere vain to paint to what his feelings grew—

It even were doubtful if their victim knew.

There is a war, a chaos of the mind,

When all its elements convulsed, combined

Lie dark and jarring with perturbed force,

And gnashing with impenitent Remorse—

That juggling fiend, who never spake before,

But cries "I warned thee!" when the deed is o'er.

Vain voice! the spirit burning but unbent,

May writhe—rebel—the weak alone repent!

Even in that lonely hour when most it feels,

And, to itself, all—all that self reveals,—

No single passion, and no ruling thought

That leaves the rest, as once, unseen, unsought,

But the wild prospect when the Soul reviews,

All rushing through their thousand avenues—

Ambition's dreams expiring, Love's regret,

Endangered Glory, Life itself beset;

The joy untasted, the contempt or hate

'Gainst those who fain would triumph in our fate;

The hopeless past, the hasting future driven

Too quickly on to guess if Hell or Heaven;

Deeds—thoughts—and words, perhaps remembered not

So keenly till that hour, but ne'er forgot;

Things light or lovely in their acted time,

But now to stern Reflection each a crime;

The withering sense of Evil unrevealed,

Not cankering less because the more concealed;

All, in a word, from which all eyes must start,

That opening sepulchre, the naked heart

Bares with its buried woes—till Pride awake,

To snatch the mirror from the soul, and break.

Aye, Pride can veil, and Courage brave it all—

All—all—before—beyond—the deadliest fall.

Each hath some fear, and he who least betrays,

The only hypocrite deserving praise:

Not the loud recreant wretch who boasts and flies

But he who looks on Death—and silent dies:

So, steeled by pondering o'er his far career,

He half-way meets Him should He menace near!

XI.

In the high chamber of his highest tower

Sate Conrad, fettered in the Pacha's power.

His palace perished in the flame—this fort

Contained at once his captive and his court.

Not much could Conrad of his sentence blame,

His foe, if vanquished, had but shared the same:—
Alone he sate—in solitude had scanned
His guilty bosom, but that breast he manned:
One thought alone he could not—dared not meet—
"Oh, how these tidings will Medora greet?"
Then—only then—his clanking hands he raised,
And strained with rage the chain on which he gazed;
But soon he found, or feigned, or dreamed relief,
And smiled in self-derision of his grief,
"And now come Torture when it will, or may—
More need of rest to nerve me for the day!"
This said, with langour to his mat he crept,
And, whatso'er his visions, quickly slept.
'Twas hardly midnight when that fray begun,
For Conrad's plans matured, at once were done,
And Havoc loathes so much the waste of time,
She scarce had left an uncommitted crime.
One hour beheld him since the tide he stemmed—
Disguised—discovered—conquering—ta'en—condemned—
A Chief on land—an outlaw on the deep—
Destroying—saving—prisoned—and asleep!

XII.

He slept in calmest seeming, for his breath
Was hushed so deep—Ah! happy if in death!
He slept—Who o'er his placid slumber bends?
His foes are gone—and here he hath no friends;
Is it some Seraph sent to grant him grace?
No, 'tis an earthly form with heavenly face!
Its white arm raised a lamp—yet gently hid,

Lest the ray flash abruptly on the lid
Of that closed eye, which opens but to pain,
And once unclosed—but once may close again.
That form, with eye so dark, and cheek so fair,
And auburn waves of gemmed and braided hair;
With shape of fairy lightness—naked foot,
That shines like snow, and falls on earth as mute—
Through guards and dunnest night how came it there?
Ah! rather ask what will not Woman dare?
Whom Youth and Pity lead like thee, Gulnare!
She could not sleep—and while the Pacha's rest
In muttering dreams yet saw his pirate-guest,
She left his side—his signet-ring she bore,
Which oft in sport adorned her hand before—
And with it, scarcely questioned, won her way
Through drowsy guards that must that sign obey.
Worn out with toil, and tired with changing blows,
Their eyes had envied Conrad his repose;
And chill and nodding at the turret door,
They stretch their listless limbs, and watch no more;
Just raised their heads to hail the signet-ring,
Nor ask or what or who the sign may bring.

XIII.

She gazed in wonder, "Can he calmly sleep,
While other eyes his fall or ravage weep?
And mine in restlessness are wandering here—
What sudden spell hath made this man so dear?
True—'tis to him my life, and more, I owe,
And me and mine he spared from worse than woe:

'Tis late to think—but soft—his slumber breaks—
How heavily he sighs!—he starts—awakes!"
He raised his head, and dazzled with the light,
His eye seemed dubious if it saw aright:
He moved his hand—the grating of his chain
Too harshly told him that he lived again.
"What is that form? if not a shape of air,
Methinks, my jailor's face shows wondrous fair!"

"Pirate! thou know'st me not, but 1 am one,
Grateful for deeds thou hast too rarely done;
Look on me—and remember her, thy hand
Snatched from the flames, and thy more fearful band.
I come through darkness—and I scarce know why—
Yet not to hurt—I would not see thee die."

"If so, kind lady! thine the only eye
That would not here in that gay hope delight:
Theirs is the chance—and let them use their right.
But still I thank their courtesy or thine,
That would confess me at so fair a shrine!"

Strange though it seem—yet with extremest grief
Is linked a mirth—it doth not bring relief—
That playfulness of Sorrow ne'er beguiles,
And smiles in bitterness—but still it smiles;
And sometimes with the wisest and the best,
Till even the scaffold[i] echoes with their jest!
Yet not the joy to which it seems akin—

It may deceive all hearts, save that within.

Whate'er it was that flashed on Conrad, now

A laughing wildness half unbent his brow:

And these his accents had a sound of mirth,

As if the last he could enjoy on earth;

Yet 'gainst his nature—for through that short life,

Few thoughts had he to spare from gloom and strife.

i. In Sir Thomas More, for instance, on the scaffold, and Anne Boleyn, in the Tower, when, grasping her neck, she remarked, that it "was too slender to trouble the headsman much." During one part of the French Revolution, it became a fashion to leave some "*mot*" as a legacy; and the quantity of facetious last words spoken during that period would form a melancholy jest-book of a considerable size.

XIV.

"Corsair! thy doom is named—but I have power

To soothe the Pacha in his weaker hour.

Thee would I spare—nay more—would save thee now,

But this—Time—Hope —nor even thy strength allow;

But all I can,—I will—at least delay

The sentence that remits thee scarce a day.

More now were ruin—even thyself were loth

The vain attempt should bring but doom to both."

"Yes!—loth indeed:—my soul is nerved to all,

Or fall'n too low to fear a further fall:

Tempt not thyself with peril—me with hope

Of flight from foes with whom I could not cope:

Unfit to vanquish—shall I meanly fly,

The one of all my band that would not die?

Yet there is one—to whom my Memory clings,

Till to these eyes her own wild softness springs.

My sole resources in the path I trod

Were these—my bark—my sword—my love—my God!

The last I left in youth!—He leaves me now—

And Man but works his will to lay me low.

I have no thought to mock his throne with prayer

Wrung from the coward crouching of Despair;

It is enough—I breathe—and I can bear.

My sword is shaken from the worthless hand

That might have better kept so true a brand;

My bark is sunk or captive—but my Love—

For her in sooth my voice would mount above:

Oh! she is all that still to earth can bind—

And this will break a heart so more than kind,

And blight a form—till thine appeared, Gulnare!

Mine eye ne'er asked if others were as fair."

"Thou lov'st another then?—but what to me

Is this—'tis nothing—nothing e'er can be:

But yet—thou lov'st—and—Oh! I envy those

Whose hearts on hearts as faithful can repose,

Who never feel the void—the wandering thought

That sighs o'er visions—such as mine hath wrought."

"Lady—methought thy love was his, for whom

This arm redeemed thee from a fiery tomb."

"My love stern Seyd's! Oh—No—No—not my love—

Yet much this heart, that strives no more, once strove

To meet his passion—but it would not be.

I felt—I feel—Love dwells with—with the free.

I am a slave, a favoured slave at best,

To share his splendour, and seem very blest!

Oft must my soul the question undergo,

Of—'Dost thou love?' and burn to answer, 'No!'

Oh! hard it is that fondness to sustain,

And struggle not to feel averse in vain;

But harder still the heart's recoil to bear,

And hide from one—perhaps another there.

He takes the hand I give not—nor withhold—

Its pulse nor checked—nor quickened—calmly cold:

And when resigned, it drops a lifeless weight

From one I never loved enough to hate.

No warmth these lips return by his imprest,

And chilled Remembrance shudders o'er the rest.

Yes—had I ever proved that Passion's zeal,

The change to hatred were at least to feel:

But still—he goes unmourned—returns unsought—

And oft when present—absent from my thought.

Or when Reflection comes—and come it must—

I fear that henceforth 'twill but bring disgust;

I am his slave—but, in despite of pride,

'Twere worse than bondage to become his bride.

Oh! that this dotage of his breast would cease!

Or seek another and give mine release,

But yesterday—I could have said, to peace!

Yes, if unwonted fondness now I feign,

Remember—Captive! 'tis to break thy chain;

Repay the life that to thy hand I owe;

To give thee back to all endeared below,

Who share such love as I can never know.

Farewell—Morn breaks—and I must now away:

'Twill cost me dear—but dread no death to-day!"

XV.

She pressed his fettered fingers to her heart,

And bowed her head, and turned her to depart,

And noiseless as a lovely dream is gone.

And was she here? and is he now alone?

What gem hath dropped and sparkles o'er his chain?

The tear most sacred, shed for others' pain,

That starts at once—bright—pure—from Pity's mine,

Already polished by the hand divine!

Oh! too convincing—-dangerously dear—

In Woman's eye the unanswerable tear!

That weapon of her weakness she can wield,

To save, subdue—at once her spear and shield:

Avoid it—Virtue ebbs and Wisdom errs,

Too fondly gazing on that grief of hers!

What lost a world, and bade a hero fly?

The timid tear in Cleopatra's eye.

Yet be the soft Triumvir's fault forgiven;

By this—how many lose not earth—but Heaven!

Consign their souls to Man's eternal foe,

And seal their own to spare some Wanton's woe!

XVI.

'Tis Morn—and o'er his altered features play

The beams—without the Hope of yesterday.

What shall he be ere night? perchance a thing

O'er which the raven flaps her funeral wing,

By his closed eye unheeded and unfelt;
While sets that Sun, and dews of Evening melt,
Chill, wet, and misty round each stiffened limb,
Refreshing earth—reviving all but him!

CANTO THE THIRD

"Come vedi—ancor non m'abbandona."
Dante, *Inferno,* v. 105.

I.

The opening lines, as far as section ii., have, perhaps, little business here, and were annexed to an unpublished (though printed) poem; but they were written on the spot, in the Spring of 1811, and—I scarce know why—the reader must excuse their appearance here—if he can.

Slow sinks, more lovely ere his race be run,

Along Morea's bills the setting Sun;

Not, as in Northern climes, obscurely bright,

But one unclouded blaze of living light!

O'er the hushed deep the yellow beam he throws,

Gilds the green wave, that trembles as it glows.

On old Ægina's rock, and Idra's isle,

The God of gladness sheds his parting smile;

O'er his own regions lingering, loves to shine,

Though there his altars are no more divine.

Descending fast the mountain shadows kiss

Thy glorious gulf, unconquered Salamis!

Their azure arches through the long expanse

More deeply purpled met his mellowing glance,

And tenderest tints, along their summits driven,

Mark his gay course, and own the hues of Heaven;

Till, darkly shaded from the land and deep,

Behind his Delphian cliff he sinks to sleep.

On such an eve, his palest beam he cast,

When—Athens! here thy Wisest looked his last.

How watched thy better sons his farewell ray,

That closed their murdered Sage's[i] latest day!

Not yet—not yet—Sol pauses on the hill—

The precious hour of parting lingers still;

But sad his light to agonising eyes,

And dark the mountain's once delightful dyes:

Gloom o'er the lovely land he seemed to pour,

The land, where Phœbus never frowned before:

But ere he sunk below Cithæron's head,

The cup of woe was quaffed—the Spirit fled;

The Soul of him who scorned to fear or fly—

Who lived and died, as none can live or die!

i. Socrates drank the hemlock a short time before sunset (the hour of execution), notwithstanding the entreaties of his disciples to wait till the sun went down.

But lo! from high Hymettus to the plain,

The Queen of night asserts her silent reign.[i]

No murky vapour, herald of the storm,

Hides her fair face, nor girds her glowing form;

With cornice glimmering as the moon-beams play,

There the white column greets her grateful ray,

And bright around with quivering beams beset,

Her emblem sparkles o'er the Minaret:

The groves of olive scattered dark and wide

Where meek Cephisus pours his scanty tide;

The cypress saddening by the sacred Mosque,

The gleaming turret of the gay Kiosk;[ii]

And, dun and sombre 'mid the holy calm,

Near Theseus' fane yon solitary palm,

All tinged with varied hues arrest the eye—

And dull were his that passed him heedless by.

i. The twilight in Greece is much shorter than in our own country: the days in winter are longer, but in summer of shorter duration.

ii. The Kiosk is a Turkish summer house: the palm is without the present walls of Athens, not far from the temple of Theseus, between which and the tree, the wall intervenes.—Cephisus' stream is indeed scanty, and Ilissus has no stream at all.

Again the Ægean, heard no more afar,

Lulls his chafed breast from elemental war;

Again his waves in milder tints unfold

Their long array of sapphire and of gold,

Mixed with the shades of many a distant isle,

That frown—where gentler Ocean seems to smile.

II.

Not now my theme—why turn my thoughts to thee?

Oh! who can look along thy native sea,

Nor dwell upon thy name, whate'er the tale,

So much its magic must o'er all prevail?

Who that beheld that Sun upon thee set,

Fair Athens! could thine evening face forget?

Not he—whose heart nor time nor distance frees,

Spell-bound within the clustering Cyclades!

Nor seems this homage foreign to its strain,

His Corsair's isle was once thine own domain—

Would that with freedom it were thine again!

III.

The Sun hath sunk—and, darker than the night,

Sinks with its beam upon the beacon height

Medora's heart—the third day's come and gone—

With it he comes not—sends not—-faithless one!

The wind was fair though light! and storms were none.

Last eve Anselmo's bark returned, and yet

His only tidings that they had not met!
Though wild, as now, far different were the tale
Had Conrad waited for that single sail.
The night-breeze freshens—she that day had passed
In watching all that Hope proclaimed a mast;
Sadly she sate on high—Impatience bore
At last her footsteps to the midnight shore,
And there she wandered, heedless of the spray
That dashed her garments oft, and warned away:
She saw not, felt not this—nor dared depart,
Nor deemed it cold—her chill was at her heart;
Till grew such certainty from that suspense—
His very Sight had shocked from life or sense!

It came at last—a sad and shattered boat,
Whose inmates first beheld whom first they sought;
Some bleeding—all most wretched—these the few—
Scarce knew they how escaped—*this* all they knew.
In silence, darkling, each appeared to wait
His fellow's mournful guess at Conrad's fate:
Something they would have said; but seemed to fear
To trust their accents to Medora's ear.
She saw at once, yet sunk not—trembled not—
Beneath that grief, that loneliness of lot,
Within that meek fair form, were feelings high,
That deemed not till they found their energy.
While yet was Hope they softened, fluttered, wept—
All lost—that Softness died not—but it slept;
And o'er its slumber rose that Strength which said,

"With nothing left to love, there's nought to dread."
'Tis more than Nature's—like the burning might
Delirium gathers from the fever's height.

"Silent you stand—nor would I hear you tell
What—speak not—breathe not—for I know it well—
Yet would I ask—almost my lip denies
The—quick your answer—tell me where he lies."
"Lady! we know not—scarce with life we fled;
But here is one denies that he is dead:
He saw him bound; and bleeding—but alive."

She heard no further—'twas in vain to strive—
So throbbed each vein—each thought—till then withstood;
Her own dark soul—these words at once subdued:
She totters—falls—and senseless had the wave
Perchance but snatched her from another grave;
But that with hands though rude, yet weeping eyes,
They yield such aid as Pity's haste supplies:
Dash o'er her deathlike cheek the ocean dew,
Raise, fan, sustain—till life returns anew;
Awake her handmaids, with the matrons leave
That fainting form o'er which they gaze and grieve;
Then seek Anselmo's cavern, to report
The tale too tedious—when the triumph short.

IV.

In that wild council words waxed warm and strange,
With thoughts of ransom, rescue, and revenge;
All, save repose or flight: still lingering there

Breathed Conrad's spirit, and forbade despair;

Whate'er his fate—the breasts he formed and led

Will save him living, or appease him dead.

Woe to his foes! there yet survive a few,

Whose deeds are daring, as their hearts are true.

V.

Within the Haram's secret chamber sate

Stern Seyd, still pondering o'er his Captive's fate;

His thoughts on love and hate alternate dwell,

Now with Gulnare, and now in Conrad's cell;

Here at his feet the lovely slave reclined

Surveys his brow—would soothe his gloom of mind;

While many an anxious glance her large dark eye

Sends in its idle search for sympathy,

His only bends in seeming o'er his beads,[i]

But inly views his victim as he bleeds.

i. The comboloio, or Mahometan rosary; the beads are in number ninety-nine.

"Pacha! the day is thine; and on thy crest

Sits Triumph—Conrad taken—fall'n the rest!

His doom is fixed—he dies; and well his fate

Was earned—yet much too worthless for thy hate

Methinks, a short release, for ransom told

With all his treasure, not unwisely sold;

Report speaks largely of his pirate-hoard—

Would that of this my Pacha were the lord!

While baffled, weakened by this fatal fray—

Watched—followed—he were then an easier prey;

But once cut off—the remnant of his band

Embark their wealth, and seek a safer strand."

"Gulnare!—if for each drop of blood a gem
Were offered rich as Stamboul's diadem;
If for each hair of his a massy mine
Of virgin ore should supplicating shine;
If all our Arab tales divulge or dream
Of wealth were here—that gold should not redeem!
It had not now redeemed a single hour,
But that I know him fettered, in my power;
And, thirsting for revenge, I ponder still
On pangs that longest rack—and latest kill."

"Nay, Seyd! I seek not to restrain thy rage,
Too justly moved for Mercy to assuage;
My thoughts were only to secure for thee
His riches—thus released, he were not free:
Disabled—shorn of half his might and band,
His capture could but wait thy first command."

"His capture *could*!—and shall I then .resign
One day to him—the wretch already mine?
Release my foe!—at whose remonstrance?—thine!
Fair suitor!—to thy virtuous gratitude,
That thus repays this Giaour's relenting mood,
Which thee and thine alone of all could spare—
No doubt, regardless—if the prize were fair—
My thanks and praise alike are due—now hear!
I have a counsel for thy gentler ear:
I do mistrust thee, Woman! and each word
Of thine stamps truth on all Suspicion heard.

Borne in his arms through fire from yon Serai—
Say, wert thou lingering there with him to fly?
Thou need'st not answer—thy confession speaks,
Already reddening on thy guilty cheeks:
Then—lovely Dame—bethink thee! and beware:
'Tis not *his* life alone may claim such care!
Another word and—nay—I need no more.
Accursed was the moment when he bore
Thee from the flames, which better far—but no—
I then had mourned thee with a lover's woe—
Now 'tis thy lord that warns—deceitful thing!
Know'st thou that I can clip thy wanton wing?
In words alone I am not wont to chafe:
Look to thyself—nor deem thy falsehood safe!"

He rose—and slowly, sternly thence withdrew,
Rage in his eye, and threats in his adieu:
Ah! little recked that Chief of womanhood—
Which frowns ne'er quelled, nor menaces subdued;
And little deemed he what thy heart, Gulnare!
When soft could feel—and when incensed could dare!
His doubts appeared to wrong—nor yet she knew
How deep the root from whence Compassion grew
She was a slave—from such may captives claim
A fellow-feeling, differing but in name;
Still half unconscious—heedless of his wrath,
Again she ventured on the dangerous path,
Again his rage repelled—until arose
That strife of thought, the source of Woman's woes!

VI.

Meanwhile—long—anxious—weary—still the same

Rolled day and night: his soul could Terror tame—

This fearful interval of doubt and dread,

When every hour might doom him worse than dead;

When every step that echoed by the gate,

Might entering lead where axe and stake await;

When every voice that grated on his ear

Might be the last that he could ever hear;

Could Terror tame—that Spirit stern and high

Had proved unwilling as unfit to die;

'Twas worn—perhaps decayed—yet silent bore

That conflict, deadlier far than all before:

The heat of fight, the hurry of the gale,

Leave scarce one thought inert enough to quail:

But bound and fixed in fettered solitude,

To pine, the prey of every changing mood;

To gaze on thine own heart—and meditate

Irrevocable faults, and coming fate—

Too late the last to shun—the first to mend—

To count the hours that struggle to thine end,

With not a friend to animate and tell

To other ears that Death became thee well;

Around thee foes to forge the ready lie,

And blot Life's latest scene with calumny;

Before thee tortures, which the Soul can dare,

Yet doubts how well the shrinking flesh may bear;

But deeply feels a single cry would shame,

To Valour's praise thy last and dearest claim;

The life thou leav'st below, denied above

By kind monopolists of heavenly love;

And more than doubtful Paradise—thy Heaven

Of earthly hope—thy loved one from thee riven.

Such were the thoughts that outlaw must sustain,

And govern pangs surpassing mortal pain:

And those sustained he—hoots it well or ill?

Since not to sink beneath, is something still!

VII.

The first day passed—he saw not her—Gulnare—

The second, third—and still she came not there;

But what her words avouched, her charms had done,

Or else he had not seen another Sun.

The fourth day rolled along, and with the night

Came storm and darkness in their mingling might.

Oh! how he listened to the rushing deep,

That ne'er till now so broke upon his sleep;

And his wild Spirit wilder wishes sent,

Roused by the roar of his own element!

Oft had he ridden on that winged wave,

And loved its roughness for the speed it gave;

And now its dashing echoed on his ear,

A long known voice—alas! too vainly near!

Loud sung the wind above; and, doubly loud,

Shook o'er his turret cell the thunder-cloud;

And flashed the lightning by the latticed bar,

To him more genial than the Midnight Star:

Close to the glimmering grate he dragged his chain,

And hoped *that* peril might not prove in vain.

He rais'd his iron hand to Heaven, and prayed
One pitying flash to mar the form it made:
His steel and impious prayer attract alike—
The storm rolled onward, and disdained to strike;
Its peal waxed fainter—ceased—he felt alone,
As if some faithless friend had spurned his groan!

VII.

The midnight passed, and to the massy door
A light step came—it paused—it moved once more;
Slow turns the grating bolt and sullen key:
'Tis as his heart foreboded—that fair She!
Whate'er her sins, to him a Guardian Saint,
And beauteous still as hermit's hope can paint;
Yet changed since last within that cell she came,
More pale her cheek, more tremulous her frame:
On him she cast her dark and hurried eye,
Which spoke before her accents—"Thou must die!
Yes, thou must die—there is but one resource,
The last—the worst—if torture were not worse."

"Lady! I look to none; my lips proclaim
What last proclaimed they—Conrad still the same:
Why should'st thou seek an outlaw's life to spare,
And change the sentence I deserve to bear?
Well have I earned—nor here alone—the meed
Of Seyd's revenge, by many a lawless deed."

"Why should I seek? because—Oh! did'st thou not
Redeem my life from worse than Slavery's lot?

Why should I seek?—hath Misery made thee blind
To the fond workings of a woman's mind?
And must I say?—albeit my heart rebel
With all that Woman feels, but should not tell—
Because—despite thy crimes—that heart is moved:
It feared thee—thanked thee—pitied—maddened—loved.
Reply not, tell not now thy tale again,
Thou lov'st another—and I love in vain:
Though fond as mine her bosom, form more fair,
I rush through peril which she would not dare.
If that thy heart to hers were truly dear,
Were I thine own—thou wert not lonely here:
An outlaw's spouse—and leave her Lord to roam!
What hath such gentle dame to do with home?
But speak not now—o'er thine and o'er my head
Hangs the keen sabre by a single thread;
If thou hast courage still, and would'st be free,
Receive this poniard—rise and follow me!"

"Aye—in my chains! my steps will gently tread,
With these adornments, o'er such slumbering head!
Thou hast forgot—is this a garb for flight?
Or is that instrument more fit for fight?"

"Misdoubting Corsair! I have gained the guard,
Ripe for revolt, and greedy for reward.
A single word of mine removes that chain:
Without some aid how here could I remain?
Well, since we met, hath sped my busy time,

If in aught evil, for thy sake the crime:
The crime—'tis none to punish those of Seyd.
That hatred tyrant, Conrad—he must bleed!
I see thee shudder, but my soul is changed—
Wronged—spurned—reviled—and it shall be avenged—
Accused of what till now my heart disdained—
Too faithful, though to bitter bondage chained.
Yes, smile!—but he had little cause to sneer,
I was not treacherous then, nor thou too dear:
But he has said it—and the jealous well,—
Those tyrants—teasing—tempting to rebel,—
Deserve the fate their fretting lips foretell.
I never loved—he bought me—somewhat high—
Since with me came a heart he could not buy.
I was a slave unmurmuring; he hath said,
But for his rescue I with thee had fled.
'Twas false thou know'st—but let such Augurs rue,
Their words are omens Insult renders true.
Nor was thy respite granted to my prayer;
This fleeting grace was only to prepare
New torments for thy life, and my despair.
Mine too he threatens; but his dotage still
Would fain reserve me for his lordly will:
When wearier of these fleeting charms and me,
There yawns the sack—and yonder rolls the sea!
What, am I then a toy for dotard's play,
To wear but till the gilding frets away?
I saw thee—loved thee—owe thee all—would save,
If but to show how grateful is a slave.

But had he not thus menaced fame and life,—
And well he keeps his oaths pronounced in strife—
I still had saved thee—but the Pacha spared:
Now I am all thine own—for all prepared:
Thou lov'st me not—nor know'st—or but the worst.
Alas! *this* love—*that* hatred—are the first—
Oh! could'st thou prove my truth, thou would'st not start,
Nor fear the fire that lights an Eastern heart;
'Tis now the beacon of thy safety—now
It points within the port a Mainote prow:
But in one chamber, where our path must lead,
There sleeps—he must not wake—the oppressor Seyd!"

"Gulnare—Gulnare—I never felt till now
My abject fortune, withered fame so low:
Seyd is mine enemy; had swept my band
From earth with ruthless but with open hand,
And therefore came I, in my bark of war,
To smite the smiter with the scimitar;
Such is my weapon—not the secret knife;
Who spares a Woman's seeks not Slumber's life.
Thine saved I gladly, Lady—not for this;
Let me not deem that mercy shown amiss.
Now fare thee well—more peace be with thy breast!
Night wears apace, my last of earthly rest!"

"Rest! rest! by sunrise must thy sinews shake,
And thy limbs writhe around the ready stake,
I heard the order—saw—I will not see—

If thou wilt perish, I will fall with thee.
My life—my love—my hatred—all below
Are on this cast—Corsair! 'tis but a blow!
Without it flight were idle—how evade
His sure pursuit?—my wrongs too unrepaid,
My youth disgraced—the long, long wasted years,
One blow shall cancel with our future fears;
But since the dagger suits thee less than brand,
I'll try the firmness of a female hand.
The guards are gained—one moment all were o'er—
Corsair! we meet in safety or no more;
If errs my feeble hand, the morning cloud
Will hover o'er thy scaffold, and my shroud."

IX.

She turned, and vanished ere he could reply,
But his glance followed far with eager eye;
And gathering, as he could, the links that bound
His form, to curl their length, and curb their sound,
Since bar and bolt no more his steps preclude,
He, fast as fettered limbs allow, pursued.
'Twas dark and winding, and he knew not where
That passage led; nor lamp nor guard was there:
He sees a dusky glimmering—shall he seek
Or shun that ray so indistinct and weak?
Chance guides his steps—a freshness seems to bear
Full on his brow as if from morning air;
He reached an open gallery—on his eye
Gleamed the last star of night, the clearing sky:
Yet scarcely heeded these—another light

From a lone chamber struck upon his sight.

Towards it he moved; a scarcely closing door

Revealed the ray within, but nothing more.

With hasty step a figure outward passed,

Then paused, and turned—and paused—'tis She at last!

No poniard in that hand, nor sign of ill—

" Thanks to that softening heart—she could not kill! "

Again he looked, the wildness of her eye

Starts from the day abrupt and fearfully.

She stopped—threw back her dark far-floating hair,

That nearly veiled her face and bosom fair,

As if she late had bent her leaning head

Above some object of her doubt or dread.

They meet—upon her brow—unknown—forgot—

Her hurrying hand had left—'twas but a spot—

Its hue was all he saw, and scarce withstood—

Oh! slight but certain pledge of crime—'tis Blood!

X.

He had seen battle—he had brooded lone

O'er promised pangs to sentenced Guilt foreshown;

He had been tempted—chastened—and the chain

Yet on his arms might ever there remain:

But ne'er from strife—captivity—remorse—

From all his feelings in their inmost force—

So thrilled, so shuddered every creeping vein,

As now they froze before that purple stain.

That spot of blood, that light but guilty streak,

Had banished all the beauty from her cheek!

Blood he had viewed—could view unmoved—but then

It flowed in combat, or was shed by men!

XI.

"'Tis done—he nearly waked—but it is done.

Corsair! he perished—thou art dearly won.

All words would now be vain—away—away!

Our bark is tossing—'tis already day.

The few gained over, now are wholly mine,

And these thy yet surviving band shall join:

Anon my voice shall vindicate my hand,

When once our sail forsakes this hated strand."

XII.

She clapped her hands, and through the gallery pour,

Equipped for flight, her vassals—Greek and Moor;

Silent but quick they stoop, his chains unbind;

Once more his limbs are free as mountain wind!

But on his heavy heart such sadness sate,

As if they there transferred that iron weight.

No words are uttered—at her sign, a door

Reveals the secret passage to the shore;

The city lies behind—they speed, they reach

The glad waves dancing on the yellow beach;

And Conrad following, at her beck, obeyed,

Nor cared he now if rescued or betrayed;

Resistance were as useless as if Seyd

Yet lived to view the doom his ire decreed.

XIII.

Embarked—the sail unfurled—the light breeze blew—

How much had Conrad's memory to review!

Sunk he in contemplation, till the Cape
Where last he anchored reared its giant shape.
Ah!—since that fatal night, though brief the time,
Had swept an age of terror, grief, and crime.
As its far shadow frowned above the mast,
He veiled his face, and sorrowed as he passed;
He thought of all—Gonsalvo and his band,
His fleeting triumph and his failing hand;
He thought on her afar, his lonely bride:
He turned and saw—Gulnare, the Homicide!

XIV.

She watched his features till she could not bear
Their freezing aspect and averted air;
And that strange fierceness foreign to her eye
Fell quenched in tears, too late to shed or dry.
She knelt beside him and his hand she pressed,
"Thou may'st forgive though Allah's self detest;
But for that deed of darkness what wert thou?
Reproach me—but not yet—Oh! spare me *now*!
I am not what I seem—this fearful night
My brain bewildered—do not madden quite!
If I had never loved—though less my guilt—
Thou hadst not lived to—hate me—if thou wilt."

XV.

She wrongs his thoughts—they more himself upbraid
Than her—though undesigned—the wretch he made;
But speechless all, deep, dark, and unexprest,
They bleed within that silent cell—his breast.
Still onward, fair the breeze, nor rough the surge,

The blue waves sport around the stern they urge;

Far on the Horizon's verge appears a speck,

A spot—a mast—a sail—an armèd deck!

Their little bark her men of watch descry,

And ampler canvass woos the wind from high;

She bears her down majestically near,

Speed on her prow, and terror in her tier;

A flash is seen—the ball beyond her bow

Booms harmless, hissing to the deep below.

Up rose keen Conrad from his silent trance,

A long, long absent gladness in his glance;

"'Tis mine—my blood-rag flag! again—again—

I am not all deserted on the main!"

They own the signal, answer to the hail,

Hoist out the boat at once, and slacken sail.

"'Tis Conrad! Conrad!" shouting from the deck,

Command nor Duty could their transport check!

With light alacrity and gaze of Pride,

They view him mount once more his vessel's side;

A smile relaxing in each rugged face,

Their arms can scarce forbear a rough embrace.

He, half forgetting danger and defeat,

Returns their greeting as a Chief may greet,

Wrings with a cordial grasp Anselmo's hand,

And feels he yet can conquer and command!

XVI.

These greetings o'er, the feelings that o'erflow,

Yet grieve to win him back without a blow;

They sailed prepared for vengeance—had they known

A woman's hand secured that deed her own,

She were their Queen—less scrupulous are they

Than haughty Conrad how they win their way.

With many an asking smile, and wondering stare,

They whisper round, and gaze upon Gulnare;

And her, at once above—beneath her sex,

Whom blood appalled not, their regards perplex.'-

To Conrad turns her faint imploring eye,

She drops her veil, and stands in silence by;

Her arms are meekly folded on that breast,

Which—Conrad safe—to Fate resigned the rest.

Though worse than frenzy could that bosom fill,

Extreme in love or hate, in good or ill,

The worst of crimes had left her Woman still!

XVII.

This Conrad marked, and felt—ah! could he less?—

Hate of that deed—but grief for her distress;

What she has done no tears can wash away,

And Heaven must punish on its angry day:

But—it was done: he knew, whate'er her guilt,

For him that poniard smote, that blood was spilt;

And he was free!—and she for him had given

Her all on earth, and more than all in heaven!

And now he turned him to that dark-eyed slave

Whose brow was bowed beneath the glance he gave,

Who now seemed changed and humbled, faint and meek,

But varying oft the colour of her cheek

To deeper shades of paleness—all its red

That fearful spot which stained it from the dead!

He took that hand—it trembled—now too late—
So soft in love—so wildly nerved in hate;
He clasped that hand—it trembled—and his own
Had lost its firmness, and his voice its tone.
"Gulnare!"—but she replied not—"dear Gulnare!"
She raised her eye—her only answer there—
At once she sought and sunk in his embrace:
If he had driven her from that resting-place,
His had been more or less than mortal heart,
But—good or ill—it bade her not depart.
Perchance, but for the bodings of his breast,
His latest virtue then had joined the rest.
Yet even Medora might forgive the kiss
That asked from form so fair no more than this,
The first, the last that Frailty stole from Faith—
To lips where Love had lavished all his breath,
To lips—whose broken sighs such fragrance fling,
As he had fanned them freshly with his wing!

XVIII.

They gain by twilight's hour their lonely isle.
To them the very rocks appear to smile;
The haven hums with many a cheering sound,
The beacons blaze their wonted stations round,
The boats are darting o'er the curly bay,
And sportive Dolphins bend them through the spray;
Even the hoarse sea-bird's shrill, discordant shriek,
Greets like the welcome of his tuneless beak!
Beneath each lamp that through its lattice gleams,
Their fancy paints the friends that trim the beams.

Oh! what can sanctify the joys of home,

Like Hope's gay glance from Ocean's troubled foam?

XIX.

The lights are high on beacon and from bower,

And 'midst them Conrad seeks Medora's tower:

He looks in vain—'tis strange—and all remark,

Amid so many, hers alone is dark.

'Tis strange—of yore its welcome never failed,

Nor now, perchance, extinguished—only veiled.

With the first boat descends he for the shore,

And looks impatient on the lingering oar.

Oh! for a wing beyond the falcon's flight,

To bear him like an arrow to that height \

With the first pause the resting rowers gave,

He waits not—looks not—leaps into the wave,

Strives through the surge, bestrides the beach, and high

Ascends the path familiar to his eye.

He reached his turret door—he paused—no sound

Broke from within; and all was night around.

He knocked, and loudly—footstep nor reply

Announced that any heard or deemed him nigh;

He knocked, but faintly—for his trembling hand

Refused to aid his heavy heart's demand.

The portal opens—'tis a well known face—

But not the form he panted to embrace.

Its lips are silent—twice his own essayed,

And failed to frame the question they delayed;

He snatched the lamp—its light will answer all—

It quits his grasp, expiring in the fall.

He would not wait for that reviving ray—

As soon could he have lingered there for day;

But, glimmering through the dusky corridor,

Another chequers o'er the shadowed floor;

His steps the chamber gain—his eyes behold

All that his heart believed not—yet foretold!

XX.

He turned not—spoke not—sunk not—fixed his look,

And set the anxious frame that lately shook:

He gazed—how long we gaze despite of pain,

And know, but dare not own, we gaze in vain!

In life itself she was so still and fair,

That Death with gentler aspect withered there;

And the cold flowers1 her colder hand contained,

In that last grasp as tenderly were strained

As if she scarcely felt, but feigned a sleep—

And made it almost mockery yet to weep:

The long dark lashes fringed her lids of snow,

And veiled—Thought shrinks from all that lurked below—

Oh! o'er the eye Death most exerts his might,

And hurls the Spirit from her throne of light;

Sinks those blue orbs in that long last eclipse,

But spares, as yet, the charm around her lips—

Yet, yet they seem as they forebore to smile,

And wished repose,—but only for a while;

But the white shroud, and each extended tress,

Long, fair—but spread in utter lifelessness,

Which, late the sport of every summer wind,

Escaped the baffled wreath that strove to bind;

These—and the pale pure cheek, became the bier—

But She is nothing—wherefore is he here?

i. In the Levant it is the custom to strew flowers on the bodies of the dead, and in the hands of young persons to place a nosegay.

XXI.

He asked no question—all were answered now

By the first glance on that still, marble brow.

It was enough—she died—what recked it how?

The love of youth, the hope of better years,

The source of softest wishes, tenderest fears,

The only living thing he could not hate,

Was reft at once—and he deserved his fate,

But did not feel it less;—the Good explore,

For peace, those realms where Guilt can never soar:

The proud, the wayward—who have fixed below

Their joy, and find this earth enough for woe,

Lose in that one their all—perchance a mite—

But who in patience parts with all delight?

Full many a stoic eye and aspect stern

Mask hearts where Grief hath little left to learn;

And many a withering thought lies hid, not lost,

In smiles that least befit who wear them most.

XXII.

By those, that deepest feel, is ill exprest

The indistinctness of the suffering breast;

Where thousand thoughts begin to end in one,

Which seeks from all the refuge found in none;

No words suffice the secret soul to show,

For Truth denies all eloquence to Woe.

On Conrad's stricken soul Exhaustion prest,
And Stupor almost lulled it into rest;
So feeble now—his mother's softness crept
To those wild eyes, which like an infant's wept:
It was the very weakness of his brain,
Which thus confessed without relieving pain.
None saw his trickling tears—perchance, if seen,
That useless flood of grief had never been:
Nor long they flowed—he dried them to depart,
In helpless—hopeless—brokenness of heart:
The Sun goes forth, but Conrad's day is dim:
And the night cometh—ne'er to pass from him.
There is no darkness like the cloud of mind,
On Grief's vain eye—the blindest of the blind!
Which may not—dare not see—but turns aside
To blackest shade—nor will endure a guide!

XXIII.

His heart was formed for softness—warped to wrong,
Betrayed too early, and beguiled too long;
Each feeling pure—as falls the dropping dew
Within the grot—like that had hardened too;
Less clear, perchance, its earthly trials passed,
But sunk, and chilled, and petrified at last.
Yet tempests wear, and lightning cleaves the rock;
If such his heart, so shattered it the shock.
There grew one flower beneath its rugged brow,
Though dark the shade—it sheltered—saved till now.
The thunder came—that bolt hath blasted both,
The Granite's firmness, and the Lily's growth:

The gentle plant hath left no leaf to tell

Its tale, but shrunk and withered where it fell;

And of its cold protector, blacken round

But shivered fragments on the barren ground!

XXIV.

'Tis morn—to venture on his lonely hour

Few dare; though now Anselmo sought his tower.

He was not there, nor seen along the shore;

Ere night, alarmed, their isle is traversed o'er:

Another morn—another bids them seek,

And shout his name till Echo waxeth weak;

Mount—grotto—cavern—valley searched in vain,

They find on shore a sea-boat's broken chain:

Their hope revives—they follow o'er the main.

'Tis idle all—moons roll on moons away,

And Conrad comes not, came not since that day:

Nor trace nor tidings of his doom declare

Where lives his grief, or perished his despair!

Long mourned his band whom none could mourn beside;

And fair the monument they gave his Bride:

For him they raise not the recording stone—

His death yet dubious, deeds too widely known;

He left a Corsair's name to other times,

Linked with one virtue, and a thousand crimes.[i]

i. That the point of honour which is represented in one instance of Conrad's character has not been carried beyond the bounds of probability, may perhaps be in some degree confirmed by the following anecdote of a brother buccaneer in the year 1814: —"Our readers have all seen the account of the enterprise against the pirates of Barataria; but few, we believe, were informed of the situation, history, or nature of that establishment. For the information of such as were unacquainted with it, we have procured from a friend the following interesting narrative of the main facts, of which he has personal knowledge, and which cannot fail to interest some of our readers:—Barataria is a bayou, or a narrow arm of the Gulf of Mexico; it runs through a rich but very flat country, until it reaches within a mile of the Mississippi river, fifteen miles below the city of New Orleans. This bayou has branches almost innumerable, in which persons can lie concealed from the severest scrutiny. It communicates with three lakes which lie on the south-west side, and these, with the lake of the same name, and which lies contiguous to the sea, where there is an island formed by the two arms of this lake and the sea. The east and west points of this island were fortified, in the year 1811, by a band of pirates, under the command of one Monsieur La Fitte. A large majority of these outlaws are of that class of the population of the state of Louisiana who fled from the island of St. Domingo during the troubles there, and took refuge in the island of Cuba; and when the last war between France and Spain commenced, they were compelled to leave that island with the short notice of a few days. Without ceremony they entered the United States, the most of them the state of Louisiana, with all the negroes they had possessed in Cuba. They were notified by the Governor of that State of the clause in the constitution which forbade the importation of slaves; but, at the same time, received the assurance of the Governor that he would obtain, if possible, the approbation of the General Government for their retaining this property.—The island of Barataria is situated about lat. 29 deg. 15 min., lon. 92. 30.; and is as remarkable for its health as for the superior scale and shell fish with which its waters abound. The chief of this horde, like Charles de Moor, had, mixed with his many vices, some transcendant virtues. In the year 1813, this party had, from its turpitude and boldness, claimed the attention of the Governor of Louisiana; and to break up the establishment he thought proper to strike at the head. He therefore, offered a reward of 500 dollars for the head of Monsieur La Fitte, who was well known to the inhabitants of the city of New Orleans, from his immediate connection, and his once having been a fencing-master in that city of great reputation, which art he learnt in Buonaparte's army, where he was a captain. The reward which was offered by the Governor for the head of La Fitte was answered by the offer of a reward from the latter of 15,000 for the head of the Governor. The Governor ordered out a company to march from the city to La Fitte's island, and to burn and destroy all the property, and to bring to the city of New Orleans all his banditti. This company, under the command of a man who had been the intimate associate of this bold Captain, approached very near to the fortified island, before he saw a man, or heard a sound, until he heard a whistle, not unlike a boatswain's call. Then it was he found himself surrounded by armed men who had emerged from the secret avenues which led to this bayou. Here it was that this modern Charles de Moor developed his few noble traits; for to this man, who had come to destroy his life and all that was dear to him, he not only spared his life, but offered him that which would have made the honest soldier easy for the remainder of his days, which was indignantly refused. He then, with the approbation of his captor, returned to the city. This circumstance, and some concomitant events, proved that this band of pirates was not to be taken by land. Our naval force having always been small in that quarter, exertions for the destruction of this illicit establishment could not be expected from them until augmented; for an officer of the navy, with most of the gun-boats on that station, had to retreat from an overwhelming force of La Fitte's. So soon as the augmentation of the navy authorised an attack, one was made; the overthrow of this banditti has been the result: and now this almost invulnerable point and key to New Orleans is clear of an

enemy, it is to be hoped the government will hold it by a strong military force."—
American Newspaper.

In Noble's continuation of "Granger's *Biographical History*", there is a singular passage in his account of Archbishop Blackbourne; and as in some measure connected with the profession of the hero of the foregoing poem, I cannot resist the temptation of extracting it.—"There is something mysterious in the history and character of Dr. Blackbourne. The former is but imperfectly known; and report has even asserted he was a buccaneer; and that one of his brethren in that profession having asked, on his arrival in England, what had become of his old chum, Blackbourne, was answered, he is Archbishop of York. We are informed, that Blackbourne was installed sub-dean of Exeter in 1694, which office he resigned in 1702; but after his successor Lewis Barnet's death, in 1704, he regained it. In the following year he became dean; and in 1714 held with it the archdeanery of Cornwall. He was consecrated Bishop of Exeter, February 24, 1716; and translated to York, November 28, 1724, as a reward, according to court scandal, for uniting George I. to the Duchess of Munster. This, however, appears to have been an unfounded calumny. As archbishop he behaved with great prudence, and was equally respectable as the guardian of the revenues of the see. Rumour whispered he retained the vices of his youth, and that a passion for the fair sex formed an item in the list of his weaknesses; but so far from being convicted by seventy witnesses, he does not appear to have been directly criminated by one. In short, I look upon these aspersions as the effects of mere malice. How is it possible a buccaneer should have been so good a scholar as Blackbourne certainly was? He who had so perfect a knowledge of the classics (particularly of the Greek tragedians), as to be able to read them with the same ease as he could Shakespeare, must have taken great pains to acquire the learned languages; and have had both leisure and good masters. But he was undoubtedly educated at Christ-church College, Oxford. He is allowed to have been a pleasant man; this, however, was turned against him, by its being said, 'he gained more hearts than souls.'"

"The only voice that could soothe the passions of the savage (Alphonso III.) was that of an amiable and virtuous wife, the sole object of his love; the voice of Donna Isabella, the daughter of the Duke of Savoy, and the grand-daughter of Philip II. King of Spain. Her dying words sunk deep into his memory; his fierce spirit melted into tears; and, after the last embrace, Alphonso retired into his chamber to bewail his irreparable loss, and to meditate on the vanity of human life."—Gibbon's *Miscellaneous Works.*

ODE TO NAPOLEON BUONAPARTE

"Expende Annibalem:—quot libras in duce summo
Invenies?"
    Juvenal, *Sat.* x. line 147.

"The Emperor Nepos was acknowledged by the *Senate,* by the *Italians,* and by the Provincials of *Gaul;* his moral virtues, and military talents, were loudly celebrated; and those who derived any private benefit from his government announced in prophetic strains the restoration of the public felicity. * * By this shameful abdication, he protracted his life about five years, in a very ambiguous state, between an Emperor and an Exile, till!!!"—Gibbon's *Decline and Fall,* two vols, notes by Milman, i. 979.

I.

'Tis done—but yesterday a King!

And armed with Kings to strive—

And now thou art a nameless thing:

So abject—yet alive!

Is this the man of thousand thrones,

Who strewed our earth with hostile bones,

And can he thus survive?

Since he, miscalled the Morning Star,

Nor man nor fiend hath fallen so far.

II.

Ill-minded man! why scourge thy kind

Who bowed so low the knee?

By gazing on thyself grown blind,

Thou taught'st the rest to see.

With might unquestioned,—power to save,—

Thine only gift hath been the grave

　　To those that worshipped thee;

Nor till thy fall could mortals guess

Ambition's less than littleness!

III.

Thanks for that lesson—it will teach

　　To after-warriors more

Than high Philosophy can preach,

　　And vainly preached before.

That spell upon the minds of men

Breaks never to unite again,

　　That led them to adore

Those Pagod things of sabre-sway,

With fronts of brass, and feet of clay.

IV.

The triumph, and the vanity,

　　The rapture of the strife—[i]

The earthquake-voice of Victory,

　　To thee the breath of life;

The sword, the sceptre, and that sway

Which man seemed made but to obey,

　　Wherewith renown was rife—

All quelled!—Dark Spirit! what must be

The madness of thy memory!

i. "Certaminis *gaudia*"—the expression of Attila in his harangue to his army, previous to the battle of Chalons, given in Cassiodorus.

V.

The Desolator desolate!

 The Victor overthrown!

The Arbiter of others' fate

 A Suppliant for his own!

Is it some yet imperial hope

That with such change can calmly cope?

 Or dread of death alone?

To die a Prince—or live a slave—

Thy choice is most ignobly brave!

VI.

He who of old would rend the oak,

 Dreamed not of the rebound;

Chained by the trunk he vainly broke—

 Alone—how looked he round?

Thou, in the sternness of thy strength,

An equal deed hast done at length,

 And darker fate hast found:

He fell, the forest prowlers' prey;

But thou must eat thy heart away!

VII.

The Roman,[i] when his burning heart

 Was slaked with blood of Rome,

Threw down the dagger—dared depart,

 In savage grandeur, home.—

He dared depart in utter scorn

Of men that such a yoke had borne,

    Yet left him such a doom!

His only glory was that hour

Of self-upheld abandoned power.

i. Sylla.

VIII.

The Spaniard, when the lust of sway

    Had lost its quickening spell,

Cast crowns for rosaries away,

    An empire for a cell;

A strict accountant of his heads,

A subtle disputant on creeds,

    His dotage trifled well:

Yet better had he neither known

A bigot's shrine, nor despot's throne.

IX.

But thou—from thy reluctant hand

    The thunderbolt is wrung—

Too late thou leav'st the high command

    To which thy weakness clung;

All Evil Spirit as thou art,

It is enough to grieve the heart

    To see thine own unstrung;

To think that God's fair world hath been

The footstool of a thing so mean;

X.

And Earth hath spilt her blood for him,
   Who thus can hoard his own!
And Monarchs bowed the trembling limb,
   And thanked him for a throne!
Fair Freedom! we may hold thee dear,
When thus thy mightiest foes their fear
   In humblest guise have shown.
Oh! ne'er may tyrant leave behind
A brighter name to lure mankind!

XI.

Thine evil deeds are writ in gore,
   Nor written thus in vain—
Thy triumphs tell of fame no more,
   Or deepen every stain:
If thou hadst died as Honour dies,
Some new Napoleon might arise.
   To shame the world again—
But who would soar the solar height,
To set in such a starless night?

XII.

Weigh'd in the balance, hero dust
   Is vile as vulgar clay;
Thy scales, Mortality! are just
   To all that pass away:
But yet methought the living great

Some higher sparks should animate.

    To dazzle and dismay:

Nor deem'd Contempt could thus make mirth

Of these, the Conquerors of the earth.

XIII.

And she, proud Austria's mournful flower,

    Thy still imperial bride;

How bears her breast the torturing hour?

    Still clings she to thy side?

Must she too bend, must she too share

Thy late repentance, long despair,

    Thou throneless Homicide?

If still she loves thee, hoard that gem,—

'Tis worth thy vanished diadem!

XIV.

Then haste thee to thy sullen Isle,

    And gaze upon the sea:

That element may meet thy smile—

    It ne'er was ruled by thee!

Or trace with thine all idle hand

In loitering mood upon the sand

    That Earth is now as free!

That Corinth's pedagogue hath now

Transferred his by-word to thy brow.

XV.

Thou Timour! in his captive's cage[i]

    What thoughts will there be thine,

While brooding in thy prisoned rage?

    But one—"The world *was* mine!"

Unless, like he of Babylon,

All sense is with thy sceptre gone,

    Life will not long confine

That spirit poured so widely forth—

So long obeyed—so little worth!

i. The cage of Bajazet, by order of Tamerlane.

XVI.

Or, like the thief of fire from heaven,[i]

    Wilt thou withstand the shock?

And share with him, the unforgiven,

    His vulture and his rock!

Foredoomed by God—by man accurst,

And that last act, though not thy worst,

    The very Fiend's arch mock;[ii]

He in his fall preserved his pride,

And, if a mortal, had as proudly died!

i. Prometheus.

ii.   "O! 'tis the spite of hell, the fiend's arch-mock,
        To lip a wanton in a secure couch,
        And to suppose her chaste!"
          Othello, act iv. sc. 1, lines 69–71.

XVII.

There was a day—there was an hour,

    While earth was Gaul's—Gaul thine—

When that immeasurable power

    Unsated to resign

Had been an act of purer fame

Than gathers round Marengo's name

    And gilded thy decline,

Through the long twilight of all time,

Despite some passing clouds of crime.

XVIII.

But thou forsooth must be a King
    And don the purple vest,
As if that foolish robe could wring
    Remembrance from thy breast.
Where is that faded garment? where
The gewgaws thou wert fond to wear,
    The star, the string, the crest?
Vain froward child of Empire! say,
Are all thy playthings snatched away?

XIX.

Where may the wearied eye repose
    When gazing on the Great;
Where neither guilty glory glows,
    Nor despicable state?
Yes—One—the first—the last—the best—
The Cincinnatus of the West,
    Whom Envy dared not hate,
Bequeathed the name of Washington,
To make man blush there was but one!

LARA: A TALE

CANTO THE FIRST

I.

The Serfs[i] are glad through Lara's wide domain,

And Slavery half forgets her feudal chain;

He, their unhoped, but unforgotten lord,

The long self-exiled Chieftain, is restored:

There be bright faces in the busy hall,

Bowls on the board, and banners on the wall;

Far checkering o'er the pictured window, plays

The unwonted faggot's hospitable blaze;

And gay retainers gather round the hearth,

With tongues all loudness, and with eyes all mirth.

i. The reader is apprised, that the name of Lara being Spanish, and no circumstance of local and natural description fixing the scene or hero of the poem to any country or age, the word "Serf," which could not be correctly applied to the lower classes in Spain, who were never vassals of the soil, has nevertheless been employed to designate the followers of our fictitious chieftain.

II.

The Chief of Lara is returned again:

And why had Lara crossed the bounding main?

Left by his Sire, too young such loss to know,

Lord of himself, —that heritage of woe,

That fearful empire which the human breast

But holds to rob the heart within of rest!—

With none to check, and few to point in time

The thousand paths that slope the way to crime;

Then, when he most required commandment, then

Had Lara's daring boyhood governed men.

It skills not, boots not step by step to trace
His youth through all the mazes of its race;
Short was the course his restlessness had run,
But long enough to leave him half undone.

III.

And Lara left in youth his father-land;
But from the hour he waved his parting hand
Each trace waxed fainter of his course, till all
Had nearly ceased his memory to recall.
His sire was dust, his vassals could declare,
'Twas all they knew, that Lara was not there;
Nor sent, nor came he, till conjecture grew
Cold in the many, anxious in the few.
His hall scarce echoes with his wonted name,
His portrait darkens in its fading frame,
Another chief consoled his destined bride,
The young forgot him, and the old had died;
"Yet doth he live!" exclaims the impatient heir,
And sighs for sables which he must not wear.
A hundred scutcheons deck with gloomy grace
The Laras' last and longest dwelling-place;
But one is absent from the mouldering file,
That now were welcome in that Gothic pile.

IV.

He comes at last in sudden loneliness,
And whence they know not, why they need not guess;
They more might marvel, when the greeting's o'er
Not that he came, but came not long before:
No train is his beyond a single page,

Of foreign aspect, and of tender age.

Years had rolled on, and fast they speed away

To those that wander as to those that stay;

But lack of tidings from another clime

Had lent a flagging wing to weary Time.

They see, they recognise, yet almost deem

The present dubious, or the past a dream.

He lives, nor yet is past his Manhood's prime,

Though seared by toil, and something touched by Time;

His faults, whate'er they were, if scarce forgot,

Might be untaught him by his varied lot;

Nor good nor ill of late were known, his name

Might yet uphold his patrimonial fame:

His soul in youth was haughty, but his sins

No more than pleasure from the stripling wins;

And such, if not yet hardened in their course,

Might be redeemed, nor ask a long remorse.

V.

And they indeed were changed—'tis quickly seen,

Whate'er he be, 'twas not what he had been:

That brow in furrowed lines had fixed at last,

And spake of passions, but of passion past:

The pride, but not the fire, of early days,

Coldness of mien, and carelessness of praise;

A high demeanour, and a glance that took

Their thoughts from others by a single look;

And that sarcastic levity of tongue,

The stinging of a heart the world hath stung,

That darts in seeming playfulness around,
And makes those feel that will not own the wound;
All these seemed his, and something more beneath
Than glance could well reveal, or accent breathe.
Ambition, Glory, Love, the common aim,
That some can conquer, and that all would claim,
Within his breast appeared no more to strive,
Yet seemed as lately they had been alive;
And some deep feeling it were vain to trace
At moments lightened o'er his livid face.

VI.

Not much he loved long question of the past,
Nor told of wondrous wilds, and deserts vast,
In those far lands where he had wandered lone,
And—as himself would have it seem—unknown:
Yet these in vain his eye could scarcely scan,
Nor glean experience from his fellow man;
But what he had beheld he shunned to show,
As hardly worth a stranger's care to know;
If still more prying such inquiry grew,
His brow fell darker, and his words more few.

VII.

Not unrejoiced to see him once again,
Warm was his welcome to the haunts of men;
Born of high lineage, linked in high command,
He mingled with the Magnates of his land;
Joined the carousals of the great and gay,
And saw them smile or sigh their hours away;
But still he only saw, and did not share,

The common pleasure or the general care;
He did not follow what they all pursued
With hope still baffled still to be renewed;
Nor shadowy Honour, nor substantial Gain,
Nor Beauty's preference, and the rival's pain:
Around him some mysterious circle thrown
Repelled approach, and showed him still alone;
Upon his eye sat something of reproof,
That kept at least Frivolity aloof;
And things more timid that beheld him near
In silence gazed, or whispered mutual fear;
And they the wiser, friendlier few confessed
They deemed him better than his air expressed.

VIII.

'Twas strange—in youth all action and all life,
Burning for pleasure, not averse from strife;
Woman—the Field—the Ocean, all that gave
Promise of gladness, peril of a grave,
In turn he tried—he ransacked all below,
And found his recompense in joy or woe,
No tame, trite medium; for his feelings sought
In that intenseness an escape from thought:
The Tempest of his Heart in scorn had gazed
On that the feebler Elements hath raised;
The Rapture of his Heart had looked on high,
And asked if greater dwelt beyond the sky:
Chained to excess, the slave of each extreme,
How woke he from the wildness of that dream!

Alas! he told not—but he did awake

To curse the withered heart that would not break.

IX.

Books, for his volume heretofore was Man,

With eye more curious he appeared to scan,

And oft in sudden mood, for many a day,

From all communion he would start away:

And then, his rarely called attendants said,

Through night's long hours would sound his hurried tread

O'er the dark gallery, where his fathers frowned

In rude but antique portraiture around:

They heard, but whispered—"*that* must not be known—

The sound of words less earthly than his own.

Yes, they who chose might smile, but some had seen

They scarce knew what, but more than should have been.

Why gazed he so upon the ghastly head

Which hands profane had gathered from the dead,

That still beside his opened volume lay,

As if to startle all save him away?

Why slept he not when others were at rest?

Why heard no music, and received no guest?

All was not well, they deemed—but where the wrong?

Some knew perchance—but 'twere a tale too long;

And such besides were too discreetly wise,

To more than hint their knowledge in surmise;

But if they would—they could"—around the board

Thus Lara's vassals prattled of their lord.

X.

It was the night—and Lara's glassy stream
The stars are studding, each with imaged beam;
So calm, the waters scarcely seem to stray,
And yet they glide like Happiness away;
Reflecting far and fairy-like from high
The immortal lights that live along the sky:
Its banks are fringed with many a goodly tree,
And flowers the fairest that may feast the bee;
Such in her chaplet infant Dian wove,
And Innocence would offer to her love.
These deck the shore; the waves their channel make
In windings bright and mazy like the snake.
All was so still, so soft in earth and air,
You scarce would start to meet a spirit there;
Secure that nought of evil could delight
To walk in such a scene, on such a night!
It was a moment only for the good:
So Lara deemed, nor longer there he stood,
But turned in silence to his castle-gate;
Such scene his soul no more could contemplate:
Such scene reminded him of other days,
Of skies more cloudless, moons of purer blaze,
Of nights more soft and frequent, hearts that now—
No—no—the storm may beat upon his brow,
Unfelt, unsparing—but a night like this,
A night of Beauty, mocked such breast as his.

XI.

He turned within his solitary hall,
And his high shadow shot along the wall:
There were the painted forms of other times,
'Twas all they left of virtues or of crimes,
Save vague tradition; and the gloomy vaults
That hid their dust, their foibles, and their faults;
And half a column of the pompous page,
That speeds the specious tale from age to age;
Where History's pen its praise or blame supplies,
And lies like Truth, and still most truly lies.
He wandering mused, and as the moonbeam shone
Through the dim lattice, o'er the floor of stone,
And the high fretted roof, and saints, that there
O'er Gothic windows knelt in pictured prayer,
Reflected in fantastic figures grew,
Like life, but not like mortal life, to view;
His bristling locks of sable, brow of gloom,
And the wide waving of his shaken plume,
Glanced like a spectre's attributes—and gave
His aspect all that terror gives the grave.

XII.

'Twas midnight—all was slumber; the lone light
Dimmed in the lamp, as loth to break the night.
Hark! there be murmurs heard in Lara's hall—
A sound—a voice—a shriek—a fearful call!
A long, loud shriek—and silence—did they hear
That frantic echo burst the sleeping ear?
They heard and rose, and, tremulously brave,

Rush where the sound invoked their aid to save;

They come with half-lit tapers in their hands,

And snatched in startled haste unbelted brands.

XIII.

Cold as the marble where his length was laid,

Pale as the beam that o'er his features played,

Was Lara stretched; his half-drawn sabre near,

Dropped it should seem in more than Nature's fear;

Yet he was firm, or had been firm till now,

And still Defiance knit his gathered brow;

Though mixed with terror, senseless as he lay,

There lived upon his lip the wish to slay;

Some half formed threat in utterance there had died,

Some imprecation of despairing Pride;

His eye was almost sealed, but not forsook,

Even in its trance, the gladiator's look,

That oft awake his aspect could disclose,

And now was fixed in horrible repose.

They raise him—bear him;—hush! he breathes, he speaks,

The swarthy blush recolours in his cheeks,

His lip resumes its red, his eye, though dim,

Rolls wide and wild, each slowly quivering limb

Recalls its function, but his words are strung

In terms that seem not of his native tongue;

Distinct but strange, enough they understand

To deem them accents of another land;

And such they were, and meant to meet an ear

That hears him not—alas! that cannot hear!

XIV.

His page approached, and he alone appeared
To know the import of the words they heard;
And, by the changes of his cheek and brow,
They were not such as Lara should avow,
Nor he interpret,—yet with less surprise
Than those around their Chieftain's state he eyes,
But Lara's prostrate form he bent beside,
And in that tongue which seemed his own replied;
And Lara heeds those tones that gently seem
To soothe away the horrors of his dream—
If dream it were, that thus could overthrow
A breast that needed not ideal woe.

XV.

Whate'er his frenzy dreamed or eye beheld,—
If yet remembered ne'er to be revealed,—
Rests at his heart: the customed morning came,
And breathed new vigour in his shaken frame;
And solace sought he none from priest nor leech,
And soon the same in movement and in speech,
As heretofore he filled the passing hours,
Nor less he smiles, nor more his forehead lowers,
Than these were wont; and if the coming night
Appeared less welcome now to Lara's sight,
He to his marvelling vassals showed it not,
Whose shuddering proved *their* fear was less forgot.
In trembling pairs (alone they dared not) crawl
The astonished slaves, and shun the fated hall;
The waving banner, and the clapping door,

The rustling tapestry, and the echoing floor;
The long dim shadows of surrounding trees,
The flapping bat, the night song of the breeze;
Aught they behold or hear their thought appals,
As evening saddens o'er the dark grey walls.
Vain thought! that hour of ne'er unravelled gloom
Came not again, or Lara could assume .
A seeming of forgetfulness, that made
His vassals more amazed nor less afraid.
Had Memory vanished then with sense restored?
Since word, nor look, nor gesture of their lord
Betrayed a feeling that recalled to these
That fevered moment of his mind's disease.
Was it a dream? was his the voice that spoke
Those strange wild accents; his the cry that broke
Their slumber? his the oppressed, o'erlaboured heart
That ceased to beat, the look that made them start?
Could he who thus had suffered so forget,
When such as saw that suffering shudder yet?
Or did that silence prove his memory fixed
Too deep for words, indelible, unmixed
In that corroding secrecy which gnaws
The heart to show the effect, but not the cause?
Not so in him; his breast had buried both,
Nor common gazers could discern the growth
Of thoughts that mortal lips must leave half told;
They choke the feeble words that would unfold.

XVII.

In him inexplicably mixed appeared
Much to be loved and hated, sought and feared;
Opinion varying o'er his hidden lot,
In praise or railing ne'er his name forgot:
His silence formed a theme for others' prate—
They guessed—they gazed—they fain would know his fate.
What had he been? what was he, thus unknown,
Who walked their world, his lineage only known?
A hater of his kind? yet some would say,
With them he could seem gay amidst the gay;
But owned that smile, if oft observed and near,
Waned in its mirth, and withered to a sneer;
That smile might reach his lip, but passed not by,
Nor e'er could trace its laughter to his eye:
Yet there was softness too in his regard,
At times, a heart as not by nature hard,
But once perceived, his Spirit seemed to chide
Such weakness, as unworthy of its pride,
And steeled itself, as scorning to redeem
One doubt from others' half withheld esteem;
In self-inflicted penance of a breast
Which Tenderness might once have wrung from Rest;
In vigilance of Grief that would compel
The soul to hate for having loved too well.

XVIII.

There was in him a vital scorn of all:
As if the worst had fallen which could befall,
He stood a stranger in this breathing world,

An erring Spirit from another hurled;
A thing of dark imaginings, that shaped
By choice the perils he by chance escaped;
But 'scaped in vain, for in their memory yet
His mind would half exult and half regret:
With more capacity for love than Earth
Bestows on most of mortal mould and birth.
His early dreams of good outstripped the truth,
And troubled Manhood followed baffled Youth;
With thought of years in phantom chase misspent,
And wasted powers for better purpose lent;
And fiery passions that had poured their wrath
In hurried desolation o'er his path,
And left the better feelings all at strife
In wild reflection o'er his stormy life;
But haughty still, and loth himself to blame,
He called on Nature's self to share the shame,
And charged all faults upon the fleshly form
She gave to clog the soul, and feast the worm;
Till he at last confounded good and ill,
And half mistook for fate the acts of will:
Too high for common selfishness, he could
At times resign his own for others' good,
But not in pity—not because he ought,
But in some strange perversity of thought,
That swayed him onward with a secret pride
To do what few or none would do beside;
And this same impulse would, in tempting time,
Mislead his spirit equally to crime;

So much he soared beyond, or sunk beneath,
The men with whom he felt condemned to breathe,
And longed by good or ill to separate
Himself from all who shared his mortal state;
His mind abhorring this had fixed her throne
Far from the world, in regions of her own:
Thus coldly passing all that passed below,
His blood in temperate seeming now would flow:
Ah! happier if it ne'er with guilt had glowed,
But ever in that icy smoothness flowed!
'Tis true, with other men their path he walked,
And like the rest in seeming did and talked,
Nor outraged Reason's rules by flaw nor start,
His Madness was not of the head, but heart;
And rarely wandered in his speech, or drew
His thoughts so forth as to offend the view.

XIX.

With all that chilling mystery of mien,
And seeming gladness to remain unseen,
He had (if 'twere not nature's boon) an art
Of fixing memory on another's heart:
It was not love perchance—nor hate—nor aught
That words can image to express the thought;
But they who saw him did not see in vain,
And once beheld—would ask of him again:
And those to whom he spake remembered well,
And on the words, however light, would dwell:
None knew, nor how, nor why, but he entwined
Himself perforce around the hearer's mind;

There he was stamped, in liking, or in hate,
If greeted once; however brief the date
That friendship, pity, or aversion knew,
Still there within the inmost thought he grew.
You could not penetrate his soul, but found,
Despite your wonder, to your own he wound;
His presence haunted still; and from the breast
He forced an all unwilling interest:
Vain was the struggle in that mental net—
His Spirit seemed to dare you to forget!

XX.

There is a festival, where knights and dames,
And aught that wealth or lofty lineage claims,
Appear—a high-born and a welcome guest
To Otho's hall came Lara with the rest.
The long carousal shakes the illumined hall,
Well speeds alike the banquet and the ball;
And the gay dance of bounding Beauty's train
Links grace and harmony in happiest chain:
Blest are the early hearts and gentle hands
That mingle there in well according bands;
It is a sight the careful brow might smooth,
And make Age smile, and dream itself to youth,
And Youth forget such hour was past on earth,
So springs the exulting bosom to that mirth!

XXI.

And Lara gazed on these, sedately glad,
His brow belied him if his soul was sad;
And his glance followed fast each fluttering fair,

Whose steps of lightness woke no echo there:
He leaned against the lofty pillar nigh,
With folded arms and long attentive eye,
Nor marked a glance so sternly fixed on his—
Ill brooked high Lara scrutiny like this:
At length he caught it—'tis a face unknown,
But seems as searching his, and his alone;
Prying and dark, a stranger's by his mien,
Who still till now had gazed on him unseen:
At length encountering meets the mutual gaze
Of keen enquiry, and of mute amaze;
On Lara's glance emotion gathering grew,
As if distrusting that the stranger threw;
Along the stranger's aspect, fixed and stern,
Flashed more than thence the vulgar eye could learn.

XXII.

"'Tis he!" the stranger cried, and those that heard
Re-echoed fast and far the whispered word.
"'Tis he!"—"'Tis who?" they question far and near,
Till louder accents rung on Lara's ear;
So widely spread, few bosoms well could brook
The general marvel, or that single look:
But Lara stirred not, changed not, the surprise
That sprung at first to his arrested eyes
Seemed now subsided—neither sunk nor raised
Glanced his eye round, though still the stranger gazed;
And drawing nigh, exclaimed, with haughty sneer,
"'Tis he!—how came he thence?—what doth he here?"

XXIII.

It were too much for Lara to pass by
Such questions, so repeated fierce and high;
With look collected, but with accent cold,
More mildly firm than petulantly bold,
He turned, and met the inquisitorial tone—
"My name is Lara—when thine own is known,
"Doubt not my fitting answer to requite
"The unlooked for courtesy of such a knight.
"'Tis Lara!—further wouldst thou mark or ask?
"I shun no question, and I wear no mask."

"Thou *shunn'st* no question! Ponder—is there none
"Thy heart must answer, though thine ear would shun?
"And deem'st thou me unknown too? Gaze again!
"At least thy memory was not given in vain.
"Oh! never canst thou cancel half her debt—
"Eternity forbids thee to forget."
With slow and searching glance upon his face
Grew Lara's eyes, but nothing there could trace
They knew, or chose to know—with dubious look
He deigned no answer, but his head he shook,
And half contemptuous turned to pass away;
But the stern stranger motioned him to stay.

"A word!—I charge thee stay, and answer here
"To one, who, wert thou noble, were thy peer,
"But as thou wast and art—nay, frown not, Lord,
"If false, 'tis easy to disprove the word—

"But as thou wast and art, on thee looks down,
"Distrusts thy smiles, but shakes not at thy frown.
"Art thou not he? whose deeds—"

                                    "Whate'er I be,
"Words wild as these, accusers like to thee,
"I list no further; those with whom they weigh
"May hear the rest, nor venture to gainsay
"The wondrous tale no doubt thy tongue can tell,
"Which thus begins so courteously and well.
"Let Otho cherish here his polished guest,
"To him my thanks and thoughts shall be expressed.
And here their wondering host hath interposed—
"Whate'er there be between you undisclosed,
"This is no time nor fitting place to mar
"The mirthful meeting with a wordy war.
"If thou, Sir Ezzelin, hast aught to show
"Which it befits Count Lara's ear to know,
"To-morrow, here, or elsewhere, as may best
"Beseem your mutual judgment, speak the rest;
"I pledge myself for thee, as not unknown,
"Though, like Count Lara, now returned alone
"From other lands, almost a stranger grown;
"And if from Lara's blood and gentle birth
"I augur right of courage and of worth,
"He will not that untainted line belie,
"Nor aught that Knighthood may accord, deny."

"To-morrow be it," Ezzelin replied, "
And here our several worth and truth be tried;

"I gage my life, my falchion to attest

"My words, so may I mingle with the blest!"

What answers Lara? to its centre shrunk

His soul, in deep abstraction sudden sunk;

The words of many, and the eyes of all

That there were gathered, seemed on him to fall;

But his were silent, his appeared to stray

In far forgetfulness away—away—

Alas! that heedlessness of all around

Bespoke remembrance only too profound.

XXIV.

"To-morrow!—aye, to-morrow!" further word

Than those repeated none from Lara heard;

Upon his brow no outward passion spoke;

From his large eye no flashing anger broke:

Yet there was something fixed in that low tone,

Which showed resolve, determined, though unknown.

He seized his cloak—his head he slightly bowed,

And passing Ezzelin, he left the crowd;

And, as he passed him, smiling met the frown

With which that Chieftain's brow would bear him down:

It was nor smile of mirth, nor struggling pride

That curbs to scorn the wrath it cannot hide;

But that of one in his own heart secure

Of all that he would do, or could endure.

Could this mean peace? the calmness of the good?

Or guilt grown old in desperate hardihood?

Alas! too like in confidence are each,

For man to trust to mortal look or speech;

From deeds, and deeds alone, may he discern
Truths which it wrings the unpractised heart to learn.

XXV.

And Lara called his page, and went his way—
Well could that stripling word or sign obey:
His only follower from those climes afar,
Where the Soul glows beneath a brighter star;
For Lara left the shore from whence he sprung,
In duty patient, and sedate though young;
Silent as him he served, his faith appears
Above his station, and beyond his years.
Though not unknown the tongue of Lara's land,
In such from him he rarely heard command;
But fleet his step, and clear his tones would come,
When Lara's lip breathed forth the words of home:
Those accents, as his native mountains dear,
Awake their absent echoes in his ear,
Friends'—kindred's—parents'—wonted voice recall,
Now lost, abjured, for one—his friend, his all:
For him earth now disclosed no other guide;
What marvel then he rarely left his side?

XXVI.

Light was his form, and darkly delicate
That brow whereon his native sun had sate,
But had not marred, though in his beams he grew,
The cheek where oft the unbidden blush shone through;
Yet not such blush as mounts when health would show
All the heart's hue in that delighted glow;
But 'twas a hectic tint of secret care

That for a burning moment fevered there;
And the wild sparkle of his eye seemed caught
From high, and lightened with electric thought,
Though its black orb those long low lashes' fringe
Had tempered with a melancholy tinge;
Yet less of sorrow than of pride was there,
Or, if 'twere grief, a grief that none should share:
And pleased not him the sports that please his age,
The tricks of Youth, the frolics of the Page;
For hours on Lara he would fix his glance,
As all-forgotten in that watchful trance;
And from his chief withdrawn, he wandered lone,
Brief were his answers, and his questions none;
His walk the wood, his sport some foreign book;
His resting-place the bank that curbs the brook:
He seemed, like him he served, to live apart
From all that lures the eye, and fills the heart;
To know no brotherhood, and take from earth
No gift beyond that bitter boon—our birth.

XXVII.

If aught he loved, 'twas Lara; but was shown
His faith in reverence and in deeds alone;
In mute attention; and his care, which guessed
Each wish, fulfilled it ere the tongue expressed.
Still there was haughtiness in all he did,
A spirit deep that brooked not to be chid;
His zeal, though more than that of servile hands,
In act alone obeys, his air commands;
As if 'twas Lara's less than *his* desire

That thus he served, but surely not for hire.
Slight were the tasks enjoined him by his Lord,
To hold the stirrup, or to bear the sword;
To tune his lute, or, if he willed it more,
On tomes of other times and tongues to pore;
But ne'er to mingle with the menial train,
To whom he showed nor deference nor disdain,
But that well-worn reserve which proved he knew
No sympathy with that familiar crew:
His soul, whate'er his station or his stem,
Could bow to Lara, not descend to them.
Of higher birth he seemed, and better days,
Nor mark of vulgar toil that hand betrays,
So femininely white it might bespeak
Another sex, when matched with that smooth cheek,
But for his garb, and something in his gaze,
More wild and high than Woman's eye betrays;
A latent fierceness that far more became
His fiery climate than his tender frame:
True, in his words it broke not from his breast,
But from his aspect might be more than guessed.
Kaled his name, though rumour said he bore
Another ere he left his mountain-shore;
For sometimes he would hear, however nigh,
That name repeated loud without reply,
As unfamiliar—or, if roused again,
Start to the sound, as but remembered then;
Unless 'twas Lara's wonted voice that spake,
For then—ear—eyes—and heart would all awake.

XXVIII.

He had looked down upon the festive hall,
And mark'd that sudden strife so marked of all:
And when the crowd around and near him told
Their wonder at the calmness of the bold,
Their marvel how the high-born Lara bore
Such insult from a stranger, doubly sore,
The colour of young Kaled went and came,
The lip of ashes, and the cheek of flame;
And o'er his brow the dampening heart-drops threw
The sickening iciness of that cold dew,
That rises as the busy bosom sinks
With heavy thoughts from which Reflection shrinks.
Yes—there be things which we must dream and dare,
And execute ere thought be half aware:
Whate'er might Kaled's be, it was enow
To seal his lip, but agonise his brow.
He gazed on Ezzelin till Lara cast
That sidelong smile upon the knight he past;
When Kaled saw that smile his visage fell,
As if on something recognised right well:
His memory read in such a meaning more
Than Lara's aspect unto others wore:
Forward he sprung—a moment, both were gone,
And all within that hall seemed left alone;
Each had so fixed his eye on Lara's mien,
All had so mixed their feelings with that scene,
That when his long dark shadow through the porch
No more relieves the glare of yon high torch,

Each pulse beats quicker, and all bosoms seem

To bound as doubting from too black a dream,

Such as we know is false, yet dread in sooth,

Because the worst is ever nearest truth.

And they are gone—but Ezzelin is there,

With thoughtful visage and imperious air;

But long remained not; ere an hour expired

He waved his hand to Otho, and retired.

XXIX.

The crowd are gone, the revellers at rest;

The courteous host, and all-approving guest,

Again to that accustomed couch must creep

Where Joy subsides, and Sorrow sighs to sleep,

And Man, o'erlaboured with his Being's strife,

Shrinks to that sweet forgetfulness of life:

There lie Love's feverish hope, and Cunning's guile,

Hate's working brain, and lulled Ambition's wile;

O'er each vain eye Oblivion's pinions wave,

And quenched Existence crouches in a grave.

What better name may Slumber's bed become?

Night's sepulchre, the universal home,

Where Weakness—Strength—Vice—Virtue—sunk supine,

Alike in naked helplessness recline;

Glad for a while to heave unconscious breath,

Yet wake to wrestle with the dread of Death,

And shun—though Day but dawn on ills increased—

That sleep,—the loveliest, since it dreams the least.

CANTO THE SECOND

I.

Night wanes—the vapours round the mountains curled
Melt into morn, and Light awakes the world,
Man has another day to swell the past,
And lead him near to little, but his last;
But mighty Nature bounds as from her birth,
The Sun is in the heavens, and Life on earth;
Flowers in the valley, splendour in the beam,
Health on the gale, and freshness in the stream.
Immortal Man! behold her glories shine,
And cry, exulting inly, "They are thine!"
Gaze on, while yet thy gladdened eye may see:
A morrow comes when they are not for thee:
And grieve what may above thy senseless bier,
Nor earth nor sky will yield a single tear;
Nor cloud shall gather more, nor leaf shall fall,
Nor gale breathe forth one sigh for thee, for all;
But creeping things shall revel in their spoil,
And fit thy clay to fertilise the soil.

II.

'Tis morn—'tis noon—assembled in the hall,
The gathered Chieftains come to Otho's call;
'Tis now the promised hour, that must proclaim
The life or death of Lara's future fame;
And Ezzelin his charge may here unfold,
And whatsoe'er the tale, it must be told.

His faith was pledged, and Lara's promise given,

To meet it in the eye of Man and Heaven.

Why comes he not? Such truths to be divulged,

Methinks the accuser's rest is long indulged.

III.

The hour is past, and Lara too is there,

With self-confiding, coldly patient air;

Why comes not Ezzelin? The hour is past,

And murmurs rise, and Otho's brow's o'ercast.

"I know my friend! his faith I cannot fear,

"If yet he be on earth, expect him here;

"The roof that held him in the valley stands

"Between my own and noble Lara's lands;

"My halls from such a guest had honour gained,

"Nor had Sir Ezzelin his host disdained,

"But that some previous proof forbade his stay,

"And urged him to prepare against to-day;

"The word I pledged for his I pledge again,

"Or will myself redeem his knighthood's stain."

He ceased—and Lara answered, "I am here

"To lend at thy demand a listening ear

"To tales of evil from a stranger's tongue,

"Whose words already might my heart have wrung,

"But that I deemed him scarcely less than mad,

"Or, at the worst, a foe ignobly bad.

"I know him not—but me it seems he knew

"In lands where—but I must not trifle too:

"Produce this babbler—or redeem the pledge;

"Here in thy hold, and with thy falchion's edge."

Proud Otho on the instant, reddening, threw
His glove on earth, and forth his sabre flew.
"The last alternative befits me best,
"And thus I answer for mine absent guest."

With cheek unchanging from its sallow gloom,
However near his own or other's tomb;
With hand, whose almost careless coolness spoke
Its grasp well-used to deal the sabre-stroke;
With eye, though calm, determined not to spare,
Did Lara too his willing weapon bare.
In vain the circling Chieftains round them closed,
For Otho's frenzy would not be opposed;
And from his lip those words of insult fell—
His sword is good who can maintain them well.

IV.

Short was the conflict; furious, blindly rash,
Vain Otho gave his bosom to the gash:
He bled, and fell; but not with deadly wound,
Stretched by a dextrous sleight along the ground.
"Demand thy life!" He answered not: and then
From that red floor he ne'er had risen again,
For Lara's brow upon the moment grew
Almost to blackness in its demon hue;
And fiercer shook his angry falchion now
Than when his foe's was levelled at his brow;
Then all was stern collectedness and art,
Now rose the unleavened hatred of his heart;
So little sparing to the foe he felled,

That when the approaching crowd his arm withheld,
He almost turned the thirsty point on those
Who thus for mercy dared to interpose;
But to a moment's thought that purpose bent;
Yet looked he on him still with eye intent,
As if he loathed the ineffectual strife
That left a foe, howe'er o'erthrown, with life;
As if to search how far the wound he gave
Had sent its victim onward to his grave.

V.

They raised the bleeding Otho, and the Leech
Forbade all present question, sign, and speech;
The others met within a neighbouring hall,
And he, incensed, and heedless of them all,
The cause and conqueror in this sudden fray,
In haughty silence slowly strode away;
He backed his steed, his homeward path he took,
Nor cast on Otho's towers a single look.

VI.

But where was he? that meteor of a night,
Who menaced but to disappear with light.
Where was this Ezzelin? who came and went,
To leave no other trace of his intent.
He left the dome of Otho long ere morn,
In darkness, yet so well the path was worn
He could not miss it: near his dwelling lay;
But there he was not, and with coming day
Came fast inquiry, which unfolded nought,
Except the absence of the Chief it sought.

A chamber tenantless, a steed at rest,

His host alarmed, his murmuring squires distressed:

Their search extends along, around the path,

In dread to meet the marks of prowlers' wrath:

But none are there, and not a brake hath borne

Nor gout of blood, nor shred of mantle torn;

Nor fall nor struggle hath defaced the grass,

Which still retains a mark where Murder was;

Nor dabbling fingers left to tell the tale,

The bitter print of each convulsive nail,

When agonisèd hands that cease to guard,

Wound in that pang the smoothness of the sward.

Some such had been, if here a life was reft,

But these were not; and doubting Hope is left;

And strange Suspicion, whispering Lara's name,

Now daily mutters o'er his blackened fame;

Then sudden silent when his form appeared,

Awaits the absence of the thing it feared

Again its wonted wondering to renew,

And dye conjecture with a darker hue.

VII.

Days roll along, and Otho's wounds are healed,

But not his pride; and hate no more concealed:

He was a man of power, and Lara's foe,

The friend of all who sought to work him woe,

And from his country's justice now demands

Account of Ezzelin at Lara's hands.

Who else than Lara could have cause to fear

His presence? who had made him disappear,

If not the man on whom his menaced charge
Had sate too deeply were he left at large?
The general rumour ignorantly loud,
The mystery dearest to the curious crowd;
The seeming friendliness of him who strove
To win no confidence, and wake no love;
The sweeping fierceness which his soul betrayed,
The skill with which he wielded his keen blade;
Where had his arm unwarlike caught that art?
Where had that fierceness grown upon his heart?
For it was not the blind capricious rage
A word can kindle and a word assuage;
But the deep working of a soul unmixed
With aught of pity where its wrath had fixed;
Such as long power and overgorged success
Concentrates into all that's merciless:
These, linked with that desire which ever sways
Mankind, the rather to condemn than praise,
'Gainst Lara gathering raised at length a storm,
Such as himself might fear, and foes would form,
And he must answer for the absent head
Of one that haunts him still, alive or dead.

VIII.

Within that land was many a malcontent,
Who cursed the tyranny to which he bent;
That soil full many a wringing despot saw,
Who worked his wantonness in form of law;
Long war without and frequent broil within
Had made a path for blood and giant sin,

That waited but a signal to begin
New havoc, such as civil discord blends,
Which knows no neuter, owns but foes or friends;
Fixed in his feudal fortress each was lord,
In word and deed obeyed, in soul abhorred.
Thus Lara had inherited his lands,
And with them pining hearts and sluggish hands;
But that long absence from his native clime
Had left him stainless of Oppression's crime,
And now, diverted by his milder sway,
All dread by slow degrees had worn away.
The menials felt their usual awe alone,
But more for him than them that fear was grown;
They deemed him now unhappy, though at first
Their evil judgment augured of the worst,
And each long restless night, and silent mood,
Was traced to sickness, fed by solitude:
And though his lonely habits threw of late
Gloom o'er his chamber, cheerful was his gate;
For thence the wretched ne'er unsoothed withdrew,
For them, at least, his soul compassion knew.
Cold to the great, contemptuous to the high,
The humble passed not his unheeding eye;
Much he would speak not, but beneath his roof
They found asylum oft, and ne'er reproof.
And they who watched might mark that, day by day,
Some new retainers gathered to his sway;
But most of late, since Ezzelin was lost,
He played the courteous lord and bounteous host:

Perchance his strife with Otho made him dread
Some snare prepared for his obnoxious head;
Whate'er his view, his favour more obtains
With these, the people, than his fellow thanes.
If this were policy, so far 'twas sound,
The million judged but of him as they found;
From him by sterner chiefs to exile driven
They but required a shelter, and 'twas given.
By him no peasant mourned his rifled cot,
And scarce the Serf could murmur o'er his lot;
With him old Avarice found its hoard secure,
With him contempt forbore to mock the poor;
Youth present cheer and promised recompense
Detained, till all too late to part from thence:
To Hate he offered, with the coming change,
The deep reversion of delayed revenge;
To Love, long baffled by the unequal match,
The well-won charms success was sure to snatch.'
All now was ripe, he waits but to proclaim
That slavery nothing which was still a name.
The moment came, the hour when Otho thought
Secure at last the vengeance which he sought:
His summons found the destined criminal
Begirt by thousands in his swarming hall;
Fresh from their feudal fetters newly riven,
Defying earth, and confident of heaven.
That morning he had freed the soil-bound slaves,
Who dig no land for tyrants but their graves!
Such is their cry—some watchword for the fight

Must vindicate the wrong, and warp the right;

Religion—Freedom—Vengeance—what you will,

A word's enough to raise Mankind to kill;

Some factious phrase by cunning caught and spread,

That Guilt may reign—and wolves and worms be fed!

IX.

Throughout that clime the feudal Chiefs had gained

Such sway, their infant monarch hardly reigned;

Now was the hour for Faction's rebel growth,

The Serfs contemned the one, and hated both .-

They waited but a leader, and they found

One to their cause inseparably bound;

By circumstance compelled to plunge again,

In self-defence, amidst the strife of men.

Cut off by some mysterious fate from those

Whom Birth and Nature meant not for his foes,

Had Lara from that night, to him accurst,

Prepared to meet, but not alone, the worst:

Some reason urged, whate'er it was, to shun

Inquiry into deeds at distance done;

By mingling with his own the cause of all,

E'en if he failed, he still delayed his fall.

The sullen calm that long his bosom kept,

The storm that once had spent itself and slept,

Roused by events that seemed foredoomed to urge

His gloomy fortunes to their utmost verge,

Burst forth, and made him all he once had been,

And is again; he only changed the scene.

Light care had he for life, and less for fame,

But not less fitted for the desperate game:
He deemed himself marked out for others' hate,
And mocked at Ruin so they shared his fate.
And cared he for the freedom of the crowd?
He raised the humble but to bend the proud.
He had hoped quiet in his sullen lair,
But Man and Destiny beset him there:
Inured to hunters, he was found at bay;
And they must kill, they cannot snare the prey.
Stern, unambitious, silent, he had been
Henceforth a calm spectator of Life's scene;
But dragged again upon the arena, stood
A leader not unequal to the feud;
In voice—mien—gesture—savage nature spoke,
And from his eye the gladiator broke.

X.

What boots the oft-repeated tale of strife,
The feast of vultures, and the waste of life?
The varying fortune of each separate field,
The fierce that vanquish, and the faint that yield?
The smoking ruin, and the crumbled wall?
In this the struggle was the same with all;
Save that distempered passions lent their force
In bitterness that banished all remorse.
None sued, for Mercy knew her cry was vain,
The captive died upon the battle-plain:
In either cause, one rage alone possessed
The empire of the alternate victor's breast;
And they that smote for freedom or for sway,

Deemed few were slain, while more remained to slay.

It was too late to check the wasting brand,

And Desolation reaped the famished land:

The torch was lighted, and the flame was spread,

And Carnage smiled upon her daily dead.

XI.

Fresh with the nerve the new-born impulse strung,

The first success to Lara's numbers clung:

But that vain victory hath ruined all;

They form no longer to their leader's call:

In blind confusion on the foe they press,

And think to snatch is to secure success.

The lust of booty, and the thirst of hate,

Lure on the broken brigands to their fate:

In vain he doth whate'er a chief may do,

To check the headlong fury of that crew:

In vain their stubborn ardour he would tame,

The hand that kindles cannot quench the flame;

The wary foe alone hath turned their mood,

And shown their rashness to that erring brood:

The feigned retreat, the nightly ambuscade,

The daily harass, and the fight delayed,

The long privation of the hoped supply,

The tentless rest beneath the humid sky,

The stubborn wall that mocks the leaguer's art,

And palls the patience of his baffled art,

Of these they had not deemed: the battle-day

They could encounter as a veteran may;

But more preferred the fury of the strife,'

And present death, to hourly suffering life:
And Famine wrings, and Fever sweeps away
His numbers melting fast from their array;
Intemperate triumph fades to discontent,
And Lara's soul alone seems still unbent;
But few remain to aid his voice and hand,
And thousands dwindled to a scanty band:
Desperate, though few, the last and best remained
To mourn the discipline they late disdained.
One hope survives, the frontier is not far,
And thence they may escape from native war:
And bear within them to the neighbouring state
An exile's sorrows, or an outlaw's hate:
Hard is the task their father-land to quit,
But harder still to perish or submit.

XII.

It is resolved—they march—consenting Night
Guides with her star their dim and torchless flight;
Already they perceive its tranquil beam
Sleep on the surface of the barrier stream:
Already they descry—Is yon the bank?
Away! 'tis lined with many a hostile rank.
Return or fly!—What glitters in the rear?
'Tis Otho's banner—the pursuer's spear!
Are those the shepherds' fires upon the height?
Alas! they blaze too widely for the flight:
Cut off from hope, and compassed in the toil,
Less blood perchance hath bought a richer spoil!

XIII.

A moment's pause—'tis but to breathe their band,

Or shall they onward press, or here withstand?

It matters little—if they charge the foes

Who by their border-stream their march oppose,

Some few, perchance, may break and pass the line,

However linked to baffle such design.

"The charge be ours! to wait for their assault

Were fate well worthy of a coward's halt."

Forth flies each sabre, reined is every steed,

And the next word shall scarce outstrip the deed:

In the next tone of Lara's gathering breath

How many shall but hear the voice of Death!

XIV.

His blade is bared,—in him there is an air

As deep, but far too tranquil for despair;

A something of indifference more than then

Becomes the bravest, if they feel for men—

He turned his eye on Kaled, ever near,

And still too faithful to betray one fear;

Perchance 'twas but the moon's dim twilight threw

Along his aspect an unwonted hue

Of mournful paleness, whose deep tint expressed

The truth, and not the terror of his breast.

This Lara marked, and laid his hand on his:

It trembled not in such an hour as this;

His lip was silent, scarcely beat his heart,

His eye alone proclaimed, "We will not part!

"Thy band may perish, or thy friends may flee,

"Farewell to Life—but not Adieu to thee!"

The word hath passed his lips, and onward driven,

Pours the linked band through ranks asunder riven:

Well has each steed obeyed the arme'd heel,

And flash the scimitars, and rings the steel;

Outnumbered, not outbraved, they still oppose

Despair to daring, and a front to foes;

And blood is mingled with the dashing stream,

Which runs all redly till the morning beam.

XV.

Commanding—aiding—animating all,

Where foe appeared to press, or friend to fall,

Cheers Lara's voice, and waves or strikes his steel,

Inspiring hope, himself had ceased to feel.

None fled, for well they knew that flight were vain;

But those that waver turn to smite again,

While yet they find the firmest of the foe

Recoil before their leader's look and blow:

Now girt with numbers, now almost alone,

He foils their ranks, or re-unites his own;

Himself he spared not—once they seemed to fly—

Now was the time, he waved his hand on high,

And shook—Why sudden droops that plumèd crest?

The shaft is sped—the arrow's in his breast!

That fatal gesture left the unguarded side,

And Death has stricken down yon arm of pride.

The word of triumph fainted from his tongue;

That hand, so raised, how droopingly it hung!

But yet the sword instinctively retains,

Though from its fellow shrink the falling reins;
These Kaled snatches: dizzy with the blow,
And senseless bending o'er his saddle-bow,
Perceives not Lara that his anxious page
Beguiles his charger from the combat's rage:
Meantime his followers charge, and charge again;
Too mixed the slayers now to heed the slain!

XVI.

Day glimmers on the dying and the dead,
The cloven cuirass, and the helmless head;
The war-horse masterless is on the earth,
And that last gasp hath burst his bloody girth;
And near, yet quivering with what life remained,
The heel that urged him and the hand that reined;
And some too near that rolling torrent lie,
Whose waters mock the lip of those that die;
That panting thirst which scorches in the breath
Of those that die the soldier's fiery death,
In vain impels the burning mouth to crave
One drop—the last—to cool it for the grave;
With feeble and convulsive effort swept,
Their limbs along the crimsoned turf have crept;
The faint remains of life such struggles waste,
But yet they reach the stream, and bend to taste:
They feel its freshness, and almost partake—
Why pause? No further thirst have they to slake—
It is unquenched, and yet they feel it not;
It was an agony—but now forgot!

XVII.

Beneath a lime, remoter from the scene,

Where but for him that strife had never been,

A breathing but devoted warrior lay:

'Twas Lara bleeding fast from life away.

His follower once, and now his only guide,

Kneels Kaled watchful o'er his welling side,

And with his scarf would staunch the tides that rush,

With each convulsion, in a blacker gush;

And then, as his faint breathing waxes low,

In feebler, not less fatal tricklings flow:

He scarce can speak, but motions him 'tis vain,

And merely adds another throb to pain.

He clasps the hand that pang which would assuage,

And sadly smiles his thanks to that dark page,

Who nothing fears—nor feels—nor heeds—nor sees—

Save that damp brow which rests upon his knees;

Save that pale aspect, where the eye, though dim,

Held all the light that shone on earth for him.

XVIII.

The foe arrives, who long had searched the field,

Their triumph nought till Lara too should yield:

They would remove him, but they see 'twere vain,

And he regards them with a calm disdain,

That rose to reconcile him with his fate,

And that escape to death from living hate:

And Otho comes, and leaping from his steed,

Looks on the bleeding foe that made him bleed,

And questions of his state; he answers not,

Scarce glances on him as on one forgot,

And turns to Kaled:—each remaining word

They understood not, if distinctly heard;

His dying tones are in that other tongue,

To which some strange remembrance wildly clung.

They spake of other scenes, but what—is known

To Kaled, whom their meaning reached alone;

And he replied, though faintly, to their sound,

While gazed the rest in dumb amazement round:

They seemed even then—that twain—unto the last

To half forget the present in the past;

To share between themselves some separate fate,

Whose darkness none beside should penetrate.

XIX.

Their words though faint were many—from the tone

Their import those who heard could judge alone;

From this, you might have deemed young Kaled's death

More near than Lara's by his voice and breath,

So sad—so deep—and hesitating broke

The accents his scarce-moving pale lips spoke;

But Lara's voice, though low, at first was clear

And calm, till murmuring Death gasped hoarsely near;

But from his visage little could we guess,

So unrepentant—dark—and passionless,

Save that when struggling nearer to his last,

Upon that page his eye was kindly cast; ino

And once, as Kaled's answering accents ceased,

Rose Lara's hand, and pointed to the East:

Whether (as then the breaking Sun from high

Rolled back the clouds) the morrow caught his eye,
Or that 'twas chance—or some remembered scene,
That raised his arm to point where such had been,
Scarce Kaled seemed to know, but turned away,
As if his heart abhorred that coming day,
And shrunk his glance before that morning light,
To look on Lara's brow—where all grew night.
Yet sense seemed left, though better were its loss;
For when one near displayed the absolving Cross,
And proffered to his touch the holy bead,
Of which his parting soul might own the need,
He looked upon it with an eye profane,
And smiled—Heaven pardon! if 'twere with disdain:
And Kaled, though he spoke not, nor withdrew
From Lara's face his fixed despairing view,
With brow repulsive, and with gesture swift,
Flung back the hand which held the sacred gift,
As if such but disturbed the expiring man,
Nor seemed to know his life but *then* began—
That Life of Immortality, secure
To none, save them whose faith in Christ is sure.

XX.

But gasping heaved the breath that Lara drew,
And dull the film along his dim eye grew;
His limbs stretched fluttering, and his head drooped o'er
The weak yet still untiring knee that bore;
He pressed the hand he held upon his heart—
It beats no more, but Kaled will not part
With the cold grasp, but feels, and feels in vain,

For that faint throb which answers not again.

"It beats!"—Away, thou dreamer! he is gone—

It once *was* Lara which thou look'st upon.

XXI.

He gazed, as if not yet had passed away

The haughty spirit of that humbled clay;

And those around have roused him from his trance,

But cannot tear from thence his fixèd glance;

And when, in raising him from where he bore

Within his arms the form that felt no more,

He saw the head his breast would still sustain,

Roll down like earth to earth upon the plain;

He did not dash himself thereby, nor tear

The glossy tendrils of his raven hair,

But strove to stand and gaze, but reeled and fell,

Scarce breathing more than that he loved so well.

Than that *he* loved! Oh! never yet beneath

The breast of *man* such trusty love may breathe!

That trying moment hath at once revealed

The secret long and yet but half concealed;

In baring to revive that lifeless breast,

Its grief seemed ended, but the sex confessed;

And life returned, and Kaled felt no shame—

What now to her was Womanhood or Fame?

XXII.

And Lara sleeps not where his fathers sleep,

But where he died his grave was dug as deep;

Nor is his mortal slumber less profound,

Though priest nor blessed nor marble decked the mound,

And he was mourned by one whose quiet grief,
Less loud, outlasts a people's for their Chief.
Vain was all question asked her of the past,
And vain e'en menace—silent to the last;
She told nor whence, nor why she left behind
Her all for one who seemed but little kind.
Why did she love him? Curious fool!—be still—
Is human love the growth of human will?
To her he might be gentleness; the stern
Have deeper thoughts than your dull eyes discern,
And when they love, your smilers guess not how
Beats the strong heart, though less the lips avow.
They were not common links, that formed the chain
That bound to Lara Kaled's heart and brain;
But that wild tale she brooked not to unfold,
And sealed is now each lip that could have told.

XXIII.

They laid him in the earth, and on his breast,
Besides the wound that sent his soul to rest,
They found the scattered dints of many a scar,
Which were not planted there in recent war;
Where'er had passed his summer years of life,
It seems they vanished in a land of strife;
But all unknown his Glory or his Guilt,
These only told that somewhere blood was spilt,
And Ezzelin, who might have spoke the past,
Returned no more—that night appeared his last.

XXIV.

The event in this section was suggested by the description of the death or rather burial of the Duke of Gandia. "The most interesting and particular account of it is given by Burchard, and is in substance as follows:—'On the eighth day of June, the Cardinal of Valenza and the Duke of Gandia, sons of the pope, supped with their mother, Vanozza, near the church of *S. Pietro ad vinculo*: several other persons being present at the entertainment. A late hour approaching, and the cardinal having reminded his brother that it was time to return to the apostolic palace, they mounted their horses or mules, with only a few attendants, and proceeded together as far as the palace of Cardinal Ascanio Sforza, when the duke informed the cardinal that, before he returned home, he had to pay a visit of pleasure. Dismissing therefore all his attendants, excepting his *staffiero,* or footman, and a person in a mask, who had paid him a visit whilst at supper, and who, during the space of a month or thereabouts, previous to this time, had called upon him almost daily at the apostolic palace, he took this person behind him on his mule, and proceeded to the street of the Jews, where he quitted his servant, directing him to remain there until a certain hour; when if he did not return, he might repair to the palace. The duke then seated the person in the mask behind him, and rode I know not whither; but in that night he was assassinated, and thrown into the river. The servant, after having been dismissed, was also assaulted and mortally wounded; and although he was attended with great care, yet such was his situation, that he could give no intelligible account of what had befallen his master. In the morning, the duke not having returned to the palace, his servants began to be alarmed; and one of them informed the pontiff of the evening excursion of his sons, and that the duke had not yet made his appearance. This gave the pope no small anxiety; but he conjectured that the duke had been attracted by some courtesan to pass the night with her, and, not choosing to quit the house in open day, had waited till the following evening to return home. When, however, the evening arrived, and he found himself disappointed in his expectations, he became deeply afflicted, and began to make inquiries from different persons, whom he ordered to attend him for that purpose. Amongst these was a man named Giorgio Schiavoni, who, having discharged some timber from a bark in the river, had remained on board the vessel to watch it; and being interrogated whether he had seen any one thrown into the river on the night preceding, he replied, that he saw two men on foot, who came down the street, and looked diligently about to observe whether any person was passing. That seeing no one, they returned, and a short time afterwards two others came, and looked around in the same manner as the former: no person still appearing, they gave a sign to their companions, when a man came, mounted on a white horse, having behind him a dead body, the head and arms of which hung on one side, and the feet on the other side of the horse; the two persons on foot supporting the body, to prevent its falling. They thus proceeded towards that part where the filth of the city is usually discharged into the river, and turning the horse, with his tail towards the water, the two persons took the dead body by the arms and feet, and with all their strength flung it into the river. The person on horseback then asked if they had thrown it in; to which they replied, *Signor, si* (yes, Sir). He then looked towards the river, and seeing a mantle floating on the stream, he enquired what it was that appeared black, to which they answered, it was a mantle; and one of them threw stones upon it, in consequence of which it sunk. The attendants of the pontiff then enquired from Giorgio, why he had not revealed this to the governor of the city; to which he replied, that he had seen in his time a hundred dead bodies thrown into the river at the same place, without any inquiry being made respecting them; and that he had not, therefore, considered it as a matter of any importance. The fishermen and seamen were then collected, and ordered to search the river, where, on the following evening, they found the body of the duke, with his habit entire, and thirty ducats in his purse. He was pierced with nine wounds, one of which was in his throat, the others in his head, body, and limbs. No sooner was the pontiff informed of the death of his son, and that he had been thrown, like filth, into the river, than, giving way to his grief, he shut himself up in a chamber, and wept bitterly. The Cardinal of Segovia, and other attendants on the pope, went to the door, and after many hours spent in persuasions and exhortations, prevailed upon him to admit them. From the evening of Wednesday till the following Saturday the pope took no food; nor did he sleep from Thursday morning till the same hour on the ensuing day. At length, however, giving way to the entreaties of his attendants, he began to restrain his sorrow, and to consider the injury which his own health might sustain by the further indulgence of his grief.'"—Roscoe's *Life and Pontificate of Leo Tenth.* 1801;. i. 265.

Upon that night (a peasant's is the tale)

A Serf that crossed the intervening vale,

When Cynthia's light almost gave way to morn,

And nearly veiled in mist her waning horn;

A Serf, that rose betimes to thread the wood,

And hew the bough that bought his children's food,

Passed by the river that divides the plain

Of Otho's lands and Lara's broad domain:

He heard a tramp—a horse and horseman broke

From out the wood—before him was a cloak

Wrapt round some burthen at his saddle-bow,

Bent was his head, and hidden was his brow.

Roused by the sudden sight at such a time,

And some foreboding that it might be crime,

Himself unheeded watched the stranger's course,

Who reached the river, bounded from his horse,

And lifting thence the burthen which he bore,

Heaved up the bank, and dashed it from the shore,

Then paused—and looked—and turned—and seemed to watch,

And still another hurried glance would snatch,
And follow with his step the stream that flowed,
As if even yet too much its surface showed;
At once he started—stooped—around him strown
The winter floods had scattered heaps of stone;
Of these the heaviest thence he gathered there,
And slung them with a more than common care.:
Meantime the Serf had crept to where unseen
Himself might safely mark what this might mean;
He caught a glimpse, as of a floating breast,
And something glittered starlike on the vest;
But ere he well could mark the buoyant trunk,
A massy fragment smote it, and it sunk:
It rose again, but indistinct to view,
And left the waters of a purple hue,
Then deeply disappeared: the horseman gazed
Till ebbed the latest eddy it had raised;
Then turning, vaulted on his pawing steed,
And instant spurred him into panting speed.
His face was masked—the features of the dead,
If dead it were, escaped the observer's dread;
But if in sooth a Star its bosom bore,
Such is the badge that Knighthood ever wore,
And such 'tis known Sir Ezzelin had worn
Upon the night that led to such a morn.
If thus he perished, Heaven receive his soul!
His undiscovered limbs to ocean roll;
And charity upon the hope would dwell
It was not Lara's hand by which he fell.

XXV.

And Kaled—Lara—Ezzelin, are gone,

Alike without their monumental stone!

The first, all efforts vainly strove to wean

From lingering where her Chieftain's blood had been:

Grief had so tamed a spirit once too proud,

Her tears were few, her wailing never loud;

But furious would you tear her from the spot

Where yet she scarce believed that he was not,

Her eye shot forth with all the living fire

That haunts the tigress in her whelpless ire;

But left to waste her weary moments there,

She talked all idly unto shapes of air,

Such as the busy brain of Sorrow paints,

And woos to listen to her fond complaints:

And she would sit beneath the very tree

Where lay his drooping head upon her knee;

And in that posture where she saw him fall,

His words, his looks, his dying grasp recall;

And she had shorn, but saved her raven hair,

And oft would snatch it from her bosom there,

And fold, and press it gently to the ground,

As if she staunched anew some phantom's wound.

Herself would question, and for him reply;

Then rising, start, and beckon him to fly

From some imagined Spectre in pursuit;

Then seat her down upon some linden's root,

And hide her visage with her meagre hand,

Or trace strange characters along the sand—

This could not last—she lies by him she loved;
Her tale untold—her truth too dearly proved.

HEBREW MELODIES

ADVERTISEMENT

The subsequent poems were written at the request of my friend, the Hon. Douglas Kinnaird, for a Selection of Hebrew Melodies, and have been published, with the music, arranged by Mr. Braham and Mr. Nathan.

January, 1815.

SHE WALKS IN BEAUTY

I.

She walks in Beauty, like the night
 Of cloudless climes and starry skies;
And all that's best of dark and bright
 Meet in her aspect and her eyes:
Thus mellowed to that tender light
 Which Heaven to gaudy day denies.

II.

One shade the more, one ray the less,
 Had half impaired the nameless grace
Which waves in every raven tress,
 Or softly lightens o'er her face:
Where thoughts serenely sweet express.
 How pure, how dear their dwelling-place.

III.

And on that cheek, and o'er that brow.

So soft, so calm, yet eloquent,

The smiles that win, the tints that glow.

But tell of days in goodness spent,

A mind at peace with all below,

A heart whose love is innocent!   June 12, 1814.

THE HARP THE MONARCH MINSTREL SWEPT

I.

The Harp the Monarch Minstrel swept,

The King of men, the loved of Heaven!

Which Music hall owed while she wept

O'er tones her heart of hearts had given—

Redoubled be her tears, its chords are riven!

It softened men of iron mould,

It gave them virtues not their own;

No ear so dull, no soul so cold,

That felt not—fired not to the tone,

Till David's Lyre grew mightier than his Throne!

II.

It told the triumphs of our King,

It wafted glory to our God:

It made our gladdened valleys ring,

The cedars bow, the mountains nod;

Its sound aspired to Heaven and there abode!

Since then, though heard on earth no more,

Devotion and her daughter Love

Still bid the bursting spirit soar

To sounds that seem as from above,

In dreams that day's broad light can not remove.

IF THAT HIGH WORLD

I.

If that high world, which lies beyond

Our own, surviving Love endears:

If there the cherished heart be fond,

The eye the same, except in tears—

How welcome those untrodden spheres!

How sweet this very hour to die!

To soar from earth and find all fears

Lost in thy light—Eternity!

II.

It must be so: 'tis not for self

That we so tremble on the brink;

And striving to o'erleap the gulf,

Yet cling to Being's severing link.

Oh! in that future let us think

To hold each heart the heart that shares,

With them the immortal waters drink,

And soul in soul grow deathless theirs!

THE WILD GAZELLE

I.

The wild gazelle on Judah's hills
    Exulting yet may bound,
And drink from all the living rills
    That gush on holy ground;
Its airy step and glorious eye
May glance in tameless transport by:—

II.

A step as fleet, an eye more bright,
    Hath Judah witnessed there;
And o'er her scenes of lost delight
    Inhabitants more fair.
The cedars wave on Lebanon,
But Judah's statelier maids are gone!

III.

More blest each palm that shades those plains
    Than Israel's scattered race;
For, taking root, it there remains
    In solitary grace:
It cannot quit its place of birth,
It will not live in other earth.

IV.

But we must wander witheringly,
    In other lands to die;
And where our fathers' ashes be,
    Our own may never lie:
Our temple hath not left a stone,
And Mockery sits on Salem's throne.

OH! WEEP FOR THOSE

I.

Oh! weep for those that wept by Babel's stream,
Whose shrines are desolate, whose land a dream;
Weep for the harp of Judah's broken shell;
Mourn—where their God hath dwelt the godless dwell!

II.

And where shall Israel lave her bleeding feet?
And when shall Zion's songs again seem sweet?
And Judah's melody once more rejoice
The hearts that leaped before its heavenly voice?

III.

Tribes of the wandering foot and weary breast,
How shall ye flee away and be at rest!
The wild-dove hath her nest, the fox his cave,
Mankind their country—Israel but the grave!

ON JORDAN'S BANKS

I.

On Jordan's banks the Arab's camels stray,
On Sion's hill the False One's votaries pray,
The Baal-adorer bows on Sinai's steep—
Yet there—even there—Oh God! thy thunders sleep

II.

There—where thy finger scorched the tablet stone!
There—where thy shadow to thy people shone!
Thy glory shrouded in its garb of fire:
Thyself—none living see and not expire!

III.

Oh! in the lightning let thy glance appear;

Sweep from his shivered hand the oppressor's spear!

How long by tyrants shall thy land be trod?

How long thy temple worshipless, Oh God?

JEPHTHA'S DAUGHTER

I.

Since our Country, our God—Oh, my Sire!

Demand that thy Daughter expire;

Since thy triumph was bought by thy vow—

Strike the bosom that's bared for thee now!

II.

And the voice of my mourning is o'er,

And the mountains behold me no more:

If the hand that I love lay me low,

There cannot be pain in the blow!

III.

And of this, oh, my Father! be sure—

That the blood of thy child is as pure

As the blessing I beg ere it flow,

And the last thought that soothes me below.

IV.

Though the virgins of Salem lament,

Be the judge and the hero unbent!

I have won the great battle for thee,

And my Father and Country are free!

V.

When this blood of thy giving hath gushed,

When the voice that thou lovest is hushed,

Let my memory still be thy pride,

And forget not I smiled as I died!

OH! SNATCHED AWAY IN BEAUTY'S BLOOM

I.

Oh! snatched away in beauty's bloom,

On thee shall press no ponderous tomb;

But on thy turf shall roses rear

Their leaves, the earliest of the year;

And the wild cypress wave in tender gloom:

II.

And oft by yon blue gushing stream

Shall Sorrow lean her drooping head,

And feed deep thought with many a dream,

And lingering pause and lightly tread;

Fond wretch! as if her step disturbed the dead!

III.

Away! we know that tears are vain,

That Death nor heeds nor hears distress:

Will this unteach us to complain?

Or make one mourner weep the less?

And thou—who tell'st me to forget,

Thy looks are wan, thine eyes are wet.

MY SOUL IS DARK

I.

My soul is dark—Oh! quickly string
    The harp I yet can brook to hear;
And let thy gentle fingers fling
    Its melting murmurs o'er mine ear.
If in this heart a hope be dear,
    That sound shall charm it forth again:
If in these eyes there lurk a tear,
    'Twill flow, and cease to burn my brain.

II.

But bid the strain be wild and deep,
    Nor let thy notes of joy be first:
I tell thee, minstrel, I must weep,
    Or else this heavy heart will burst;
For it hath been by sorrow nursed,
    And ached in sleepless silence long;
And now 'tis doomed to know the worst,
    And break at once—or yield to song.

I SAW THEE WEEP

I.

I saw thee weep—the big bright tear
    Came o'er that eye of blue;
And then methought it did appear
    A violet dropping dew:

I saw thee smile—the sapphire's blaze
Beside thee ceased to shine;
It could not match the living rays
That filled that glance of thine.

II.

As clouds from yonder sun receive
A deep and mellow dye,
Which scarce the shade of coming eve
Can banish from the sky,
Those smiles unto the moodiest mind
Their own pure joy impart;
Their sunshine leaves a glow behind
That lightens o'er the heart.

THY DAYS ARE DONE

I.

Thy days are done, thy fame begun;
Thy country's strains record
The triumphs of her chosen Son,
The slaughters of his sword!
The deeds he did, the fields he won,
The freedom he restored!

II.

Though thou art fall'n, while we are free
Thou shalt not taste of death!
The generous blood that flowed from thee
Disdained to sink beneath:
Within our veins its currents be,
Thy spirit on our breath!

III.

Thy name, our charging hosts along,
  Shall be the battle-word!
Thy fall, the theme of choral song
  From virgin voices poured!
To weep would do thy glory wrong:
  Thou shalt not be deplored.

SAUL

I.

Thou whose spell can raise the dead,
  Bid the Prophet's form appear.
"Samuel, raise thy buried head!
  King, behold the phantom Seer!"
Earth yawned; he stood the centre of a cloud:
Light changed its hue, retiring from his shroud.
Death stood all glassy in his fixèd eye;
His hand was withered, and his veins were dry;
His foot, in bony whiteness, glittered there,
Shrunken and sinewless, and ghastly bare;
From lips that moved not and unbreathing frame,
Like cavemed winds, the hollow accents came.
Saul saw, and fell to earth, as falls the oak,
At once, and blasted by the thunder-stroke."

II.

"Why is my sleep disquieted?
Who is he that calls the dead?
Is it thou, O King? Behold,
Bloodless are these limbs, and cold:

Such are mine; and such shall be
Thine to-morrow, when with me:
Ere the coming day is done,
Such shalt thou be—such thy Son.
Fare thee well, but for a day,
Then we mix our mouldering clay.
Thou—thy race, lie pale and low,
Pierced by shafts of many a bow;
And the falchion by thy side
To thy heart thy hand shall guide:
Crownless—breathless—headless fall,
Son and Sire—the house of Saul!"   Seaham, Feb., 1815.

SONG OF SAUL BEFORE HIS LAST BATTLE

I.

Warriors and chiefs! should the shaft or the sword
Pierce me in leading the host of the Lord,
Heed not the corse, though a King's, in your path:
Bury your steel in the bosoms of Gath!

II.

Thou who art bearing my buckler and bow,
Should the soldiers of Saul look away from the foe,
Stretch me that moment in blood at thy feet!
Mine be the doom which they dared not to meet.

III.

Farewell to others, but never we part,
Heir to my Royalty—Son of my heart!
Bright is the diadem, boundless the sway,
Or kingly the death, which awaits us to-day!   Seaham, 1815.

"ALL IS VANITY, SAITH THE PREACHER"

I.

Fame, Wisdom, Love, and Power were mine,
 And Health and Youth possessed me;
My goblets blushed from every vine,
 And lovely forms caressed me;
I sunned my heart in Beauty's eyes,
 And felt my soul grow tender;
All Earth can give, or mortal prize,
 Was mine of regal splendour.

II.

I strive to number o'er what days
 Remembrance can discover,
Which all that Life or Earth displays
 Would lure me to live over.
There rose no day, there rolled no hour
 Of pleasure unembittered;
And not a trapping decked my Power
 That galled not while it glittered.

III.

The serpent of the field, by art
 And spells, is won from harming;
But that which coils around the heart,
 Oh! who hath power of charming?
It will not list to Wisdom's lore,
 Nor Music's voice can lure it;
But there it stings for evermore
 The soul that must endure it.

Seaham, 1815.

WHEN COLDNESS WRAPS THIS SUFFERING CLAY

I.

When coldness wraps this suffering clay,
    Ah! whither strays the immortal mind?
It cannot die, it cannot stay,
    But leaves its darkened dust behind.
Then, unembodied, doth it trace
    By steps each planet's heavenly way?
Or fill at once the realms of space,
    A thing of eyes, that all survey?

II.

Eternal—boundless,—undecayed,
    A thought unseen, but seeing all,
All, all in earth, or skies displayed,
    Shall it survey, shall it recall:
Each fainter trace that Memory holds
    So darkly of departed years,
In one broad glance the Soul beholds,
    And all, that was, at once appears.

III.

Before Creation peopled earth,
    Its eye shall roll through chaos back;
And where the farthest heaven had birth,
    The Spirit trace its rising track.
And where the future mars or makes,
    Its glance dilate o'er all to be,
While Sun is quenched—or System breaks,
    Fixed in its own Eternity.

IV.

Above or Love—Hope—Hate—or Fear,
　　It lives all passionless and pure:
An age shall fleet like earthly year;
　　Its years as moments shall endure.
Away—away—without a wing,
　　O'er all—through all—its thought shall fly,
A nameless and eternal thing,
　　Forgetting what it was to die.　　　　　　Seaham, 1815.

VISION OF BELSHAZZAR

I.

The King was on his throne,
　　The Satraps thronged the hall:
A thousand bright lamps shone
　　O'er that high festival.
A thousand cups of gold,
　　In Judah deemed divine—
Jehovah's vessels hold
　　The godless Heathen's wine!

II.

In that same hour and hall,
　　The fingers of a hand
Came forth against the wall.
　　And wrote as if on sand;
The fingers of a man;—
　　A solitary hand
Along the letters ran,
　　And traced them like a wand.

III.

The monarch saw, and shook,
 And bade no more rejoice;
All bloodless waxed his look,
 And tremulous his voice.
"Let the men of lore appear,
 The wisest of the earth,
And expound the words of fear,
 Which mar our royal mirth."

IV.

Chaldea's seers are good,
 But here they have no skill;
And the unknown letters stood
 Untold and awful still.
And Babel's men of age
 Are wise and deep in lore;
But now they were not sage,
 They saw—but knew no more.

V.

A captive in the land,
 A stranger and a youth,
He heard the King's command,
 He saw that writing's truth.
The lamps around were bright,
 The prophecy in view;
He read it on that night,—
 The morrow proved it true.

VI.

"Belshazzar's grave is made,
　His kingdom passed away,
He, in the balance weighed,
　Is light and worthless clay;
The shroud, his robe of state,
　His canopy the stone;
The Mede is at his gate!
　The Persian on his throne!"

SUN OF THE SLEEPLESS!

Sun of the sleepless! melancholy star!
Whose tearful beam glows tremulously far,
That show'st the darkness thou canst not dispel,
How like art thou to Joy remembered well!
So gleams the past, the light of other days,
Which shines, but warms not with its powerless rays:
A night-beam Sorrow watcheth to behold,
Distinct, but distant—clear—but, oh how cold!

WERE MY BOSOM AS FALSE AS THOU DEEM'ST IT TO BE

I.

Were my bosom as false as thou deem'st it to be,
I need not have wandered from far Galilee;
It was but abjuring my creed to efface
The curse which, thou say'st, is the crime of my race.

II.

If the bad never triumph, then God is with thee!

If the slave only sin—thou art spotless and free!

If the Exile on earth is an Outcast on high,

Live on in thy faith—but in mine I will die.

III.

I have lost for that faith more than thou canst bestow,

As the God who permits thee to prosper doth know;

In his hand is my heart and my hope—and in thine

The land and the life which for him I resign.   Seaham, 1815.

HEROD'S LAMENT FOR MARIAMNE

I.

Oh, Mariamne! now for thee

    The heart for which thou bled'st is bleeding;

Revenge is lost in Agony

    And wild Remorse to rage succeeding.

Oh, Mariamne! where art thou?

    Thou canst not hear my bitter pleading:

Ah! could'st thou—thou would'st pardon now,

    Though Heaven were to my prayer unheeding.

II.

And is she dead?—and did they dare

    Obey my Frenzy's jealous raving?

My Wrath but doomed my own despair:

    The sword that smote her's o'er me waving.—

But thou art cold, my murdered Love!

    And this dark heart is vainly craving

For he who soars alone above,

    And leaves my soul unworthy saving.

III.

She's gone, who shared my diadem;

    She sunk, with her my joys entombing;

I swept that flower from Judah's stem,

    Whose leaves for me alone were blooming;

And mine's the guilt, and mine the hell,

    This bosom's desolation dooming;

And I have earned those tortures well,

    Which unconsumed are still consuming!   Jan. 15, 1815.

ON THE DAY OF THE DESTRUCTION OF JERUSALEM BY TITUS

I.

From the last hill that looks on thy once holy dome,

I beheld thee, oh Sion! when rendered to Rome:

'Twas thy last sun went down, and the flames of thy fall

Flashed back on the last glance I gave to thy wall.

II.

I looked for thy temple—I looked for my home,

And forgot for a moment my bondage to come;

I beheld but the death-fire that fed on thy fane,

And the fast-fettered hands that made vengeance in vain.

III.

On many an eve, the high spot whence I gazed
Had reflected the last beam of day as it blazed;
While I stood on the height, and beheld the decline
Of the rays from the mountain that shone on thy shrine.

IV.

And now on that mountain I stood on that day,
But I marked not the twilight beam melting away;
Oh! would that the lightning had glared in its stead,
And the thunderbolt burst on the Conqueror's head!

V.

But the Gods of the Pagan shall never profane
The shrine where Jehovah disdained not to reign;
And scattered and scorned as thy people may be,
Our worship, oh Father! is only for thee.   1S15.

BY THE RIVERS OF BABYLON WE SAT DOWN AND WEPT

I.

We sate down and wept by the waters
    Of Babel, and thought of the day
When our foe, in the hue of his slaughters,
    Made Salem's high places his prey;
And Ye, oh her desolate daughters!
    Were scattered all weeping away.

II.

While sadly we gazed on the river
   Which rolled on in freedom below,
They demanded the song; but, oh never
   That triumph the Stranger shall know!
May this right hand be withered for ever,
   Ere it string our high harp for the foe!

III.

On the willow that harp is suspended,
   Oh Salem! its sound should be free;
And the hour when thy glories were ended
   But left me that token of thee:
And ne'er shall its soft tones be blended
With the voice of the Spoiler by me!   Jan. 15, 1813.

"BY THE WATERS OF BABYLON"

I.

In the valley of waters we wept on the day
When the host of the Stranger made Salem his prey;
And our heads on our bosoms all droopingly lay,
And our hearts were so full of the land far away!

II.

The song they demanded in vain—it lay still
In our souls as the wind that hath died on the hill—
They called for the harp—but our blood they shall spill
Ere our right hands shall teach them one tone of their skill.

III.

All stringlessly hung in the willow's sad tree,

As dead as her dead-leaf, those mute harps must be:

Our hands may be fettered—our tears still are free

For our God—and our Glory—and Sion, Oh *Thee*!   1815.

THE DESTRUCTION OF SENNACHERIB

I.

The Assyrian came down like the wolf on the fold,

And his cohorts were gleaming in purple and gold;

And the sheen of their spears was like stars on the sea,

When the blue wave rolls nightly on deep Galilee.

II.

Like the leaves of the forest when Summer is green,

That host with their banners at sunset were seen:

Like the leaves of the forest when Autumn hath blown,

That host on the morrow lay withered and strown.

III.

For the Angel of Death spread his wings on the blast,

And breathed in the face of the foe as he passed;

And the eyes of the sleepers waxed deadly and chill,

And their hearts but once heaved—and for ever grew still!

IV.

And there lay the steed with his nostril all wide,

But through it there rolled not the breath of his pride;

And the foam of his gasping lay white on the turf,

And cold as the spray of the rock-beating surf.

V.

And there lay the rider distorted and pale,

With the dew on his brow, and the rust on his mail:

And the tents were all silent—the banners alone—

The lances unlifted—the trumpet unblown.

VI.

And the widows of Ashur are loud in their wail,

And the idols are broke in the temple of Baal;

And the might of the Gentile, unsmote by the sword,

Hath melted like snow in the glance of the Lord!   Seaham, Feb. 17, 1815.

A SPIRIT PASSED BEFORE ME
FROM JOB.

I.

A spirit passed before me: I beheld

The face of Immortality unveiled—

Deep Sleep came down on every eye save mine—

And there it stood,—all formless—but divine:

Along my bones the creeping flesh did quake;

And as my damp hair stiffened, thus it spake:

II.

"Is man more just than God? Is man more pure

Than he who deems even Seraphs insecure?

Creatures of clay—vain dwellers in the dust!

The moth survives you, and are ye more just?

Things of a day! you wither ere the night,

Heedless and blind to Wisdom's wasted light!"

POEMS 1814–1816

FAREWELL! IF EVER FONDEST PRAYER

1.

Farewell! if ever fondest prayer
    For other's weal availed on high,
Mine will not all be lost in air,
    But waft thy name beyond the sky.
'Twere vain to speak—to weep—to sigh:
    Oh! more than tears of blood can tell,
When wrung from Guilt's expiring eye,
    Are in that word—Farewell!—Farewell!

2.

These lips are mute, these eyes are dry;
    But in my breast and in my brain,
Awake the pangs that pass not by,
    The thought that ne'er shall sleep again.
My soul nor deigns nor dares complain,
    Though Grief and Passion there rebel:
I only know we loved in vain—
    I only feel—Farewell!—Farewell!

WHEN WE TWO PARTED

1.

When we two parted
   In silence and tears,
Half broken-hearted
   To sever for years,
Pale grew thy cheek and cold,
   Colder thy kiss;
Truly that hour foretold
   Sorrow to this.

2.

The dew of the morning
   Sunk chill on my brow—
It felt like the warning
   Of what I feel now.
Thy vows are all broken,
   And light is thy fame:
I hear thy name spoken,
   And share in its shame.

3.

They name thee before me,
   A knell to mine ear;
A shudder comes o'er me—
   Why wert thou so dear?
They know not I knew thee,
   Who knew thee too well:—
Long, long shall I rue thee,
   Too deeply to tell.

4.

In secret we met—

   In silence I grieve,

That thy heart could forget,

   Thy spirit deceive.

If I should meet thee

   After long years,

How should I greet thee?—

   With silence and tears.

[LOVE AND GOLD]

1.

I cannot talk of Love to thee,

   Though thou art young and free and fair!

There is a spell thou dost not see,

   That bids a genuine love despair.

2.

And yet that spell invites each youth,

   For thee to sigh, or seem to sigh;

Makes falsehood wear the garb of truth,

   And Truth itself appear a lie.

3.

If ever Doubt a place possest

   In woman's heart, 'twere wise in thine:

Admit not Love into thy breast,

   Doubt others' love, nor trust in mine.

4.

Perchance 'tis feigned, perchance sincere,
    But false or true thou canst not tell;
So much hast thou from all to fear,
    In that unconquerable spell.

5.

Of all the herd that throng around,
    Thy simpering or thy sighing train,
Come tell me who to thee is bound
    By Love's or Plutus' heavier chain.

6.

In some 'tis Nature, some 'tis Art
    That bids them worship at thy shrine;
But thou deserv'st a better heart,
    Than they or I can give for thine.

7.

For thee, and such as thee, behold,
    Is Fortune painted truly—blind!
Who doomed thee to be bought or sold,
    Has proved too bounteous to be kind.

8.

Each day some tempter's crafty suit
    Would woo thee to a loveless bed:
I see thee to the altar's foot
    A decorated victim led.

9.

Adieu, dear maid! I must not speak

Whate'er my secret thoughts may be;

Though thou art all that man can reck

I dare not talk of Love to *thee.*

STANZAS FOR MUSIC

1.

I speak not, I trace not, I breathe not thy name,

There is grief in the sound, there is guilt in the fame:

But the tear which now burns on my cheek may impart

The deep thoughts that dwell in that silence of heart.

2.

Too brief for our passion, too long for our peace,

Were those hours—can their joy or their bitterness cease?

We repent, we abjure, we will break from our chain,—

We will part, we will fly to—unite it again!

3.

Oh! thine be the gladness, and mine be the guilt!

Forgive me, adored one!—forsake, if thou wilt;—

But the heart which is thine shall expire undebased

And *man* shall not break it—whatever *thou* mayst.

4.

And stern to the haughty, but humble to thee,

This soul, in its bitterest blackness, shall be:

And our days seem as swift, and our moments more sweet,

With thee by my side, than with worlds at our feet.

5.

One sigh of thy sorrow, one look of thy love,

Shall turn me or fix, shall reward or reprove;

And the heartless may wonder at all I resign—

Thy lip shall reply, not to them, but to *mine*.   May 4, 1814.

ADDRESS INTENDED TO BE RECITED AT THE CALEDONIAN MEETING

Who hath not glowed above the page where Fame

Hath fixed high Caledon's unconquered name;

The mountain-land which spurned the Roman chain,

And baffled back the fiery-crested Dane,

Whose bright claymore and hardihood of hand

No foe could tame—no tyrant could command?

That race is gone—but still their children breathe,

And Glory crowns them with redoubled wreath:

O'er Gael and Saxon mingling banners shine,

And, England! add their stubborn strength to thine.

The blood which flowed with Wallace flows as free,

But now 'tis only shed for Fame and thee!

Oh! pass not by the northern veteran's claim,

But give support—the world hath given him, fame!.

The humbler ranks, the lowly brave, who bled

While cheerly following where the Mighty led—

Who sleep beneath the undistinguished sod

Where happier comrades in their triumph trod,

To us bequeath—'tis all their fate allows—
The sireless offspring and the lonely spouse:
She on high Albyn's dusky hills may raise
The tearful eye in melancholy gaze,
Or view, while shadowy auguries disclose
The Highland Seer's anticipated woes,
The bleeding phantom of each martial form
Dim in the cloud, or darkling in the storm;
While sad, she chaunts the solitary song,
The soft lament for him who tarries long—
For him, whose distant relics vainly crave
The Coronach's wild requiem to the brave!

'Tis Heaven—not man—must charm away the woe,
Which bursts when Nature's feelings newly flow;
Yet Tenderness and Time may rob the tear
Of half its bitterness for one so dear;
A Nation's gratitude perchance may spread
A thornless pillow for the widowed head;
May lighten well her heart's maternal care,
And wean from Penury the soldier's heir;
Or deem to living war-worn Valour just
Each wounded remnant—Albion's cherished trust—
Warm his decline with those endearing rays,
Whose bounteous sunshine yet may gild his days—
So shall that Country—while he sinks to rest—
His hand hath fought for—by his heart be blest!

May, 1814.

ELEGIAC STANZAS ON THE DEATH OF SIR PETER PARKER, BART.

1.

There is a tear for all that die,

A mourner o'er the humblest grave;

But nations swell the funeral cry,

And Triumph weeps above the brave.

2.

For them is Sorrow's purest sigh

O'er Ocean's heaving bosom sent:

In vain their bones unburied lie,

All earth becomes their monument!

3.

A tomb is theirs on every page,

An epitaph on every tongue:

The present hours, the future age,

For them bewail, to them belong.

4.

For them the voice of festal mirth

Grows hushed, *their name* the only sound;

While deep Remembrance pours to Worth

The goblet's tributary round.

5.

A theme to crowds that knew them not,

Lamented by admiring foes,

Who would not share their glorious lot?

Who would not die the death they chose?

6.

And, gallant Parker! thus enshrined
   Thy life, thy fall, thy fame shall be;
And early valour, glowing, find
   A model in thy memory.

7.

But there are breasts that bleed with thee
   In woe, that glory cannot quell;
And shuddering hear of victory,
   Where one so dear, so dauntless, fell.

8.

Where shall they turn to mourn thee less?
   When cease to hear thy cherished name?
Time cannot teach forgetfulness,
   While Griefs full heart is fed by Fame.

9.

Alas! for them, though not for thee,
   They cannot choose but weep the more;
Deep for the dead the grief must be,
   Who ne'er gave cause to mourn before.   October 7, 1814.

JULIAN

1.

The Night came on the Waters—all was rest
On Earth—but Rage on Ocean's troubled Heart.
The Waves arose and rolled beneath the blast;
The Sailors gazed upon their shivered Mast.
In that dark Hour a long loud gathered cry

From out the billows pierced the sable sky,

And borne o'er breakers reached the craggy shore—

The Sea roars on—that Cry is heard no more.

2.

There is no vestige, in the Dawning light,

Of those that shrieked thro' shadows of the Night.

The Bark—the Crew—the very Wreck is gone,

Marred—mutilated—traceless—all save one.

In him there still is Life, the Wave that dashed

On shore the plank to which his form was lashed,

Returned unheeding of its helpless Prey—

The lone survivor of that Yesterday—

The one of Many whom the withering Gale

Hath left unpunished to record their Tale.

But who shall hear it? on that barren Sand

None comes to stretch the hospitable hand.

That shore reveals no print of human foot,

Nor e'en the pawing of the wilder Brute;

And niggard vegetation will not smile,

All sunless on that solitary Isle.

3.

The naked Stranger rose, and wrung his hair,

And that first moment passed in silent prayer.

Alas! the sound—he sunk into Despair—

He was on Earth—but what was Earth to him,

Houseless and homeless—bare both breast and limb?

Cut off from all but Memory he curst

His fate—his folly—but himself the worst.

What was his hope? he looked upon the Wave—
Despite—of all—it still may be his Grave!

4.

He rose and with a feeble effort shaped
His course unto the billows—late escaped:
But weakness conquered—swam his dizzy glance,
And down to Earth he sunk in silent trance.
How long his senses bore its chilling chain,
He knew not—but, recalled to Life again,
A stranger stood beside his shivering form—
And what was he? had he too scaped the storm?

5.

He raised young Julian. "Is thy Cup so full
"Of bitterness—thy Hope—thy heart so dull
"That thou shouldst from Thee dash the Draught of Life,
"So late escaped the elemental strife!
"Rise—tho' these shores few aids to Life supply,
"Look upon me, and know thou shalt not die.
"Thou gazest in mute wonder—more may be
"Thy marvel when thou knowest mine and me.
"But come—The bark that bears us hence shall find
"Her Haven, soon, despite the warning Wind."

6.

He raised young Julian from the sand, and such
Strange power of healing dwelt within the touch,
That his weak limbs grew light with freshened Power,
As he had slept not fainted in that hour,
And woke from Slumber—as the Birds awake,
Recalled at morning from the branched brake,

When the day's promise heralds early Spring,
And Heaven unfolded woos their soaring wing:
So Julian felt, and gazed upon his Guide,
With honest Wonder what might next betide.   Dec. 12, 1814.

TO BELSHAZZAR

1.

Belshazzar! from the banquet turn,
   Nor in thy sensual fulness fall;
Behold! while yet before thee burn
   The graven words, the glowing wall,
Many a despot men miscall
   Crowned and anointed from on high;
But thou, the weakest, worst of all—
   Is it not written, thou must die?

2.

Go! dash the roses from thy brow—
   Grey hairs but poorly wreathe with them;
Youth's garlands misbecome thee now,
   More than thy very diadem,
Where thou hast tarnished every gem:—
   Then throw the worthless bauble by,
Which, worn by thee, ev'n slaves contemn;
   And learn like better men to die!

3.

Oh! early in the balance weighed,
   And ever light of word and worth,
Whose soul expired ere youth decayed,
   And left thee but a mass of earth.

To see thee moves the scorner's mirth:

But tears in Hope's averted eye

Lament that even thou hadst birth—

Unfit to govern, live, or die.   February 12, 1815.

STANZAS FOR MUSIC

"O Lachrymarum fons, tenero sacros
Ducentium ortus ex animo: quater
    Felix! in imo qui scatentem
        Pectore te, pia Nympha, sensit."
—GRAY'S *Poemata.*

1.

There's not a joy the world can give like that it takes away,

When the glow of early thought declines in Feeling's dull decay;

'Tis not on Youth's smooth cheek the blush alone, which fades so fast,

But the tender bloom of heart is gone, ere Youth itself be past.

2.

Then the few whose spirits float above the wreck of happiness

Are driven o'er the shoals of guilt or ocean of excess:

The magnet of their course is gone, or only points in vain

The shore to which their shivered sail shall never stretch again.

3.

Then the mortal coldness of the soul like Death itself comes down;

It cannot feel for others' woes, it dare not dream its own;

That heavy chill has frozen o'er the fountain of our tears,

And though the eye may sparkle still, 'tis where the ice appears.

4.

Though wit may flash from fluent lips, and mirth distract the breast,

Through midnight hours that yield no more their former hope of rest;

'Tis but as ivy-leaves around the ruined turret wreath,

All green and wildly fresh without, but worn and grey beneath.

5.

Oh, could I feel as I have felt,—or be what I have been,

Or weep as I could once have wept, o'er many a vanished scene;

As springs in deserts found seem sweet, all brackish though they be,

So, midst the withered waste of life, those tears would flow to me.

March, 1815.

ON THE DEATH OF THE DUKE OF DORSET

1.

I heard thy fate without a tear,

    Thy loss with scarce a sigh;

And yet thou wast surpassing dear,

    Too loved of all to die.

I know not what hath seared my eye—

    Its tears refuse to start;

But every drop, it bids me dry,

    Falls dreary on my heart.

2.

Yes, dull and heavy, one by one,

    They sink and turn to care,

As caverned waters wear the stone,

    Yet dropping harden there:

They cannot petrify more fast,

　Than feelings sunk remain,

Which coldly fixed regard the past,

　But never melt again.

STANZAS FOR MUSIC

1.

Bright be the place of thy soul!

　No lovelier spirit than thine

E'er burst from its mortal control,

　In the orbs of the blessed to shine.

On earth thou wert all but divine,

　As thy soul shall immortally be;

And our sorrow may cease to repine

　When we know that thy God is with thee.

2.

Light be the turf of thy tomb!

　May its verdure like emeralds be!

There should not be the shadow of gloom

　In aught that reminds us of thee.

Young flowers and an evergreen tree

　May spring from the spot of thy rest:

But nor cypress nor yew let us see;

　For why should we mourn for the blest?

NAPOLEON'S FAREWELL

1.

Farewell to the Land, where the gloom of my Glory
Arose and o'ershadowed the earth with her name—
She abandons me now—but the page of her story,
The brightest or blackest, is filled with my fame.
I have warred with a World which vanquished me only
When the meteor of conquest allured me too far;
I have coped with the nations which dread me thus lonely,
The last single Captive to millions in war.

2.

Farewell to thee, France! when thy diadem crowned me,
I made thee the gem and the wonder of earth,—
But thy weakness decrees I should leave as I found thee,
Decayed in thy glory, and sunk in thy worth.
Oh! for the veteran hearts that were wasted
In strife with the storm, when their battles were won
Then the Eagle, whose gaze in that moment was blasted
Had still soared with eyes fixed on Victory's sun!

3.

Farewell to thee, France!—but when Liberty rallies
Once more in thy regions, remember me then,—
The Violet still grows in the depth of thy valleys;
Though withered, thy tear will unfold it again—
Yet, yet, I may baffle the hosts that surround us,
And yet may thy heart leap awake to my voice—
There are links which must break in the chain that has bound us,
Then turn thee and call on the Chief of thy choice!

July 25, 1815. London.

FROM THE FRENCH

I.

Must thou go, my glorious Chief,
   Severed from thy faithful few?
Who can tell thy warrior's grief,
   Maddening o'er that long adieu?
Woman's love, and Friendship's zeal,
   Dear as both have been to me—
What are they to all I feel,
   With a soldier's faith for thee?

II.

Idol of the soldier's soul!
   First in fight, but mightiest now;
Many could a world control;
   Thee alone no doom can bow.
By thy side for years I dared
   Death; and envied those who fell,
When their dying shout was heard,
   Blessing him they served so well.

III.

Would that I were cold with those,
   Since this hour I live to see;
When the doubts of coward foes
   Scarce dare trust a man with thee,
Dreading each should set thee free!
   Oh! although in dungeons pent,
All their chains were light to me,
   Gazing on thy soul unbent.

IV.

Would the sycophants of him

   Now so deaf to duty's prayer,

Were his borrowed glories dim,

   In his native darkness share?

Were that world this hour his own,

   All thou calmly dost resign,

Could he purchase with that throne

   Hearts like those which still are thine?

V.

My Chief, my King, my Friend, adieu!

   Never did I droop before;

Never to my Sovereign sue,

   As his foes I now implore:

All I ask is to divide

   Every peril he must brave;

Sharing by the hero's side

   His fall—his exile—and his grave.

ODE FROM THE FRENCH

1.

We do not curse thee, Waterloo!

Though Freedom's blood thy plain bedew;

There 'twas shed, but is not sunk—

Rising from each gory trunk,

Like the water-spout from ocean,

With a strong and growing motion—

It soars, and mingles in the air,

With that of lost La Bédoyère—

With that of him whose honoured grave

Contains the "bravest of the brave."

A crimson cloud it spreads and glows,

But shall return to whence it rose;

When 'tis full 'twill burst asunder—

Never yet was heard such thunder

As then shall shake the world with wonder—

Never yet was seen such lightning

As o'er heaven shall then be bright'ning!

Like the Wormwood Star foretold

By the sainted Seer of old,

Show'ring down a fiery flood,

Turning rivers into blood.[i]

i. See *Rev.* Cbap. viii. V. 7, etc., "The first angel sounded, and there followed hail and fire mingled with blood," etc. V. 8, "And the second angel sounded, and as it were a great mountain burning with fire was cast into the sea: and the third part of the sea became blood," etc. V. 10, "And the third angel sounded, and there fell a great star from heaven, burning as it were a lamp, and it fell upon the third part of the rivers, and upon the fountains of waters." V. 11," And the name of the star is called *Wormwood:* and the third part of the waters became *wormwood;* and many men died of the waters, because they were made bitter."

II.

The Chief has fallen, but not by you,

Vanquishers of Waterloo!

When the soldier citizen

Swayed not o'er his fellow-men—

Save in deeds that led them on

Where Glory smiled on Freedom's son—

Who, of all the despots banded,

With that youthful chief competed?

Who could boast o'er France defeated,

Till lone Tyranny commanded?
Till, goaded by Ambition's sting,
The Hero sunk into the King?
Then he fell:—so perish all,
Who would men by man enthral!

III.

And thou, too, of the snow-white plume!
Whose realm refused thee ev'n a tomb;[i]
Better hadst thou still been leading
France o'er hosts of hirelings bleeding,
Than sold thyself to death and shame
For a meanly royal name;
Such as he of Naples wears,
Who thy blood-bought title bears.
Little didst thou deem, when dashing
 On thy war-horse through the ranks,
 Like a stream which burst its banks,
While helmets cleft, and sabres clashing,
Shone and shivered fast around thee—
Of the fate at last which found thee:
Was that haughty plume laid low
By a slave's dishonest blow?
Once—as the Moon sways o'er the tide,
It rolled in air, the warrior's guide;
Through the smoke-created night
Of the black and sulphurous fight,
The soldier raised his seeking eye
To catch that crest's ascendancy,—
And, as it onward rolling rose,

So moved his heart upon our foes.

There, where death's brief pang was quickest,

And the battle's wreck lay thickest,

Strewed beneath the advancing banner

   Of the eagle's burning crest—

(There with thunder-clouds to fan her,

   Who could then her wing arrest—

   Victory beaming from her breast?)

While the broken line enlarging

   Fell, or fled along the plain;

There be sure was Murat charging!

   There he ne'er shall charge again!

i. Murat's remains are said to have been torn from the grave and burnt.

IV.

O'er glories gone the invaders march,

Weeps Triumph o'er each levelled arch—

But let Freedom rejoice,

With her heart in her voice;

But, her hand on her sword,

Doubly shall she be adored;

France hath twice too well been taught

The "moral lesson" dearly bought—

Her safety sits not on a throne,

With Capet or Napoleon!

But in equal rights and laws,

Hearts and hands in one great cause—

Freedom, such as God hath given

Unto all beneath his heaven,

With their breath, and from their birth,

Though guilt would sweep it from the earth;

With a fierce and lavish hand

Scattering nations' wealth like sand;

Pouring nations' blood like water,

In imperial seas of slaughter!

V.

But the heart and the mind,

And the voice of mankind,

Shall arise in communion—

And who shall resist that proud union?

The time is past when swords subdued—

Man may die—the soul's renewed:

Even in this low world of care

Freedom ne'er shall want an heir;

Millions breathe but to inherit

Her for ever bounding spirit—

When once more her hosts assemble,

Tyrants shall believe and tremble—

Smile they at this idle threat?

Crimson tears will follow yet.

STANZAS FOR MUSIC

1.

There be none of Beauty's daughters

With a magic like thee;

And like music on the waters

Is thy sweet voice to me:

When, as if its sound were causing
The charmèd Ocean's pausing,
The waves lie still and gleaming,
And the lulled winds seem dreaming:

2.

And the midnight Moon is weaving
    Her bright chain o'er the deep;
Whose breast is gently heaving,
    As an infant's asleep:
So the spirit bows before thee,
To listen and adore thee;
With a full but soft emotion,
Like the swell of Summer's ocean.   March 28.

ON THE STAR OF "THE LEGION OF HONOUR"

1.

Star of the brave!—whose beam hath shed
Such glory o'er the quick and dead—
Thou radiant and adored deceit!
Which millions rushed in arms to greet,—
Wild meteor of immortal birth!
Why rise in Heaven to set on Earth?

2.

Souls of slain heroes formed thy rays;
Eternity flashed through thy blaze;
The music of thy martial sphere
Was fame on high and honour here;
And thy light broke on human eyes,
Like a Volcano of the skies.

3.

Like lava rolled thy stream of blood,
And swept down empires with its flood;
Earth rocked beneath thee to her base,
As thou didst lighten through all space;
And the shorn Sun grew dim in air,
And set while thou wert dwelling there.

4.

Before thee rose, and with thee grew,
A rainbow of the loveliest hue
Of three bright colours,[i] each divine,
And fit for that celestial sign;
For Freedom's hand had blended them,
Like tints in an immortal gem.

i. The tricolor.

5.

One tint was of the sunbeam's dyes;
One, the blue depth of Seraph's eyes;
One, the pure Spirit's veil of white
Had robed in radiance of its light:
The three so mingled did beseem
The texture of a heavenly dream.

6.

Star of the brave! thy ray is pale,
And darkness must again prevail!
But, oh thou Rainbow of the free!
Our tears and blood must flow for thee.
When thy bright promise fades away,
Our life is but a load of clay.

7.

And Freedom hallows with her tread
The silent cities of the dead;
For beautiful in death are they
Who proudly fall in her array;
And soon, oh, Goddess! may we be
For evermore with them or thee!

STANZAS FOR MUSIC

I.

They say that Hope is happiness;
   But genuine Love must prize the past,
And Memory wakes the thoughts that bless:
   They rose the first—they set the last;

II.

And all that Memory loves the most
   Was once our only Hope to be,
And all that Hope adored and lost
   Hath melted into Memory.

III.

Alas! it is delusion all:
   The future cheats us from afar,
Nor can we be what we recall,
   Nor dare we think on what we are.

THE SIEGE OF CORINTH

"Guns, Trumpets, Blunderbusses, Drums and Thunder."
Pope, *Sat.* i. 26.'

TO

JOHN HOBHOUSE, ESQ.,

THIS POEM IS INSCRIBED,

BY HIS

FRIEND.

January 22nd, 1816.

ADVERTISEMENT

"The grand army of the Turks (in 1715), under the Prime Vizier, to open to themselves a way into the heart of the Morea, and to form the siege of Napoli di Romania, the most considerable place in all that country,ⁱ thought it best in the first place to attack Corinth, upon which they made several storms. The garrison being weakened, and the governor seeing it was impossible to hold out such a place against so mighty a force, thought it fit to beat a parley: but while they were treating about the articles, one of the magazines in the Turkish camp,

wherein they had six hundred barrels of powder, blew up by accident, whereby six or seven hundred men were killed; which so enraged the infidels, that they would not grant any capitulation, but stormed the place with so much fury, that they took it, and put most of the garrison, with Signior Minotti, the governor, to the sword. The rest, with Signior or Antonio Bembo, Proveditor Extraordinary, were made prisoners of war."—*A Compleat History of the Turks*, iii. 151.

i. Napoli di Romania is not now the most considerable place in the Morea, but Tripolitza, where the Pacha resides, and maintains his government. Napoli is near Argos. I visited all three in 1810-n; and, in the course of journeying through the country from my first arrival in 1809, I crossed the Isthmus eight times in my way from Attica to the Morea, over the mountains; or in the other direction, when passing from the Gulf of Athens to that of Lepanto. Both the routes are picturesque and beautiful, though very different: that by sea has more sameness; but the voyage, being always within sight of land, and often very near it, presents many attractive views of the islands Salamis, Ægina, Poros, etc., and the coast of the Continent.

In the year since Jesus died for men,

Eighteen hundred years and ten,

We were a gallant company,

Riding o'er land, and sailing o'er sea.

Oh! but we went merrily!

We forded the river, and clomb the high hill,

Never our steeds for a day stood still;

Whether we lay in the cave or the shed,

Our sleep fell soft on the hardest bed;

Whether we couched in our rough capote,

On the rougher plank of our gliding boat,

Or stretched on the beach, or our saddles spread,

As a pillow beneath the resting head,

Fresh we woke upon the morrow:

    All our thoughts and words had scope,

    We had health, and we had hope,

Toil and travel, but no sorrow.

We were of all tongues and creeds;—

Some were those who counted beads,

Some of mosque, and some of church,

    And some, or I mis-say, of neither;

Yet through the wide world might ye search,

    Nor find a motlier crew nor blither.

But some are dead, and some are gone,

And some are scattered and alone,

And some are rebels on the hills[i]

    That look along Epirus' valleys,

    Where Freedom still at moments rallies,

And pays in blood Oppression's ills;

    And some are in a far countree,

And some all restlessly at home;

But never more, oh! never, we

Shall meet to revel and to roam.

But those hardy days flew cheerily!

And when they now fall drearily,

My thoughts, like swallows, skim the main,

And bear my spirit back again

Over the earth, and through the air,

A wild bird and a wanderer.

'Tis this that ever wakes my strain,

And oft, too oft, implores again

The few who may endure my lay,

To follow me so far away.

Stranger, wilt thou follow now,

And sit with me on Acro-Corinth's brow?

i. The last tidings recently heard of Dervish (one of the Arnauts who followed me) state him to be in revolt upon the mountains, at the head of some of the bands common in that country in times of trouble.

I.

Many a vanished year and age,

And Tempest's breath, and Battle's rage,

Have swept o'er Corinth; yet she stands,

A fortress formed to Freedom's hands.

The Whirlwind's wrath, the Earthquake's shock,

Have left untouched her hoary rock,

The keystone of a land, which still,

Though fall'n, looks proudly on that hill,

The landmark to the double tide

That purpling rolls on either side,

As if their waters chafed to meet,

Yet pause and crouch beneath her feet.

But could the blood before her shed

Since first Timoleon's brother bled,

Or baffled Persia's despot fled,

Arise from out the Earth which drank

The stream of Slaughter as it sank,

That sanguine Ocean would o'erflow

Her isthmus idly spread below:

Or could the bones of all the slain,

Who perished there, be piled again.

That rival pyramid would rise

More mountain-like, through those clear skies

Than yon tower-capp'd Acropolis,

Which seems the very clouds to kiss.

II.

On dun Citheron's ridge appears

The gleam of twice ten thousand spears;

And downward to the Isthmian plain,

From shore to shore of either main,

The tent is pitched, the Crescent shines

Along the Moslem's leaguering lines;

And the dusk Spahi's hands advance

Beneath each bearded Pacha's glance;

And far and wide as eye can reach

The turbaned cohorts throng the beach:

And there the Arab's camel kneels.

And there his steed the Tartar wheels;

The Turcoman[i] hath left his herd,

The sabre round his loins to gird;

And there the volleying thunders pour,
Till waves grow smoother to the roar.
The trench is dug, the cannon's breath
Wings the far hissing globe of death;
Fast whirl the fragments from the wall,
Which crumbles with the ponderous ball;
And from that wall the foe replies,
O'er dusty plain and smoky skies,
With fires that answer fast and well
The summons of the Infidel.

i. The life of the Turcomans is wandering and patriarchal: they dwell in tents.

III.

But near and nearest to the wall
Of those who wish and work its fall,
With deeper skill in War's black art,
Than Othman's sons, and high of heart
As any Chief that ever stood
Triumphant in the fields of blood;
From post to post, and deed to deed,
Fast spurring on his reeking steed,
Where sallying ranks the trench assail,
And make the foremost Moslem quail;
Or where the battery, guarded well,
Remains as yet impregnable,
Alighting cheerly to inspire
The soldier slackening in his fire:
The first and freshest of the host
Which Stamboul's Sultan there can boast,
To guide the follower o'er the field,

To point the tube, the lance to wield,
Or whirl around the bickering blade;—
Was Alp, the Adrian renegade!

IV.

From Venice—once a race of worth
His gentle Sires—he drew his birth;
But late an exile from her shore,'-
Against his countrymen he bore
The arms they taught to bear; and now
The turban girt his shaven brow.
Through many a change had Corinth passed
With Greece to Venice' rule at last;
And here, before her walls, with those
To Greece and Venice equal foes,
He stood a foe, with all the zeal
Which young and fiery converts feel,
Within whose heated bosom throngs
The memory of a thousand wrongs.
To him had Venice ceased to be
Her ancient civic boast—"the Free;"
And in the palace of St. Mark
Unnamed accusers in the dark
Within the "Lion's mouth" had placed
A charge against him uneffaced:
He fled in time, and saved his life,
To waste his future years in strife,"
That taught his land how great her loss
In him who triumphed o'er the Cross,

'Gainst which he reared the Crescent high,

And battled to avenge or die.

V.

Coumourgi[i]—he whose closing scene

Adorned the triumph of Eugene,

When on Carlowitz' bloody plain,

The last and mightiest of the slain,

He sank, regretting not to die,

But cursed the Christian's victory—

Coumourgi—can his glory cease,

That latest conqueror of Greece,

Till Christian hands to Greece restore

The freedom Venice gave of yore?

A hundred years have rolled away

Since he refixed the Moslem's sway;

And now he led the Mussulman,

And gave the guidance of the van

To Alp, who well repaid the trust

By cities levelled with the dust;

And proved, by many a deed of death,

How firm his heart in novel faith.

i. Ali Coumourgi, the favourite of three sultans, and Grand Vizier to Achmet III., after recovering Peloponnesus from the Venetians in one campaign, was mortally wounded in the next, against the Germans, at the battle of Peterwaradin (in the plain of Carlowitz), in Hungary, endeavouring to rally his guards. He died of his wounds next day. His last order was the decapitation of General Breuner, and some other German prisoners, and his last words, "Oh that I could thus serve all the Christian dogs!" a speech and act not unlike one of Caligula. He was a young man of great ambition and unbounded presumption: on being told that Prince Eugene, then opposed to him, "was a great general," he said, "I shall become a greater, and at his expense."

VI.

The walls grew weak; and fast and hot
Against them poured the ceaseless shot,
With unabating fury sent
From battery to battlement;
And thunder-like the pealing din
Rose from each heated culverin;
And here and there some crackling dome
Was fired before the exploding bomb;
And as the fabric sank beneath
The shattering shell's volcanic breath,
In red and wreathing columns flashed
The flame, as loud the ruin crashed,
Or into countless meteors driven,
Its earth-stars melted into heaven;
Whose clouds that day grew doubly dun,
Impervious to the hidden sun,
With volumed smoke that slowly grew
To one wide sky of sulphurous hue.

VII.

But not for vengeance, long delayed,
Alone, did Alp, the renegade,
The Moslem warriors sternly teach
His skill to pierce the promised breach:
Within these walls a Maid was pent
His hope would win, without consent
Of that inexorable Sire,
Whose heart refused him in its ire,
When Alp, beneath his Christian name,

Her virgin hand aspired to claim.

In happier mood, and earlier time,

While unimpeached for traitorous crime,

Gayest in Gondola or Hall,

He glittered through the Carnival;

And tuned the softest serenade

That e'er on Adria's waters played

At midnight to Italian maid.

VIII.

And many deemed her heart was won;

For sought by numbers, given to none,

Had young Francesca's hand remained

Still by the Church's bonds unchained:

And when the Adriatic bore

Lanciotto to the Paynim shore,

Her wonted smiles were seen to fail,

And pensive waxed the maid and pale;

More constant at confessional,

More rare at masque and festival;

Or seen at such, with downcast eyes,

Which conquered hearts they ceased to prize:

With listless look she seems to gaze:

With humbler care her form arrays;

Her voice less lively in the song;

Her step, though light, less fleet among

The pairs, on whom the Morning's glance

Breaks, yet unsated with the dance.

IX.

Sent by the State to guard the land,
(Which, wrested from the Moslem's hand,
While Sobieski tamed his pride
By Buda's wall and Danube's side,
The chiefs of Venice wrung away
From Patra to Euboea's bay,)
Minotti held in Corinth's towers
The Doge's delegated powers,
While yet the pitying eye of Peace
Smiled o'er her long forgotten Greece:
And ere that faithless truce was broke
Which freed her from the unchristian yoke,
With him his gentle daughter came;
Nor there, since Menelaus' dame
Forsook her lord and land, to prove
What woes await on lawless love,
Had fairer form adorned the shore
Than she, the matchless stranger, bore.

X.

The wall is rent, the ruins yawn;
And, with to-morrow's earliest dawn,
O'er the disjointed mass shall vault
The foremost of the fierce assault.
The bands are ranked—the chosen van
Of Tartar and of Mussulman,
The full of hope, misnamed "forlorn,"
Who hold the thought of death in scorn,
And win their way with falchion's force,

Or pave the path with many a corse,
O'er which the following brave may rise,
Their stepping-stone—the last who dies!

XI.

'Tis midnight: on the mountains brown
The cold, round moon shines deeply down;
Blue roll the waters, blue the sky
Spreads like an ocean hung on high,
Bespangled with those isles of light,
So wildly, spiritually bright;
Who ever gazed upon them shining
And turned to earth without repining,
Nor wished for wings to flee away,
And mix with their eternal ray?
The waves on either shore lay there
Calm, clear, and azure as the air;
And scarce their foam the pebbles shook,
But murmured meekly as the brook.
The winds were pillowed on the waves;
The banners drooped along their staves,
And, as they fell around them furling,
Above them shone the crescent curling;
And that deep silence was unbroke,
Save where the watch his signal spoke,
Save where the steed neighed oft and shrill,
And echo answered from the hill,
And the wide hum of that wild host
Rustled like leaves from coast to coast,
As rose the Muezzin's voice in air

In midnight call to wonted prayer;

It rose, that chanted mournful strain,

Like some lone Spirit's o'er the plain:

'Twas musical, but sadly sweet,

Such as when winds and harp-strings meet,

And take a long unmeasured tone,

To mortal minstrelsy unknown.

It seemed to those within the wall

A cry prophetic of their fall:

It struck even the besieger's ear

With something ominous and drear,

An undefined and sudden thrill,

Which makes the heart a moment still,

Then beat with quicker pulse, ashamed

Of that strange sense its silence framed;

Such as a sudden passing-bell

Wakes, though but for a stranger's knell.

XII.

The tent of Alp was on the shore;

The sound was hushed, the prayer was o'er;

The watch was set, the night-round made,

All mandates issued and obeyed:

'Tis but another anxious night,

His pains the morrow may requite

With all Revenge and Love can pay,

In guerdon for their long delay.

Few hours remain, and he hath need

Of rest, to nerve for many a deed

Of slaughter; but within his soul

The thoughts like troubled waters roll.

He stood alone among the host;

Not his the loud fanatic boast

To plant the Crescent o'er the Cross,

Or risk a life with little loss,

Secure in paradise to be

By Houris loved immortally:

Nor his, what burning patriots feel,

The stern exaltedness of zeal,

Profuse of blood, untired in toil,

When battling on the parent soil.

He stood alone—a renegade

Against the country he betrayed;

He stood alone amidst his band,

Without a trusted heart or hand:

They followed him, for he was brave,

And great the spoil he got and gave;

They crouched to him, for he had skill

To warp and wield the vulgar will:

But still his Christian origin

With them was little less than sin.

They envied even the faithless fame

He earned beneath a Moslem name;

Since he, their mightiest chief, had been

In youth a bitter Nazarene.

They did not know how Pride can stoop,

When baffled feelings withering droop;

They did not know how Hate can burn

In hearts once changed from soft to stern;

Nor all the false and fatal zeal

The convert of Revenge can feel.

He ruled them—man may rule the worst,

By ever daring to be first:

So lions o'er the jackals sway;

The jackal points, he fells the prey,

Then on the vulgar, yelling, press,

To gorge the relics of success.

XIII.

His head grows fevered, and his pulse

The quick successive throbs convulse;

In vain from side to side he throws

His form, in courtship of repose;

Or if he dozed, a sound, a start

Awoke him with a sunken heart.

The turban on his hot brow pressed,

The mail weighed lead-like on his breast,

Though oft and long beneath its weight

Upon his eyes had slumber sate,

Without or couch or canopy,

Except a rougher field and sky

Than now might yield a warrior's bed,

Than now along the heaven was spread.

He could not rest, he could not stay

Within his tent to wait for day,

But walked him forth along the sand,

Where thousand sleepers strewed the strand.

What pillowed them? and why should he

More wakeful than the humblest be,

Since more their peril, worse their toil?
And yet they fearless dream of spoil;
While he alone, where thousands passed
A night of sleep, perchance their last,
In sickly vigil wandered on,
And envied all he gazed upon.

XIV.

He felt his soul become more light
Beneath the freshness of the night.
Cool was the silent sky, though calm,
And bathed his brow with airy balm:
Behind, the camp—before him lay,
In many a winding creek and bay,
Lepanto's gulf; and, on the brow
Of Delphi's hill, unshaken snow,
High and eternal, such as shone
Through thousand summers brightly gone,
Along the gulf, the mount, the clime;
It will not melt, like man, to time:
Tyrant and slave are swept away,
Less formed to wear before the ray;
But that white veil, the lightest, frailest,
Which on the mighty mount thou hailest,
While tower and tree are torn and rent,
Shines o'er its craggy battlement;
In form a peak, in height a cloud,
In texture like a hovering shroud,
Thus high by parting Freedom spread,
As from her fond abode she fled,

And lingered on the spot, where long
Her prophet spirit spake in song,
Oh! still her step at moments falters
O'er withered fields, and ruined altars,
And fain would wake, in souls too broken,
By pointing to each glorious token:
But vain her voice, till better days
Dawn in those yet remembered rays,
Which shone upon the Persian flying,
And saw the Spartan smile in dying.

XV.

Not mindless of these mighty times
Was Alp, despite his flight and crimes;
And through this night, as on he wandered,
And o'er the past and present pondered,
And thought upon the glorious dead
Who there in better cause had bled,
He felt how faint and feebly dim
The fame that could accrue to him,
Who cheered the band, and waved the sword,
A traitor in a turbaned horde;
And led them to the lawless siege,
Whose best success were sacrilege.
Not so had those his fancy numbered,
The chiefs whose dust around him slumbered;
Their phalanx marshalled on the plain,
Whose bulwarks were not then in vain.
They fell devoted, but undying;
The very gale their names seemed sighing;

The waters murmured of their name;
The woods were peopled with their fame;
The silent pillar, lone and grey,
Claimed kindred with their sacred clay;
Their spirits wrapped the dusky mountain,
Their memory sparkled o'er the fountain;
The meanest rill, the mightiest river
Rolled mingling with their fame for ever.
Despite of every yoke she bears,
That land is Glory's still and theirs!
'Tis still a watch-word to the earth:
When man would do a deed of worth
He points to Greece, and turns to tread,
So sanctioned, on the tyrant's head:
He looks to her, and rushes on
Where life is lost, or Freedom won.

XVI.

Still by the shore Alp mutely mused,
And wooed the freshness Night diffused.
There shrinks no ebb in that tideless sea,[i]
Which changeless rolls eternally;
So that wildest of waves, in their angriest mood,
Scarce break on the bounds of the land for a rood;
And the powerless moon beholds them flow,
Heedless if she come or go:
Calm or high, in main or bay,
On their course she hath no sway.
The rock unworn its base doth bare,
And looks o'er the surf, but it comes not there;

And the fringe of the foam may be seen below,

On the line that it left long ages ago:

A smooth short space of yellow sand

Between it and the greener land.

i. The reader need hardly be reminded that there are no perceptible tides in the Mediterranean.

He wandered on along the beach,

Till within the range of a carbine's reach

Of the leaguered wall; but they saw him not,

Or how could he 'scape from the hostile shot?

Did traitors lurk in the Christians' hold?

Were their hands grown stiff, or their hearts waxed cold?

I know not, in sooth; but from yonder wall

There flashed no fire, and there hissed no ball,

Though he stood beneath the bastion's frown,

That flanked the seaward gate of the town;

Though he heard the sound, and could almost tell

The sullen words of the sentinel,

As his measured step on the stone below

Clanked, as he paced it to and fro;

And he saw the lean dogs beneath the wall

Hold o'er the dead their Carnival,

Gorging and growling o'er carcass and limb;

They were too busy to bark at him!

From a Tartar's skull they had stripped the flesh,

As ye peel the fig when its fruit is fresh;

And their white tusks crunched o'er the whiter skull,[i]

As it slipped through their jaws, when their edge grew dull,

As they lazily mumbled the bones of the dead,

When they scarce could rise from the spot where they fed;

So well had they broken a lingering fast

With those who had fallen for that night's repast.

And Alp knew, by the turbans that rolled on the sand,

The foremost of these were the best of his band:

Crimson and green were the shawls of their wear,

And each scalp had a single long tuft of hair,[ii]

All die rest was shaven and bare.

The scalps were in the wild dog's maw,

The hair was tangled round his jaw:

But close by the shore, on the edge of the gulf,

There sat a vulture flapping a wolf,

Who had stolen from the hills, but kept away,

Scared by the dogs, from the human prey;

But he seized on his share of a steed that lay,

Picked by the birds, on the sands of the bay.

i. This spectacle I have seen, such as described, beneath the wall of the Seraglio at Constantinople, in the little cavities worn by the Bosphorus in the rock, a narrow terrace of which projects between the wall and the water. I think the fact is also mentioned in Hobhouse's *Travels*. The bodies were probably those of some refractory Janizaries.

ii. This tuft, or long lock, is left from a superstition that Mahomet will draw them into Paradise by it.

XVII.

Alp turned him from the sickening sight:

Never had shaken his nerves in fight;

But he better could brook to behold the dying,

Deep in the tide of their warm blood lying,

Scorched with the death-thirst, and writhing in vain,

Than the perishing dead who are past all pain.

There is something of pride in the perilous hour,

Whate'er be the shape in which Death may lower;

For Fame is there to say who bleeds,

And Honour's eye on daring deeds!

But when all is past, it is humbling to tread

O'er the weltering field of the tombless dead,

And see worms of the earth, and fowls of the air,

Beasts of the forest, all gathering there;

All regarding man as their prey,

All rejoicing in his decay.

XVIII.

There is a temple in ruin stands,

Fashioned by long forgotten hands;

Two or three columns, and many a stone,

Marble and granite, with grass o'ergrown!

Out upon Time! it will leave no more

Of the things to come than the things before!

Out upon Time! who for ever will leave

But enough of the past for the future to grieve

O'er that which hath been, and o'er that which must be:

What we have seen, our sons shall see;

Remnants of things that have passed away,

Fragments of stone, reared by creatures of clay!

XIX.

He sate him down at a pillar's base,

And passed his hand athwart his face;

Like one in dreary musing mood,

Declining was his attitude;

His head was drooping on his breast,

Fevered, throbbing, and oppressed;

And o'er his brow, so downward bent,

Oft his beating fingers went,

Hurriedly, as you may see

Your own run over the ivory key,

Ere the measured tone is taken

By the chords you would awaken.

There he sate all heavily,

As he heard the night-wind sigh.

Was it the wind through some hollow stone,

Sent that soft and tender moan?[i]

He lifted his head, and he looked on the sea,

But it was unrippled as glass may be;

He looked on the long grass—it waved not a blade:

How was that gentle sound conveyed?

He looked to the banners—each flag lay still,

So did the leaves on Cithæron's hill,

And he felt not a breath come over his cheek;

What did that sudden sound bespeak?

He turned to the left—is he sure of sight?

There sate a lady, youthful and bright!

i. I must here acknowledge a close, though unintentional, resemblance in these twelve lines to a passage in an unpublished poem of Mr. Coleridge, called "Christabel." It was not till after these lines were written that I heard that wild and singularly original and beautiful poem recited; and the MS. of that production I never saw till very recently, by the kindness of Mr. Coleridge himself, who, I hope, is convinced that I have not been a wilful plagiarist. The original idea undoubtedly pertains to Mr. Coleridge, whose poem has been composed above fourteen years. Let me conclude by a hope that he will not longer delay the publication of a production, of which I can only add my mite of approbation to the applause of far more competent judges.

XX.

He started up with more of fear

Than if an armèd foe were near.

"God of my fathers! what is here?

Who art thou? and wherefore sent
So near a hostile armament?"
His trembling hands refused to sign
The cross he deemed no more divine:
He had resumed it in that hour,"-
But Conscience wrung away the power.
He gazed, he saw; he knew the face
Of beauty, and the form of grace;
It was Francesca by his side,
The maid who might have been his bride!

The rose was yet upon her cheek,
But mellowed with a tenderer streak:
Where was the play of her soft lips fled?
Gone was the smile that enlivened their red.
The Ocean's calm within their view,
Beside her eye had less of blue;
But like that cold wave it stood still,
And its glance, though clear, was chill.
Around her form a thin robe twining,
Nought concealed her bosom shining;
Through the parting of her hair,
Floating darkly downward there,
Her rounded arm showed white and bare:
And ere yet she made reply,
Once she raised her hand on high;
It was so wan, and transparent of hue,
You might have seen the moon shine through.

XXI.

"I come from my rest to him I love best,

That I may be happy, and he may be blessed.

I have passed the guards, the gate, the wall;

Sought thee in safety through foes and all.

'Tis said the lion will turn and flee

From a maid in the pride of her purity

And the Power on high, that can shield the good

Thus from the tyrant of the wood,

Hath extended its mercy to guard me as well

From the hands of the leaguering Infidel.

I come—and if I come in vain,

Never, oh never, we meet again!

Thou hast done a fearful deed

In falling away from thy fathers' creed:

But dash that turban to earth, and sign

The sign of the cross, and for ever be mine;

Wring the black drop from thy heart,

And to-morrow unites us no more to part."

"And where should our bridal couch be spread?

In the midst of the dying and the dead?

For to-morrow we give to the slaughter and flame

The sons and the shrines of the Christian name.

None, save thou and thine, I've sworn,

Shall be left upon the morn:

But thee will I bear to a lovely spot,

Where our hands shall be joined, and our sorrow forgot.

There thou yet shalt be my bride,

When once again I've quelled the pride
Of Venice; and her hated race
Have felt the arm they would debase
Scourge, with a whip of scorpions, those
Whom Vice and Envy made my foes."

Upon his hand she laid her own—
Light was the touch, but it thrilled to the bone,
And shot a chillness to his heart,
Which fixed him beyond the power to start.
Though slight was that grasp so mortal cold,
He could not loose him from its hold;
But never did clasp of one so dear
Strike on the pulse with such feeling of fear,
As those thin fingers, long and white,
Froze through his blood by their touch that night.
The feverish glow of his brow was gone,
And his heart sank so still that it felt like stone,
As he looked on the face, and beheld its hue,
So deeply changed from what he knew:
Fair but faint—without the ray
Of mind, that made each feature play
Like sparkling waves on a sunny day;
And her motionless lips lay still as death,
And her words came forth without her breath,
And there rose not a heave o'er her bosom's swell,
And there seemed not a pulse in her veins to dwell.
Though her eye shone out, yet the lids were fixed,
And the glance that it gave was wild and unmixed

With aught of change, as the eyes may seem
Of the restless who walk in a troubled dream;
Like the figures on arras, that gloomily glare,
Stirred by the breath of the wintry air
So seen by the dying lamp's fitful light,
Lifeless, but life-like, and awful to sight;
As they seem, through the dimness, about to come down
From the shadowy wall where their images frown;
Fearfully flitting to and fro,
As the gusts on the tapestry come and go.

"If not for love of me be given
Thus much, then, for the love of Heaven,—
Again I say—that turban tear
From off thy faithless brow, and swear
Thine injured country's sons to spare,
Or thou art lost; and never shalt see—
Not earth—that's past—but Heaven or me.
If this thou dost accord, albeit
A heavy doom 'tis thine to meet,
That doom shall half absolve thy sin,
And Mercy's gate may receive thee within:
But pause one moment more, and take
The curse of Him thou didst forsake;
And look once more to Heaven, and see
Its love for ever shut from thee.
There is a light cloud by the moon—[i]
'Tis passing, and will pass full soon—
If, by the time its vapoury sail

Hath ceased her shaded orb to veil,

Thy heart within thee is not changed,

Then God and man are both avenged;

Dark will thy doom be, darker still

Thine immortality of ill."

i. I have been told that the idea expressed in this and the five following lines has been admired by those whose approbation is valuable. I am glad of it; but it is not original—at least not mine; it may be found much better expressed in pages 182–3–4 of the English version of "Vathek" (I forget the precise page of the French), a work to which I have before referred; and never recur to, or read, without a renewal of gratification.

Alp looked to heaven, and saw on high

The sign she spake of in the sky;

But his heart was swollen, and turned aside,

By deep interminable pride.

This first false passion of his breast

Rolled like a torrent o'er the rest.

He sue for mercy! *He* dismayed

By wild words of a timid maid!

He, wronged by Venice, vow to save

Her sons, devoted to the grave!

No—though that cloud were thunder's worst,

And charged to crush him—let it burst!

He looked upon it earnestly,

Without an accent of reply;

He watched it passing; it is flown:

Full on his eye the clear moon shone,

And thus he spake—"Whate'er my fate,

I am no changeling—'tis too late:

The reed in storms may bow and quiver,

Then rise again; the tree must shiver.

What Venice made me, I must be,

Her foe in all, save love to thee:

But thou art safe: oh, fly with me!"

He turned, but she is gone!

Nothing is there but the column stone.

Hath she sunk in the earth, or melted in air?

He saw not—he knew not—but nothing is there.

XXII.

The night is past, and shines the sun

As if that morn were a jocund one.

Lightly and brightly breaks away

The Morning from her mantle grey,

And the Noon will look on a sultry day.

Hark to the trump, and the drum,

And the mournful sound of the barbarous horn,

And the flap of the banners, that flit as they're borne,

And the neigh of the steed, and the multitude's hum,

And the clash, and the shout, "They come! they come!"

The horsetails[i] are plucked from the ground, and the sword

From its sheath; and they form, and but wait for the word.

Tartar, and Spahi, and Turcoman,

Strike your tents, and throng to the van;

Mount ye, spur ye, skirr the plain,

That the fugitive may flee in vain,

When he breaks from the town; and none escape,

Agèd or young, in the Christian shape;

While your fellows on foot, in a fiery mass,

Bloodstain the breach through which they pass.

The steeds are all bridled, and snort to the rein;

Curved is each neck, and flowing each mane;

White is the foam of their champ on the bit;

The spears are uplifted; the matches are lit;

The cannon are pointed, and ready to roar,

And crush the wall they have crumbled before:

Forms in his phalanx each Janizar;

Alp at their head; his right arm is bare,

So is the blade of his scimitar;

The Khan and the Pachas are all at their post;

The Vizier himself at the head of the host.

When the culverin's signal is fired, then on;

Leave not in Corinth a living one—

A priest at her altars, a chief in her halls,

A hearth in her mansions, a stone on her walls.

God and the prophet—Alla Hu!

Up to the skies with that wild halloo!

"There the breach lies for passage, the ladder to scale;

And your hands on your sabres, and how should ye fail?

He who first downs with the red cross may crave

His heart's dearest wish; let him ask it, and have!"

Thus uttered Coumourgi, the dauntless Vizier;

The reply was the brandish of sabre and spear,

And the shout of fierce thousands in joyous ire:—

Silence—hark to the signal—fire!

i. The horsetails, fixed upon a lance, a pacha's standard.

XXIII.

As the wolves, that headlong go

On the stately buffalo,

Though with fiery eyes, and angry roar,

And hoofs that stamp, and horns that gore,

He tramples on earth, or tosses on high

The foremost, who rush on his strength but to die

Thus against the wall they went,

Thus the first were backward bent;

Many a bosom, sheathed in brass,

Strewed the earth like broken glass,

Shivered by the shot, that tore

The ground whereon they moved no more:

Even as they fell, in files they lay,

Like the mower's grass at the close of day,

When his work is done on the levelled plain;

Such was the fall of the foremost slain.

XXIV.

As the spring-tides, with heavy plash,

From the cliffs invading dash

Huge fragments, sapped by the ceaseless flow,

Till white and thundering down they go,

Like the avalanche's snow

On the Alpine vales below;

Thus at length, outbreathed and worn,

Corinth's sons were downward borne

By the long and oft renewed

Charge of the Moslem multitude.

In firmness they stood, and in masses they fell,

Heaped by the host of the Infidel,

Hand to hand, and foot to foot:

Nothing there, save Death, was mute;

Stroke, and thrust, and flash, and cry

For quarter, or for victory,

Mingle there with the volleying thunder,

Which makes the distant cities wonder

How the sounding battle goes,

If with them, or for their foes;

If they must mourn, or may rejoice

In that annihilating voice,

Which pierces the deep hills through and through

With an echo dread and new:

You might have heard it, on that day,

O'er Salamis and Megara;

(We have heard the hearers say,)

Even unto Piræus' bay.

XXV.

From the point of encountering blades to the hilt,

Sabres and swords with blood were gilt;

But the rampart is won, and the spoil begun,

And all but the after carnage done.

Shriller shrieks now mingling come

From within the plundered dome:

Hark to the haste of flying feet,

That splash in the blood of the slippery street;

But here and there, where 'vantage ground

Against the foe may still be found,

Desperate groups, of twelve or ten,

Make a pause, and turn again—

With banded backs against the wall,

Fiercely stand, or fighting fall.

There stood an old man—his hairs were white,
But his veteran arm was full of might:
So gallantly bore he the brunt of the fray,
The dead before him, on that day,
In a semicircle lay;
Still he combated unwounded,
Though retreating, unsurrounded.
Many a scar of former fight
Lurked beneath his corslet bright:
But of every wound his body bore,
Each and all had been ta'en before:
Though agèd, he was so iron of limb,
Few of our youth could cope with him,
And the foes, whom he singly kept at bay,
Outnumbered his thin hairs of silver grey.
From right to left his sabre swept:
Many an Othman mother wept
Sons that were unborn, when dipped
His weapon first in Moslem gore,
Ere his years could count a score.
Of all he might have been the sire
Who fell that day beneath his ire:
For, sonless left long years ago,
His wrath made many a childless foe;
And since the day, when in the strait[i]
His only boy had met his fate,
His parent's iron hand did doom
More than a human hecatomb.
If shades by carnage be appeased,

Patroclus' spirit less was pleased

Than his, Minotti's son, who died

Where Asia's bounds and ours divide.

Buried he lay, where thousands before

For thousands of years were inhumed on the shore

What of them is left, to tell

Where they lie, and how they fell?

Not a stone on their turf, nor a bone in their graves;

But they live in the verse that immortally saves.

i. In the naval battle at the mouth of the Dardanelles, between the Venetians and the Turks.

XXVI.

Hark to the Allah shout! a band

Of the Mussulman bravest and best is at hand;

Their leader's nervous arm is bare,

Swifter to smite, and never to spare—

Unclothed to the shoulder it waves them on;

Thus in the fight is he ever known:

Others a gaudier garb may show,

To tempt the spoil of the greedy foe;

Many a hand's on a richer hilt,

But none on a steel more ruddily gilt;

Many a loftier turban may wear,—

Alp is but known by the white arm bare;

Look through the thick of the fight, 'tis there!

There is not a standard on that shore

So well advanced the ranks before;

There is not a banner in Moslem war

Will lure the Delhis half so far;

It glances like a falling star!

Where'er that mighty arm is seen,

The bravest be, or late have been;

There the craven cries for quarter

Vainly to the vengeful Tartar;

Or the hero, silent lying,

Scorns to yield a groan in dying;

Mustering his last feeble blow

'Gainst the nearest levelled foe,

Though faint beneath the mutual wound,

Grappling on the gory ground.

XXVII.

Still the old man stood erect,

And Alp's career a moment checked.

"Yield thee, Minotti; quarter take,

For thine own, thy daughter's sake."

"Never, Renegade-, never!

Though the life of thy gift would last for ever."

"Francesca!—Oh, my promised bride!

Must she too perish by thy pride!"

"She is safe."—"Where? where?"—"In Heaven;

From whence thy traitor soul is driven—

Far from thee, and undefiled."

Grimly then Minotti smiled,

As he saw Alp staggering bow

Before his words, as with a blow.

"Oh God! when died she?"—"Yesternight—
Nor weep I for her spirit's flight:
None of my pure race shall be
Slaves to Mahomet and thee—
Come on!"—That challenge is in vain —
Alp's already with the slain!
While Minotti's words were wreaking
More revenge in bitter speaking
Than his falchion's point had found,
Had the time allowed to wound,
From within the neighbouring porch
Of a long defended church,
Where the last and desperate few
Would the failing fight renew,
The sharp shot dashed Alp to the ground;
Ere an eye could view the wound
That crashed through the brain of the infidel,
Round he spun, and down he fell;
A flash like fire within his eyes
Blazed, as he bent no more to rise,
And then eternal darkness sunk
Through all the palpitating trunk;
Nought of life left, save a quivering
Where his limbs were slightly shivering:
They turned him on his back; his breast
And brow were stained with gore and dust,
And through his lips the life-blood oozed,
From its deep veins lately loosed;
But in his pulse there was no throb,

Nor on his lips one dying sob;
Sigh, nor word, nor struggling breath
Heralded his way to death:
Ere his very thought could pray,
Unaneled he passed away,
Without a hope from Mercy's aid,—
To the last a Renegade.

XXVIII.

Fearfully the yell arose
Of his followers, and his foes;
These in joy, in fury those:
Then again in conflict mixing,
Clashing swords, and spears transfixing,
Interchanged the blow and thrust,
Hurling warriors in the dust.
Street by street, and foot by foot,
Still Minotti dares dispute
The latest portion of the land
Left beneath his high command;
With him, aiding heart and hand,
The remnant of his gallant band.
Still the church is tenable,
Whence issued late the fated ball
That half avenged the city's fall,
When Alp, her fierce assailant, fell:
Thither bending sternly back,
They leave before a bloody track;
And, with their faces to the foe,
Dealing wounds with every blow,

The chief, and his retreating train,
Join to those within the fane;
There they yet may breathe awhile,
Sheltered by the massy pile.

XXIX.

Brief breathing-time! the turbaned host,
With added ranks and raging boast,
Press onwards with such strength and heat,
Their numbers balk their own retreat;
For narrow the way that led to the spot
Where still the Christians yielded not;
And the foremost, if fearful, may vainly try
Through the massy column to turn and fly;
They perforce must do or die.
They die; but ere their eyes could close,
Avengers o'er their bodies rose;
Fresh and furious, fast they fill
The ranks unthinncd. though slaughtered still;
And faint the weary Christians wax
Before the still renewed attacks:
And now the Othmans gain the gate;
Still resists its iron weight,
And still, all deadly aimed and hot,
From every crevice comes the shot;
From every shattered window pour
The volleys of the sulphurous shower:
But the portal wavering grows and weak —
The iron yields, the hinges creak—

It bends—it falls—and all is o'er;
Lost Corinth may resist no more!

XXX.

Darkly, sternly, and all alone,
Minotti stood o'er the altar stone:
Madonna's face upon him shone,
Tainted in heavenly hues above,
With eyes of light and looks of love;
And placed upon that holy shrine
To fix our thoughts on things divine,
When pictured there, we kneeling see
Her, and the boy-God on her knee,
Smiling sweetly on each prayer
To Heaven, as if to waft it there.
Still she smiled; even now she smiles,
Though slaughter streams along her aisles:
Minotti lifted his agèd eye,
And made the sign of a cross with a sigh,
Then seized a torch which blazed thereby;
And still he stood, while with steel and flame,
Inward and onward the Mussulman came.

XXXI.

The vaults beneath the mosaic stone
Contained the dead of ages gone;
Their names were on the graven floor,
But now illegible with gore;
The carvèd crests, and curious hues
The varied marble's veins diffuse,
Were smeared, and slippery—stained, and strown

With broken swords, and helms o'erthrown:
There were dead above, and the dead below
Lay cold in many a coffined row;
You might see them piled in sable state,
By a pale light through a gloomy grate;
But War had entered their dark caves,
And stored along the vaulted graves
Her sulphurous treasures, thickly spread
In masses by the fleshless dead:
Here, throughout the siege, had been
The Christians' chiefest magazine;
To these a late formed train now led,
Minotti's last and stern resource
Against the foe's o'erwhelming force.

XXXII.

The foe came on, and few remain
To strive, and those must strive in vain:
For lack of further lives, to slake
The thirst of vengeance now awake,
With barbarous blows they gash the dead,
And lop the already lifeless head,
And fell the statues from their niche,
And spoil the shrines of offerings rich,
And from each other's rude hands wrest
The silver vessels Saints had blessed.
To the high altar on they go;
Oh, but it made a glorious show!
On its table still behold
The cup of consecrated gold;

Massy and deep, a glittering prize,

Brightly it sparkles to plunderers' eyes:

That morn it held the holy wine,

Converted by Christ to his blood so divine,

Which his worshippers drank at the break of day,

To shrive their souls ere they joined in the fray.

Still a few drops within it lay;

And round the sacred table glow

Twelve lofty lamps, in splendid row,

From the purest metal cast;

A spoil—the richest, and the last.

XXXIII.

So near they came, the nearest stretched

To grasp the spoil he almost reached

When old Minotti's hand

Touched with the torch the train—

'Tis fired!

Spire, vaults, the shrine, the spoil, the slain,

The turbaned victors, the Christian band,

All that of living or dead remain,

Hurled on high with the shivered fane,

In one wild roar expired!

The shattered town—the walls thrown down—

The waves a moment backward bent—

The hills that shake, although unrent,

As if an Earthquake passed—

The thousand shapeless things all driven

In cloud and flame athwart the heaven,

By that tremendous blast—

Proclaimed the desperate conflict o'er

On that too long afflicted shore:

Up to the sky like rockets go

All that mingled there below:

Many a tall and goodly man,

Scorched and shrivelled to a span,

When he fell to earth again

Like a cinder strewed the plain:

Down the ashes shower like rain:

Some fell in the gulf, which received the sprinkles

With a thousand circling wrinkles:

Some fell on the shore, but, far away,

Scattered o'er the isthmus lay;

Christian or Moslem, which be they?

Let their mothers see and say!

When in cradled rest they lay,

And each nursing mother smiled

On the sweet sleep of her child,

Little deemed she such a day

Would rend those tender limbs away.

Not the matrons that them bore

Could discern their offspring more

That one moment left no trace

More of human form or face

Save a scattered scalp or bone:

And down came blazing rafters, strown

Around, and many a falling stone,

Deeply dinted in the clay,

All blackened there and reeking lay.

All the living things that heard

The deadly earth-shock disappeared:

The wild birds flew: the wild dogs fled,

And howling left the unburied dead;

The camels from their keepers broke;

The distant steer forsook the yoke—

The nearer steed plunged o'er the plain,

And burst his girth, and tore his rein;

The bull-frog's note, from out the marsh,

Deep-mouthed arose, and doubly harsh;

The wolves yelled on the caverned hill

Where Echo rolled in thunder still:

The jackal's troop, in gathered cry,[i]

Bayed from afar complainingly,

With a mixed and mournful sound,

Like crying babe, and beaten hound:

With sudden wing, and ruffled breast,

The eagle left his rocky nest,

And mounted nearer to the sun,

The clouds beneath him seemed so dun;

Their smoke assailed his startled beak,

And made him higher soar and shriek—

   Thus was Corinth lost and won!

i. I believe I have taken a poetical licence to transplant the jackal from Asia. In Greece I never saw nor heard these animals; but among the ruins of Ephesus I have heard them by hundreds. They haunt ruins, and follow armies.

PARISINA

ADVERTISEMENT

The following poem is grounded on a circumstance mentioned in Gibbon's "Antiquities of the House of Brunswick." I am aware, that in modern times, the delicacy or fastidiousness of the reader may deem such subjects unfit for the purposes of poetry. The Greek dramatists, and some of the best of our old English writers, were of a different opinion: as Alfieri and Schiller have also been, more recently, upon the Continent. The following extract will explain the facts on which the story is founded. The name of *Azo* is substituted for Nicholas, as more metrical.

"Under the reign of Nicholas III. Ferrara was polluted with a domestic tragedy. By the testimony of a maid, and his own observation, the Marquis of Este discovered the incestuous loves of his wife Parisina, and Hugo his bastard son, a beautiful and valiant youth. They were beheaded in the castle by the sentence of a father and husband, who published his shame, and survived the execution. he was unfortunate, if they were guilty: if they were innocent, he was still more unfortunate; nor is they any possible situation in which I can sincerely approve the last act of the justice of a parent."—GIBBON's *Miscellaneous Works*, vol. iii. p. 470.

"This turned out a calamitous year for the people of Ferrara, for there occurred a very tragical event in the court of their sovereign. Our annals, both printed and in manuscript, with the exception of the unpolished and negligent work of Sardi, and one other, have given the following relation of it,—from which, however, are rejected many details, and especially the narrative of Bandelli, who wrote a century afterwards, and who does not accord with the contemporary historians.

"By the above-mentioned Stella dell' Assassino, the Marquis, in the year 1405, had a son called Ugo, a beautiful and ingenuous youth. Parisina Malatesta, second wife of Niccolo, like the generality of step-mothers, treated him with little kindness, to the infinite regret of the Marquis, who regarded him with fond partiality. One day she asked leave of her husband to undertake a certain journey, to which he consented, but upon condition that Ugo should bear her company; for he hoped by these means to induce her, in the end, to lay aside the obstinate aversion which she had conceived against him. And indeed his intent was accomplished but too well, since, during the journey, she not only divested herself of all her hatred, but fell into the opposite extreme. After their return, the Marquis had no longer any occasion to renew his former reproofs. It happened one day that a servant of the Marquis, named Zoese, or, as some call him, Giorgio, passing before the apartments of Parisina, saw going out from them one of her chamber-maids, all terrified and in tears. Asking the reason, she told him that her mistress, for some slight offence, had been beating her; and, giving vent to her rage, she added, that she could easily be revenged, if she chose to make known the criminal familiarity which subsisted between Parisina and her step-son. The servant took note of the words, and related them to his master. He was astounded thereat, but, scarcely believing his ears, he assured himself of the fact, alas! too clearly, on the 18th of May, by looking through a hole made in the ceiling of his wife's chamber. Instantly he broke into a furious rage, and arrested both of them, together with Aldobrandino Rangoni, of Modena, her gentleman, and also, as some say, two of the women of her chamber, as abettors of this sinful act. He ordered them to be brought to a hasty trial, desiring the judges to pronounce sentence, in the accustomed forms, upon the culprits. This sentence was death. Some there were that bestirred themselves in favour of the delinquents, and, amongst others, Ugoccion Contrario, who was all-powerful with Niccolo, and also his aged and much deserving minister Alberto dal Sale. Both of these, their tears flowing down their cheeks, and upon their knees, implored him for mercy; adducing whatever reasons they could suggest for sparing the offenders, besides those motives of honour and decency which might persuade him to conceal from the public so scandalous a deed. But his rage made him inflexible, and, on the instant, he commanded that the sentence should be put in execution.

"It was, then, in the prisons of the castle, and exactly in those frightful dungeons which are seen at this day beneath the chamber called the Aurora, at the foot of the Lion's tower, at the top of the street Giovecca, that on the night of the 21st of May were beheaded, first, Ugo, and afterwards Parisina. Zoese, he that accused her, conducted the latter under his arm to the place of punishment. She, all along, fancied that she was to be thrown into a pit, and asked at every step, whether she was yet come to the spot? She was told that her punishment was the axe. She enquired what was become of Ugo, and received for answer, that he was already dead; at which, sighing grievously, she exclaimed, 'Now, then, I wish not myself to live;' and, being come to the block, she stripped herself, with her own hands, of all her ornaments, and, wrapping a cloth round her head, submitted to the fatal stroke, which terminated the cruel scene. The same was done with Rangoni, who, together with the others, according to two calendars in the library of St. Francesco, was buried in the cemetery of that convent. Nothing else is known respecting the women.

"The Marquis kept watch the whole of that dreadful night, and, as he was walking backwards and forwards, enquired of the captain of the castle if Ugo was dead yet? who answered him, Yes. He then gave himself up to the most desperate lamentations, exclaiming, 'Oh! that I too were dead, since I have been hurried on to resolve thus against my own Ugo!' And then gnawing with his teeth a cane which he had in his hand, he passed the rest of the night in sighs and in tears, calling frequently upon his own dear Ugo. On the following day, calling to mind that it would be necessary to make public his justification, seeing that the transaction could not be kept secret, he ordered the narrative to be drawn out upon paper, and sent it to all the courts of Italy.

"On receiving this advice, the Doge of Venice, Francesco Foscari, gave orders, but without publishing his reasons, that stop should be put to the preparations for a tournament, which, under the auspices of the Marquis, and at the expense of the city of Padua, was about to take place, in the square of St. Mark, in order to celebrate his advancement to the ducal chair.

"The Marquis, in addition to what he had already done, from some unaccountable burst of vengeance, commanded that as many of the married women as were well known to him to be faithless, like his Parisina, should, like her, be beheaded. Amongst others, Barberina, or, as some call her, Laodamia Romei, wife of the court judge, underwent this sentence, at the usual place of execution; that is to say, in the quarter of St. Giacomo, opposite the present fortress, beyond St. Paul's. It cannot be told how strange appeared this proceeding in a prince, who, considering his own disposition, should, as it seemed, have been in such cases most indulgent. Some, however, there were who did not fail to commend him."

I.

It is the hour when from the boughs

    The nightingale's high note is heard;

It is the hour when lovers' vows

    Seem sweet in every whispered word;

And gentle winds, and waters near,

Make music to the lonely ear.

Each flower the dews have lightly wet,

And in the sky the stars are met,

And on the wave is deeper blue,

And on the leaf a browner hue,

And in the heaven that clear obscure,

So softly dark, and darkly pure,

Which follows the decline of day,

As twilight melts beneath the moon away.[i]

i. The lines contained in this section were printed as set to music some time since,
but belonged to the poem where they now appear; the greater part of which was
composed prior to *Lara*, and other compositions since published.

II.

But it is not to list to the waterfall

That Parisina leaves her hall,

And it is not to gaze on the heavenly light

That the Lady walks in the shadow of night;

And if she sits in Este's bower,

'Tis not for the sake of its full-blown flower;

She listens—but not for the nightingale—

Though her ear expects as soft a tale.

There glides a step through the foliage thick,

And her cheek grows pale, and her heart beats quick.

There whispers a voice through the rustling leaves,

And her blush returns, and her bosom heaves:

A moment more—and they shall meet—

'Tis past—her Lover's at her feet.

III.

And what unto them is the world beside,

With all its change of time and tide?

Its living things—its earth and sky—

Are nothing to their mind and eye.

And heedless as the dead are they

  Of aught around, above, beneath;

As if all else had passed away,

  They only for each other breathe;

Their very sighs are full of joy

So deep, that did it not decay,

That happy madness would destroy

The hearts which feel its fiery sway:

Of guilt, of peril, do they deem

In that tumultuous tender dream?

Who that have felt that passion's power,

Or paused, or feared in such an hour?

Or thought how brief such moments last?

But yet—they are already past!

Alas! we must awake before

We know such vision comes no more.

IV.

With many a lingering look they leave

The spot of guilty gladness past:

And though they hope, and vow, they grieve,

As if that parting were the last.

The frequent sigh—the long embrace—

The lip that there would cling for ever,

While gleams on Parisina's face

The Heaven she fears will not forgive her,

As if each calmly conscious star

Beheld her frailty from afar—

The frequent sigh, the long embrace,

Yet binds them to their trysting-place.

But it must come, and they must part

In fearful heaviness of heart,

With all the deep and shuddering chill

Which follows fast the deeds of ill.

V.

And Hugo is gone to his lonely bed,
　　To covet there another's bride;
But she must lay her conscious head
　　A husband's trusting heart beside.
But fevered in her sleep she seems,
And red her cheek with troubled dreams,
　　And mutters she in her unrest
A name she dare not breathe by day,
　　And clasps her Lord unto the breast
Which pants for one away:
And he to that embrace awakes,
And, happy in the thought, mistakes
That dreaming sigh, and warm caress,
For such as he was wont to bless;
And could in very fondness weep
O'er her who loves him even in sleep.

VI.

He clasped her sleeping to his heart,
　　And listened to each broken word:
He hears—Why doth Prince Azo start,
　　As if the Archangel's voice he heard?
And well he may--a deeper doom
Could scarcely thunder o'er his tomb,
When he shall wake to sleep no more,
And stand the eternal throne before.
And well he may—his earthly peace
Upon that sound is doomed to cease.
That sleeping whisper of a name

Bespeaks her guilt and Azo's shame.

And whose that name? that o'er his pillow

Sounds fearful as the breaking billow,

Which rolls the plank upon the shore,

    And dashes on the pointed rock

The wretch who sinks to rise no more,—

    So came upon his soul the shock.

And whose that name?—'tis Hugo's,—his—,

In sooth he had not deemed of this!—

'Tis Hugo's,—he, the child of one

He loved—his own all-evil son—

The offspring of his wayward youth,

When he betrayed Bianca's truth,

  The maid whose folly could confide

In him who made her not his bride.

VII.

He plucked his poniard in its sheath,

    But sheathed it ere the point was bare;

Howe'er unworthy now to breathe,

    He could not slay a thing so fair—

    At least, not smiling—sleeping—there—

Nay, more:—he did not wake her then,

    But gazed upon her with a glance

    Which, had she roused her from her trance,

Had frozen her sense to sleep again;

And o'er his brow the burning lamp

Gleamed on the dew-drops big and damp.

She spake no more—but still she slumbered—

While, in his thought, her days are numbered.

And with the morn he sought and found,
In many a tale from those around,
The proof of all he feared to know,
Their present guilt—his future woe;
The long-conniving damsels seek
  To save themselves, and would transfer
  The guilt—the shame—the doom—to her:
Concealment is no more—they speak
All circumstance which may compel
Full credence to the tale they tell:
And Azo's tortured heart and ear
Have nothing more to feel or hear.

                IX.

He was not one who brooked delay:
  Within the chamber of his state,
The Chief of Este's ancient sway
  Upon his throne of judgement sate;
His nobles and his guards are there,—
Before him is the sinful pair;
Both young,—and *one* how passing fair!
With swordless belt, and fettered hand,
Oh, Christ! that thus a son should stand
  Before a father's face!
Yet thus must Hugo meet his sire,
And hear the sentence of his ire,
  The tale of his disgrace!
And yet he seems not overcome,
Although, as yet, his voice be dumb.

X.

And still,—and pale—and silently
    Did Parisina wait her doom;
How changed since last her speaking eye
    Glanced gladness round the glittering room,
Where high-born men were proud to wait—
Where Beauty watched to imitate
    Her gentle voice—her lovely mien—
And gather from her air and gait
    The graces of its Queen:
Then,—had her eye in sorrow wept,
A thousand warriors forth had leapt,
A thousand swords had sheathless shone,
And made her quarrel all their own.
Now,—what is she? and what are they
Can she command, or these obey?
All silent and unheeding now,
With downcast eyes and knitting brow,
And folded arms, and freezing air,
And lips that scarce their scorn forbear,
Her knights, her dames, her court—is there:
And he—the chosen one, whose lance
Had yet been couched before her glance,
Who—were his arm a moment free—
Had died or gained her liberty;
The minion of his father's bride,—
He, too, is fettered by her side;
Nor sees her swoln and full eye swim
Less for her own despair than him:

Those lids—o'er which the violet vein
Wandering, leaves a tender stain,
Shining through the smoothest white
That e'er did softest kiss invite—
Now seemed with hot and livid glow
To press, not shade, the orbs below;
Which glance so heavily, and fill,
As tear on tear grows gathering still.

XI.

And he for her had also wept,
    But for the eyes that on him gazed:
His sorrow, if he felt it, slept;
    Stern and erect his brow was raised.
Whate'er the grief his soul avowed,
He would not shrink before the crowd;
But yet he dared not look on her;
Remembrance of the hours that were—
His guilt—his love—his present state—
His father's wrath, all good men's hate—
His earthly, his eternal fate—
And hers,—oh, hers! he dared not throw
One look upon that death-like brow!
Else had his rising heart betrayed
Remorse for all the wreck it made.

XII.

And Azo spake:—"But yesterday
    I gloried in a wife and son;
That dream this morning passed away;
    Ere day declines, I shall have none.

My life must linger on alone;

Well,—let that pass,—there breathes not one

Who would not do as I have done:

Those ties are broken—not by me;

    Let that too pass;—the doom's prepared!

Hugo, the priest awaits on thee,

    And then—thy crime's reward!

Away! address thy prayers to Heaven;

    Before its evening stars are met,

Learn if thou there canst be forgiven;

    Its mercy may absolve thee yet.

But here, upon the earth beneath,

    There is no spot where thou and I

Together for an hour could breathe:

    Farewell! I will not see thee die—

But thou, frail thing! shalt view his head—

    Away! I cannot speak the rest:

    Go! woman of the wanton breast;

Not I, but thou his blood dost shed:

Go! if that sight thou canst outlive,

And joy thee in the life I give."

XIII.

And here stern Azo hid his face—

    For on his brow the swelling vein

    Throbbed as if back upon his brain

    The hot blood ebbed and flowed again;

And therefore bowed he for a space,

    And passed his shaking hand along

    His eye, to veil it from the throng;

While Hugo raised his chainèd hands,
And for a brief delay demands
His father's ear: the silent sire
Forbids not what his words require.
  "It is not that I dread the death—
For thou hast seen me by thy side
All redly through the battle ride,
And that—not once a useless brand—
Thy slaves have wrested from my hand
Hath shed more blood in cause of thine,
Than e'er can stain the axe of mine:
    Thou gav'st, and may'st resume my breath,
A gift for which I thank thee not;
Nor are my mother's wrongs forgot,
Her slighted love and ruined name,
Her offspring's heritage of shame;
But she is in the grave, where he,
Her son—thy rival—soon shall be.
Her broken heart—my severed head—
Shall witness for thee from the dead
How trusty and how tender were
Thy youthful love—paternal care.
'Tis true that I have done thee wrong—
    But wrong for wrong:—this,—deemed thy bride,
    The other victim of thy pride,—
Thou know'st for me was destined long;
Thou saw'st, and coveted'st her charms;
    And with thy very crime—my birth,—
    Thou taunted'st me—as little worth;

A match ignoble for her arms;

Because, forsooth, I could not claim

The lawful heirship of thy name,

Nor sit on Este's lineal throne;

    Yet, were a few short summers mine,

    My name should more than Este's shine

With honours all my own.

I had a sword—and have a breast

That should have won as haught1 a crest

As ever waved along the line

Of all these sovereign sires of thine.

Not always knightly spurs are worn

The brightest by the better born;

And mine have lanced my courser's flank

Before proud chiefs of princely rank,

When charging to the cheering cry

Of 'Este and of Victory!'

I will not plead the cause of crime,

Nor sue thee to redeem from time

A few brief hours or days that must

At length roll o'er my reckless dust;—

Such maddening moments as my past,

They could not, and they did not, last;—

Albeit my birth and name be base,

And thy nobility of race

Disdained to deck a thing like me—

    Yet in my lineaments they trace

    Some features of my father's face,

And in my spirit—all of thee.

From thee this tamelessness of heart—
From thee—nay, wherefore dost thou start?—
From thee in all their vigour came
My arm of strength, my soul of flame—
Thou didst not give me life alone,
But all that made me more thine own.
See what thy guilty love hath done!
Repaid thee with too like a son!
I am no bastard in my soul,
For that, like thine, abhorred control;
And for my breath, that hasty boon
Thou gav'st and wilt resume so soon,
I valued it no more than thou,
When rose thy casque above thy brow,
And we, all side by side, have striven,
And o'er the dead our coursers driven:
The past is nothing—and at last
The future can but be the past;
Yet would I that I then had died:
    For though thou work'dst my mother's ill,
And made thy own my destined bride,
    I feel thou art my father still:
And harsh as sounds thy hard decree,
'Tis not unjust, although from thee.
Begot in sin, to die in shame,
My life begun and ends the same:
As erred the sire, so erred the son,
And thou must punish both in one.

My crime seems worst to human view,

But God must judge between us too!"

i. Haught—haughty. "Away, *haught* man, thou art insulting me."—SHAKESPEARE.

XIV.

He ceased—and stood with folded arms,

On which the circling fetters sounded;

And not an ear but felt as wounded,

Of all the chiefs that there were ranked,

When those dull chains in meeting clanked:

Till Parisina's fatal charms

Again attracted every eye—

Would she thus hear him doomed to die!

She stood, I said, all pale and still,

The living cause of Hugo's ill:

Her eyes unmoved, but full and wide,

Not once had turned to either side—

Nor once did those sweet eyelids close,

Or shade the glance o'er which they rose,

But round their orbs of deepest blue

The circling white dilated grew—

And there with glassy gaze she stood

As ice were in her curdled blood;

But every now and then a tear

So large and slowly gathered slid

From the long dark fringe of that fair lid,

It was a thing to see, not hear!

And those who saw, it did surprise,

Such drops could fall from human eyes.

To speak she thought—the imperfect note

Was choked within her swelling throat,
Yet seemed in that low hollow groan
Her whole heart gushing in the tone.
It ceased—again she thought to speak,
Then burst her voice in one long shriek,
And to the earth she fell like stone
Or statue from its base o'erthrown,
More like a thing that ne'er had life,—
A monument of Azo's wife,—
Than her, that living guilty thing,
Whose every passion was a sting,
Which urged to guilt, but could not bear
That guilt's detection and despair.
But yet she lived—and all too soon
Recovered from that death-like swoon—
But scarce to reason—every sense
Had been o'erstrung by pangs intense
And each frail fibre of her brain ' '"
(As bowstrings, when relaxed by rain,
The erring arrow launch aside)
Sent forth her thoughts all wild and wide—
The past a blank, the future black,
With glimpses of a dreary track,
Like lightning on the desert path,
When midnight storms are mustering wrath.
She feared—she felt that something ill
Lay on her soul, so deep and chill;
That there was sin and shame she knew,
That some one was to die—but who?

She had forgotten:—did she breathe?

Could this be still the earth beneath,

The sky above, and men around;

Or were they fiends who now so frowned

On one, before whose eyes each eye

Till then had smiled in sympathy?

All was confused and undefined

To her all-jarred and wandering mind;

A chaos of wild hopes and fears:

And now in laughter, now in tears,

But madly still in each extreme,

She strove with that convulsive dream;

For so it seemed on her to break:

Oh! vainly must she strive to wake!

XV.

The Convent bells are ringing,

    But mournfully and slow;

In the grey square turret swinging,

    With a deep sound, to and fro.

    Heavily to the heart they go!

Hark! the hymn is singing—

    The song for the dead below,

    Or the living who shortly shall be so!

For a departed being's soul

The death-hymn peals and the hollow bells knoll:

He is near his mortal goal;

Kneeling at the Friar's knee,

Sad to hear, and piteous to see—

Kneeling on the bare cold ground,

With the block before and the guards around;
And the headsman with his bare arm ready,
That the blow may be both swift and steady,
Feels if the axe be sharp and true
Since he set its edge anew:
While the crowd in a speechless circle gather
To see the Son fall by the doom of the Father!

XVI.

It is a lovely hour as yet
Before the summer sun shall set,
Which rose upon that heavy day,
And mock'd it with his steadiest ray;
And his evening beams are shed
Full on Hugo's fated head,
As his last confession pouring
To the monk, his doom deploring
In penitential holiness,
He bends to hear his accents bless
With absolution such as may
Wipe our mortal stains away.
That high sun on his head did glisten
As he there did bow and listen,
And the rings of chestnut hair
Curled half down his neck so bare;
But brighter still the beam was thrown
Upon the axe which near him shone
With a clear and ghastly glitter—
Oh! that parting hour was bitter!
Even the stern stood chilled with awe:

Dark the crime, and just the law—
Yet they shuddered as they saw.

XVII.

The parting prayers are said and over
Of that false son, and daring lover!
His beads and sins are all recounted,
His hours to their last minute mounted;
His mantling cloak before was stripped,
His bright brown locks must now be clipped;
'Tis done—all closely are they shorn;
The vest which till this moment worn—
The scarf which Parisina gave—
Must not adorn him to the grave.
Even that must now be thrown aside,
And o'er his eyes the kerchief tied;
But no—that last indignity
Shall ne'er approach his haughty eye.
All feelings seemingly subdued,
In deep disdain were half renewed,
When headsman's hands prepared to bind
Those eyes which would not brook such blind,
As if they dared not look on death.
"No—yours my forfeit blood and breath;
These hands are chained, but let me die
At least with an unshackled eye—
Strike:"—and as the word he said,
Upon the block he bowed his head;
These the last accents Hugo spoke:
"Strike"—and flashing fell the stroke—

Rolled the head—and, gushing, sunk
Back the stained and heaving trunk,
In the dust, which each deep vein
Slaked with its ensanguined rain;
His eyes and lips a moment quiver,
Convulsed and quick—then fix for ever.

He died, as erring man should die,
   Without display, without parade;
   Meekly had he bowed and prayed,
   As not disdaining priestly aid,
Nor desperate of all hope on high.
And while before the Prior kneeling,
His heart was weaned from earthly feeling;
His wrathful Sire—his Paramour—
What were they in such an hour?
No more reproach,—no more despair,—
No thought but Heaven,—no word but prayer—
Save the few which from him broke,
When, bared to meet the headsman's stroke,
He claimed to die with eyes unbound,
His sole adieu to those around.

XVIII.

Still as the lips that closed in death,
Each gazer's bosom held his breath:
But yet, afar, from man to man,
A cold electric shiver ran,
As down the deadly blow descended
On him whose life and love thus ended;

And, with a hushing sound compressed,

A sigh shrunk back on every breast;

But no more thrilling noise rose there,

Beyond the blow that to the block

Pierced through with forced and sullen shock,

Save one:—what cleaves the silent air

So madly shrill, so passing wild?

That, as a mother's o'er her child,

Done to death by sudden blow,

To the sky these accents go,

Like a soul's in endless woe.

Through Azo's palace-lattice driven,

That horrid voice ascends to heaven,

And every eye is turned thereon;

But sound and sight alike are gone!

It was a woman's shriek—and ne'er

In madlier accents rose despair;

And those who heard it, as it past,

In mercy wished it were the last.

XIX.

Hugo is fallen; and, from that hour,

No more in palace, hall, or bower,

Was Parisina heard or seen:

Her name—as if she ne'er had been—

Was banished from each lip and ear,

Like words of wantonness or fear;

And from Prince Azo's voice, by none

Was mention heard of wife or son;

No tomb—no memory had they;

Theirs was unconsecrated clay—

At least the Knight's who died that day.

But Parisina's fate lies hid

Like dust beneath the coffin lid:

Whether in convent she abode,

And won to heaven her dreary road,

By blighted and remorseful years

Of scourge, and fast, and sleepless tears;

Or if she fell by bowl or steel,

For that dark love she dared to feel;

Or if, upon the moment smote,

She died by tortures less remote,

Like him she saw upon the block

With heart that shared the headsman's shock

In quickened brokenness that came,

In pity o'er her shattered frame,

None knew—and none can ever know:

But whatsoe'er its end below,

Her life began and closed in woe!

XX.

And Azo found another bride,

And goodly sons grew by his side;

But none so lovely and so brave

As him who withered in the grave;

Or if they were—on his cold eye

Their growth but glanced unheeded by,

Or noticed with a smothered sigh.

But never tear his cheek descended,

And never smile his brow unbended;

And o'er that fair broad brow were wrought
The intersected lines of thought;
Those furrows which the burning share
Of Sorrow ploughs untimely there;
Scars of the lacerating mind
Which the Soul's war doth leave behind.
He was past all mirth or woe:
Nothing more remained below
But sleepless nights and heavy days,
A mind all dead to scorn or praise,
A heart which shunned itself—and yet
That would not yield, nor could forget,
Which, when it least appeared to melt,
Intensely thought—intensely felt:
The deepest ice which ever froze
Can only o'er the surface close;
The living stream lies quick below,
And flows, and cannot cease to flow.
Still was his sealed-up bosom haunted
By thoughts which Nature hath implanted;
Too deeply rooted thence to vanish,
Howe'er our stifled tears we banish;
When struggling as they rise to start,
We check those waters of the heart,
They are not dried—those tears unshed
But flow back to the fountain head,
And resting in their spring more pure,
For ever in its depth endure,
Unseen—unwept—but uncongealed,

And cherished most where least revealed.
With inward starts of feeling left,
To throb o'er those of life bereft,
Without the power to fill again
The desert gap which made his pain;
Without the hope to meet them where
United souls shall gladness share;
With all the consciousness that he
Had only passed a just decree;
That they had wrought their doom of ill;
Yet Azo's age was wretched still.
The tainted branches of the tree,
     If lopped with care, a strength may give,
     By which the rest shall bloom and live
All greenly fresh and wildly free:
But if the lightning, in its wrath,
The waving boughs with fury scathe,
The massy trunk the ruin feels,
And never more a leaf reveals.

POEMS OF THE SEPARATION

FARE THEE WELL

"Alas! they had been friends in youth;
But whispering tongues can poison truth:
And Constancy lives in realms above;
And Life is thorny; and youth is vain:
And to be wroth with one we love,
Doth work like madness in the brain;
　　　　*　　*　　*　　*　　*

But never either found another
To free the hollow heart from paining—
They stood aloof, the scars remaining,
Like cliffs which had been rent asunder;
A dreary sea now flows between,
But neither heat, nor frost, nor thunder,
Shall wholly do away, I ween,
The marks of that which once hath been."
　　COLERIDGE's *Christabel.*

Fare thee well! and if for ever,

　　Still for ever, fare *thee well*:

Even though unforgiving, never

　　'Gainst thee shall my heart rebel.

Would that breast were bared before thee

　　Where thy head so oft hath lain,

While that placid sleep came o'er thee

　　Which thou ne'er canst know again:

Would that breast, by thee glanced over,

　　Every inmost thought could show!

Then thou would'st at last discover

　　'Twas not well to spurn it so.

Though the world for this commend thee—
  Though it smile upon the blow,
Even its praises must offend thee,
  Founded on another's woe:
Though my many faults defaced me,
  Could no other arm be found,
Than the one which once embraced me,
  To inflict a cureless wound?

Yet, oh yet, thyself deceive not—
  Love may sink by slow decay,
But by sudden wrench, believe not
  Hearts can thus be torn away:
Still thine own its life retaineth—
  Still must mine, though bleeding, beat;
And the undying thought which paineth
  Is—that we no more may meet.

These are words of deeper sorrow
  Than the wail above the dead;
Both shall live—but every morrow
  Wake us from a widowed bed.
And when thou would'st solace gather—
  When our child's first accents flow—
Wilt thou teach her to say "Father!"
  Though his care she must forego?

When her little hands shall press thee—
  When her lip to thine is pressed—
Think of him whose prayer shall bless thee—
  Think of him thy love *had* blessed!
Should her lineaments resemble

Those thou never more may'st see,

Then thy heart will softly tremble

With a pulse yet true to me.

All my faults perchance thou knowest—

All my madness—none can know;

All my hopes—where'er thou goest—

Wither—yet with *thee* they go.

Every feeling hath been shaken;

Pride—which not a world could bow—

Bows to thee—by thee forsaken,

Even my soul forsakes me now.

But 'tis done—all words are idle—

Words from me are vainer still;

But the thoughts we cannot bridle

Force their way without the will.

Fare thee well! thus disunited—

Torn from every nearer tie—

Seared in heart—and lone—and blighted—

More than this I scarce can die.

A SKETCH

"Honest—honest Iago!
If that thou be'st a devil, I cannot kill thee."
SHAKESPEARE.

Born in the garret, in the kitchen bred,

Promoted thence to deck her mistress' head;

Next—for some gracious service unexpressed,

And from its wages only to be guessed—

Raised from the toilet to the table,—where

Her wondering betters wait behind her chair.

With eye unmoved, and forehead unabashed,

She dines from off the plate she lately washed.

Quick with the tale, and ready with the lie,

The genial confidante, and general spy—

Who could, ye gods! her next employment guess—

An only infant's earliest governess!

She taught the child to read, and taught so well,

That she herself, by teaching, learned to spell.

An adept next in penmanship she grows,

As many a nameless slander deftly shows:

What she had made the pupil of her art,

None know—but that high Soul secured the heart,

And panted for the truth it could not hear,

With longing breast and undeluded ear.

Foiled was perversion by that youthful mind,

Which Flattery fooled not, Baseness could not blind,

Deceit infect not, near Contagion soil,

Indulgence weaken, nor Example spoil,

Nor mastered Science tempt her to look down

On humbler talents with a pitying frown,

Nor Genius swell, nor Beauty render vain,

Nor Envy ruffle to retaliate pain,

Nor Fortune change, Pride raise, nor Passion bow,

Nor Virtue teach austerity—till now.

Serenely purest of her sex that live,

But wanting one sweet weakness—to forgive;

Too shocked at faults her soul can never know,

She deems that all could be like her below:

Foe to all vice, yet hardly Virtue's friend,
For Virtue pardons those she would amend.

But to the theme, now laid aside too long,
The baleful burthen of this honest song,
Though all her former functions are no more,
She rules the circle which she served before.
If mothers—none know why—before her quake;
If daughters dread her for the mothers' sake;
If early habits—those false links, which bind
At times the loftiest to the meanest mind—
Have given her power too deeply to instil
The angry essence of her deadly will;
If like a snake she steal within your walls,
Till the black slime betray her as she crawls;
If like a viper to the heart she wind,
And leave the venom there she did not find;
What marvel that this hag of hatred works
Eternal evil latent as she lurks,
To make a Pandemonium where she dwells,
And reign the Hecate of domestic hells?
Skilled by a touch to deepen Scandal's tints
With all the kind mendacity of hints,
While mingling truth with falsehood—sneers with smiles—
A thread of candour with a web of wiles;
A plain blunt show of briefly-spoken seeming,
To hide her bloodless heart's soul-hardened scheming;
A lip of lies; a face formed to conceal,
And, without feeling, mock at all who feel:

With a vile mask the Gorgon would disown,—
A cheek of parchment, and an eye of stone.
Mark, how the channels of her yellow blood
Ooze to her skin, and stagnate there to mud,
Cased like the centipede in saffron mail,
Or darker greenness of the scorpion's scale—
(For drawn from reptiles only may we trace
Congenial colours in that soul or face)—
Look on her features! and behold her mind
As in a mirror of itself defined:
Look on the picture! deem it not o'ercharged—
There is no trait which might not be enlarged:
Yet true to "Nature's journeymen," who made
This monster when their mistress left off trade—
This female dog-star of her little sky,
Where all beneath her influence droop or die.
Oh! wretch without a tear—without a thought,
Save joy above the ruin thou hast wrought—
The time shall come, nor long remote, when thou
Shalt feel far more than thou inflictest now;
Feel for thy vile self-loving self in vain,
And turn thee howling in unpitied pain.
May the strong curse of crushed affections light
Back on thy bosom with reflected blight!
And make thee in thy leprosy of mind
As loathsome to thyself as to mankind!
Till all thy self-thoughts curdle into hate,
Black—as thy will for others would create:
Till thy hard heart be calcined into dust,

And thy soul welter in its hideous crust.

Oh, may thy grave be sleepless as the bed,

The widowed couch of fire, that thou hast spread!

Then, when thou fain wouldst weary Heaven with prayer,

Look on thine earthly victims—and despair!

Down to the dust!—and, as thou rott'st away,

Even worms shall perish on thy poisonous clay.

But for the love I bore, and still must bear,

To her thy malice from all ties would tear—

Thy name—thy human name—to every eye

The climax of all scorn should hang on high,

Exalted o'er thy less abhorred compeers—

And festering in the infamy of years.

STANZAS TO AUGUSTA

When all around grew drear and dark,

    And reason half withheld her ray—

And Hope but shed a dying spark

    Which more misled my lonely way;

In that deep midnight of the mind,

    And that internal strife of heart,

When dreading to be deemed too kind,

    The weak despair—the cold depart;

When Fortune changed—and Love fled far,

    And Hatred's shafts flew thick and fast,

Thou wert the solitary star

    Which rose and set not to the last.

Oh! blest be thine unbroken light!

   That watched me as a Seraph's eye,

And stood between me and the night,

   For ever shining sweetly nigh.

And when the cloud upon us came,

   Which strove to blacken o'er thy ray—

Then purer spread its gentle flame,

   And dashed the darkness all away.

Still may thy Spirit dwell on mine,

   And teach it what to brave or brook—

There's more in one soft word of thine

   Than in the world's defied rebuke.

Thou stood'st, as stands a lovely tree,

   That still unbroke, though gently bent,

Still waves with fond fidelity

   Its boughs above a monument.

The winds might rend—the skies might pour,

   But there thou wert—and still wouldst be

Devoted in the stormiest hour

   To shed thy weeping leaves o'er me.

But thou and thine shall know no blight,

   Whatever fate on me may fall;

For Heaven in sunshine will requite

   The kind—and thee the most of all.

Then let the ties of baffled love

   Be broken—thine will never break;

Thy heart can feel—but will not move;

   Thy soul, though soft, will never shake.

And these, when all was lost beside,

Were found and still are fixed in thee;—
And bearing still a breast so tried,
Earth is no desert— ev'n to me.